CW01239486

ALSO BY WILL WIGHT

THE LAST HORIZON
The Captain

THE TRAVELER'S GATE TRILOGY
House of Blades
The Crimson Vault
City of Light

The Traveler's Gate Chronicles

THE ELDER EMPIRE

Of Sea & Shadow   *Of Shadow & Sea*
Of Dawn & Darkness   *Of Darkness & Dawn*
Of Kings & Killers   *Of Killers & Kings*

For the most up-to-date bibliography, please visit **WillWight.com**

CRADLE

I
UNSOULED

II
SOULSMITH

III
BLACKFLAME

IV
SKYSWORN

V
GHOSTWATER

VI
UNDERLORD

VII
UNCROWNED

VIII
WINTERSTEEL

IX
BLOODLINE

X
REAPER

XI
DREADGOD

XII
WAYBOUND

SKYSWORN

CRADLE : VOLUME FOUR

WILL WIGHT

SKYSWORN

Copyright © 2017, 2023 Hidden Gnome Publishing

Book and cover design by Patrick Foster
Illustrations by Ashley Mackenzie and Teigan Mudle
Limited Edition Hardcover cover illustration by Teigan Mudle

All rights reserved. No part of this book may be reproduced in any form by any electronic or mechanical means including photocopying, recording, or information storage and retrieval without permission in writing from the author.

This is a work of fiction. Names, characters, places, and incidents either are the product of the author's imagination or are used fictitiously, and any resemblance to actual persons, living or dead, businesses, companies, events, or locales is entirely coincidental.

www.WillWight.com

1 2 3 4 5 6 7

LIMITED EDITION HARDCOVER: 978-1-959001-25-6
HARDCOVER: 978-1-959001-24-9
TRADE PAPERBACK: 978-1-959001-23-2

PUBLISHED BY

HIDDEN GNOME PUBLISHING

PRINTED IN CHINA

To Lyla Anna, who is slightly older than this book.
By the time you're old enough to read this,
our robot overlords will have already outlawed reading.

All hail the machines.

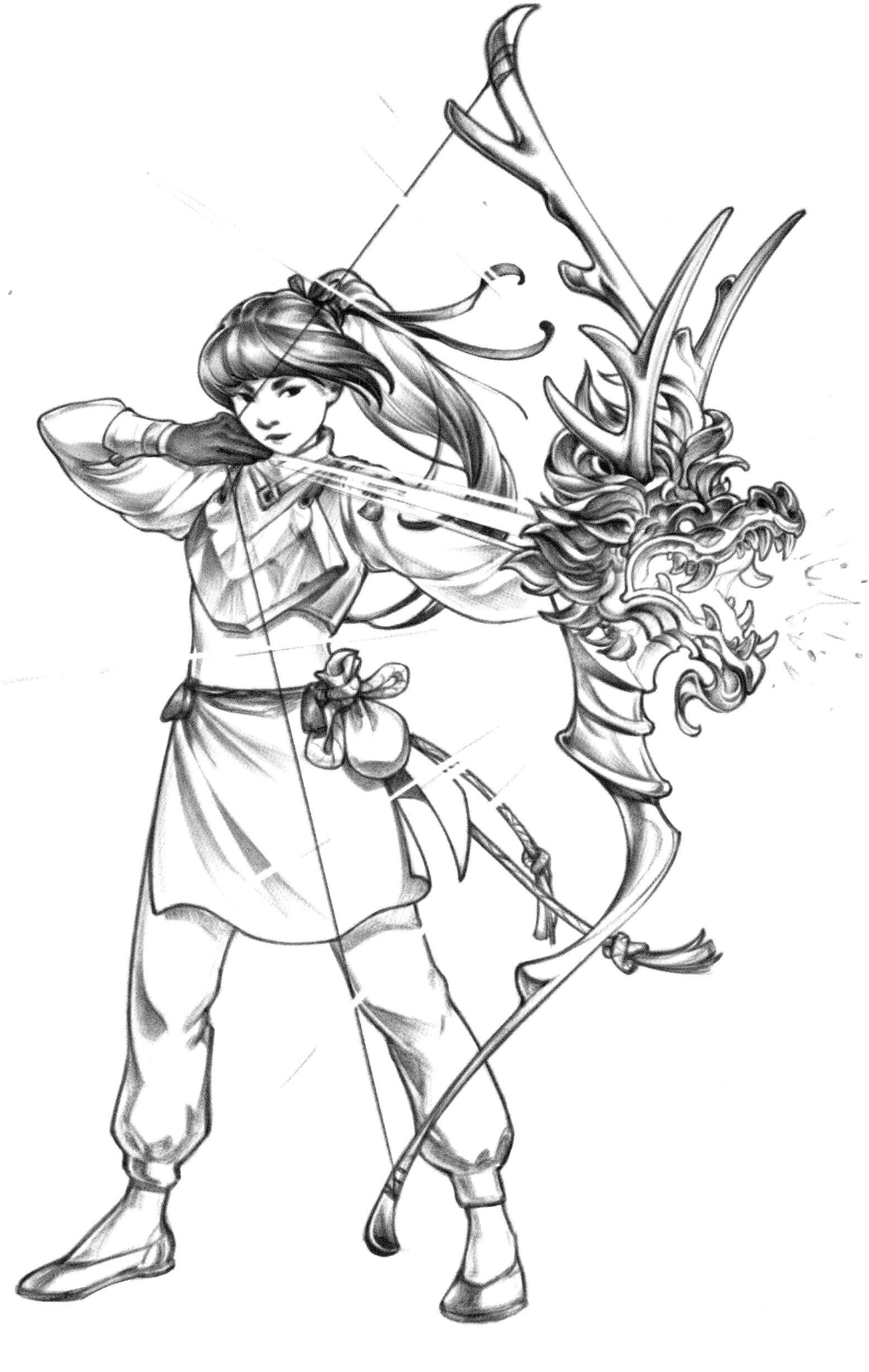

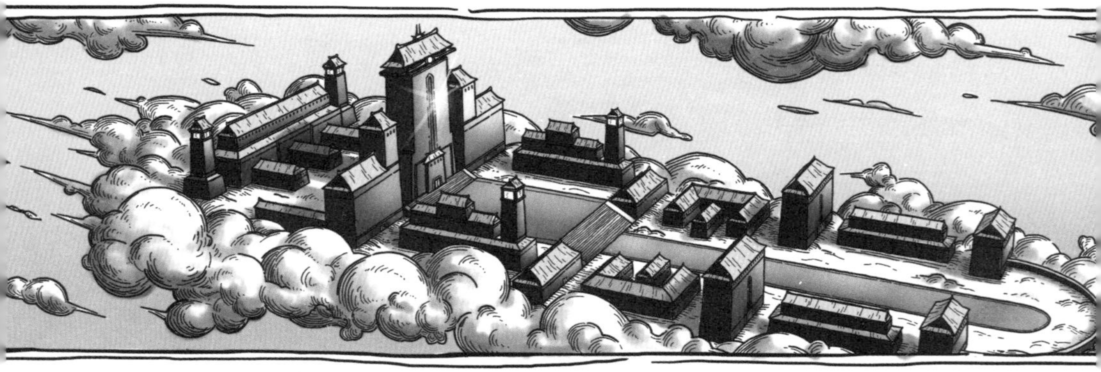

I

Jai Daishou labored up the side of the sharp peak alone, madra trickling through his body in a pathetic dribble. The white metal strands of his hair flogged his back with each step as he pressed against the wind, moving higher with every step.

Remnants blacker than the night sky lined his path. They were voids against the stars, their caws like shattering glass, their feathers drifting down like shredded shadows. The feathers hissed as they landed on the rocks, eating into the stone. They had dissolved his shoes already, but an Underlord's flesh was not so easily seared away.

He felt his weakness in every step, as agony traveled up his ankles and into his spine like lightning. His spirit was no longer strong enough to prop up his fragile body.

A month ago, he could have made this journey without pain. But back then, he'd still had options. Many plans in play, many pieces on the board. He had already been dying, but not so quickly.

Now, he only wanted his clan to outlive him. Anything that prolonged the life of the Jai clan was a virtue. No matter what it cost.

As raven Remnants screeched at him, he climbed toward a gamble he never would have made, had he any other choice.

This was the first of his last hopes.

He reached the end of the road, a sharp cliff overlooking an ocean of clouds. It stretched out before him as though he stood before the end of the world, and overhead the stars glared down at him.

Mist swirled before the cliff as *something* moved beneath the cloud's surface. An instant later, wings of shadow rose from the gray cloud. Each of these wings was the size of a ship's sail, and the head that followed was bigger than a horse. It looked like a bird formed from living ink.

The vast raven filled his vision, floating in the air with still wings. It remained motionless, not disturbing the icy wind with a single flap, drifting like a ghost instead of a living thing. Curls of darkness rose from its feathers.

Jai Daishou inclined his head. As a supplicant, he should have bowed, but his back had locked up so tight he thought he might fold over backwards. His lack of respect might kill him, and that thought chilled him as much as the Remnant's presence. No matter how much he had prepared to throw his own life away if necessary, nothing could prepare him to come face-to-face with a spirit of death.

"I greet you, Lord of Specters, and I come with an offering."

From his robes, he produced an ebony box, holding it out in both hands. He could only hope the spirit heard him over the screeching of its flock.

Not all those who sought the Remnant's services brought an offering, but the wise did. It was quite separate from the raven's price, but a freely given offering bought a measure of protection. Returning a gift with betrayal incurred a soul-debt, which the Remnant should want to avoid.

A gift would not save Jai Daishou if he truly offended the Lord of Specters, but it couldn't hurt his chances.

Two of the raven Remnants fluttered down from their rocky perches, landing on his arms. They radiated a cold that infected him, stealing his warmth, seeping even into his spirit.

With an identical motion of two beaks, they flipped open the box.

A severed head lay on a bed of stained velvet, its skin waxy and blue, its tongue swollen out of its mouth. This was a servant of the Arelius family whose name Jai Daishou had never learned—he had needed a head, and so he had taken one. Better to steal from his enemies than from his friends.

The great raven opened its beak and inhaled. In the Jai Underlord's sight, a dark and nebulous mist lifted from the corpse's head like smoke from a fire. Death aura had once been difficult for him to see, until he had learned the trick of it. Until he had become accustomed to its presence.

Once the Remnant had its mouthful, Jai Daishou threw the box—head and all—out over the cliff. It would have been more polite to kneel and place the container on the ground, but his knees were giving him almost as much trouble as his back.

The Lord of Specters opened its beak once more, and a voice issued forth like a distant chorus singing a dirge. *"Tell us the name of your enemy."* The screeching bird-spirits grew louder, their discordant song scraping his ears.

In the Blackflame Empire, when you wanted an Underlord dead, you had precious few options.

There were weapons that could do it, but killing an Underlord yourself risked reprisal from their family and friends. And most assassins were Truegold at best. Any poisons that could affect a body forged in soulfire would cost a fortune, and the refiners with the skill to make such poisons were difficult to silence.

Still, there were a few specialists, if you had the resources and the fortitude to hire them. Among them, the Lord of Specters was the most...palatable.

"The feud between us cannot be solved except by blood," Jai Daishou said, raising his voice over the smaller, squawking Remnants. "I cannot kill him, and I fear that when I die, his family will tear mine apart."

The raven remained silent, listening. Some legends said that if the Lord found your reasons insufficient, it would feed you to its flock.

"His name is Eithan Arelius."

Instantly, the broken-glass screeching of the ravens died. The night was silent but for the wind, which gasped across the spear-sharp peaks of the mountain.

"Eithan Arelius will not be taken," the Lord of Specters sang. *"Choose another, or be gone."*

Jai Daishou stood in shock, like he'd taken a step forward to find his foot poised over a chasm. He had come prepared for a failure of negotiations, or for hostility, or for the Lord of Specters to demand a price too high. But not for an immediate, flat-out refusal.

"Lord of Specters, your servant can prepare a handsome price. Blood essences from life-Remnants more than a century old. Spirits sworn to your service by oath. Scales of death and shadow from the Path of the Twisting Abyss. Name any wish, and if it is within your servant's power, I will fulfill it."

The Lord finally flapped its great wings, and ice crawled along Jai Daishou's spirit. His madra pulsed brightly in his channels, fighting against the darkness—a weaker sacred artist might have withered in that one gust.

"Eithan Arelius is a friend to the flock. He has given us great gifts."

"Only to protect himself," Jai Daishou insisted. "He wants to tie you down so that none can hire you against him; he has no loyalty to you."

"Even so," the great raven said. *"To act against him would bind our soul with chains of debt. You may name another, but not a feather of ours will harm Eithan Arelius."*

"Let me tell you something about that family," Mo She said, slamming his clay mug back down on the tavern table. "You don't ever take a contract against an Arelius. Not a *real* Arelius, anyway. They always see you coming." Mo She looked like a desiccated corpse someone had unearthed from an ancient tomb: a skeletal, shriveled man with skin tight over his bones and hair like drifting scraps of mist.

His eyes were mismatched; one a blind, milky white, and the other a statue's eye carved of green jade.

"And then there's *this* Arelius in particular," Mo She continued. "He doesn't just see you when you strike. He saw you when you got up this morning."

Jai Daishou stiffened in his chair. He may be on the last leg of his mortal journey, but he was still an Underlord. He had enough power to punish insolence. "You speak of him as though he were above me."

In the half-empty tavern, quite a few eyes turned to Jai Daishou. The barkeeper, polishing his counter with a towel, chuckled. A one-legged boy in the corner grinned at him, mocking.

They knew exactly who he was. They knew of his pride, but they showed open contempt for him anyway.

You did not join the Path of the Last Breath if you cared about staying alive.

Mo She held up his hand for peace, taking another drink as he did so. "Me and my boys would take a contract out on the heavens themselves, if the price was right. Worst that could happen is we die, right? But going up against somebody who knows you're coming and can do something about it…well, there's a difference between gambling and throwing your money down a well."

From his robes, Jai Daishou withdrew a gilded box the size of his palm. He clapped it down onto the table, then slid it across to Mo She.

With his thumb, Mo She cracked the lid. As he did so, a gust of wind pushed the box all the way open, along with a pale green light. Wind aura gathered around the box, a gentle storm of green, and air rushed and spun all around the box. Mo She's brown robes rippled in the wind, and his hair blew away from his face.

"A top-grade scale," Jai Daishou said. "Forged by the Emperor himself. I have collected seven of these over the years, for my services to the Empire." He had never meant to use them as currency, carrying them instead as badges of honor. But when the enemy was at the gates, you used any weapon at your disposal.

Mo She didn't have anyone who could swallow the scale directly—it would take an Underlord to process even a fraction of this scale's energy—but it could be used to power weapons of wind madra, to fuel a massive boundary formation, or to nurture wind-aspect sacred herbs. Failing that, Mo She could just sell it. This was the most valuable coin in the Blackflame Empire.

With clear reluctance on his face, Mo She forced the lid shut. "It's a pretty offer, but you'd have to prove to me that he's not watching us *right now.* You want somebody for a suicidal mission, sure, we're your guys. But this is just suicide."

Even in the depths of night, the jungle air was still hot and choking. Water aura swirled in Jai Daishou's spiritual sight, almost equal to the power of wind. But brighter than both was the vivid green of life aura, which made the dense mesh of vines and trees around him look like an emerald bonfire.

The trees loomed over him, swallowing the sky, filtering the sunlight through their wide leaves. The noise from the jungle's inhabitants was like a force itself. As ever-present as the heat, that mass of chirps, growls, screeches, and screams crushed his ears.

At the southern edge of the Blackflame Empire, this lush green expanse had once belonged to the Tanaban clan. Before they had been driven to extinction by the mad Blackflames.

Now, this was the home of a thousand squabbling families, none large or important enough to be called a clan. If the heavens provided, he could enter and leave without anyone ever knowing he'd been here.

A crash echoed through the jungle, and he tightened his veil: the technique that hid and contained his power as an Underlord. He forced his body to hurry despite the sharp pain in his knees, huddling behind a thick bush.

A tree lifted one mass of roots like a leg, taking another step forward, wading through the foliage like a man through shallow water. It crushed a sapling underfoot, and a panicked squeal cut through the noises of the jungle.

A plump creature the size of a dog shot away from the walking tree, whimpering loudly. A tenderfoot scurried off, thankfully not in Jai Daishou's direction. If he had to unveil himself and destroy one of these ancestral trees, the Underlady of the southern jungles would sense him in a blink.

Tenderfoots were like wild pigs with the long, floppy ears of rabbits. They bred quickly, fed on roots and leaves, and served as prey for most of the jungle.

A hand of vines reached down from the tree and snatched up the tenderfoot, which kicked its legs wildly as it was shoved into a widening gap in the bark. When the tree crunched down, blood and one severed leg fell to the ground.

There were thousands of ancestral trees in this jungle, and most of them fed on blood and flesh. When Jai Daishou had flown in on his Thousand-Mile Cloud, he had seen a dozen of them circling the ocean of leaves like sharks in the surf.

He had to withdraw his spiritual senses in order to maintain his veil, but he estimated this tree was only Jade. The Lowgolds could move faster, and some of them had developed eyes. The Truegolds could be crafty, in their way. Above that...

This was a vast and wild land. Some of these trees were truly ancient, and truly powerful.

When the tree had finished feeding, a flock of colorful birds fluttered down from its branches, fighting over the bits of flesh that had fallen from the plant's meal. They tugged the meat between their beaks, glaring at one another. As they fought, the nearby soil swirled up as though caught in a sudden wind.

Sacred beasts. They lived in the branches of the ancestral trees, feeding on leftovers and the occasional spirit-fruit the tree produced. In return, they helped defend their tree against rivals.

When the tree had finally gone, Jai Daishou progressed. The scripted eight-sided plate in his hands glowed softly blue to the north-northwest, so he headed that way.

He wasn't supposed to know the exact location of this prison, and it would go badly for him if anyone knew he'd marked it for later return. The Deepwalker Ape had killed thousands before it was finally subdued by the previous Empress, and officially it had been executed.

Unofficially, the bloodthirsty creature had been given to the Underlady of the South to imprison. One did not simply throw away an Underlord-level sacred beast. Not when it could be turned to the good of the Empire someday.

Jai Daishou intended to turn it to the good of the Jai clan instead.

He finally reached his goal in a clearing: a massive boulder the size of a house, dropped into a ring of trees as though it had fallen from the sky. Now that he was out of the shade, the sun beat down so hard that even *he* began to sweat. A human without a robust Iron body might have been killed by this heat.

The Underlord struck one unremarkable knob of rock, and a hidden circle lit white. He repeated that process six times in different places, and finally the aura in the area shimmered and dispersed.

A formation designed to lock the boulder in place. If he hadn't helped design this prison, he would never have been able to remove this lid. And only careful interrogation of some of his old friends, who had actually placed the seal, allowed him to find its location.

Now, though...

He braced his hands against the blistering hot rock, Enforcing his body with madra. The flow of power strained against his veil, almost revealing him, but he limited himself to the level of a Truegold. Even so, his soulfire-forged body had advantages no Gold could ever hope to imitate.

Jai Daishou shouted, both to chase away the pain in his joints and to focus his attention. He pushed against the rocky soil, shoving the boulder forward.

His feet started to dig down into the ground, and he used a quick Ruler technique to add force aura to his push. Force was not quite his chosen Path—sword aura was a specific adaptation of force aura, but in practice, they were cousins at best—but his mastery was such that it was enough. The stone slid away from its resting-place, slamming into a pair of trees with a crunch and knocking them over.

The lid's removal revealed a wide, circular pit ten yards across. A stench billowed up from within, like blood and sweat and carrion left to rot in the sun, but its contents were shrouded in absolute darkness.

Jai Daishou drew himself up despite the aching in his back, Enforcing his lungs. "Ape!" he shouted down. "Jai Daishou, Underlord of the Jai clan, brings you freedom!"

Except for the buzz of insects and scream of a distant cat, silence reigned.

He looked to the edges of the hole, where chains thicker than his wrists were still securely anchored. They were steel with veins of halfsilver, and they should anchor the ape's madra as well as its massive strength.

The last he'd seen the creature, it was half-mad with rage, and had sworn bloody revenge against the Imperial clan and every Underlord in the Empire. This beast would be a disaster, one that he was reluctant to unleash on the Empire, but it shouldn't be too hard to steer it toward the Arelius family first. Afterwards, it could be dealt with.

But he had expected it to howl and rage at the sight of him. Instead, it was quiet. Was it dead? Or had it learned patience in its long imprisonment?

Jai Daishou reached out to the power of the sunlight around him. There was no light aura in the pit, but it was strong up here. He gathered the light with his Ruler technique, focusing it, shining it down into the pit as though he were magnifying it through a telescope.

The beam shone down, revealing the distant bottom of the pit. The prison was a long cylinder, many stories deep, its walls circled with security scripts. The Deepwalker Ape should have waited at the bottom, staring up at him in rage. Or its body should have lain there, broken after decades of isolation.

Instead, the floor was spotlessly clean. No fur, no muck, no blood. Nothing.

Only two characters scratched into the stone floor, so large that they were visible from the entrance so far above.

Two words: "Nice try."

Jai Daishou didn't need to have seen the characters before to recognize Eithan Arelius' handwriting.

He staggered back from the edge of the pit, clutching his stomach. All his life, he had heard of people coughing up blood in anger. He had always thought of it as an expression, an artistic way of illustrating the toxic feel of anger.

But now, he really felt as though he were choking back blood. It had taken him weeks to reach this jungle, far from his lands. And it cost him a small fortune to keep it secret.

All the while, he had been nothing but a fool dancing in Eithan's hand.

Jai Daishou actually did cough then, and he spat into his palm. The saliva was stained red.

So you *could* cough up blood in rage. Or perhaps his time was even closer than he'd thought.

In a fury, Jai Daishou tore away the veil over his core, uncaring of the consequences. He cycled his madra to its limit, and white blades of light shredded the trees, tearing apart the forest in time with his rage.

The Deepwalker Ape had been the last piece he could play with only one life on the line. The last weapon he could buy so cheaply.

But now? Now, he would see Eithan dead at any cost. If his clan had to burn, if the Empire *itself* did, Eithan Arelius would burn with it.

Lindon sat with legs crossed, surrounded by a ring of fifty candles. With his eyes shut, he could feel the aura around him.

Fire aura, bright and red, radiated from each of the candles. He pulled wisps of it into his core, pushing it through his madra channels in time with each of his slow, measured breaths.

In his time here—however long that had been—he had reached a deeper understanding of the Path of Black Flame. At first, he had seen fire and destruction as two entirely separate powers. He had wondered how he could possibly train both, without access to a dragon's den like the one in Serpent's Grave.

But the aura of fire and destruction went hand-in-hand. Even now, tiny sparks of black power surrounded the wicks of the fifty candles as they were burned away by the flames. Destruction aura. He could harvest almost five times as much fire aura as destruction, but he limited himself. Balance was important...or so he'd learned after his madra had revolted and he'd scorched the back of his hand.

In his core, he visualized a stone wheel grinding away with a deliberate, agonizingly slow rhythm. It pushed at the boundaries of his core, stretching him, expanding his spirit.

Even after all this time, the Heaven and Earth Purification Wheel still felt like breathing through a thin straw. Sweat covered his forehead, his lungs burned, and each inhale was ragged. Only determination kept him breathing in time with the cycling technique.

Of course, it was more than just the restrictive technique that was making him feel trapped. There was also the fact that he was, quite literally, in prison. Not that you'd know it from his surroundings.

The Skysworn had brought him here directly after leaving Serpent's Grave. They had dumped him into this room and left without answering a single question. If not for his twice-daily meals, he would assume that they had forgotten him.

At first, he hadn't thought of these rooms as a prison cell. They didn't look like one. For one thing, they were *rooms*. He had a privy equipped with water-generating constructs, a small bedroom, and a sitting-room. The furniture was polished and finely carved, and the walls were smooth wood. His meals were simple but varied, and he was served tea with each one.

He wanted to burn through the walls and escape.

Every time he shut his eyes to cycle, it felt as though the walls shrunk to an inch from his skin. He remembered his time sealed in the Transcendent Ruins, and sometimes he had to snap his eyes open to remind himself that he wasn't still there.

He actually had burned through a panel of the wooden wall to see if escape was possible. The wood was only a finger thick, with scripted stone beneath that did not give way to Blackflame. If he became more desperate, he might try blasting through even that.

He needed out. He didn't even know how long he'd been here—he had no window by which to judge the passing of time, and they'd confiscated his pack. He could have counted meal deliveries, but he hadn't thought of that until it was too late. The duel with Jai Long was approaching, and he wasn't ready. They might wrench open his door one day and haul him to his death.

It couldn't have been more than a week. Could it?

Even if freedom was too much to ask, he just needed a word. He could speak to his jailors through the door as they delivered his meal, and they would provide him with any reasonable request. They'd given him a few books on cycling theory, several loads of candles, and a new teacup when he'd broken his first. But they wouldn't *speak* to him. He was at the point where he would trade one of his meals for a single—

Boots tapped against the stone outside. Mealtime already.

The steps grew louder, and he snapped out of his cycling trance. He jumped to his feet, wiping the sweat from his face and preparing a smile. They glanced in sometimes, and he wanted them to see him in control and friendly, not desperate. They might take desperation as hostility, and treat him as an enemy. An enemy might never get out.

The boots stopped. The top half of his wooden door could swing open separately, leaving the bottom half in place. There were bars behind the top half, and they could hand him his food and tea through the bars. Unfortunately, that always gave him a clear look at the person who was refusing to talk to him. If they were faceless, sliding his meals under the door, maybe he could forget that they were humans at all. Pretend that his food was delivered by construct.

As he had for every other meal delivery, he stood with back straight and waited with a smile for the top half to swing open.

This time, he was left smiling at his door. Firmly shut.

He kept his expression in place as each breath stretched on. He hadn't heard anyone walk away, so surely someone was still there. Was this silence designed to make him uncomfortable? Or had it only been a few seconds, and his frantic mind was stretching each instant into an eternity?

He took three deliberate breaths and confirmed that no, they really were making him wait. Why? Every other day, they had simply delivered the food.

An instant later, he was given his answer.

The door swung open.

Normally, a balding old man delivered a box with his meal in it, collected his old box, and left without a word. Lindon had deliberately not picked up his old box today, in the hopes of prodding a sentence out of the man—a demand, a curse, anything. It hadn't worked when he'd tried that before, as the man had simply gestured and the wind had carried Lindon's empty box to him, but surely anything worth trying was worth trying twice.

Eithan and Yerin stood outside, both smiling.

The Underlord had a smug grin on his face, hands in the pockets of his blue silk robes, long yellow hair tied behind him. He looked like a child who had the satisfaction of seeing a trick he'd pulled work flawlessly.

Yerin's smile came with a breath of relief, as though she hadn't expected to find him here. He stared at her like he hadn't seen her for months: her skin covered by razor-thin scars, her black robes sliced and tattered, and two silver blades hanging over her shoulders. A sword was buckled onto her hip, strapped onto a red belt that seemed to be made of liquid...or perhaps a living Remnant.

Even after all the times she'd saved his life, he'd still never been happier to see her.

Eithan...he couldn't be quite so happy to see Eithan. Usually, when the Arelius Patriarch popped up unannounced, that meant he was about to put Lindon through something dangerous.

Lindon stared at them for longer than was appropriate. He knew his eyes were wide and his lips parted, but he still couldn't quite believe that they were *here*. Now, with no hint and no warning.

"You like looking at me so much, I might get the wrong idea," Yerin said, grinning and rapping her knuckles on the lower half of the door, which was still shut. "You going to ask us in, or what?"

Lindon stammered for a few moments before saying, "...in? You're not coming to get me out?"

Eithan put on an offended look even as he levered the handle and slid the rest of the door open. "Get you out? After all the trouble we went through breaking in here? That would just be rude."

He shut both halves of the door behind them when they entered.

Yerin glanced around the room and nodded approvingly. "Not bad. Can't even call this a proper prison, can you?"

Eithan ran his hands over the scorched hole in the wall paneling. "Ah, what happened here? Training accident?"

"No, I was trying to *escape*. I stopped because I thought you might come for me."

"Just to visit you," Eithan said, leaning against the wall and folding his arms. "Looks like you have a cozy place to call your own. I wouldn't want to ruin that."

Lindon had no response.

Yerin kicked the side of Eithan's leg so hard that it sounded like a hammer hitting the ground, but the Underlord didn't so much as flinch.

"The Skysworn say they haven't arrested you," Yerin explained. "They like to fiddle with words. Basically, they're keeping you like a fish in a pond so they can keep an eye on you. You're not in danger."

That was a relief, but it didn't explain why they weren't freeing him.

Eithan buffed his fingernails on the edge of his robe. "I'd prefer not to antagonize the Skysworn more than I already have, but I couldn't let your training stagnate with such an important deadline looming. So I decided to bring the training to you! We can all three continue our pursuits in this very room. Convenient, isn't it?"

Lindon wouldn't have called it convenient, but he still had to admit he was greatly relieved to see them here. At least he wouldn't be alone anymore. And there were some burning questions he finally had the chance to ask.

From his pocket, he withdrew a glass ball that burned with a blue flame in the very center. The Skysworn had confiscated it from him—along with most of his belongings—when they brought him here, but it had appeared beside him one morning when he woke up.

"You showed me something like this before," Lindon said, voice low. "Where did you get it?"

Eithan tapped his fingers together. "That's an interesting first question. You don't want to know about my Path, perhaps? The techniques I could teach you?"

"Of course, yes. But this first."

"Very well. I inherited it from my family."

Lindon waited for more, but none came.

"Did you know all along?" He asked. "Is that why you...picked me?"

This was one of the questions that had needled him ever since he'd seen Eithan produce the marble with the void at its heart. Had Eithan really singled him out because he saw a singular opportunity, or because he'd recognized Suriel's marble? Was Lindon only special because of the glass ball in his hand?

Eithan patted the pocket on his right hip. "I keep mine in here. Close your eyes and stretch out your perception, if you would."

Lindon followed instructions, reaching out to sense Eithan with the extra sense he'd developed when he grew to Jade. He was still growing used to the impressions given by his spiritual sense—it seemed to only feel the nature of madra, ignoring anything physical, so something could feel as though it was right next to you even if it was blocked off by a brick wall.

At first, he felt Yerin's power: sharp, cold, and somehow not fully formed, like a gemstone halfway through cutting. The sword on her hip gave off a different power, distant and cold as a far-off mountain. He couldn't get a grasp of exactly how powerful that weapon was. Her belt...he pulled his perception away from the belt. It always made him think of murder, of blood-drenched hands and the scent of a slaughterhouse.

He felt almost nothing from Eithan, as though the man were made of air. Eithan had mentioned before that he wrapped his core in a veil: a technique that allowed him to mask his power. Lindon wondered if Eithan would teach him, now that he had enough power to mask.

Sharpening his focus, he dove into Eithan's pocket and encountered...a gap.

He wouldn't have noticed anything strange if he hadn't been specifically looking for it, but it was like something in Eithan's pocket was *hidden*, concealed so that he couldn't sense a hint. He pushed further, tightening his perception, trying to penetrate it.

He may as well have saved his effort. Confused, he ran his perception into the marble he carried. Suriel's marble was warm and comforting, even to his spiritual sense, and it also brought a sense of order, of rightness. Like the flame added something into the world, rather than taking it away.

When Lindon opened his eyes, Eithan dipped into his pocket and withdrew the void marble. He held it up so that Lindon could see: a perfectly clear orb the size of a man's thumbnail with a perfectly dark hole in the center. Lindon still *felt* nothing, as though the object had no power whatsoever.

"The legacy of my bloodline works slightly differently," Eithan explained. "An Arelius sees things as though with our physical senses, seeing and hearing and smelling rather than picking up on spiritual perception. As such, I saw the marble in your pocket like a ball of glass...but I could see nothing inside."

He closed his own eyes and nodded. "Even now, I can see you holding a transparent ball, but I can see no blue flame." He tossed his own marble up and caught it. "As for mine, however, I can pierce it quite easily with both my bloodline powers and my perception. It is the same for you, yes?"

Lindon nodded slowly. "So what did you think it was?"

"Naturally, I assumed there was something inside. I thought it was a Lord-stage barrier meant to protect a small treasure, or perhaps a pill or construct. And I was very curious to learn what Copper had caught the eye of an Underlord. It was only later that I began to suspect it had been produced by someone far above any Underlord."

He held up the void marble, inspecting it. "As far as I knew, this was the only example of such a heavenly relic in the world. If I ran into another, I would have expected it to look like mine. How interesting that I was wrong."

"I would love to hear that story," Lindon said, sensing an opportunity. "I'm only too happy to share mine."

"He is," Yerin confirmed, fiddling with one of the edges of her outer robe. She must have been bored. "Shared it with me more than once."

"And I would be delighted to listen," Eithan said, closing his fist around his marble. "Later. Unless this heavenly messenger told you something urgent?"

Suriel had said he had thirty years, and he'd spent slightly more than one. He supposed he could wait a little longer, though the curiosity might kill him in the meantime. He sighed and shook his head.

The glass ball vanished into Eithan's pocket. "Excellent! Consider our conversation a prize for when you defeat Jai Long, hm? Something to look forward to."

Lindon dipped his head in acknowledgement, but he wasn't satisfied. Suriel had seen something in him, even if he wasn't quite sure what that was. She must have seen something in Eithan as well, or at least someone else up there had.

Eithan had said more than once that he wanted to pursue the sacred arts to their height. And he thought Lindon and Yerin had what it took to join him.

Maybe the heavens thought so too.

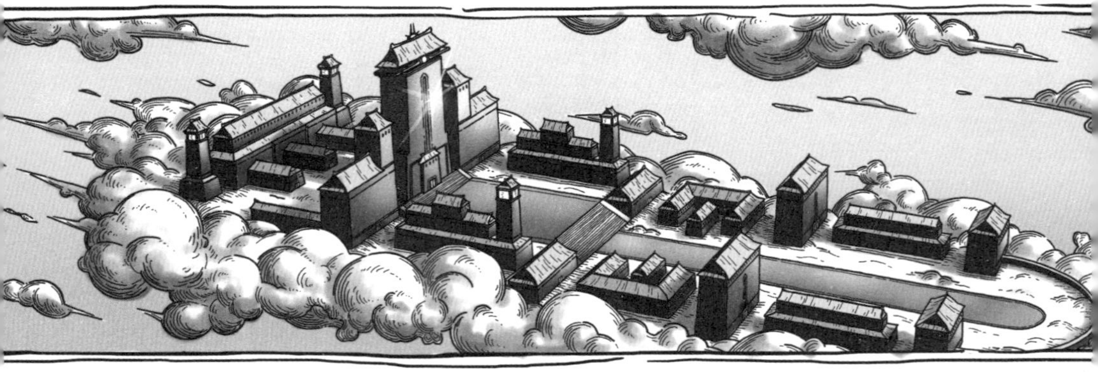

Outpost 01: Oversight

People from various worlds often likened the Way to a tree, or a branching vine. Suriel had always thought of it more as a network of veins, stretching out in all directions from a central heart. The Way touched everything, bringing order, stability, and protection from the ravages of the void. Only in the shelter of the Way could life and reason exist.

In the center of that heart of the Way, at the nexus of everything that existed, was Oversight.

As she drifted in endless blue, thousands of kilometers away, she could see the entire station: one blue-and-green planet of standard size orbited by no less than sixteen moons. Each of the moons was so close that it almost looked like they skated along the planet's surface, and she could see city lights blanketing every surface over all seventeen spheres.

This was the headquarters of Makiel's First Division: the Hounds.

He had created this system himself, hand-selecting the fragments from the void and binding them together with the force of his will. He had positioned it here, manipulating the Way to enforce natural laws. The inhabitants of Outpost lived as naturally as they would in an Iteration, but with an endless blue sky devoid of sun or stars.

Twelve billion people lived here, and the vast majority of them were not Abidan. They were simply people. They went about their lives, living and dying with no knowledge of the greater cosmos.

These were *his* ties to Fate. Every sentient being was a tie to the Way, and even here at the heart of it all, Makiel wanted to be closer.

As staggered as she was every time she thought about the vast expenditure of time and personal power that must have gone into the creation of this outpost, it frightened her as much as it impressed her. Every other division of the Abidan was headquartered on Sanctum, so they shared a cultural understanding that facilitated interaction.

Not the Hounds. The First Division was centered here.

They tracked targets forward and backwards in time, reading Fate to find criminals and predict disasters, and their official excuse for their location was a desire to see as clearly as possible.

Suriel had no doubt that was true. From Oversight, a sufficiently talented Hound could glimpse the destiny of every Iteration in existence. It was especially easy to locate those places where one Iteration's fate overlapped another's, and investigate for violations.

But even here, she couldn't sense Cradle.

She touched the Way—so easy here—and simply adjusted her position in space. One blue flash later, she stood on an endless arctic plain, a layer of gray clouds overhead and snow drifting in the wind.

The north pole of Oversight's main planet. Makiel's home.

She glanced down at the two hundred meters of snow and ice beneath her: this was Makiel's front door.

Suriel tapped the Way, flexing her authority as the sixth Judge of the Abidan Court. Blue power flared from her back like wings, and the seal on the door responded.

A symbol shone blue in response: a three-headed dog, one hundred meters in diameter. The symbol of the Hounds.

The ice cracked, sliding apart, snow trickling down in white waterfalls. The ice split beneath her feet, but she stayed floating in the air until it had parted enough for her shoulders. Then she let herself drift downwards.

Into Makiel's lair.

The room beneath her was huge, hundreds of meters, its tiles marked in a giant circle of runes meant to focus sight. It was lit by a diffuse purple glow, all emanating from violet-edged "screens" that floated in the air at various heights. These were celestial lenses, used by Judges and most high-ranking Abidan for monitoring Iterations from the Way. They displayed images of the future, which looked odd to the naked eye, as though they showed dreams. Actions would have two results, or would rewind and play again on a loop. Numbers flashed with each image: chance of occurrence, temporal deviation, Iteration number, and so on.

The lenses opened like eyes even as others blinked shut. They were rectangles, some as small as a palm and others as big as a barn wall, all angled toward the center of the room. The chamber was packed with them, such that no one could possibly see them all at once.

Unless you were both powerful and very skilled.

Makiel stood in the center, surrounded by eyes. Manifestations of his Presence. His white-gauntleted hands were a blur of motion as he tapped one eye and another, transmitting messages to one sector or another. When he tapped an eye, it flashed blue and disappeared, transferred through the Way to its destination. For every eye that disappeared, a celestial lens vanished.

By her brief count, he was tracking over a thousand threads of Fate at once, over hundreds of different worlds. Any other Judge would have delegated this work, in order to focus their power and attention only where it was needed. Not Makiel. The only busier Judge should be Telariel, the Spider, who coordinated communications for all the Abidan and simultaneously scouted for invasions...but he used his subordinates to cover practically every one of his duties.

No wonder Makiel's Hounds worshiped him so. He was worth a division all on his own.

The First Judge himself had an unremarkable appearance. He looked like a natural human, as though his genetics had remained the same since birth. Suriel, and every other Abidan she knew, had altered themselves in some way to improve their performance. Rumor said that Makiel never had, and that he worked solely on natural talent, but of course he would never allow a scan to confirm those rumors.

He had dark brown skin, slightly wrinkled like a man in his fifties, and silver at the wings of his black, short hair. He was trim and solidly built, with a square jaw; as a girl, she would have said he looked like a soldier. Only his eyes stood out, blazing a brighter violet than the celestial lenses around him, as he watched Fate.

"Suriel," he said, and his voice resonated through the room. "Will you verify for the record that Ozriel is dead?"

Her Presence had prepared her for this. Suriel had not told Sector Twenty-one the story of the survivors she'd pulled from Ozriel's shelter, but Makiel's mandate included watching the past as well as the future. Her actions would have alerted him, and he would be able to piece together a picture of the truth, even from the ashes of a dead world.

"I cannot," she responded, finally settling down on the tiled floor. "I am not myself convinced." She could feel the energy passing through the circle beneath her feet, urging her to gaze into the future.

Makiel's hands were still a blur, eyes fluttering into existence and then vanishing several times a second. He didn't seem to be looking at her, but she knew he saw everything. "Yet he was already missing. Why stage his death?"

The First Judge would have considered all the possibilities already. He was asking her for her opinion, so she gave it.

"To encourage us to look for a replacement," she said. "He has left us in a scenario where we have no choice but to act as though he is dead. He may have thought that we would simply wait for him to return, even as the cosmos crumbled around us."

[Based on models of Ozriel's personality, this explanation is sixty-two percent convincing,] her Presence told her. [And only eighteen percent likely to be the sole explanation.]

Makiel's hands paused for half a second, and she felt a ripple in Fate as possibilities began tumbling like a handful of dice. For her to feel such a working even in the midst of his normal activity meant he had exerted himself. To check something, or to change something? She would have to investigate later.

"It seems your task has ended, Suriel," he said at last. "That took much less time than I anticipated. Ninety-two out of a hundred projections had you on his trail for decades."

Her own predictions had suggested as much. "And a twelve percent chance of finding him eventually," she added. "In those cases, I had a ninety-one percent chance of persuading him to return. How were *your* odds?"

Makiel gestured, and his Presence stopped manifesting. The arc of eyeballs in front of him vanished, with a single purple eye hovering over his shoulder just as the gray ghost hovered on Suriel's. The celestial lenses in the room all remained frozen in the air, emitting violet light and flickering with images and scrolling numbers.

His eyes blazed as he faced her, crossing his hands behind his back. "Tell me. What were you doing in Harrow?"

Anger flooded her system, but she flushed it out. He was provoking her, just as Gadrael had when he had *sent* her to Harrow. On Makiel's orders.

"Is the Hound's eye so blind that he can no longer see his own actions?"

"Gadrael was ordered to show you the cost of Ozriel's absence. You chose to stay and cleanse the world yourself."

Which he had *surely* known she would do, but she remained silent. She would not give him excuses.

"It only cost you a handful of standard months, but those were months in which you were *not* seeking Ozriel. That you stumbled on evidence of him was due to his foresight, not your own success as a hunter. And where were you before that?"

It was dangerous, here in the heart of Makiel's power, but she couldn't let him play her like a puppet. She activated her eyes and scanned Fate.

Immediately, she saw where he was headed with this line of questioning. He hadn't bothered to hide it. Her stomach twisted, and her anger gained greater heat before she choked it off.

"You were in Cradle," he continued, overlooking her glimpse into the future. "Where you knew you would not find Ozriel, because he could not hide there. He would have a better chance of hiding in Sanctum itself than in Cradle, but you knew you had a plausible excuse for checking his home world."

"I want to *restore* the Abidan," she said, her power crackling blue in the air between them. "You have been tearing the wound deeper for centuries."

She was trying to distract him, to pull him away from his plan, but he remained doggedly focused. "You went to Cradle for a breath of fresh air, to consider your options, to decide if you wanted to hunt Ozriel at all. Convenient, then, that your search has ended *before you ever started looking for him.*"

He would go on for another minute if she didn't stop him. He would say that she had been manipulated by the Reaper, and allowed him his freedom. That if Ozriel was still on their side, he would have told Suriel before his departure. She was his closest friend on the Court, after all. There was no need to hide it from her, and then place an elaborate distraction to keep her from looking for him.

He was controlling her. Looking down on her. Exploiting her sympathy.

That was the Hound's objective. Since she couldn't deflect him, she cut straight to it. "If he didn't want me looking for him, there were easier ways to stop me."

"He knew you could find him," Makiel said. "Your odds of finding him must have been much higher without this plan. Since I didn't know about his fake death scene, I couldn't factor it into my projections. He blinded me, and he kept you sidetracked."

"Then he succeeded. I'm returning to my division." She tapped into the Way, preparing to depart directly. Leaving this way was disrespectful, but she was beyond caring. She always left Makiel irritated if not disgusted. He had only summoned her here to produce the results he wanted, and then he had the nerve to accuse someone *else* of manipulation.

The worst part was, he was probably right. Ozriel could have warned her about his departure, but he hadn't. He had moved her like a pawn to be manipulated.

She would feel better if he really *were* dead.

"The quarantine," Makiel said, before she left. "I would like your vote."

"Ozriel said he left a total of sixteen shelters," she said, light tearing into a blue-edged portal overlooking Iteration 001: Sanctum. "Evacuate the other fifteen, prepare those worlds for corruption, and you have my vote."

"Already done." When she turned back to the portal, he continued. "Now, let's talk about the changes you made to Cradle."

Behind her, all the screens vanished except one, which swelled to take up the whole wall.

It showed Wei Shi Lindon. He was tall and broad-shouldered, with short black hair and his expression locked in a glower. He looked sullen even when he was fast asleep, and she knew his face alone had provoked more than one fight.

That face was even more unpleasant now.

His eyes were solid black but for the irises, which were solid red. They shone as black fire gathered within his hands. He was practicing a new Path.

[The Path of Black Flame,] her Presence supplied. [Its sacred artists imitate the power of a tribe of black dragons.]

Suriel didn't care about those details at the moment. Why had Makiel shown her this?

She turned, allowing her portal to close.

Makiel fully faced the image on the lens, his hands still behind his back, looking away from her. "What changes did you make in this young man's life?" he asked.

She told the truth, as it would not matter. The Eledari Pact only prevented Abidan from changing the destiny of a healthy Iteration. Saving one young man's life wouldn't have altered anything. "He was caught in a spatial violation, which I reverted. After conversing with him, I determined that he was fated to die in a disaster, and I set him on a course to prevent it."

"*You* stayed within the bounds of the Pact," Makiel agreed. "But someone *else* did not."

Cradle's deviation. It hadn't been her interference after all. But who...

The answer came to her before she even finished answering the question.

"Ozriel left something behind, it seems," Makiel went on. "For his descendants."

The picture changed to show a man in his early thirties, handsome and smiling, with blond hair trailing behind him. He wore a silk robe of fine blue, and he looked down fondly on someone: Yerin, the girl that Suriel had told Lindon to seek. She scowled at a pale white sword as she knelt on the ground, invisible blades cutting at the dirt around her and nicking the edges of her robes. Two silver blades hung on thin arms over her shoulders: Goldsigns.

The man was training her. Eithan Arelius, an Underlord in the Arelius family.

A touch of anger entered Makiel's voice. "Ozriel's bloodline, from before he *was* Ozriel. He worked against us before he ever gained his Mantle."

Now it was starting to come together in Suriel's mind. Some artifact of Ozriel's had been recently found by one of his descendants, altering that man's destiny. Then Suriel's actions had changed Lindon's direction.

And the two had collided.

On their own, neither of those changes had been significant. Together, they would be exponentially more dangerous. And more difficult to predict.

"Their actions would have affected all of Cradle," the Hound said. "They would work for decades, changing the Iteration, and eventually derailing it entirely. I cannot see any further than thirty years in Cradle's future."

That was chilling. Either it meant that Cradle would be destroyed so soon, or it would have changed so drastically that its relationship to Fate shifted. Either way, they couldn't jeopardize their Cradle. It produced an Abidan candidate every century or so: far more than any other Iteration.

"I will resolve this," Suriel said heavily.

"This is a violation of Fate. It is the mandate of Makiel." He shifted his gaze to her. "However, I will act with a gentle hand. I intend to accelerate events so that they cannot stay within the confines of the world for so long. The faster they are gone, the lesser the damage."

"You have a solution?"

"I believe I do. If I am successful, their world itself will eventually force them to leave, and will not tolerate their staying and making alterations. However, this does increase the personal risk to both subjects."

The odds were already stacked against Lindon, but the alternative was manipulating his memory and sending him home. This was a peace offering from Makiel to her, fixing the problem she had helped create while keeping her favored mortal intact. All the while demonstrating the damage that Ozriel's meddling could cause.

She appreciated the gesture. Perhaps Makiel was willing to work together for unity after all.

Suriel nodded, and the Hound reached up to his Presence.

Jai Daishou stood before a stone door, weighing his life in his mind.

The door was marked with a familiar symbol, one that had remained embedded in his memory for decades. It was etched with four beasts: on the top, a coiling dragon surrounded by rain and crackling with lightning. On the bottom, a phoenix with feathers like drops of blood. To the right, an armored warrior with the shell of a turtle and a sword so rough it was almost a club. To the left, a tiger seated on treasure and crowned with light.

This was more than just a decoration. It was a warning.

By his oath to the Empire, he should not open this door. It was located inside Jai clan territory, beneath a lake and past miles of underground tunnel. This was the deepest into the labyrinth he—or anyone else—had ever dared to delve since the demise of the old Blackflame Empire.

Behind him, in the shallow chambers, had once been a series of Gold-stage weapons and devices left by ancient Soulsmiths. His clan had plundered that chamber decades ago.

But here...past this door were weapons for Lords. Ancient records described a few of their number, and with any one of them, he could shoot to the top of the Underlord rankings. With some, he could declare himself Emperor.

Of course, opening this door was punishable by the death of one's entire clan. Part of his mandate as Patriarch of the Jai clan was to prevent anyone from entering.

It was forbidden not because of the power of its contents, but because of their danger. When this door had been opened before, it had called disaster down on the entire continent.

But then, it had remained open for years. Now, he would be in and out in a flash. No one would ever know.

The Dreadgods wouldn't be watching so closely.

He had even consulted some oracles, who confirmed that there was no hint of the Dreadgods in their dreams. At least not for several decades.

That was good enough for him. But still he hesitated.

Every day of his life, he had been taught to serve his clan so that his clan could serve the Empire. In his earlier rage against Eithan Arelius, he had been willing to risk this, but now that he faced it... was he really willing to put everything at risk?

He thought of his clan, doomed to slide into obscurity without him to lead them. If he opened this door and was detected, they would be executed by either the Dreadgods or the Empire. No matter how good his odds, was he really willing to roll the dice with his family's lives?

But what kind of lives would they be, without an Underlord at their helm? They would not enjoy the respect, the standard of living to which they had become accustomed. They would have to live like paupers.

Dithering over a decision for so long wasn't like him. He was a man of action.

And he couldn't wait to see the smile torn from Eithan Arelius' face.

With a ward key in each hand, he pressed them against the

script-circles to the sides of the door. He had to pour most of his madra into the circles before they activated—far more than he anticipated, enough that the loss of power left him gasping for air—and those didn't even open the door. They caused a pedestal to rise from the floor, set with yet another circle of script.

On his fingertips, he ignited soulfire. The gray, almost colorless flame danced for a moment before being sucked into the script.

It drew more, enough that he was glad he had woven extra soulfire before coming. When it had finished devouring a stream of dull fire, it flickered once and then slid back down into the ground.

This time, the door swung silently open.

Power washed out, flooding him with awe. He glanced at the aura, which seemed both shining white and utter black at the same time, as though he couldn't see through the doorway because it was both too bright and too dark. Either way, the aura blinded his spiritual sight, and he had to close down that sense as he stepped inside the ancient storehouse.

He couldn't shut the door behind him while he was inside, or he'd be sealed within to die alone, so he had to be quick.

It had taken them years to notice before, so he could probably take his time, but he thought he might as well minimize his risk.

The room was a hallway, set on either side with walls of polished wooden cabinets from floor to the ceiling, fifteen feet above his head. That hallway continued as far as he could see…and as an Underlord, he could see quite far indeed.

For a moment, he felt as though he'd stumbled onto a dragon's hoard. He was shocked by the sheer value of what was presented before him, overwhelmed by the weight of wealth.

He wanted it all.

He was surprised at his own greed, but his hands trembled as he reached to open the first cabinet. The bottom row of cubbies was the largest, big enough to contain a large dog, but each row got progressively smaller up to the top, far above his head. Those were only the size of his fist.

If each of these cabinets, down this endless hallway, contained precious treasures of the ancients...there might be millions of weapons down here. He might have enough to buy the entire Empire.

Or to destroy it.

The cabinet was smooth to the touch, and he seized the wooden handle and pulled it open.

It was empty.

So was its neighbor, and the eighteen others he checked in an instant. He was sweating by this point, his gut heavy with disappointment. Where had all his wealth gone?

He shook himself. He wasn't worried about riches, but about the fate of his family.

He had to tell himself that very firmly.

Ten more empty cabinets went by before he found something: a ring of pure white, scripted inside and out, set with a single black gemstone. He had no records of this, so he swept his spirit through it.

He couldn't sense anything. It would be an Overlord weapon, then, or perhaps even one for Archlords.

Reluctantly, he set it back and shut the door. He left all the empty ones open.

He moved to the next cabinet feeling like an idiot. Why couldn't he take the ring? Surely he should stuff his pockets.

He knew why: because everything he took was another chance to get caught, and he could only carry one object at a time in his soulspace. He had to find a weapon he recognized if he wanted to kill Eithan Arelius. Anything else would only weigh him down.

Ten more minutes passed before he found something that initially excited him: a duplicate of the Ancestor's Spear.

Until he realized it was cracked in the middle. The scripts around the edges of the cabinet were preserving it, keeping it from dissolving, but he would need a Soulsmith to repair it. Which may or may not succeed.

He tucked the two halves of the spear away; it wouldn't be enough on its own, but at least he wasn't leaving empty-handed.

Finally, when he was almost ready to give up, he pulled open a cabinet the size of his head. The object inside was so unremarkable at first glance that it wouldn't have grabbed his attention anywhere else. Only that it was here, important enough to seal up, drew his focus.

It was a crystal ball slightly bigger than a hand, filled with a dim, diffuse light. The light swirled like smoke, as though something invisible swam within.

He touched it with his spirit, and felt an endless will to devour that almost consumed him. He wanted to tear through every cabinet, cramming his pockets full. So what if he died in here? He would die the richest man in the world. The will of an Underlord was not so easily swayed, and he resisted.

But he recognized this device from the records. It was perfect.

He focused his power onto it, then took in a deep breath. As though he had inhaled it, the stone vanished and reappeared inside his spirit.

Inside him, above his core and behind the cage of his tangled madra channels, a crystal ball floated. It seemed to orbit his soulfire, as though the two attracted one another but could draw no closer.

His soulspace was full, and he may have even obtained a replacement for the Ancestor's Spear. This may have been the most profitable day of his life; it was cause for celebration.

No matter how much he might be leaving behind.

Feeling as though he were leaving behind his own limbs, he left the chamber and sealed it once again behind him. The satisfaction of success carried him away, and allowed him to break the hold of whatever feelings had swallowed him back in the storehouse.

Armed with this Archstone, he couldn't lose.

INFORMATION REQUESTED: MAKIEL'S INFLUENCE ON CRADLE

BEGINNING REPORT...

The Jai Patriarch exits the labyrinth proud of his prize. The facility's unique aura shone like a beacon for the duration of his visit: twenty-six minutes.

In ninety-nine out of a hundred projections, this aura goes unnoticed. Jai Daishou returns from his trip safely. There is only a negligible chance that a Dreadgod will notice this aura, which calls to them like the scent of meat to a predator, and choose to investigate. His gamble has paid off.

INFLUENCE DETECTED: DESIGNATION ZERO-ZERO-ONE, MAKIEL.

MAKIEL'S INFLUENCE CONFIRMED. RECALCULATING...

The possibility of a Dreadgod noticing increases in likelihood as the probability shifts. The will of the Hound bends Fate, twisting chance.

Currently, there is only one Dreadgod within range: the Bleeding Phoenix. Hundreds of miles to the south, it rests beneath a city of tattered cloth. Its servants, the Redmoon Hall, attend to its feeding as it sleeps.

During the first twenty-five minutes, the Dreadgod tosses and turns, sending shivers through the members of Redmoon Hall. They sense their master's needs through the parasites embedded in their bodies, and they seek the cause of its distress.

On the twenty-sixth minute, as the aura fades, the Bleeding Phoenix regains a fraction of its consciousness. It catches the scent of power it has almost forgotten, power long lost. It calls to a memory buried deep in the creature's awareness.

For the first time in centuries, its bloody feathers stir.

The members of Redmoon Hall, from Jade to Herald, fall to their knees in supplication. Their master has spoken to them through its Blood Shadows, preparing them.

They must head north and pave the way.

SUGGESTED TOPIC: YERIN, RELUCTANT HOST OF A SEALED BLOOD SHADOW. CONTINUE?

TOPIC ACCEPTED, CONTINUING REPORT...

Yerin is seeking the voice of the Sword Sage as she cycles. She has uncovered four of his memories since achieving Highgold, and combs over them every day for fragments of his wisdom. The remaining memories in his Remnants will help polish her techniques, if not advance her to Truegold.

At the moment the Bleeding Phoenix contacts its subordinates, she feels a sudden restlessness, an urge to rise to her feet and destroy everything around her. The call seems to be pushing her north.

She shifts in her meditation, uncomfortable, but she knows where this compulsion comes from.

An idle hand moves behind her, to feel the knot tied in her Blood Shadow, which she wears as a belt. Her fingertips pass through it as though through a liquid, though nothing remains on her skin.

The thought is pushed aside, a momentary distraction, and she returns to her training.

REPORT COMPLETE.

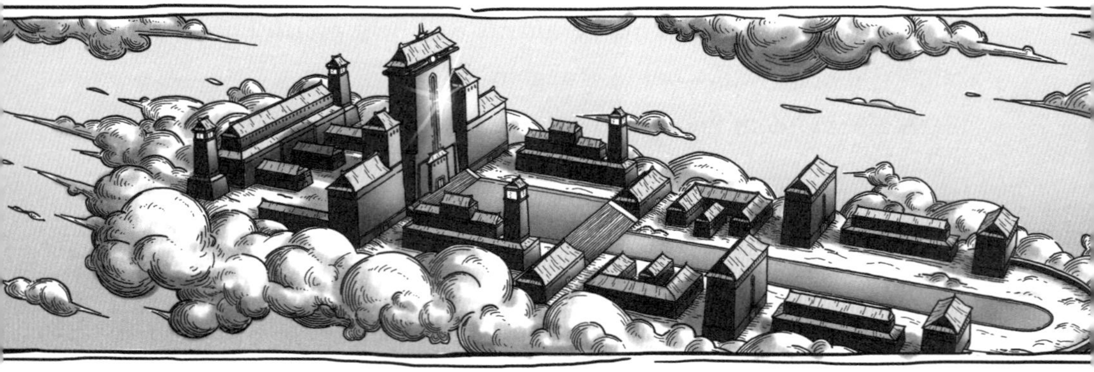

III

Renfei finished buckling on the green plates of her Skysworn armor, clipped the dark hammer to her belt, and sent a whisper of spiritual awareness to test the Thousand-Mile Cloud preserved inside her armor. It was fully powered and ready to deploy.

And so was she.

She pulled her hair back and tied it into a tail, then walked to the door. As she expected, Bai Rou was waiting on the other side. He had to bend down to see her through the doorframe.

"Ready?" he asked.

"Time's up," she responded. "Let's go get him."

Bai Rou, her partner in the Skysworn, was two feet taller than she was and twice as broad. He always wore a hat woven from dried stalks, which cast a shadow across his face. Only his eyes shone from within the darkness, bright yellow—his Goldsign. He wore the same armor she did, though his was three sizes bigger and he carried no hammer.

They had to travel down cramped hallways lit only by flickering, damaged rune-lights—no one had done the maintenance on these scripts for years.

Fortunately, their destination was nearby.

They reached the end of the hallway in a minute, in front of a... well, it wasn't a door. More like a thick metal plate bolted to the wall, with a script in the center.

This script wasn't derelict, like the others. The custodians of the prison knew better than to allow actual security to lapse.

From inside a pocket at her belt, Renfei pulled out her half of the key—a ceramic half-disc etched with one part of a script-circle. Bai Rou handed over the other half, and she fit the two halves of the disc together.

When the script was completed, she let her madra flow through it. Another security measure: this key was created anew for each new jailer, and would shatter if power from the wrong Path flowed through it.

She pressed it against the circle on the metal slab, and power spun through the door. The metal lit up in lines, as hidden scripts activated.

The bolts around the edges, each marked with a script-circle of its own, began to spin out of their mounts. An instant later, they pinged to the ground, followed by the thick metal plate swinging soundlessly open.

Renfei walked through the doorway, Bai Rou ducking after her.

They found themselves in a room of twisting mist. Images

seemed to swirl and die within the mist, as sounds haunted the very edges of her hearing. She heard something like children whispering, a gong sounding, the cries of a thousand birds.

It was easy to ignore the illusions, as she and Bai Rou carried ward keys to this formation. The two of them saw only mist and heard only distant sounds, but anyone without ward keys would be snared in convincing visions.

They walked across a narrow bridge with no railing, a sheer drop on either side.

Though it looked bottomless, Renfei knew that more than simply air and darkness waited beneath. Anyone trapped in the tricks of this world would live only long enough to hit the bottom, whereupon they would be devoured by what waited there.

"This is too much," Bai Rou said, his deep voice drowning out the whispers.

"Too much to secure him," Renfei replied. "But not enough to keep him isolated."

"Not enough?"

She sighed. "You know it won't be."

The next door was wooden and opened to a simple physical key and lock. It opened into a dark stone room, lit only by light spilling in from the room of illusions. A pair of crimson lions waited at the end of the room, embers burning in their eyes, flames building in their throats. Remnants, sealed to the defense of this room.

The Remnants had been Truegold when they were imprisoned here, but were fed weekly to make them even more formidable. If she and Bai Rou had to fight their way through, they might be able to do it, but they would have to pay a heavy cost.

Fortunately, the Remnants recognized them and parted, allowing them to walk through. That didn't lessen the tension—their heat pressed against her like she was locked in an oven, and their burning gazes made them look anything but tame. She brushed her fingertips against the hammer at her waist.

Remnants could be bound, but they weren't predictable. These looked like swirls of bright color painted onto the world, their eyes like balls of fire. They glared at her, and she found herself wondering if they might make a fight of this after all.

She could feel Bai Rou's madra, like water and nightmares, gathering behind her. She realized she was cycling her own Cloud Hammer madra, and picked up her pace.

The next door was made of heavy stone, moved by brute strength. This might be the least secure entrance, but it was made so that it only opened slowly. Anyone who tried to ignore the lions and open the door would find themselves trapped and delayed.

This room was thick with water aura, a pale green waterfall splitting the hall in two. It wasn't water, not really—instead, it was liquid madra, water fused with the essences of death and venom. A truly vile combination.

A construct provided by the prison allowed them to pass through this one—a personal shield that repelled this exact Path of madra. Renfei was still nervous as she walked through the green waterfall, even though she could feel the shield intact. Bai Rou might survive contact with this liquid, though even he wouldn't enjoy it, but she would die without a doubt.

The next room was full of security constructs. The floor was a web of etched circles, and brightly colored devices made of Remnant parts stuck from every wall and the ceiling. Eyes on purple stalks pushed away from a mass of muscle-like madra stuck to one wall, examining them. The ceiling bristled with spiked tails, clenched claws, sparking fangs, and pieces she couldn't identify. She could, however, sense the power of the Striker bindings in all of them.

If the scripts beneath them were triggered, the constructs would unleash enough power to vaporize an Underlord.

Her heart rate picked up every time, but they were once again allowed to pass.

"No sign of entry," Bai Rou noted, as they approached the last door.

"There wasn't last time either," she said.

"This is different."

Renfei had to admit that she couldn't imagine these defenses being penetrated. Their prisoner wasn't too dangerous on his own—he was locked in more as a political statement than to protect others from him. The Skysworn had received orders to keep him isolated, but that had proven more difficult than they anticipated. Everywhere they put him, no matter how secret or protected, had been infiltrated within days.

This time, with the approval of their Underlord, they had placed him in the most isolated facility that could hold him without killing him. Having just passed through the security herself, she had to admit, she couldn't imagine how someone could pass through each of those measures without the keys. Or without blowing a hole through each wall in sequence.

Maybe this time will be different, she thought.

It wasn't.

This cell was originally designed for top-level security threats that couldn't be executed by usual means. Its door was shot through with halfsilver veins, and the room itself was broad and brightly lit. There was a separate prison in the center of the room: a box of bars, at least twenty feet away from each wall. The box itself was fairly roomy for one prisoner, with a bed, a chair, and a pit with a water construct that flushed away his waste twice per day. The only thing a prisoner wouldn't have was privacy—anyone who entered the cell would see everything from every angle, through the gaps in the bars. Even the bars had flecks of halfsilver in them—the empire spent a fortune finishing this place, and a smaller fortune powering and maintaining it.

Wei Shi Lindon Arelius stood outside those bars, his white sacred artist's robe scuffed and torn. He was on the balls of his feet, madra flowing through his body in an Enforcer technique, and blood trailed down from a split lip.

His eyes weren't black-and-red, as they had been when Renfei had first seen him. Now he didn't look quite so horrifying, but he had that rough look to him that she associated with lawbreakers. He looked like the kind of young man who started fights for fun.

Over her interactions with him in the last several months, she had grown to realize that he was practically the opposite. A troublemaker, certainly, but of a very different type.

He was supposed to be inside his cage, but she didn't wonder how he'd gotten out.

Instead, she wondered—not for the first time—how all these other people had gotten *in*.

Yerin Arelius stood opposite Lindon, a pale sword held casually in one hand. The Skysworn had obviously interrupted a training session between them—they were facing one another, and Lindon had a few more cuts than just his lip.

She had not taken a single injury that Renfei could see. At least, not in *this* fight. Yerin's whole appearance was a map of battles won and lost, her skin crisscrossed by thin scars, her black robes sliced and tattered, her hair cut straight above her eyes. A pair of silver arms stretched up from behind her, flattening into sword-blades that poised over each shoulder: her Goldsign. A red rope of living madra had been wrapped around her waist, with a complicated knot at her back, and Renfei instinctively kept her spiritual awareness away. The rope was rank with blood aura.

A huge black turtle waited in the back of the room, as long as a horse from tip-to-tail, and the peak of his shell as tall as a man. Orthos regarded her with black eyes that burned with circles of red, and then snorted out a puff of smoke, ignoring her. Dull red light smoldered in the facets of his shell, and smoke drifted up from him as though from a dying fire. As she watched, he stretched his neck out and took a bite from the nearby stone.

Fisher Gesha was the only one to greet the Skysworn with respect, drawing herself to her feet and bowing over her fists pressed together. The old woman was tiny and almost impossibly wrinkled, her hair drawn up into a tight bun. She carried a sharp-edged hook of goldsteel strapped to her back, and the weapon was almost as large as her entire body. From the bottom of her robes, long purple spider legs stretched out, evidence of her drudge. The Fisher Goldsign, a web of madra between her fingers that slowly gave them webbed fingers, was difficult to make out at this distance.

Renfei had checked Gesha's background after finding her with Lindon that first time. The woman was an ordinary Highgold Soulsmith, having spent her entire life in the remote Desolate Wilds out west. If there was anything strange about her, it was finding her in the Empire proper.

Body parts of vivid color, so bright they looked unreal, had been spread out on the floor behind Fisher Gesha. She had abandoned these Remnant parts when Renfei came in, and the pieces behaved oddly when left alone: one claw scuttled in circles, a sapphire lock of hair started to fade as though it were starting to vanish, and a loop of twisted violet entrails reached out a questing tendril as though to slither away.

Was she here to work as a Soulsmith, or had she just turned to her specialty to pass the time?

A man leaned back from an easel and a half-finished swirl of color, holding a brush in one hand and a shallow clay bowl of paint in the other. With a brilliant smile, he turned to her.

Steadying her breath and the flow of her madra, Renfei met his eyes.

Eithan Arelius wore a brilliant blue outer robe, though he had tucked a long towel into his collar to protect his clothes from the stray splatters of paint. His blond hair flowed freely down his back, his smile was brilliant, and his eyes were as bright as if he had just spotted a long-lost friend.

A tiny blue spirit clung to the top of his head, tilting its head to regard Renfei and Bai Rou with childish curiosity. It was like a girl the size of a hand, blue as the deep ocean. She looked human in fine detail except for her legs, which trailed off into a shape like a dress.

"Ah, the Skysworn! What a pleasure you could join us today!"

"How?" Bai Rou asked, astonished.

Eithan waved his brush. "Well, I took painting lessons as a child, but I admit it's not coming back to me as quickly as I would have hoped."

"How are you *here?*" Renfei said. She couldn't let him escape this.

No matter where they had taken Lindon, from the most ordinary dungeon to the safe house of their Underlord himself, they had found Eithan Arelius and the others waiting for them. None of the security measures had ever been disturbed, and there was no sign that it had cost them any effort at all.

The bloodline powers of the Arelius would explain how he had found them in the first place, but even *that* explanation strained belief. They had moved Lindon to different *cities*, sometimes. And even if you assumed Eithan had simply sensed and followed them every time, even an Underlord shouldn't have been able to break the security on this place. It was made to hold Overlords.

There was a trick here, and Renfei didn't dare to hope Eithan would share it with them. If he designed to tell them how he'd done it, perhaps the Skysworn would have an excuse to save them from the anger of their Captain. He was not happy that Eithan Arelius could come and go as he pleased anytime, anywhere.

"Well, we were in the neighborhood when I happened to notice that Lindon was in need of some company. What kind of Patriarch would I be if I didn't serve the least of my family in this fashion?"

Underlord Arelius didn't serve the *least* of his family at all, as far as Renfei could tell. He focused his attention on a few individuals, and recently Lindon was his pet project. It must have taken a great investment of time and resources to raise him to Lowgold in the Path of Black Flame. And after only a few months, Yerin had broken through to Highgold as well. An early advancement—she couldn't be more than eighteen.

Supposedly, she had been the disciple of a Sage before Eithan had found her, but Renfei regarded that rumor with a skeptical eye. There were only three Sages on the entire continent, as far as she knew, and Sages never took disciples. Everyone knew that.

Regardless, Yerin and Eithan were part of some plot, and Renfei had the sick feeling that she and the Skysworn were playing their role just as Eithan had planned.

"Tell me how you avoided our security," Renfei said coldly, refusing to let him evade. She couldn't intimidate this man, not even with the weight of her office—Underlords were too valuable to the Empire to have their freedom restricted, barring great offenses. But she exerted as much pressure as she could to squeeze some kind of answer out of him.

The natural spirit perched on his head shrank back as though frightened of Renfei's voice, but Eithan's smile brightened if anything. "Ah, but I think there's more pressing business, isn't there? You can't be here for my stimulating conversation."

Lindon had his head respectfully down, but now he looked to her. "Is it time already?" he asked. "I thought I was to have two more days." She supposed he was nervous about the answer, but with his tight jaw and wide eyes, he looked more like he was spoiling for a fight instead.

"We must take you to the arena ahead of the others," she explained, turning from Eithan and trying to suppress her frustration with the Underlord. If he would just cooperate, he could make life easier for her, but *no*. The higher-ups of the clans did what they wished, without concern for those beneath them. It was a large reason her parents had sent her to join the Cloud Hammer sect, as a child.

The cloud hovering over her head was boiling, she was sure.

"We can't disclose the location of the venue ahead of time," she said. "To prevent tampering. We will notify the respective Underlords when the venue has been prepared, and then give them time to travel there."

These were standard procedures when the representatives of two great clans or families dueled with real stakes, but since both Underlords had personal pride in this, the Skysworn had to have an Underlord of their own to ensure parity. That was a large part of the reason her Captain was in such a foul mood lately; he hated having to waste his time supervising a fight between children.

That, and he had to deal with Eithan Arelius.

Lindon turned to the others, and even on his contentious face, there was a look of uncertainty. Yerin walked up and tapped him on the chest with her fist. "Your path's as straight as a good road," she said. "Kill him if you can. Try not to die."

The words sounded casual, but Renfei detected a tremble in Yerin's spirit. For the briefest instant, her madra was disrupted in its flow.

A smile pulled at Lindon's lips, as though Yerin had said something touching, but Orthos bulled in a second later. "Destroy him!" the turtle said, through a mouthful of gravel. "Scatter his ashes around the arena! Crush your enemy, drive him before you, hear the lamentations of his—"

"I will do what I can, Orthos," Lindon said, resting his hand on the turtle's head.

The sacred beast snorted, pulling back. "Cycle Blackflame and say that to me again."

Lindon complied, his spirit going from a tranquil pool to a rolling chaos of dark fire in an instant. Renfei pulled her awareness back slightly—destruction was a difficult power to sense too closely. It always reminded her of insects swarming over their prey, and gave her a headache.

His eyes now matched Orthos', giving his features a sinister cast. He had a solid build, such that he looked older than he really was, and the eyes gave him a menacing edge.

"I will do what I can," Lindon said again, but Orthos snapped at the air between them.

"No! The dragon destroys! Victory is not good enough, you have to *finish* him."

Lindon straightened himself, his Blackflame madra suddenly boiling. "I'll send his ashes back to the Jai clan in a jar." His dark eyes faded, and he smiled sheepishly. "...if I can."

Orthos snorted. "We need to have a Soulsmith make you a spine." He wandered away, muttering to himself, and Fisher Gesha approached next.

"All right," she said, slapping her palms together. "To business, hm? Which would you like to take?"

To Renfei's surprise, she led Lindon to a huge trunk at the corner of his cell. Renfei hadn't noticed it before; she had been too preoccupied watching the people. That was a mistake, and she chided herself for it. She had worked for the Skysworn long enough to know that it was the detail you missed that killed you.

The Fisher threw open the chest, pulling out devices of bright color: constructs and weapons. The products of a Soulsmith.

"Well, hurry it up," she said. "Tell me what you want."

"Everything," Lindon said. He sounded much more certain than when he had spoken with Orthos.

Fisher Gesha's eyebrows shot up. "Everything? You want to fight with your pockets bulging like a squirrel's cheeks?"

"Everything," he said again.

When he was finally ready to leave, he turned to the Skysworn with a bright blue band around his head, a purple bracelet on one wrist, a black bracer on the other, three rods of varying length and color at his waist, a gelatinous red mass that pulsed like a heart stuck to his chest, a bright green dagger in an ankle sheath, and—sure enough—his pockets swollen, spilling multi-colored light into the air.

He looked like a clown. More weapons did not mean a more prepared warrior, and everyone present had to know that.

She looked to the others as though they would stop him, but even Yerin looked resigned. Eithan beamed as though watching his proud son leave for the first day at a School of sacred arts.

"We will send a messenger to contact you when the fight is ready to begin," Renfei said. "Each Underlord is of course allowed a retinue, though we hope that you will conduct yourself with honor, as befitting your respected rank and station."

Eithan turned back to his painting. It depicted a tall, lonely mountain, jutting from the surrounding landscape like a gray spear. The top was flat, as though the summit of the mountain had been sliced off, and it was capped by an ancient stone building supported by columns.

Renfei stared at the picture. She was afraid her mouth might be hanging open.

"See you there!" Eithan said.

***

On the top of a gray mountain, Lindon waited, cycling Blackflame madra to fight off the chill of the relentless wind. The gusts shoved at him, stronger than he would have thought possible—even with his Iron body reinforced by Lowgold madra, he had to bend down and grip the edge of a nearby boulder to stay in place.

The power of wind was strong here, covering his spiritual sight in green swirls. A Jade wouldn't be able to survive alone under these conditions; they would eventually exhaust their madra fighting against the wind and be shoved off the sheer edge of the nearby cliff.

Lindon had grown up in Sacred Valley, surrounded by mountains, and *this* mountain was a strange one. It had been sliced off at the top as though by a sword, so it now terminated in a flat plane. A vast stone structure had been built at the center, squat and ancient, supported by granite pillars.

It was impossible to reach this place without flying, and even the Skysworn who had carried them here on their Thousand-Mile

Cloud had been forced to fight their way up. Sacred eagles with emerald talons had harassed them all the way.

Lindon didn't even know where in the Blackflame Empire he was. South, they said, but he had no way to tell.

He had traveled with the Skysworn for a full day, spent the night huddled in a tiny valley, and then taken off again the next day at dawn. When they finally reached this barren peak, the two green-armored Truegolds had stuffed him into a room carved into the base of the mountain for two more nights, leaving him to marinate in nerves.

Today, of all days, they'd taken him out only to abandon him on the edge of the cliff while they checked inside the "sanctuary," as they called it, for potential tampering.

The Blackflame madra warmed his spirit and his flesh, protecting him from the cold of the wind, but he shivered anyway.

The day had finally come.

He hadn't seen Jai Long for months, not since the Skysworn had taken him away to prevent him from causing a panic with his identity as a Blackflame. At first, he had almost been relieved, thinking that his imprisonment meant the duel would be canceled.

Then Eithan had shown up and told him otherwise.

Eithan had brought Yerin and the others to him more than ten times, and each time the Skysworn either moved him or increased security. It never seemed to matter.

Lindon stared up at the stone columns, wind whipping at his hair and his outer robe. Though his heart pounded and his breath was coming faster, he felt a strange calm.

The others, especially Yerin and Fisher Gesha, had done everything they could to prepare him for this day. He was as ready as he could be.

There were still no guarantees, of course. But this was just another obstacle he had to overcome. Just one more step.

...of course, he was still armed to the teeth.

The constructs felt strange against his skin. The blue headband tickled, the purple loop around his wrist squeezed, the mass on his chest pulsed in time with his heartbeat. He had helped Fisher Gesha make every one of these constructs...though perhaps "helped" was too strong a word. She had provided the bindings and the dead matter to make the constructs, and he had simply assisted her and maintained them afterwards.

Their essence bled into the air, like tiny motes of colored light rising from the surface of the constructs as their madra dissolved. Lindon couldn't help but worry when he saw that. They would degrade over time, and probably wouldn't be useful in any fight after this one, but they *should* last at least that long. Still, he couldn't help feeling like they'd crumble at any second.

He looked up as two figures walked out of the cavernous entrance to the sanctuary. Bai Rou loomed over his partner, his green armor making him seem as steady as a statue, his glowing yellow eyes in the shadow of his hat striking and intimidating. He seemed to radiate menace.

He was overwhelming, but Lindon preferred the impression Renfei gave: she was calm, composed, ready to act at a moment's notice. Her black hair was pulled back in a tail, a gray cloud hovering inches over her head, hammer bouncing on her hip. She didn't seem threatening, just in control.

That was how Lindon wanted to feel.

She met him with a direct, unblinking gaze. "We're to confiscate your weapons," she said.

Lindon's hands instinctively moved to cover his pockets. The Skysworn had taken his pack when they first captured him and had yet to return it to him, and he felt almost helpless without it. The constructs returned some measure of that control.

"Jai Long will have a weapon," he said reasonably. "Surely you won't deny me mine, if this duel is to be entertaining at all."

He had some strategies he could attempt against Jai Long. Eithan put Lindon's chance of winning at thirty or forty percent. *"Those aren't the worst odds I've ever bet on!"* he'd said.

But Lindon's chances went down significantly if he had to walk in unarmed. All of the ideas he'd come up with for rigging the fight had involved altering the arena in some way, but it seemed that the Skysworn had anticipated him. Unless he could still get some time alone with the stage...

"We will return any weapons appropriate to your stage of advancement," Renfei said. "We can't have you bringing an Underlord weapon into a fight between Golds."

Lindon shifted so that his outer robe covered up the pulsing mass attached to his chest. It had been worth a try.

They peeled the constructs off him one at a time, and though he put up a few more halfhearted attempts at bargaining, he didn't struggle. They would sense any object of power he had on him, regardless of how he tried to hide.

This was within his expectations. During one of their planning sessions, Eithan had warned him that they would likely confiscate anything too powerful, though he had hoped they would match his weapons to the level of his opponent. In that case, Lindon would have been left Highgold and Truegold tools as well.

Renfei did give him a reproachful look when she discovered that one of his launcher constructs was made from Underlord-grade parts. As was the artificial heart on his chest. And the band around his forehead.

Two more of his constructs were Truegold, and four were Highgold. They sealed all those into a scripted box that Bai Rou produced, but kept the Lowgold devices in a sack. Those would be returned to him quickly, he assumed. He hoped.

"Your first core is..." Renfei flicked her spirit through Lindon's, and he froze, wondering if she would see past the first of his surprises. But she said "...Jade," and he relaxed. "Your second core is Lowgold, so you go on record as a Lowgold. You can take in weapons appropriate to your stage."

As expected, they missed Suriel's marble. The glass ball sat tucked into his pocket, burning with a steady blue candle-flame. Had they looked inside, they would have seen it, but they had done all their searching with their spiritual sense.

They also left him his badge, which was heavy and cold against his chest. It was made of gold, etched with a hammer, and it reminded him of home. Nothing reminded him that he was a sacred artist of Sacred Valley like that badge.

The two Skysworn ushered him inside, and Lindon took a deep breath.

As far as he was concerned, the duel had begun. From here on out, he had to take any advantage he could.

"What about my sacred beast?" Lindon asked them. "I have a contracted partner. Correct me if I'm wrong, but I believe sacred artists are allowed to do battle alongside their partners."

Bai Rou gave a single, deep laugh.

"Traditionally, contracted partners are allowed to duel as a single unit," Renfei confirmed. "However, Orthos is too far above you. That makes you *his* partner, and if he were to participate, this would be officially recorded as a duel between Jai Long of the Jai clan and Orthos, guardian of the Arelius family. This is not what we were permitted to allow, nor what either side wants."

They walked through the entrance, the wind cutting off as though sliced with a knife, and Lindon started to sweat. It was quite cool inside, but every possibility they denied him reduced his chance of winning.

This was still within his predictions, though. At least they'd left him *some* weapons.

The hall was a vast, empty space, and Lindon suspected it was rare to see a visitor in a year. Dust had piled up in the corners, cobwebs on the ceiling, and the stone was worn with the passage of time. More, there was no sign of any inhabitants other than the fresh boot-prints in the dust that must have been left by the Skysworn.

A single heavy, wooden door waited at the end of the hall, and Bai Rou pushed it open. Yellow eyes bright, he ushered Lindon inside.

Or rather, outside.

The room was fairly spacious, but the far wall was open. Only pillars held up the ceiling, and the spaces between them were filled with views of a snowy mountain range. The sight brought back a sudden, unexpected longing for home.

Wind rushed in again, though not as fierce as it had been on the edge of the cliff. This room was about a hundred yards square, and had no furnishings at all. Besides the wall behind Lindon, with its single door, everything else was open to the sky.

The Underlords were already waiting.

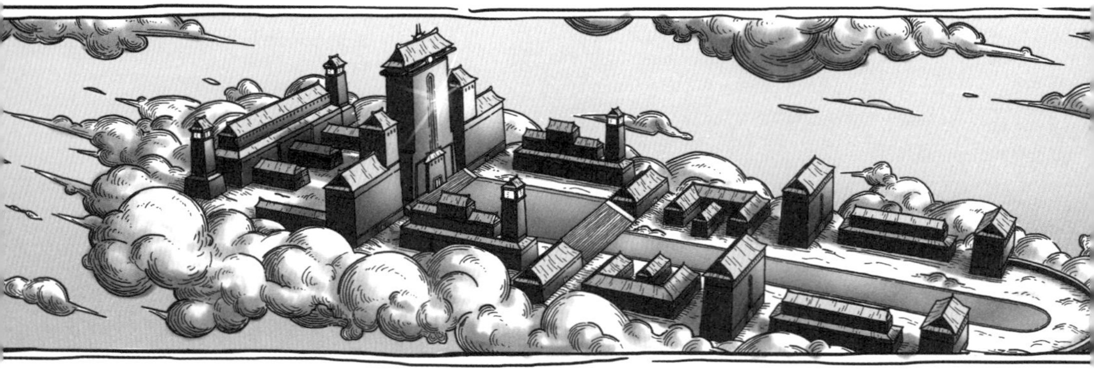

IV

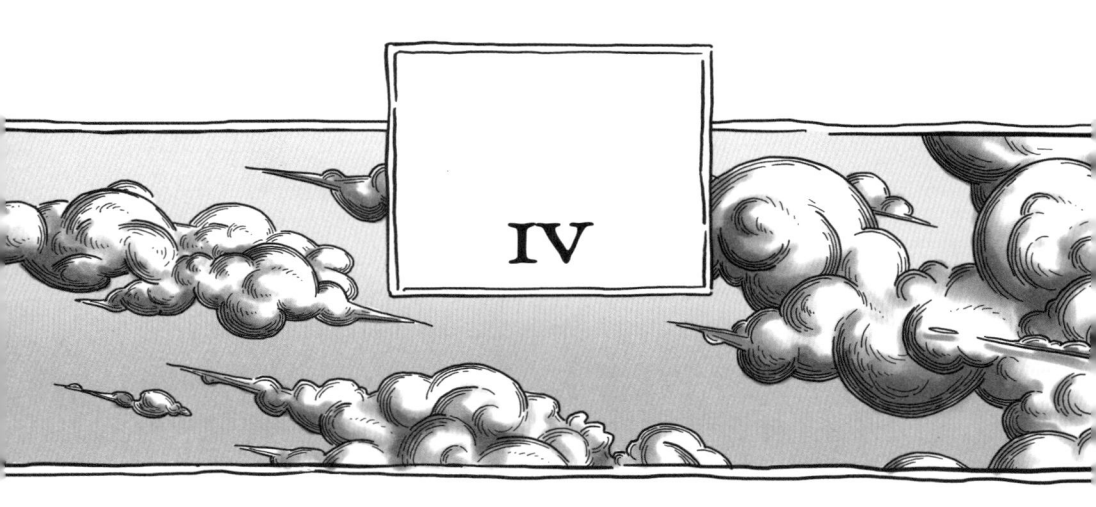

Eithan stood on Lindon's right, and he gave a cheery wave when he saw Lindon, his smile as bright as ever.

Opposite him was Jai Daishou, the Patriarch of the Jai clan. An old man, he wore white robes with highlights of blue, and his white hair ran in a straight river down his back. Thanks to the Goldsign of the Path of the Stellar Spear, his hair was a collection of metal strands that reflected bright in the sunlight. He gripped a blue-hafted spear in his right hand, grinding its butt against the stone of the floor.

He had deteriorated since Lindon had last seen him.

The last time, Jai Daishou had looked like a fit man in his eighties. His back had been as straight as his spear, and his eyes were sharp. Now, his back was curved as the branch of an old tree, and his eyes were half-lidded, as though it was a strain to keep them open. He held his spear, not like he was ready to use it, but as though it was the only thing holding him up.

He may have been an Underlord, but he had one foot in the underworld. Lindon had spent long hours hoping he would die before this duel—if he was gone, the Arelius family would have nothing at stake here. It would purely be a duel between Lindon and Jai Long.

In that case, the Skysworn wouldn't have checked the surroundings for traps. Lindon could have cheated to his heart's content.

They must have just arrived, because Eithan didn't greet his opposite until Lindon was close enough to hear. "Jai Daishou! You're in good health, it seems. Better than last I saw you."

The Jai Underlord's hand shot up to his chest, clawing at the center, as though his heart were seizing up at that moment. His wrinkled face twisted in hatred, but his voice was clear as he responded. "This is a waste of my time. Without your tricks, this duel is already over. You should have had the boy's head delivered to me on a plate and saved us all a day's travel."

"I asked him about that," Eithan said. "He told me he prefers his head where it is."

That was a true story. While Lindon had been practicing with Fisher Gesha, Eithan had looked up from his book and suggested that this whole thing could be resolved if they just delivered Lindon's severed head to the enemy. It would look bad for the Arelius, but losing an official duel would be worse, because there would be a public record of their shame.

Lindon had politely requested to keep his head attached.

There were three other people in the room, but Lindon had focused on the two Patriarchs first.

Another old man stood in the center, equally distant from both Underlords. He wore the green armor of the Skysworn, but there was something on his back sticking up from his shoulders. Was he wearing a backpack?

He wasn't as ancient as Jai Daishou seemed to be, but he still looked like he could be Lindon's grandfather. His build was still powerful, and he wore his green Skysworn armor more naturally than Renfei or Bai Rou, as though he had been born in it. Its plates were so scuffed and dented that the armor might well be as old as he was.

His gray hair was long and matted, hanging down in tangled curtains. A large patch of his face was scarred and twisted, as though it had been burned, and he wore a large sword strapped to his back.

His scratched armor, dirty hair, and scorched face didn't make him look weak to Lindon. It was the opposite, if anything. He looked like a man who belonged on a battlefield.

The old man chewed on a leaf that stuck halfway out of his mouth, regarding Lindon with a weary expression. "All right, all right. On behalf of the Blackflame Empire, I witness this duel between Jai Daishou of the Jai clan and Eithan Arelius of the Arelius family. As an Underlord and Captain of the Skysworn sect, I, Naru Gwei, certify upon my word of honor that no tampering has occurred at the venue before my arrival, and I will not tolerate any further interference by outside parties during the duel itself."

Every word was hammered in like a nail, as though he were reciting something while desperately wishing he could be anywhere else.

"It's a joy to have you here, Gwei," Eithan said happily. "Of all the duel adjudicators in the Empire, you're still the highest-ranked, aren't you? It's honestly a pleasure, a *pleasure*, to have such an esteemed—"

"Eithan, one more word out of you and I will personally beat you down into the center of the mountain." Naru Gwei gnawed on his leaf as he spoke, still looking as though he'd rather be in bed. "I don't have any love for the Jai clan, but as for *you*, if I saw you on fire I'd hold an umbrella for you so the rain didn't put you out."

"I don't feel like that's *entirely* warranted."

Lindon's heart was already hammering as the duel loomed over him and he tried not to look at the red-masked man standing behind Jai Daishou, but his heartbeat quickened and his stomach soured when he realized that Eithan had antagonized the *judge*. What had he done? Would Naru Gwei interfere on Jai Long's behalf?

"Wei Shi Lindon Arelius," the Skysworn Captain said, "go stand next to your Underlord and face your opposite. Wipe that smile off your face, Eithan. Heavens above, it sickens me to look at you."

Lindon stood shoulder-to-shoulder with Eithan...but slid away slightly. The less he could associate himself with Eithan in the judge's mind, the better. For Eithan's part, he looked as though he were enjoying himself immensely.

With no other choice, Lindon finally looked at the two people standing behind Jai Daishou.

He didn't mind seeing Jai Chen. About his age, she was small and pale, with soft black hair that tumbled down past her shoulders. Her wide eyes were fixed on the judge in an expression of concern, but when she saw Lindon looking at her, she turned to him. She was dressed in powder-blue robes cut longer and looser than the traditional sacred artist's robes, and her sleeves hid her hands until she raised one in his direction.

She didn't smile—she still looked worried—but at least she had acknowledged him. That was a friendly gesture, right? He hoped the Blackflame Empire didn't have a history of acknowledging enemies with the wave of a hand.

He smiled tightly, the closest to a friendly expression he could manage with his stomach twisting, and nodded to her.

Then, for the first time since entering, he finally looked straight at his opponent.

Jai Long was already watching him.

His dark eyes glistened through a gap in the strips of red cloth that wrapped his head completely. He was tall and lithe, his robes dark blue, and he held his spear at his side.

Lindon brightened when he saw that spear—it wasn't a shaft of pure white, the signature weapon of the Jai clan's ancestor. *That* spear could steal madra, and this one was a mundane weapon of wood and metal.

Jai Long raised his own hand to Lindon, which returned concerns that perhaps this gesture was meant to show respect to an enemy. He couldn't see anything of his opponent's expression beneath the mask, but he decided to take the gesture as cordial and raised his own right hand.

Naru Gwei looked from Lindon to Jai Long, ensuring their attention was on him, before he took the leaf out of his mouth and spoke. "This is a duel for pride. As such, the champions will fight to death or incapacitation. I am here to ensure that the Underlords cannot interfere, so fight without reserve. The bounds of your battle shall be confined to this room; if it seems you will breach those bounds, I will return you by force."

He slid the leaf back into his lips and continued talking, but now it no longer sounded like he was quoting. "Even though this is a...Lowgold with a second, weaker core...against a Truegold, it's still a fight between two great families. It will reflect official rankings, as well as the reputation of both powers. If you can resolve your differences, do so now."

He didn't sound like he had much hope for that to happen.

Lindon thought back to what he'd heard from the others over the intervening months of his imprisonment. The Arelius family was dangerously under-funded since the attack of the Jai clan, but the Jai clan's reputation was at an all-time low. Some merchant organizations refused to deal with the Jai clan anymore, either because of their weakness or because of the poor form they'd shown in suddenly attacking the Arelius family's workers.

Attacking them and *failing* was the real sin, as Lindon understood it. If Jai Daishou had succeeded in killing Eithan, and the rest of his fighters had crippled the Arelius family work force, the other Underlords of the Blackflame Empire would have considered it a clever move.

On top of all that, their Underlord didn't have long to live. In this case, it would only take one pebble to start an avalanche that buried them.

But it was down to Lindon to be that pebble.

He gathered himself, mentally running down the four construct-weapons that he had been allowed to keep. They would be of limited use compared to the ones he had been denied, but his plans would still work with them. He hoped.

"Step to the center of the room and face your enemy," Naru Gwei said, walking over to the open side of the room. He crossed his arms and leaned one shoulder against a column, not seeming to care about the sheer drop behind him. "Everyone else, back up. I'll be protecting the duel from you, not you from the duel."

Eithan not only backed up, but sat down, propping his back against the wall and stretching his legs out in front of him, crossing one ankle over another. He looked like he was making himself comfortable at a picnic.

Casting worried glances at the participants, Jai Chen followed Jai Daishou as he slowly made his way over to another end of the room.

They left Jai Long and Lindon with plenty of open space around them. And nothing to watch but each other. For Lindon's part, his enemy seemed to swell and fill the entire world.

It felt too soon.

It had been a year, an entire *year* since he stood at the peak of the Transcendent Ruins. That didn't feel real. Where had the time gone? It couldn't possibly have been a year; he felt cheated.

Suddenly, he felt like running to Eithan and begging out. Someone had made a mistake—he wasn't ready yet. He needed more time.

"Exchange greetings," Naru Gwei commanded.

Jai Long pressed his fists together, holding his spear in the crook of his elbow, and gave a shallow bow. His eyes didn't leave Lindon.

Mechanically, Lindon's body returned the gesture. His mind was still floating in disbelief. Was he really here?

"I have to thank you for healing my sister," Jai Long said. "You killed my brother, but you gave me my sister back. For my part, we're even."

That jostled Lindon awake, and he rushed to speak. "We can walk away! I have no grudge against *you*."

"If it were up to me, I would have called it off already. I would never fight for the Jai clan at all." He spun his spear up to grip it in both hands, lowering himself into a stance and pointing the spearhead at Lindon. "But it isn't up to me. I will be as gentle as I can."

Some of Lindon's nerves retreated. If his enemy was taking it easy on him, then maybe he had a better chance than he'd imagined.

"Ready yourselves," Naru Gwei said. Lindon leaned forward onto the balls of his feet, flexing his knees, ready to run. Jai Long's fists tightened on his weapon. Madra spun through Lindon's channels even as wind spun through the open space.

Whether he liked it or not, the time was here. And he was ready.

"Begin," the Skysworn Underlord said, and a thunderclap tore the air between the two fighters.

Lindon shot forward.

I'd contend he thinks of you like a Blackflame, Yerin had told him. *He'll want to hold off and block your first technique. Break through it.*

Lindon activated the purple bracelet wrapping his right wrist, casting his hand forward. A bright purple line shot forward like a whip, its tip blue-white.

Back in the Desolate Wilds, the Fishers had a technique they called the Snare. It used their connection madra to stick to prey, which they could then reel in with raw strength. Fisher Gesha had brought a Fisher Remnant from home, and when she and Lindon dissected it, they had found a Snare binding.

When they made it into a construct, they built some modifications. Now, the technique inside the purple bracelet was called the Void Snare.

Jai Long had the speed to intercept the technique, of course. He was a Truegold. He swept his spear through it, but his weapon only passed through the line of Fisher madra and was stuck. The string had no physical substance, but drew objects toward Lindon.

And the tip of the whip, the shining blue-white tip, struck Jai Long in the shoulder.

Inserting pure madra into an opponent's body wouldn't work exactly like the Empty Palm. That technique was designed to disrupt an enemy's body, interrupting their control over their entire spirit, and it had to land on the core.

This was more of a localized pulse, like the sting of a needle compared to the stab of a sword. When the tip of the whip hit Jai Long's shoulder, it discharged its payload of pure madra.

The power in his shoulder was disrupted. Not enough to prevent him from using his sacred arts, but enough to keep him from breaking the line for just a moment.

A moment was enough. With all his strength, Lindon pulled.

His strength was nothing next to Jai Long's, and of course the Truegold resisted. But Lindon wasn't trying to pull his enemy to *him*.

Quite the opposite.

Lindon pulled himself forward, launching himself toward his opponent.

Struck by the Void Snare, it took half a breath before Jai Long could muster his madra and blow the purple line apart with white light. By the time he managed it, breaking the technique, Lindon was already inside spear range.

"A good fight is a short fight," Orthos said. *"A dragon uses his full strength, whether he's fighting a Sage or a mouse."*

End it quickly.

Lindon had already pulled the launcher from his waist: a crackling bar of living lightning that had once been the wrist-bones of a Remnant. The binding inside snapped with power; it wasn't just lightning, there was more to it, but Lindon didn't need to understand the Path of this strange Remnant to use its power.

He activated the construct, and an arrow of sizzling light blasted Jai Long.

Jai Long's motions blurred as he pulled his spear back, sweeping it vertically in front of himself, leaving a trail of white light on the air. That white light bloomed into a hissing serpent, which was instantly torn apart by the blast from Lindon's launcher.

Lindon could feel the construct snap as he used it—he wouldn't get a second shot. That was the risk of using a construct after having it exposed for so long to let its essence dissolve.

Fortunately, he didn't need a second shot. The launcher was just to keep Jai Long on the defensive; if he had used that speed to take a step backward and attack instead, he would have skewered Lindon through the gut by now.

Instead, he had been prepared for an attack by Blackflame. He had been hit by unknown attacks from unexpected angles, and he was trying to treat Lindon 'gently.'

He hadn't come into this fight with a willingness to kill.

That didn't mean he wouldn't end up killing Lindon if he was in a position to do so, or if things went wrong, but Lindon had been counting on that moment of hesitation to cause Jai Long to decide to defend instead of attack. That was Lindon's chance of victory, and he seized it.

He already had his next move ready.

Even as his right hand cast the ruined launcher construct aside, his left had already withdrawn an object from his pocket: a rounded skull the size of his fist. It was the brown of old parchment and felt greasy in his hand. A single-use, simple construct.

"Warriors focus on weapons too much, you see," Gesha had taught him. *"Powerful treasures, legendary swords, yes? In a duel, the winner is not the one with the strongest weapon."*

Lindon dropped the Nether-drain Swamp construct at Jai Long's feet. The skull cackled as it struck the ground, filled with Lindon's madra. Now free from restrictions, the Remnant skull acted according to its nature: it exploded into a technique.

This technique covered the ground like brown paint in an instant, splattering on Lindon's legs, but covering Jai Long to the ankles. The paint stuck to the floor like glue, but Lindon had expected it—he tore free of the few drops that reached him.

Jai Long was not only caught off his guard, but the technique had originated between his feet. He was stuck fast, at least for the instant before the paint drew itself up into a thousand grasping, scaly brown hands, grabbing his legs and pulling him down toward them.

His eyes left Lindon as he jerked his head down. Now he was not only stuck, but the hands pulled at his feet, keeping him off balance, drawing his attention.

"You may have noticed I don't have a Goldsign," Eithan had said. "No Remnant, you see."

Jai Long's core was open. He was swinging the butt of his spear up, intending to crack Lindon in the head, but Lindon was already close enough.

"I reached Gold purely through accumulated power. We can do the same for you, if you like."

With just a thought, Lindon removed the veil around his Lowgold pure core.

He couldn't disable Jai Long completely. His Truegold madra was too difficult for Lindon's weaker spirit to disrupt. But Lindon could buy himself an instant with a much-weaker opponent. If he were still Jade, his technique would have slid harmlessly off Jai Long's spirit.

Before the butt of the spear reached him, Lindon slammed his Empty Palm into Jai Long's core.

Driven along with the motion, his pure madra slammed like a spike into the heart of Jai Long's spirit. The madra washed through his channels, disrupting the natural rhythm of his soul, choking out his techniques. Madra that could not be controlled by a pattern was useless.

The spear smacked into Lindon's forehead, and his world flashed white. If Jai Long had Enforced the blow or his weapon, that could have been a lethal strike. But the Empty Palm had broken his Enforcer techniques.

Lindon stumbled back, agony stabbing through his head, his eyes blinded by pain and tears. He couldn't even be sure if the effect of his Empty Palm had lasted, or if Jai Long had shaken it off immediately.

He had to assume it had worked, so he focused his breathing on his core. The pain in his skull made it hard to focus, but if the Empty Palm *had* worked, it would only last for so long.

He had to make it count.

In a breath, he reeled his pure madra back to one of his cores. The one that, in his spiritual vision, shone a soft blue-white.

On his next breath, he drew from his other core.

Black fire ran along his madra channels. His eyes warmed as they changed color, and Lindon focused. He couldn't have put much distance between himself and Jai Long, but the Truegold must be still off-balance from the spiritual disruption. Otherwise, the fight would have ended already.

Under Lindon's direction, Blackflame madra slithered like roots to every corner of his body. According to the ancient Enforcer technique, it ran into his skin, penetrated his muscles, and burned his bones. It felt like his body had begun to dissolve from the inside-out, and the heat was uncomfortable.

He ignited the madra, activating the technique.

The Burning Cloak sprung to life around him, the air blazing with a hazy, translucent shell of black-and-red fire.

His madra would run out quickly, with the Cloak active. The Enforcer technique burned his muscles, and his Bloodforged Iron body activated to restore him. The combined effect felt as though his limbs were constantly sizzling, and both the technique and the Iron body required madra.

He couldn't keep this up for long, but he didn't need to. He had an Enforcer technique, and for the moment Jai Long didn't.

Under the power of the Burning Cloak, Lindon kicked off the

stone. He exploded with motion, covering the distance between himself and Jai Long in an instant.

There was a long, frozen moment where Lindon's eyes and his opponent's met.

Then Lindon stabbed him.

This was the fourth and final construct he'd been allowed to keep. Made from only a Remnant's claw, with no binding involved, it was what she called a "dead construct." It had no abilities apart from the properties of the madra it was made of and any script you carved into it.

In the case of this dagger, there was no script. Its structure wasn't solid enough to be carved, and even if it were, the pressure of a script would have torn it apart immediately.

It was black as ink, the length of one of Lindon's hands, and shaped like a long fang. It felt like a waterskin full of worms, stretching in Lindon's fingers, as everything except the tip was soft and pliant. The point was sharp as a spearhead, and it pierced Jai Long's robes at the chest.

With no Enforcer technique to protect him, the Truegold couldn't resist. Blood sprayed from him as his skin broke.

The dagger wasn't strong enough to penetrate any deeper, but that was enough. As it tasted Jai Long's blood, the dagger squirmed eagerly in Lindon's grip, worming its way into the wound and slithering into Jai Long's bloodstream.

Lindon leaped away, then let the Burning Cloak die.

Jai Long grunted, but he didn't scream as Lindon had expected. Instead he stood, gripping his spear, as he fought the foreign madra inside of him.

If Lindon hadn't broken his defense with the Empty Palm first, this would never have worked. The sheer power of Jai Long's spirit wouldn't have allowed the dagger inside.

Now, the Path of Twisted Blood went to work.

Fisher Gesha had determined that the madra was harvested primarily from life, shadow, and blood aura, but it had been twisted even further by the Path's practitioner. The Remnant from which she took the claw had been sliding inside animals' veins and twisting them from the inside out, breaking every bone in their body at once.

She hadn't been able to determine why it did so. Remnants didn't feed on blood or flesh, but on madra, so killing would only be an expenditure of its energy. Nonetheless, that was what every part of its body did, even when separated from the others. This Remnant's guiding purpose was to kill.

The same was true of its claw.

After a moment, Jai Long's arms both twisted backwards. It looked like he was a toy a child had decided to break. His neck slid to the right, despite his obvious effort to fight. His legs were still snared by the grasping brown hands emerging from the swamp, but the rest of his body had begun to contort.

"You...fight...like...a coward..." Jai Long's words were choked out one at a time, but they emerged tinged with rage from a tightening jaw.

Lindon didn't expect this weapon to actually kill Jai Long. The Remnant had been at the Highgold level, so Jai Long's madra would eventually exert control again.

But he had planned for one of two things to happen: either rendering the opponent helpless would count as a win, or it would give him an opportunity.

Lindon looked to Naru Gwei, but the Skysworn Captain was still watching through the filthy curtain of his matted gray hair, the burn scar around his left eye giving him a sinister cast. He chewed on a leaf and looked completely unconcerned. Not at all as though he were about to stop the match.

Reluctantly, Lindon gathered black fire into a ball between his hands.

The red-streaked black flame built, wild and difficult to control. It stressed his concentration and his spirit to gather, and only a few months ago he would have had to use some pure madra props to execute this technique at all. After practicing during his enforced isolation, he had improved...though a technique that required several seconds to gather would be of limited use in a fight.

"Surrender," Lindon said, voice strained with the effort of controlling the dragon's breath.

A white light flashed beneath Jai Long's clothes. It was fitful and weak, struggling against the intrusion of the Path of Twisted Blood, but Jai Long's head snapped straight again. He dropped his spear, but pulled both his arms back under control. The brown hands holding his ankles started to dissolve, the Nether-drain Swamp dissolving under white light.

Lindon released the dragon's breath.

He had no grudge against Jai Long. The man was an obstacle, and one he had to pass to continue, but not quite a true *enemy*. And he would hate to think that he had healed Jai Chen only to kill her brother.

He hadn't asked for this duel. But over the intervening year, one thing had become clear: he was the weaker party. He didn't have the luxury of pulling his punches.

If he didn't come at Jai Long intending to kill, he couldn't win.

The dragon's fire blasted toward Jai Long, not soft and billowing like a cloud, but a tight bar of almost liquid-looking red-and-black flame. It skewed right, and Lindon had an instant to hope that perhaps it would only take off Jai Long's arm, but leave him alive.

Then there came a blinding flash of white.

Jai Long blocked the bar of red and black with a shaft of pure white madra. The spear was almost seven feet long, smooth, and etched with a web of scripts that Lindon could only see because of their bright glow. The spearhead accounted for a foot of its length, flat and white.

The Ancestor's Spear. He'd taken it from nowhere.

Lindon's heart dropped.

How had he gotten it back? *Where* had he gotten it? Lindon thought *Eithan* had taken it. Had his own Underlord returned it?

"I think you have a decent chance of winning," Eithan had told him. *"As long as Jai Long is only a Truegold."*

"If he's an Underlord, then surely they won't continue with the duel," Lindon had said. *"It's only remotely fair in the first place because we're both technically Gold."*

"It's true; if Jai Long has truly reached Underlord, he will become my *problem. But there is a...third option."*

Jai Long swept his spear through the dragon's breath, splashing tongues of Blackflame onto the stone floor and ceiling. They hissed when the stone dissolved as though under acid.

"Reaching Underlord requires a Truegold to clear three distinct stages. If he has cleared the second, weaving soulfire from aura, then he will defeat you instantly. The first stage, however, is opening a space in your soul."

In the same motion as he disrupted Lindon's technique, Jai Long retaliated. An arm-long snake of white madra was born, its jaws agape as it flew toward Lindon. He reactivated the Burning Cloak, cycling madra to his limbs.

"If he pulls a weapon out of nowhere, he's cleared the first stage. That means he has taken half a step into the Lord realm.."

Lindon pivoted into a punch, spraying Blackflame out of the punch in a half-formed Striker technique. The force of the flame met the serpent, and the two clashed in a burst of light. But it wasn't enough to stop the Truegold attack.

From the cloud of Blackflame, the serpent emerged, avoiding Lindon's fist and sliding over his hand.

It *burned*.

Lindon screamed as the snake slid over the back of his hand and up his forearm, scoring the skin and burning, slicing him like a red-hot knife. The technique's madra dissipated in a blink and the snake disappeared, but it had already traveled up to his elbow, leaving a twisting trail of blood all the way up his arm.

He held up his other hand in defense, though he had no technique gathered. It was just the instinctive panic of a wounded animal. It was hard to see through the pain, and the rising tide of fear that threatened to choke him.

All of his preparation had come to nothing. His weapons were gone. His plans had failed.

He was at Jai Long's mercy.

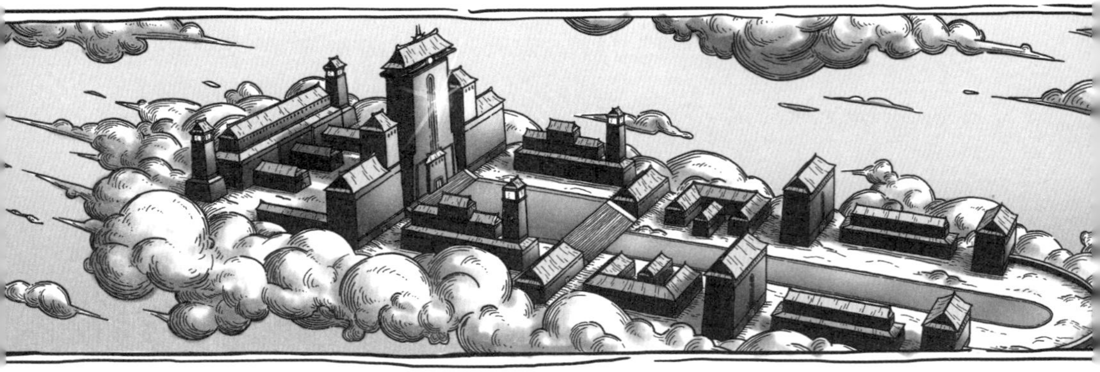

V

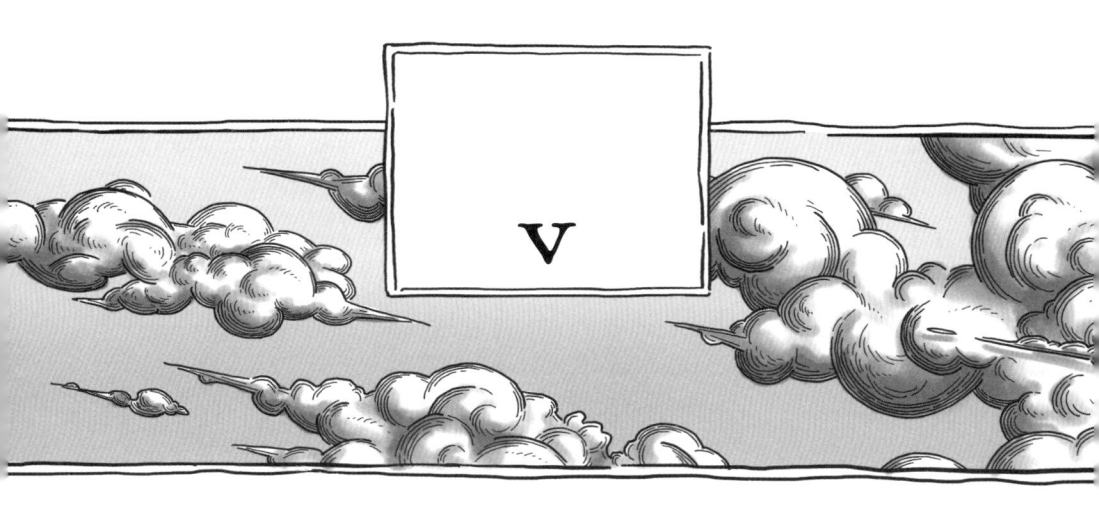

Jai Long moved in a flash. His red-wrapped face was only two feet from Lindon's own, his pale spear raised, poised to plunge down. Lindon scrambled backward, but the weapon wasn't pointed at his head or chest. Jai Long paused a moment to take aim at...his leg.

He was trying to spear Lindon through the leg. That was probably a mercy, but Lindon certainly didn't feel like it at the moment. His arm already felt like it had been chewed up and spat out, and now his enemy was trying to *cut off his leg*. He almost fell as he scrambled to escape.

"Enough," Eithan said. His voice wasn't stern, but it echoed through the room like the command of an emperor.

Jai Long's spear froze. Lindon backed up another few steps, keeping a wary eye on the spear, but he still turned slightly to see Eithan.

The Arelius Underlord was standing now, hands in his pockets, a slightly pained smile on his face. "It's clear the Arelius family has lost this duel. Congratulations, Jai Daishou. You have found a worthy replacement...though I'm sorry you had to use such a tight leash."

Lindon didn't understand that, but Jai Long tensed. Jai Daishou's wrinkled face twisted with disgust, and he barked at his champion: "It isn't over yet. Kill him."

Jai Long tightened his grip on the spear as though straining against something. "I carried out your command," he said, through gritted teeth. "He surrendered; we're done." Jai Chen let out a breath of relief at almost the same time Lindon did.

"It's not a duel to surrender," came an aged, lazy voice from the cliff overlooking the drop. Naru Gwei's dirty gray hair drifted in the wind as he rested against the column, arms still crossed. He chewed on his leaf as though unconcerned.

Jai Long stopped. He turned slowly, lifting the Ancestor's Spear.

Behind him, Jai Daishou looked as though the heavens had opened and given him a gift.

Lindon clenched his jaw at the pain in his arm, but his Bloodforged Iron body had already started pulling madra to heal it. He cycled the Path of Black Flame, preparing the Burning Cloak.

Eithan raised both hands from his pockets. "Hey now, let's not go too far. I've admitted my loss, Captain, openly and without reservation. I will accept the cost of losing."

"Not how it works, Arelius," Naru Gwei said, spitting out his leaf and replacing it with another. "I'm the adjudicator. Surrender all you want, but the boy isn't killed or crippled."

Lindon could feel the world tightening around him. Jai Long gathered his madra, white light spreading from beneath his robes.

He wasn't going to get out of this. He couldn't cheat. He wouldn't catch Jai Long off guard again. Eithan couldn't save him.

Lindon was on his own. He was walking out of this killed... or crippled.

His Burning Cloak ignited.

"We've had our differences," Eithan said, his voice becoming more serious. "Don't make this about me."

The Skysworn Captain turned back to the two champions.

"Fight," he said.

Jai Long blurred as he moved, and Lindon struck to the side with his good arm. It was a bad punch—he was off-balance, and his stance was sloppy; Yerin would have mocked him for it—but his knuckles met the edge of the Ancestor's Spear.

It sliced his skin.

The force of his punch knocked Jai Long's blow aside, so the spear swept harmlessly by his shoulder, but Lindon hardly noticed. The pain from this tiny cut was almost as overwhelming as the agony from his shredded arm.

This spear cut not just the flesh, but the spirit. Spiritual damage, as he had experienced several times before, was deeper and harder to ignore than physical pain. It cut him to his core, and his Blackflame core shivered.

Black-and-red light slithered down the spear, and Jai Long took a step back. He jabbed the spear backwards, thrusting the butt into the floor behind him. The Blackflame madra spurted out with the motion, venting into the floor, scorching a pothole into the stone.

So that was how it worked.

Fisher Gesha still hadn't given him back the Soulsmith papers he'd taken from the Transcendent Ruins, but he'd been allowed to study them for the purpose of preparing for the upcoming match. Just in case Jai Long were to use the Ancestor's Spear.

He hadn't known how the weapon would work—if the spear took in madra that was incompatible with the user's Path, would it absorb the madra anyway? Thus perhaps ruining the user's core? That would have been a double-edged sword, and one Lindon could exploit. He had considered intentionally allowing himself to be cut, so that Jai Long would corrupt his own core.

But there was a safety valve built into the script of the spear. Fisher Gesha had theorized there would be, otherwise it wouldn't be a useful weapon in battle.

That was one more hope struck dead. His Blackflame core had dimmed slightly with that cut, and his Iron body was still trying to heal his right arm. He would run out of madra very quickly at this rate, even with both his cores raised according to months of the Heaven and Earth Purification Wheel.

Without that cycling technique, perhaps his Blackflame core would *already* be dangerously low. He had expanded the capacity of both his cores to the point that he had almost made up for the weakness of splitting his cores in the first place: each core held almost as much madra as any Lowgold sacred artist's core should.

But he didn't have vast reserves to draw on, especially with his Bloodforged Iron body draining madra with every injury and every second he used the Burning Cloak.

That spear would be his downfall...and Jai Long could probably beat him without it.

Jai Long moved with such speed that Lindon couldn't track his movements. Only the explosive speed provided by the Burning Cloak let him keep up, and each of his dodges was a guess. He leaped to the left, hoping to avoid a thrust from the right, and the Ancestor's Spear sliced across his ribs. It took another chunk from his spirit at the same time.

A stab above, a sweep from the left, and a probing attack at his legs. He guessed the first one was coming and ducked, accidentally hit the second with a blind punch, and missed the third completely. The white spearhead buried itself in his calf, and he screamed as he jerked his leg away.

Jai Long vented enough Blackflame from the butt of his spear to gouge a ditch in the rock, Lindon swaying with exhaustion on a body of pure pain. His Blackflame madra was about to run out, though his pure core was still fat and bright, and there was something wrong with his wounds.

His Bloodforged Iron body was still working on his right arm, but it hadn't sent any madra to the other wounds. Why not? Was it working on the worst injury first? No, the stab to his calf was deep enough that his shoes were already soaked in blood. Then...

His heart clenched as he realized the truth. The Ancestor's Spear was blocking his Iron body from healing him.

When it drained madra away from the affected areas, some property he didn't understand prevented his Iron body from sending power back into the flesh. He could still cycle madra through those areas, but he couldn't use it to affect the wounds at all. Maybe bits of the spear's substance, left behind after each thrust?

Even when it looked like he was about to lose one of his limbs, he was trying to understand. Some part of his mind was still trying to capture details about the spear; any information he gained would help him understand the binding he'd taken from that ancient Soulsmith foundry.

That was one year ago today.

Jai Long had finished venting his madra, but something caught his eye. Lindon stumbled to the side so he could see too.

Eithan was on his feet, frozen mid-step by chains of green wind aura that were only visible in spiritual sight. To the mundane eye, he was as still as though he'd been locked in glass.

It was a Ruler technique. The Skysworn Captain had controlled the wind to lock him in place.

"We didn't pick this place on accident, Underlord," Naru Gwei said, chewing on his leaf. "Continue, boys."

Jai Long stood with the Ancestor's Spear held loose in one hand, the Blackflame gone from its shaft. He didn't attack immediately. "You're a coward, and you have no shame. I've killed people who deserved it less than you, and slept soundly afterwards." Coming from a red-masked monster, the icy words were even more chilling.

Then he glanced back at his sister. "...but I still don't want to kill you. Give up the arm."

If nothing else, Lindon thought, *helping Jai Chen paid off.* He had wanted to try and help her because he knew what it was like to have no control over your own soul, but he had almost ignored that feeling when he realized she was Jai Long's sister.

He had continued in order to build up some goodwill with Jai Long, hoping to cancel the duel entirely.

That hadn't worked *quite* as well as he'd hoped, but without Jai Long's mercy, he would have died already. Now...

He shivered as he extended his shredded right arm. It hurt so badly that raising it every inch was a new stab of agony, but the fact that he could move it at all was testament to the power of his Iron body.

Jai Long nodded, a businesslike acknowledgement, and moved his spear in a smooth blur.

Lindon projected Blackflame out of his hand, pulling it away from the weapon.

It wasn't a proper Striker technique, and projecting madra outside of his body without a real technique was always both difficult and inefficient. This time, a puff of madra burst from his fist in all directions, dying almost immediately like a bubble popping.

So instead of his hand, the spear swept through a cloud of Blackflame madra.

It was much easier to cope with Jai Long's superior speed when he knew exactly where the next strike would land.

The spearhead flashed as it absorbed the cloud of madra...but as Lindon had hoped, a lick of the diffusing flame landed on the spear's haft. And a small puff of essence burned upward.

Not much. Just a spark like one would see from a campfire, instead of the dust-sized motes that usually drifted from decomposing madra. But it taught Lindon one thing: the spear *could* be destroyed. And the Path of Black Flame could do it.

He gathered Blackflame into his cupped hand as Jai Long thrust his own hand forward. Another white snake bloomed out of nothing, lunging for Lindon.

A wave of madra tore through the entire building.

It passed Lindon like a curtain of cool water, rippling smoothly through his spirit. Not a single hair was affected, nor a pebble disturbed; only the spirit trembled at the touch of this power.

Pure madra. That one pulse was more than Lindon could contain in his entire body.

Jai Long's serpent dispersed into a cloud of harmless white motes and vanished. The fistful of Blackflame guttered and went out like a candle, and even his Burning Cloak was blown away like dust in a strong wind.

And Eithan was free.

His pulse of pure madra had disrupted the madra Naru Gwei had used to control the wind aura, and as soon as he lost that control, the wind was once again nothing more than air. Eithan covered another ten feet of ground in a blink, black scissors flashing in the sun.

Then he froze again. His face was grim, all smile gone. His yellow hair streamed behind him—each strand undulating slowly, as though underwater. He had both hands on his scissors, held in front as though he were about to drive them into flesh, and his body was low as he'd been caught in the middle of a dash.

The green-armored man's leaf had fallen from his lips, and now he was giving Eithan his full attention.

The blond Underlord's jaw worked, and he forced words out. "I will not allow this," Eithan said, his voice cold as the grave.

"Not yours to allow," Naru Gwei said, but he seemed to be waking up. "I follow the rules, Arelius. Our laws are etched in steel."

The chains of aura binding Eithan were much brighter in Lindon's spiritual sight now, like thick bands of green steel wrapping the Underlord. It was clear that the Skysworn Captain was putting everything he could into it.

Another sacred artist could respond with a Ruler technique of their own, but there was no such thing as pure aura. Eithan would have to break free physically...or disrupt the Skysworn's control again, as he had done before.

But even if he arrived at Naru Gwei, would he be in time to help Lindon?

Lindon returned his full attention to Jai Long, gathering Blackflame in his palm once again. He had to fight as though he were all on his own.

Jai Long seemed distracted. Behind him, the Jai Underlord walked forward steadily, spear gripped in both hands. He seemed to regain ten years at the sight of a helpless Eithan. "Please, Captain, allow me to assist you."

"Get back, Jai," Naru Gwei barked. Jai Daishou stopped, confused.

"Do not mistake this as a favor to you. The Arelius Underlord thinks he is the exception to all rules. He trespasses on the Imperial Palace and escapes without punishment. He moves behind the scenes of the empire, pulling strings, violating the laws of the realm without fear. He raised a *Blackflame* and expected to get away with it. Because he always does."

He thrust two green-armored hands forward, and a green gust of madra visible to the naked eye blew toward Eithan. It looked like wind dyed green, and it wrapped in a circle around Eithan's shoulders, pulling his arms into his sides.

Now Eithan was trapped by both madra and natural wind, but the Skysworn stayed focused on him.

"I will uphold the laws of this empire," Naru Gwei said. "If you violate them as well, you will join him."

Jai Daishou looked as though he'd swallowed a lemon, but his expression brightened when he looked back at Jai Long. *His* champion had been barely scratched, while Lindon looked like he shouldn't be able to stand up.

Lindon himself was surprised that he could still stand. His calf had started to slowly heal, but the pain infected every thought, affecting his concentration. It was twice as hard to gather madra in his palm as it should have been.

Without a word, the Underlord strode back to his place next to Jai Chen. The girl had gone pale, but she was no longer concentrating on the fight. She held her palms a few inches apart and was focusing between them, as though she were struggling to use a technique.

Before Jai Daishou had returned to his seat, Lindon threw his hand forward as though hurling a fistful of water. The Blackflame madra wasn't concentrated enough to hurt Jai Long—it burned a few holes in his clothes, but it vanished as soon as it touched the Truegold madra flowing through his skin.

But the sloppy technique did its job. More sparks sprayed up from the haft of the Ancestor's Spear, though the spearhead absorbed part of the power safely. That madra spiraled down the weapon's script, gathering at the butt until Jai Long vented it.

Jai Long continued with his attack, stepping into the thrust, but Lindon stepped back with surprising ease. That had been the easiest move so far to dodge. Maybe Jai Long was getting tired, just as he was.

Lindon should have seen it coming.

In the same motion as his 'failed' attack, Jai Long swept the spear up and back until the butt was pointed at Lindon.

Then he expelled Blackflame into Lindon's face.

Lindon crossed his arms in front of his head, cycling the Path of Black Flame. He'd spent enough time fighting Orthos to know what to expect; as a Blackflame artist, he could resist the madra with his own, but it still burned. Such a small amount of madra, released with no technique, couldn't kill him.

But it put another burden on his core. The madra he used to resist came from his Blackflame core, and his Bloodforged Iron body activated at the burns...draining yet more power.

As the dark fire washed over him, his core sputtered. He only had a spark of Blackflame left.

A fist-sized hole had been burned in Jai Long's mask, exposing one corner of his mouth. His lips stretched inhumanly wide in a smile that stretched all the way back to his ears...but it wasn't a *real* smile. Not a human one.

It was a crocodile's smile. The baring of fangs. And those were actual fangs showing in his mouth, blue and sharp as a shark's. Yerin had described what she'd seen beneath his mask before, but Lindon found that seeing with his own eyes was different.

Patches of skin were showing through the small, burned holes in Jai Long's robes, and lines of white snaked over his skin as he advanced. "That is the way my ancestor used this spear," he said, calmly walking forward. "I'll show you the proper—"

Another wave of pure madra lashed the room.

This time, Lindon was ready. He switched to his pure core immediately. Jai Long wasn't disabled by the pulse, but his Enforcer technique had been banished, so he'd lost his advantage in speed.

Lindon lunged forward, driving the Empty Palm into Jai Long's core.

For a second time, it connected.

There was a loud explosion from somewhere out of sight, and something pushed him from behind like a pillow hitting him in the back, but that only thrust his body into Jai Long's.

Jai Long grabbed him to push him off, one hand still holding the Ancestor's Spear.

And Lindon switched to Blackflame.

He was close enough that he might have been able to kill his opponent, but in the moment, he didn't even consider it. He had already set his target.

With both hands, Lindon grabbed the white shaft of the Ancestor's Spear and let Blackflame flow.

The fire spread through the weapon as though through a dry log, sending sparks spraying into the air like blood from a severed artery. Jai Long cast the red-hot weapon aside, shouting in horror.

Lindon stood panting, his pain turning his emotions numb. He watched with a sort of dull fascination as the white spear melted like ice, its light dulling steadily as scripts broke and died.

In mere moments, the Ancestor's Spear was a pile of white dust, and even that was disintegrating by the second. Only the spearhead remained, white and glinting, a single script on its surface shining.

Lindon noted its position. If there was any way for him to get out of here with that, he should try—it would be an invaluable material for Soulsmithing.

Not that it seemed like he was getting out of here at all.

Jai Daishou roared, his face actually turning red, and his lips were speckled with...was that blood? He drew up his spear, and white light shone from his skin. Jai Chen glanced at him nervously, but she was still concentrating on a space between her hands. Something swirled there, like one of Jai Long's snakes, but smaller and so faded it was barely visible.

Her Patriarch didn't spare her a glance. He cocked his spear back over his shoulder, preparing to throw at Lindon.

Suddenly, it was hard to breathe.

At first, Lindon thought it was fear and blood loss. He had been on the brink of death often enough to know that his body could betray him in unexpected ways.

But it wasn't just his breath. There was pressure on every inch of his skin, as though someone had wrapped him in a sheet and pulled it tight. Each movement was difficult, like he was pushing his way through mud.

Judging from Jai Long's stiff position, Lindon wasn't the only one affected. Jai Daishou seemed even worse, as his spear dropped from a suddenly slack grip—and drifted through midair, falling like a feather. Jai Chen seemed like she had been touched the least, her hair lifting but her posture changing not at all.

Lindon looked to the Skysworn Underlord.

Sure enough, he had thrust both his hands out to the sides, and green madra spilled from them like gas. The power faded into invisibility, affecting the wind aura and commanding the air to obey him.

This was a Ruler technique. He had locked everyone in place, though it didn't seem as thorough as what he'd used on Eithan earlier. Lindon could still move, if with difficulty, and he saw the others shifting position slightly as well.

He must be concentrating it differently on each of us, he thought. If he was binding them according to their relative threat level, that explained why Lindon and Jai Chen were least disrupted.

Of course, the primary target was Eithan.

In Lindon's spiritual sight, Eithan glowed in a sun of green wind aura. The wind howled in from all the open sides of the building, pushing against him, building a prison of air.

He was only a step from the Skysworn Captain, his scissors poised.

Naru Gwei's filthy gray locks were whipped in the wind, his eyes savage, the burn scars on his face crinkled and red. He shouted, and from his back spread two enormous, emerald wings.

They glistened like jewels, bright as the most stable Remnants, but each feather had as much detail as a real bird's wings. His Goldsign.

"Interfering with a Skysworn in the course of his duties!" Naru Gwei announced. "No matter your background, even you can't—"

A pulse of madra blasted out of Eithan.

Lindon could *see* it, twisting the air like a heat haze. It burst from Eithan's chest, the size of a galloping horse, sweeping through Naru Gwei in an instant. The cage around Eithan vanished, as the technique passed through Gwei's body.

It did not, however, pass through his wings.

The spread Goldsign caught the blast of pure madra like a sail catching the full force of a hurricane's wind. The Underlord was ripped back by his own wings, hurtling out over the abyss.

And dropping.

Where he had stood a moment before, the majestic range of snowy peaks now reigned. Everyone in the room stared.

Lindon wanted to say something, but it was a struggle to stay conscious. He began shuffling toward the head of the Ancestor's Spear—now that the Skysworn's restriction had vanished, he could move under his own power again, but he barely had the strength to do it.

Before anyone had a chance to react, there came a sound like a flag snapping in the wind and the huge emerald wings reappeared. The green-armored Skysworn rose up to the building's height, bobbing up and down with every flap of his wings.

There was a dark gray sword in his hand, its blade long and thick. Its surface was notched and dull, just like the Underlord's armor, but its edge was clean and sharp.

Eithan's smile was back, and he regarded Naru Gwei with arms folded. He looked like his normal, cheerful self, as though the icy demeanor from before was only a lie. "You really want to use your Goldsign to fly? If I take them away, you'll fall three hundred feet."

The Skysworn's face hardened. "Do *you* really want to make an enemy of the entire empire by fighting me? I'm the second-ranked Underlord on these shores, Arelius. You'll be lucky to escape the Emperor's wrath already."

"You...almost made me lose my temper, I'll admit," Eithan said. "But no harm done. No, I'm not here to fight you. I just want to delay you." A little of that ice returned to his voice. "I have a different target."

One step, a swirl of his wrist, and a punch.

Pure madra rippled out of his fist, so dense as to be visible. It caught Naru Gwei in the center of his chest, and he plummeted like a brick.

Jai Daishou scrambled on the ground, pulling up his spear as though his life depended on it. His white metal hair fell around his face in disarray, and he watched Eithan in panic. White light began to glow from the tip of his spear...but the light was fitful and weak.

Eithan turned to him. Not quickly or slowly—he was the picture of a man in control. "I rarely have to kill someone twice," he said. "A third time? Never."

Jai Long shoved Lindon away and ran over toward the Patriarch... then he scooped up his sister and backed away.

He was leaving Jai Daishou on his own.

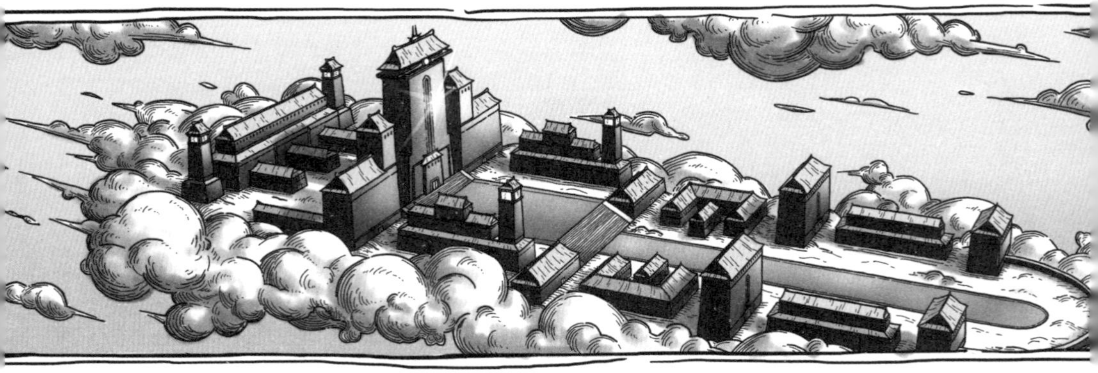

VI

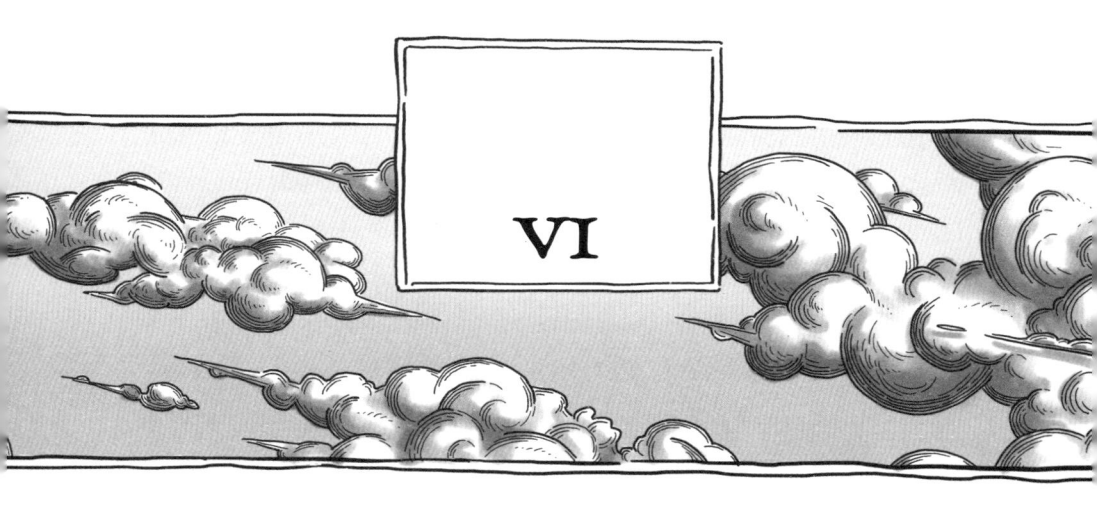

Jai Chen, for her part, didn't seem to realize that her brother had pulled her away for her own safety. She released the technique from between her hands, and a finger-sized worm of pink-tinged white light slithered into the air.

Though it was smaller, it seemed somehow more...real than Jai Long's attacks. The serpents he created while fighting were bare outlines, like the sketches of snakes, but this tiny dragon drew itself up in front of Jai Chen, sniffing at her face like a dog.

It was like a tiny Remnant. Like a real spirit.

Like Little Blue.

Lindon had only turned his head for a second, but he looked back when the sound of crashing steel tore the air louder than thunder. Eithan had smashed the Jai Underlord's spear aside with his scissors.

They traded another half-dozen blows in an instant, each one loud as a ship crashing into rocks. The air itself rippled around their blows, and Lindon thought he could see flashes of a gray, almost colorless fire: soulfire. The hallmark of an Underlord. They were surely using it in their attacks, but he couldn't see how.

In the first second of their engagement, it was clear that Eithan was toying with his opponent. Despite having the advantage in reach, Jai Daishou was always on the back foot. He could barely move his spear enough to intercept the blows, and at any moment, Eithan could take away his sacred arts.

He was done. Lindon had made it.

The relief—that sweet sensation of having walked away from a situation that should have killed him—settled onto Lindon. It was growing to be a familiar sensation.

He lowered himself to pick up the head of the Ancestor's Spear. It took him entirely too long, as his entire body screamed in pain, and even his pure core was strained trying to provide enough madra to fuel the Bloodforged Iron body's restoration. With or without it, he was running low on blood, and he was going to need some real medical attention. The wounds caused by the Ancestor's Spear still weren't healing right.

Something snatched the spearhead out of his hand.

It was a small, worm-sized figure of pink and white. The blade was bigger than its entire body, but it still seized the spearhead in its jaws and hauled it back, like a snake trying to drag a bear's carcass.

Lindon watched it with bleary eyes, the sight so bizarre that it took a moment to register.

Jai Chen was taking it.

He grabbed for it out of slow-witted reaction more than anything else, but the little worm turned and snapped at him. It was actually a little dragon, he realized; a serpentine figure with a flowing mane and four undersized legs.

Lindon hesitated before grabbing for the spearhead again. He hated to let it go, but he didn't need it exactly, and he didn't have the strength to fight anyone for it. And the last thing he needed was to provoke Jai Long again.

Besides, the tiny dragon was amusing. It was still having trouble dragging the blade across the floor, every once in a while raising its head to give Lindon a wary look.

He swayed on his feet, and he realized he couldn't feel his left leg anymore. That couldn't be good. At least his right arm was almost useable again, though it still looked like mincemeat.

Eithan still hammered away at Jai Daishou, keeping the old man stumbling backwards, occasionally throwing a barely-visible pulse of pure madra that whizzed past the Jai Underlord's shoulder or between his legs.

Though the battle had only continued for a few seconds, Lindon could already tell: Eithan was drawing it out on purpose. Why? What was he waiting for?

As Lindon wondered, Jai Daishou caught his eye.

"Jai Long!" the Patriarch screamed. *"Serve the clan!"*

Jai Long stiffened.

Lindon's stomach hollowed out.

He had wondered why Jai Long would fight for the Jai clan, who had exiled him to the Desolate Wilds. Lindon had gotten the impression that he and his sister had grudges against the clan proper, but after they began working for the Underlord, he'd assumed he was mistaken.

Now it made sense: Jai Long was under an oath.

Dredging up the last of his strength, Lindon raised his fists to defend himself. He ran madra through his muscles to Enforce himself, though his Path of Twin Stars did not have an actual Enforcer technique.

"Hold on just a moment," Lindon said, as Jai Long approached. Light had already started slithering over his skin, even the lips of his stretched-out grin. "Let's talk this out. You can serve the clan without—"

Jai Long blurred forward.

Lindon didn't have the speed of the Burning Cloak anymore. He didn't have the time to switch to his Blackflame core, and even if he did, that core was empty anyway.

He triggered his Void Snare, but Jai Long didn't even try to avoid it. The purple line caught him in the forehead and simply pulled him forward. It would have disrupted his Enforcer technique in his head, as well, and Lindon wondered if there were some way to use that to his advantage.

He was still wondering when the razor-edged white light took off his arm.

For the second time, Jai Daishou was being driven backward by a pair of *scissors*.

He had hoped Eithan would be distracted by Lindon's impending death, but the Arelius was as cold as an Underlord should be. He stayed focused on his enemy, raining blows down on Jai Daishou's spear.

On the spear itself. As though he were aiming for the weapon, and not to kill.

"I have beaten you," Eithan said, knocking the spear aside and ignoring a gap that could easily have reached his enemy's throat. "I could kill you any second." He slapped the weapon down this time with his bare hand, contemptuously.

"You're a weak—" He broke a Striker technique, shattering the beam of white light. "—old—" Eithan kicked Jai Daishou's wrist, sending the pain of shattered bone through his arm. "—man." Jai Daishou's spear clattered to the ground, and Eithan kicked it away.

Jai Daishou crouched, panting, his entire body aching. His spirit was a dull spark, and darkness closed in around his eyes. He tasted blood in his mouth, and his breath came rough. Even if he survived this day, it wouldn't be for long.

His time was up.

"Unless you have *something left*," Eithan said, smiling.

He knew.

Somehow, he knew.

Blood sprayed up from behind the Arelius Underlord, and Lindon's arm fell to the ground. Jai Daishou felt a surge of elation before the crushing despair reminded him that a crippled Lindon changed nothing.

He should have made Jai Long swear a tighter oath. Absolute loyalty to him, not just obedience to the letter of his commands. That would have saved him today.

If he could have ordered Jai Long to "kill" instead of to "serve the clan," then surely Eithan would have turned aside and saved his young disciple. Surely.

Instead, the young Lowgold fell to his knees, staring at his stump. Then he folded like a rag as consciousness failed him.

Jai Daishou envied him.

Only rage kept him awake. If spite could give him power, Eithan would have already crumbled to ash and blown away.

Now, he only had one option left: the Archstone. Eithan had cornered him into using it. Naru Gwei would be back any moment. This could ruin the Jai clan...

...but how could he worry about consequences in a time like this?

From his soulspace, he withdrew the fist-sized crystal orb. It flickered with a swirling light, as though something invisible swirled through it. Its palpable sensation of power tickled his spirit, as it would for anyone within range. Even Eithan's eyes widened for a moment in sheer awe.

A flap of emerald wings, and Naru Gwei emerged from below the cliff. He looked furious, but his anger could compare nothing to Jai Daishou's.

Now? *Now* the Skysworn finally managed to make it back up the mountain? Now that it was too late?

Jai Daishou triggered the Archstone.

Color drained from the entire world. It appeared gray and lifeless, as though he had painted everything in charcoal. Aura still appeared as colorful as ever, if he looked through his spiritual sight, but all madra and mundane matter now appeared in shades of gray.

An instant later, streams of color burst from everyone in the room. A twisting, white light flowed from Jai Long's chest, thick as his wrist. A thin string of pink-tinged white came from Jai Chen, and an even thinner stream of pale blue from Lindon's unconscious form.

That was strange; the Archstone should have drawn from everyone according to their power. Either Lindon simply had that little power left, or the artifact drew less madra from unconscious targets. Jai Daishou didn't know; records about these weapons were imprecise, and he hadn't been able to test it for fear of discovery.

But those three streams were only teasers. They were appetizers before the main course.

A breath later, streams of power burst from the Underlords.

These were rivers, thick as the bodies from which they came. Naru Gwei's was green and nebulous, but bright, funneling into the Archstone and from the Archstone into Jai Daishou. It came to him in a torrent, overloading his madra channels, stuffing him full.

And even that was nothing next to the tide of madra from Eithan.

It surged from him in a wave that was mostly colorless and tinged with blue-white. The pure madra blended and strengthened every other type, diluting it like a flow of water.

Jai Daishou took in so much madra that his spirit began to strain at the seams. It vented madra, white light bleeding from his skin, and *still* Eithan's power kept coming. How much madra did the man have?

Though the Jai Underlord had already permanently damaged his spirit, he cackled. What did he have to lose? He was dying.

He took more, and the world lit up.

It was as though there were invisible strings leading from him to the rest of the world, and each string carried his hearing and sight along with it. He could see in all directions, though only a tiny strip at a time: he could hear worms crawling through the dirt in the mountain, and Lindon's heart beating weakly. He could see the two Skysworn guarding the outer door, hear snatches of their whispered conversation about whether they should intervene. He could taste the wood of the door between them, smell the clean snow on the roof.

The legendary power of the Arelius bloodline power. It was beautiful.

So beautiful that it overwhelmed him.

He tried to move, but where was his body? He was standing on the wings of a sacred eagle, perched on the edge of a cliff, deep beneath the ground...

Vaguely, he could feel that he needed to take a breath, but he couldn't remember how.

Eithan staggered forward, unused to a body without madra, but his scissors were still sharp. Naru Gwei had managed to land before his wings failed him, but he couldn't move in his armor any longer.

Then a piercing pain bit into Jai Daishou's neck.

He screamed, snapping back to himself, and lashed out with his madra. A chaotic mess of madra stained with different colors tore out of him, a stream blinding in its brilliance, but it was too great for him to control. He was like a child trying to swing his father's sword.

The rough Striker technique blasted through the stone of the building, tearing a gouge in the wall, slowly carving outward until it was blasting column after column. The roof sagged, but the pain in his neck didn't subside.

If anything, it got stronger.

His soul was tearing itself apart, but he realized part of his massive power was missing. His core had dimmed, and now he was bleeding from a hole *through* his neck.

He was choking on blood. He couldn't breathe. Couldn't speak. But he could still see.

Jai Chen was behind him.

She clutched the spearhead of the Ancestor's Spear in both hands, the weapon still planted in his neck.

Power surged through her, flooding her core. She released the blade quickly, her core swelling, her madra channels strained to bursting. As she panted, eyes wide, he could see white light rising in the back of her throat.

He tried to ask her what she was doing, but he still couldn't say anything. His hands went numb, and the Archstone fell from his fingers.

He reached out for it, and realized he was lying on stone. He couldn't lose that. He had risked too much to get it.

Without it, he had no chance. It was his only hope.

His only...

◯

Eithan saw everything at once, and it was a mess. Things had gotten out of hand.

Naru Gwei held the Archstone in two gauntleted hands as though it were a writhing spider, his heartbeat picking up as he realized the implications. The Captain of the Skysworn would see that Jai Daishou had violated an imperial command to retrieve that weapon, and had placed the entire realm in danger. Being who he was, he would provide an accurate account to the Emperor.

That much, at least, had gone according to plan.

Jai Chen crackled with stolen madra; it stretched her core, straining her channels. Her back arched, her eyes rolling back into her head, her jaw locked open. But she didn't fall. Her brother held her, the chaotic mix of madra blended by the Archstone slicing pieces of his clothes away. But still he held her, Enforcing his own flesh to protect himself, his muscles tense and eyes locked on his sister.

And Lindon...Lindon lay a foot away from his right arm, his Bloodforged Iron body drawing madra to stop the bleeding. Jai Long had cut him evenly at the elbow, for which Eithan was grateful. It would be easier to attach a prosthetic at the joint.

This will be an opportunity for him, Eithan thought. *A chance for him to grow.*

That was true, but it was also an excuse. He was honest enough with himself to recognize that.

This was all Eithan's fault. And Lindon had suffered for it.

The other two Skysworn kicked in the door just in time to see a white tendril rise from Jai Daishou's body. A dozen tendrils followed, and Renfei and Bai Rou were horrified, gathering their power to defend. A cloud boiled up from the hammer in Renfei's right hand, and Bai Rou Forged three fist-sized drops of yellow water: Amberwell madra.

An Underlord's Remnant was no joke, and this one had been swollen by the Archstone. Under different conditions, Eithan and

Naru Gwei would have had to join their powers together in order to prevent this spirit from tearing the building apart.

Instead, Eithan didn't even turn around, keeping his eyes on Lindon. Naru Gwei tucked the smoky crystal Archstone into his armor, paying no attention to the Remnant. He knew.

The two Truegolds ran as though to battle, even as a dozen fat tentacles of white light pushed at the ground around Jai Daishou's corpse, hauling the main body of the Remnant out of his chest...

There was one instant where the outline of the Remnant was visible, a bulbous pale creature that looked like it belonged at the bottom of the sea. Then it fell apart.

Chunks of wet, slick-looking madra fell to the ground, dissolving to essence almost immediately. The tentacles shook with spasms as they squirmed on the floor, then they too faded to nothing. Only seconds after Jai Daishou's Remnant had begun to reveal itself, it was nothing more than a cloud of white dust hanging in the air.

The Archstone itself was capable of siphoning much more power than it had demonstrated today, but its wielder had limits. Jai Daishou had drawn everything he could with no attention to his own safety. He had eroded the foundation of his own soul, so his madra wasn't stable enough to form a whole Remnant. If he had lived a little longer with his spirit shredding itself apart, his core would have shattered so completely that a Remnant wouldn't have formed at all.

The two surviving Underlords had realized what would happen, but the others didn't have enough experience. Bai Rou's yellow eyes were wide as he stared at Eithan as though wondering what he'd done. Renfei returned her hammer to her hip, but her brow was creased in confusion.

Eithan tilted his head to Naru Gwei. "He must have been desperate, to go so deep into the labyrinth."

"He should have died with courage," the Skysworn Captain barked. He scratched roughly at his dirty hair. "Do you know what this...no, you do. Of course you do."

"To protect himself, he put us all in danger. If we caught the attention of the Bleeding Phoenix, Redmoon Hall will show themselves inside a week."

"That's the *best* case," Naru Gwei said, looking as though he wanted to kick Jai Daishou's body. "If the Titan or the Dragon caught a whiff, then our lives depend on the whims of the Monarchs."

"The Weeping Dragon was sighted only last year in the Iceflower Continent. No reason to think it should be making its way here."

Naru Gwei looked like a man running on three sleepless nights who was staring down three more. "Dreadgods...I never thought I'd see the day. I'll bring word to the Emperor, but if it is Redmoon Hall, he will require all of us. You'll have to do your duty this time, Arelius."

Eithan put a hand on his chest and staggered as though Naru Gwei had wounded him. "How dare you suggest that I wouldn't do my duty for my beloved Empire?"

The Skysworn Captain wasn't in the mood for levity, it seemed. His jaw clenched, the muscles in his arms and legs tensed, and madra swirled through his soul. He had to be weighing the costs and benefits of attacking Eithan once again.

Eithan raised his hands. "No need for that, I apologize. I'm aware of the weight of this situation."

Naru Gwei's look was still bleak, and his madra kept cycling.

Eithan resisted the urge to roll his eyes. The Captain wouldn't kill him, not before a potential Dreadgod attack. This was just irritation boiling over—Eithan saw it quite often. An Underlord should have more control over his emotions than this.

If there *were* another fight, Eithan would not fare well. He'd been forced to waste an absurd amount of madra to break Naru Gwei's Ruler techniques, and the Archstone had taken even more out of him. Despite his years of practicing the Heaven and Earth Purification Wheel, his core was almost dry. He couldn't afford another fight here.

Finally, help came from an unexpected corner. Jai Long raised his head, crying out in a hoarse voice. "Please, help her!"

Eithan ran his spiritual sense through her soul. Thanks to Sylvan Riverseed's touch, her madra channels had been rebalanced, cleansed, and purified. Without that, she would have lost control of her madra and died already.

As it was, she was just *barely* holding on. A sack stuffed to capacity and coming apart at the seams, but not in danger of bursting.

"Unfortunately, there's nothing we can do for her," Eithan said, and Jai Long's twisted face began to fall behind his mask. "...but *fortunately*, there's also no need. She will survive this. And her core will be filled with quite unique madra, so that's a treat. You were quite lucky that Lindon and I were here, and that Lindon's Blackflame core was empty, otherwise the madra would have reached a critical imbalance. As it is, none of our madra conflicted too badly with each other. They will blend together in her."

She would also gain some measure of the Arelius bloodline ability, though she would have to expend madra to use it, while Eithan's happened naturally. She really had ended up in quite a unique situation, and he looked forward to seeing how she handled it.

"She will have difficulty controlling her madra for a while," he continued. "But then...well, she has a unique Path ahead of her."

And he was very interested in that Path, though he didn't express it. The siblings needed space, so he could keep his distance.

For now.

While he spoke, he reached down and casually took an object from the floor. Jai Long didn't notice, consumed as he was with his sister's fate, so Eithan had no trouble slipping the head of the Ancestor's Spear into his pocket.

He could certainly find a use for that. He still had the original, locked away in Serpent's Grave...but there was no such thing as too many priceless weapons.

Naru Gwei stretched out his wings and walked over to the edge of the room. "I'll be reporting the results of this duel, Arelius."

"You don't think we have more important concerns?"

"It was still a legal match with a valid conclusion. When this all blows over, you'll be facing the consequences."

"I understand," Eithan said, affecting a solemn tone. The family elders and branch heads would irritate him after this. The reputation of the Arelius name would take a hit, and that would result in economic pressure on the family all across the country. The rest of the family would use this to put restrictions on him, and if Redmoon Hall really did invade, he wouldn't have time to deal with family business.

This would tie his hands for a while, but in the end, he found it hard to care. The world was so much more than anyone on this continent imagined, and there were still more worlds beyond.

He reached into his pocket and rolled the glass marble between his fingers. As always, the feel of its cool surface comforted him.

Naru Gwei walked over to the edge, where the wind tossed his dirty hair. "Will you follow me to the Emperor, or will I have to drag you?"

"I will follow as soon as I have seen to family business. I have a disciple who has just lost an arm."

Muscles all over Naru Gwei's body tensed, though he didn't change on the outside. *He needs to learn to relax,* Eithan thought.

"Even now, you still won't cooperate? When a Dreadgod might be headed our way with all its little cult in tow?"

"If I have to choose between disappointing you or my disciple... well, I'm sorry, but I don't like you very much."

Eithan gave him a cheery wave and turned his back on the Skysworn, strolling away.

"I won't wait long," Naru Gwei said.

Eithan walked through the door without a response.

He needed to take Lindon to shelter, and surround him with friendly faces. When he woke up, he wouldn't be happy.

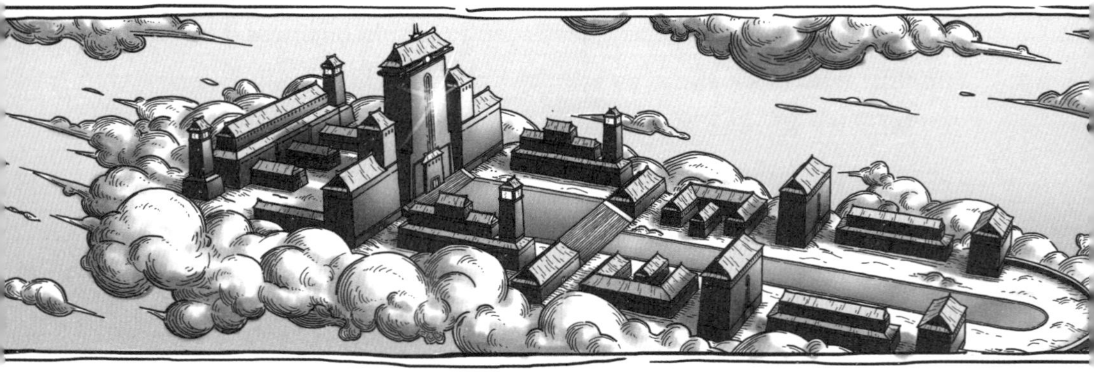

VII

"Prosthetic limbs," Fisher Gesha said, "are among the easiest constructs for a Soulsmith to create. You were lucky. If we had to replace one of your organs, I would be singing a very different tune right now, hm?"

They were still inside the mountain, five or six floors beneath the arena where he'd fought. Apparently this whole place was honeycombed with shelters—it had once been the home of a sect living in secrecy, but had been abandoned for years. Or so the Fisher had told him in the last few minutes.

Lindon remembered nothing of the trip down here, and very little of the fight. He didn't even ask how Fisher Gesha had gotten there, though he assumed Eithan had brought her. Yerin and Orthos were nowhere to be seen, but he didn't ask about them. His attention was swallowed entirely by his right arm.

Which was lying somewhere above him, he assumed.

Now, it ended abruptly above the elbow. Gesha had wrapped his stump with scripted bandages, which weren't stained with as much blood as he had expected. This script must work the same as the one his mother had once used on him: it guided his spirit through an Enforcer technique that blocked out pain. Certainly, he didn't feel any physical pain. It was more like the opposite. He felt normal, as though he could reach out with his right arm just as always.

But he couldn't seem to peel his eyes away from the space where his hand should be.

The Fisher firmly grasped his chin and turned his head back toward her. Her wrinkled face was set in a stern expression, but a few strands of gray hair had escaped their normal tight bun. "Whatever state you're in, you listen to me when I'm talking to you, yes?" Involuntarily, he tried to turn back to his arm, but her grip was steel.

"Don't think," she warned him. "After an injury like this, it is your thoughts that are most deadly. Your fears, your pain, your despair, they are deadly poison. Do not let them rule you."

From somewhere, he mustered up a nod.

"Good. Now, limbs are simple. We simply take an arm from a Remnant that is compatible with your Path—or *Paths*, I suppose, since you always have to make things complicated—and we attach it to you with a combination of scripting and Forging. I happen to have some Remnant arms with me right now."

She knelt by his bed, rummaging around in her chest, which gave

Lindon a chance to look around the room. It was a rounded room carved out of the stone, giving it the impression that a mole had dug it out of solid rock. His bed was more of a cot, made of trembling wood and scratchy sheets. A single candle sat on a shelf bolted to the wall. There was one more source of light: a glowing script-circle on the wall behind a square of paper painted with an abstract landscape. Meant to replace a window, he was certain.

His pack leaned against the wall, which was a relief. Next to it was the Sylvan Riverseed's case, a box of glass with a tiny island inside. Little Blue herself, now almost too big for her enclosure, stood on the island and stared at him with her hands pressed against the glass. Though she was made entirely from ocean-blue madra, she had gained enough definition that he could read her face: she was worried.

Her concern almost broke him, but he tore his eyes away and took in a deep breath. *Don't think about it.* He was fine. Better than fine, really. He had expected to die if he lost, so walking away with three limbs out of four was a bargain.

Fisher Gesha straightened, carrying a wide wooden tray set with three limbs.

As Remnant arms, they didn't look quite real, like they were paintings come to three-dimensional life.

"These are the ones I have on hand for you," she said, "and be grateful I have this many. It's not every day I have to match a limb to not one, but *two* cores." She gestured to the first, a slick-looking purple arm with webbing between the fingers. "From a Fisher Remnant, this one has a Snare binding like the one you used against Jai Long. It is more compatible with your pure Path than with Blackflame, so you might have some trouble cycling Blackflame for the next few weeks, but it won't trigger a critical incompatibility."

Lindon had seen Fisher Gesha use some of her techniques before, and of course he'd practiced with his Void Snare construct. He could imagine lashing himself to a wall to pull himself up the side of a building, trapping enemies who tried to escape, swinging across a chasm...

The thought cheered him. Just a little.

"The problem will be what the binding becomes when it absorbs your Path of Black Flame, you see? I see two possibilities: either it will become a sort of burning whip instead of an actual Snare technique, or it will work as usual, but carry a measure of Blackflame with it that burns whatever you attach to. It depends on how the madra balances out, and there's no way to test without slapping it on."

She moved to the second offering on the table, a gray mass of cloud molded into the shape of a limb that looked as though it could blow apart any second. "You'll have to concentrate to keep this firm enough to interact with solid objects, but it's made from Cloud Hammer madra. It was one of their Enforcer techniques in a binding, though I'm afraid I don't know the name. It may have been a custom technique belonging to the artist who left this Remnant. Anyway, you'll pack quite the punch, especially once it equalizes with your Blackflame madra."

He reached out and passed his fingers through the cloud. As he expected, it only felt like mist. He could find a use for this just as much as the binding inside—an arm that could reach through solid objects.

"I like the physical properties of this one," he said, reaching for a set of goldsteel tongs at the edge of the tray. But he reached with his right hand, so nothing happened besides his stump twitching.

He blinked.

Gesha snapped up the goldsteel tongs and used them to grip the limb of cloud. You needed goldsteel to manipulate Remnant parts like this one, because anything else would pass straight through. Madra couldn't pass through goldsteel.

The golden tools flashed unnaturally milk-white in the light as she grabbed the cloud hand and stretched. The hand grabbed at her tool while she pulled, trying to wrestle against her. Remnant limbs often retained some life and will of their own.

She ignored the hand's attempt to fight back and stretched the limb, pulling it out to a good three feet before the cloud started to thin. The severed end stayed on the tray, but now the fingertips were halfway across the room.

"It can be stretched, you see," she said, holding it there for a moment. "This is something you could learn to do in time, though keeping it solid while you do so would take quite the force of madra."

Lindon had already forgotten about the Fisher arm. *This* one had endless possibilities. He could stretch it, reach through doors, and hit with the force of a Cloud Hammer Enforcer technique...

Maybe he hadn't lost as much as he'd thought.

Gesha folded the arm back onto the tray and placed down her goldsteel tongs, moving to the third limb.

"Now, this one...you're lucky I favor you, hm? I made this one myself."

This hand had six fingers with an extra joint on each one, making them look somewhat like an insect's legs. They were tipped as though clawed, and the arm was inhumanly thin. It seemed to be made of glass, with the slightest hint of color shooting through it. The color changed every second, a wisp of green brightening to a hint of yellow before darkening to orange.

"Path of the Shifting Skies," she said proudly, as though it was her own Path. "I caught this Remnant almost four years ago, and I recognized its potential immediately. Years of experience should not be underestimated," she said, shooting him a glance as though he had been questioning her expertise. "It was an interesting blend of cloud, wind, and water madra, but I found it especially intriguing when I found that it was also extremely close to pure. It was only barely tinged with other aspects of madra, as though the artist who left it had cycled aura for no more than a month. Though this is a Highgold arm, so that certainly could not be the case. I do wish I knew the story of this sacred artist," she said with a regretful sigh.

Lindon stared at the transparent arm. If he understood her correctly, then she had easily saved the best for last. Finding a pure Remnant in the wild was next to impossible, because there were so few pure madra Paths. Unless Eithan died, there was very little chance of Lindon ever encountering one. That was the whole reason Eithan had gone through the effort of raising him to Lowgold without hunting down a Remnant—because finding a Remnant would have been even more difficult and expensive.

But Fisher Gesha had found a piece of the next best thing.

"I say *I* created this because I've fed it with pure madra for almost the last two years," she said. "It was difficult to do so without compromising the balance of the binding or the structure of the limb, but I did it, didn't I? If we join this to you, it should—should, I say—match perfectly with the Path of Black Flame while you're drawing on your Blackflame core, but lose that influence and match with your pure core while you cycle the Path of Twin Stars. Eventually, it will carry a slight Blackflame influence, but it won't affect the performance of the limb."

"It can't be so perfect for me," Lindon said. If it were, she wouldn't have given him a choice, and would have simply brought this limb out from the beginning.

She pointed to him. "And so it isn't. Very good. Always be wary of anything that seems to fit too well. There is no binding in this limb, so it will not bring any technique along with it. Only the properties of its madra. It will serve you perfectly well as an arm, but it will carry you no capabilities you don't already have."

Lindon nodded absently, looking from one arm to another. So he had a choice between compatibility and utility. The cloud arm looked the best, but there was an argument for the Fisher arm. Though tying himself to a surface didn't sound terribly exciting, it would allow him some creative options. Of course, he was still worried about its interaction with Blackflame.

How could he only choose one?

"What about all three?" Lindon asked. "I could change them out according to the situation."

Fisher Gesha raised two fingers as though she were about to smack him on the head, but grumbled to herself for a moment and lowered them. "You think binding a Remnant arm to your spirit is so simple of a process, do you? You think you can just stick it in and remove it whenever you want to?"

"Pardon, Fisher Gesha, but you said it *was* simple."

She opened her mouth, but then closed it again. "I suppose I did. Well, attaching one is the simplest process in the world, but by the time you can use it naturally, it will be *your* arm. It will be attached to your body and spirit, you see. Losing it will be the same as losing the limb you were born with."

Lindon's eyes drifted back to his stump before he jerked them away. "I see. I'll be sure to choose carefully, then."

A thought occurred to him, and he nodded to his pack sitting in the corner of the room. "What if we added a binding of our own? To the Shifting Skies arm, I mean." That one was clearly the best selection, if only it came with a technique.

Fisher Gesha clearly understood what he meant, because she hesitated. "You should know that we've studied bindings like that one for generations. Dreadbeasts have plagued our lands long enough that we wanted to know what kind of madra created such monsters."

She waited for him to ask a question, but he remained silent, so she reached into her robes and pulled out a sheaf of papers bound together with string. The Soulsmith notes he'd taken from the foundry back in the Desolate Wilds.

"We never had a name for the white madra in dreadbeast bindings," she continued. "Our drudges could measure some of its properties, you see, but not enough to identify it. These notes call it *hunger* madra, which is perhaps one of the most absurd names for a power that I've ever heard. Though it seems to fit."

"Hunger madra," Lindon repeated. He'd read the notes, so he had heard the expression before, but he hadn't put the phrase together with the binding he'd carried around for the past year. "Is it compatible with my Paths?"

"As far as we can tell, it's compatible with everything," she said wryly. "Dreadbeasts attack us with madra of all aspects, and they all have one of those bindings inside them. Although it could be that the ones with incompatible spirits die off..."

She waved a hand in the air. "You're distracting me. These notes reference an origin for this madra, a single source from which they got all their samples. They were trying to breed sacred beasts that left Remnants of this aspect, but they never made it. At least, not by the time these notes were written."

Lindon nodded. If they didn't have a reliable source of Remnants, then the bindings and madra for the Ancestor's Spear must have come from somewhere else. "So where did the bindings come from?"

"That is what disturbs me," she said. She shook her head as though shaking off cobwebs. "But it doesn't matter, does it? I could put your binding into this arm, certainly, but there would be no framework for it. We would need more hunger madra to reinforce and adapt the arm to handle the binding. Besides, do you really want a hand that devours madra? It could start feeding on the spirit of anyone you touch."

To Lindon, that sounded incredible.

"If it worked like the Ancestor's Spear, my Paths would be much easier to advance," he said delicately, keeping his enthusiasm from his voice. If she knew how excited he was, she would try and talk him out of it. "Reaching the peak of Truegold would be no problem. I could even split my core again, and train yet a third Path." He nodded to the color-tinged glass arm, which was tapping its pointed fingertips on the tray like a woodpecker. "We have such a fine sample here. Why not try an experiment?"

He was trying to appeal to her curiosity as a Soulsmith, but she shook her head. "The Ancestor's Spear worked thanks to its script as much as its binding. Without those scripts, we can't be certain *what* it will do, and testing out the binding might destroy it, and render our tests useless. Besides, we need more hunger madra if we're to build it into your arm without collapsing it, and the spear has dissolved already. There's no—"

She was cut off when the steel-banded wooden door creaked open, revealing Eithan grinning and holding up a pure white knife.

Gesha pinched the bridge of her nose and let out a heavy breath, but soon composed herself and bowed. "Underlord."

Lindon started to greet Eithan, but no words came out. The man's easy smile stabbed him.

"It seems you need further materials," Eithan said cheerily, striding into the room. "I just so happen to have some to spare."

He tossed her the spearhead, but instead of reaching out her hands to catch it, she jerked them back as though afraid. Lines of purple madra lashed out from her, lashing the blade to the ceiling and slowly lowering it down to her eye level like a spider on a line. Clearly, she didn't want to risk having her madra drained away, even if Eithan had been holding it in his bare hands with no apparent problems.

When she saw that her technique had remained intact despite its contact with the weapon, she gingerly plucked it out of the web with two fingers.

The spearhead was about a foot long and a hand wide. She studied it for a moment, and then two long purple spider's legs reached up from beneath her. Her drudge.

The two legs snatched the blade from her, juggling and spinning it between them for a good two minutes before the spider-construct let out a hiss.

Finally, she gave a single nod. "There's enough here to...try. I'll have to break this binding down to its materials to avoid a conflict, and once we have the fragments of this weapon, we can begin merging them with the Shifting Skies limb." She jabbed a finger at Eithan. "I cannot promise anything, you understand. And you'll be giving up this weapon."

"I expect to gain a better one," Eithan said, his gaze on Lindon.

Fisher Gesha gathered up her tray, returning the limbs to her script-sealed box before the madra decayed any further. "I'll need my assistant for this," she said. "I don't want to muddy this with more aspects than we need, so Fisher madra is not the most suitable. We'll need his pure madra to link it all together, and perhaps Blackflame to break down the extra binding."

Lindon was eager to begin working, and he started to struggle out of the bed—no matter how weak he felt, this was something to do. Something to focus on besides what he had lost.

Eithan held up a hand, stopping him.

"I apologize, Fisher, but I need a word with him for a moment. Do what you can on your own, for now, and I'll send him to you when he's ready."

Gesha hesitated, looking between Lindon and the Underlord.

"Don't you give him any trouble, now," she said firmly, and

to Lindon's shock, she wasn't speaking to him. She was looking straight at Eithan.

He raised his eyebrows. "I'll try my best not to."

"He ought to get some time to rest after a day like this. You hear me? He's not a construct. Even if he were, you couldn't push him every day like you do without ever giving him time to rest."

"I don't intend to—" Eithan began, but Fisher Gesha interrupted him.

"A whole year I've been here," she said. Her spider-legs carried her forward, and she actually rapped her knuckles against the Underlord's chest. "A whole year of my life I've given up, and I don't have many of those left, do I? Well, I've always wanted to see the Empire, and so I have. I've tried foods I'd never heard of before, I've worked on Remnants I couldn't imagine, I've met strange people and seen strange sights."

She reached up as though to smack him in the face, but seemed to remember who she was talking to, and pointed at him instead. "How much of that has *he* done, hm?"

Lindon started. He hadn't given much thought to what Fisher Gesha had been doing while he was training. He supposed he thought she just...worked all the time.

Like he did.

"He's spent more time underground than a mole. At least he's got Yerin with him, she's a good girl, but she wouldn't rest if someone killed her. You have to slow them down, you hear me? They're not Underlords." She lowered her hand and sighed. "Not yet."

Eithan's eyes were wide and his mouth slightly open. After a moment, his smile came back, but this time it was soft. "Honored grandmother, I will take your words to heart. I'm sorry for worrying you." Then he pressed his fists together into a salute and bowed low.

Gesha cleared her throat and reddened slightly. "Well. So long as you know."

Before Lindon could gather his thoughts, she'd already scooped up her chest and scurried out the door.

Eithan stared after her, chin in his hands. "You know," he said, "I don't believe I've paid enough attention to her."

"I apologize for her," Lindon said, dipping his head slightly. "I have no complaints about my work over the past year. I know it was done for my benefit."

"Not *entirely* for your benefit," Eithan said. "I was initially hoping that Jai Long would serve as a motivation for you, of course, but the situation evolved as soon as Jai Daishou inserted himself. I was hoping to reap some benefits for the Arelius family, and though I didn't get everything I wanted, I still made some measurable progress. I'll chalk this whole thing up to a win, though we *may* have indirectly led to the destruction of the entire Empire."

Lindon was meant to ask about the destruction part of that sentence, he knew. It was bait, set by Eithan, trying to capture Lindon's interest and attention. Normally, it would have worked.

This time, Lindon shrugged his right shoulder, drawing attention to his missing arm. "You could have finished off Jai Daishou immediately."

Eithan's smile faded. "I could have, yes."

"You drew it out. You were trying to get him to bring out that crystal ball."

"The Archstone. It's a—"

Lindon cut him off. "He took my arm."

Eithan clasped his hands behind his back and studied his disciple. Instead of deflecting or pointing out that technically Jai Long was the one who had removed the arm, which would be typical Eithan tactics, the Underlord simply nodded. "He did. If he hadn't given the order, Jai Long would have left you alone. If I hadn't put him under such pressure, he wouldn't have given the order."

The admission both made Lindon feel better and much, much worse. It tore open the bandage he'd wrapped around his anger, and he could feel tears welling up in the corners of his eyes.

"Why?" he said. "Why did you have to push him? I just…want to know it was worth it."

Eithan looked to the ceiling for a moment, considering, then looked back down to Lindon. "What do you know about the Dreadgods?"

"Nothing," Lindon said. "I don't know that I've ever heard the word. Are they like dreadbeasts?"

"Yes. Yes, they are." Eithan chewed on his words for a second, as though trying to gather his thoughts. Or trying to decide how much to tell Lindon. "They are…disasters. Four monsters, big enough to blot out the sky, hungry for destruction, and so powerful that the most advanced sacred artists in the world have to join forces to drive them off. *Drive them off*, you understand. None of the Dreadgods have ever been killed."

"They're sacred beasts?"

"Corrupted ones. Like the dreadbeasts of the Desolate Wilds, they were warped and twisted by their own powers."

"Where do they come from?" Lindon asked, caught up in the

legend. He briefly wondered if this was another tactic to distract him...but if it was, it was working.

"They're scattered all over the world. They burrow into a secure location and wait for decades...but when they wake up, they're hungry. Fortunately for humanity, no two have woken at the same time in centuries.

"But the last time they did, they destroyed the original Blackflame Empire."

From Orthos and Eithan, Lindon had heard of the fall of the Blackflame family. But from what he could piece together, even that family had taken over the remains of another, more powerful Empire.

And even that ancient nation had fallen to these Dreadgods.

"The original Empire was ruled by dragons, not men," Eithan said, with a tone that suggested dragons building an empire was nothing unusual. "As they advanced as a culture, they began to study civilizations even older than theirs. And they stumbled on a...vast, underground complex. It was abandoned even then, and it was so massive and so dangerous that not even the greatest of the dragons could map it fully."

That reminded Lindon of something, but before he could voice it, Eithan nodded to him. "You've seen one of the shallowest corners of this massive labyrinth in the Desolate Wilds. What they called the Transcendent Ruins was, in reality, just a corner of this huge maze that stretches all over the Empire. There are entrances all over, but to have seen one is your good fortune."

"Two," Lindon said. "There was one in my homeland."

He remembered the ancient tomb from the Heaven's Glory sect, and a stone door marked with four beasts.

Now, that carving carried an eerie significance.

"Is that so?" Eithan asked, surprised. "Well, you're lucky indeed. And even luckier that you didn't explore too far inside. The dragons of the first Blackflame Empire found that out firsthand when they plundered weapons from the depths of the labyrinth. At first, they only took Highgold or Truegold devices, wanting to study them, but they became greedy for more when they learned that the weapons had such miraculous effects."

"The Ancestor's Spear," Lindon said.

"One of the weakest objects in the maze. The spear wasn't even unique, you know, though it *is* enough to dazzle the eyes of anyone below Truegold." Eithan stared longingly into the distance. "The labyrinth is a true treasure trove, but there's a reason we've left it undisturbed for so long, only nibbling at the corners every once in a while in places like the Desolate Wilds. Because when the dragons delved deeper, withdrawing Lord treasures like the Archstone..."

He paused, picking up from a different point. "You should understand that the dragons left the doors open for years as they explored the labyrinth, making war on one another and settling petty grudges with their new weaponry. They didn't realize that something in that place drew the Dreadgods like wolves to fresh meat.

"Records of that disaster are very spotty, as you might expect. But the warnings they left are clear. Most of this continent was reduced to a blasted wasteland, from which it has not entirely recovered even to this day. *Billions* of people and sacred beasts died, and the former Blackflame Empire was nothing more than a Remnant haunt for generations."

Eithan slowly shook his head. "We can't know how many dragons survived, but it wasn't more than a handful. The survivors returned all their weapons to the labyrinth, leaving dire warnings to future generations. To delve past the shallows of this maze is to invite death. They destroyed as many of the entrances as they could, and sealed up the rest."

"And Jai Daishou opened one?" Lindon asked.

"Desperate men cannot see beyond their own desperation," Eithan said, with the air of a man quoting. "There was an entrance to the labyrinth in his territory. He would have kept the door open for less than a day. A minor risk, he must have thought, though a risk to the entire Empire. When he brought out the Archstone, Naru Gwei and I knew what he had done. We knew that he had risked bringing the Dreadgods down on us once again."

A wisp of Lindon's anger rose up again. "You pushed him to it."

Eithan held up a finger. "I closed off his options to push him to do *something* foolish. Otherwise, I'd have been leaving my reputation entirely on the outcome of a single fight. I don't prefer to gamble without an overwhelming advantage."

"But you knew exactly what he had. You *knew* it was a hidden weapon, you weren't guessing."

"Yes, well, I was watching when he opened the door. I was shocked he would go so far as to risk the wrath of the Dreadgods, but there it is. That was my plan: to get him to incriminate himself in front of the Skysworn. Even if he had survived, with Jai Long victorious, his reputation—and that of the Jai clan—would never recover. They are the lowest-ranked of the great clans, and the Arelius are ranked number one among the major families. They will lose their spot in the Empire, and we will take it."

He grimaced, looking uncertain for just a moment. "I am...sorry that you lost what you did. Only know that you were a part of something greater. The Arelius family will rise because of you, and you can only benefit from that."

Lindon nodded, but his gut was still a little twisted. He shouldn't be complaining about a lost arm. Back in Sacred Valley, if Eithan had offered to raise him to Gold in exchange for a lost arm, he would have handed the man a saw himself.

But this didn't feel like he'd sacrificed something for a greater goal. It felt like he had been a pawn in the plans of the powerful.

"The Dreadgods," Lindon said at last, trying to change the subject. "Are they coming for us?"

"Most likely not," Eithan said. "But just in case, the Emperor is gathering his Underlords to him."

"Will you fight them?"

Eithan let out a bark of a laugh. "As an Underlord? No, they could evaporate my blood from a hundred miles away. We'll be working to keep the populace under control in a state of emergency, should we see signs of a Dreadgod's approach. And we'll be messengers to the people that might actually help."

Before Lindon could ask who, Eithan explained.

"The Monarchs. They're the most powerful individuals in our world, though the best they could hope for would be a stalemate. None could win a fight against a Dreadgod alone. Not Seshethkunaaz, not Akura Malice, not the Eight-Man Empire or the entire Ninecloud Court."

Lindon's breath caught. He remembered two of those names, but he had never expected to hear them from Eithan.

How much did Eithan know about them? *Monarchs*, he'd said. Lindon had never heard the term applied to sacred arts. It sounded like there was a whole group of people at that stage, not just the three examples Suriel had shown him.

He took the thought to its natural conclusion, and a fist seemed to squeeze his lungs. Suriel had given him the names of three people with the power to save Sacred Valley: Sha Miara the Queen of the Ninecloud Court, Northstrider the dragon-eater, and the Eight-Man Empire.

If those were the most powerful people in the world, that meant whatever was approaching Sacred Valley was even more horrifying than he had imagined.

It might not be one of these Dreadgods, but it would be something equally destructive. He couldn't even imagine it.

"I've heard of them before," Lindon said.

"I would imagine so. They're very famous."

"No, in a vision. Suriel showed me. She said…they were the ones that could save my homeland."

Eithan nodded slowly. Over the months, he had scraped most of the details of Suriel's visit from Lindon. All without giving up the details of his own vision. But Lindon had never been specific enough to name the individuals Suriel had shown him.

But that brought up another point, and Lindon could sense an opportunity. He seized it.

"Speaking of visions…" he began, and Eithan's back straightened.

"Later," Eithan promised.

"I lost an *arm* for your plans," Lindon said, the heat of Blackflame leaking into his voice. "I have earned your trust."

It was perhaps the most firmly Lindon had ever spoken to Eithan, and a trembling part of Lindon's mind—the part that still remembered being Unsouled—begged him to apologize. But Lindon kept staring into Eithan's blue eyes.

"I owe you a full explanation," Eithan said. "And I will give you one. The more you grow, the more I can share with you. For now, I beg *you* to trust *me*."

That was an irritating non-answer, but Eithan spoke more earnestly and openly than he almost ever did.

Reluctantly, Lindon nodded.

"That's good," Eithan said, and his grin returned. "Cassias will be here in *Sky's Mercy* to retrieve you any day now. Rest. Fisher Gesha was right; you've trained like a madman for a year, but that's no way to live forever. There will be plenty of time to advance when I return."

"When will that be?" Lindon asked. The idea of staying in bed for months horrified him. What if he fell behind his advancement?

"That depends," Eithan said, "on whether or not there's a Dreadgod coming to kill us all."

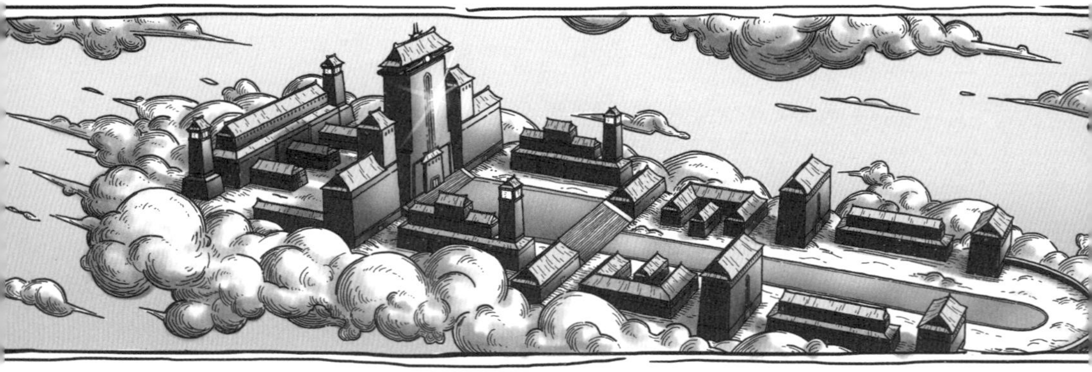

VIII

Sky's Mercy was a cloudship maintained by the Arelius family: a large blue cloud with a house in the center, flying through the air. Yerin had seen stranger things before—stranger cloudships, too—but there was something about a floating house that especially knocked her off-kilter.

There used to be a second building on the cloud, and Yerin missed the barn. She had more room. Instead, she and Cassias were inside a single bedroom-sized cultivation room, surrounded by wooden walls that had been reinforced by scripts so they didn't fall apart with every flying Striker technique.

He was showing her what it took to be the second-ranked Highgold in the Empire.

She kicked off from the wall, slashing the air in a Rippling Sword technique: a wave of silver madra that sliced through the air like an extension of her sword.

Cassias stood before her, back straight, one hand on his thin saber. He looked like Eithan's more serious younger brother: his golden hair was curly and short, his blue eyes calm, and he wore no smile.

He sidestepped her technique, raising his weapon to return a strike. But she had counted on that. She'd gathered enough aura around her sword, and she struck that aura with her madra as hard as she could.

Her sword rang like a bell.

A ripple ran through the sword aura in the room, exciting it, causing invisible cuts to appear on her robes...and then the wave of aura reached Cassias.

When it hit his sword, the weapon *should* have burst into a wave of slicing sword-energy that cut him to pieces, but instead he gathered aura himself as he pulled his saber back. The aura she'd affected with the Endless Sword was drawn in like straw into a cyclone, and it swirled around his sword in a silver cloud visible to her Copper sight.

Then he stabbed forward, carrying all that aura with it.

The thrust stabbed across the room in an instant, piercing the air and passing an inch over Yerin's shoulder. A few strands of her hair fell away, and she shivered as she felt the air disturbed by her ear. His technique landed on the wall, where a script shone and dispersed the aura, leaving only a slight scratch on the paneling.

Cassias sheathed his saber and frowned. "If you haven't recovered from last time, I'd be happy to wait."

Yerin's ankle was still sore, but nothing that would slow her down in a real fight. "You never woke up with a dull edge? Happens to everyone, sometimes." Cassias had defeated her in no more than three moves each time today, and normally she could hold him off for six or seven. She was a Highgold now, technically his equal, but he had experience and skill that she couldn't match. Yet.

Cassias nodded, expression softening as though he understood. "Don't worry. Eithan has taken too much interest in Lindon to let him die so easily. And in you too."

Yerin snorted in disbelief, but she turned her head so as not to meet his eyes. What did he know? Sacred artists risked their lives every day. That wasn't enough to worry her.

Even though people died all the time where they weren't meant to. Her master had died in Sacred Valley, maybe the safest place in the world. It wasn't the trap you saw that killed you.

Without her around, Lindon wouldn't know what to watch for. Would Eithan look out for him?

Cassias pulled an intricately carved wooden device out of his outer robe and checked it, tucking it back inside after a glance. "It's almost time. Before we go, Yerin, would you mind if I asked you a personal question?"

"How personal?"

"No one pushes as hard as you do without a goal. Pardon me if I'm overstepping my bounds, but I'd like to know what destination you have in mind."

She'd started wondering that herself recently.

"To become a Sage," she said.

His eyebrows lifted. "I wouldn't have thought you were so ambitious."

"Most Sages don't take disciples. Not real ones, anyway. They don't want to pass on their Path. My master trusted me, and now he's gone." She ran her hand over the hilt of her master's sword. "I'm not letting his Path go to waste."

Cassias moved to the door, gesturing for her to follow. "That's a noble goal, and an impressive one. I met a Sage as a child, back in my family's homeland. It was a humbling experience. But it took him centuries to reach that height. Most people can't handle the pressure of training at that level, day after day, year after year, with no guarantee that they'll ever make it."

They passed through the door on the second floor of the house, moving to the stairs. Through the tall arched windows, she caught a glimpse of the deep blue Thousand-Mile Cloud that was their foundation, as well as the islands of white that surrounded them.

"Never understood that myself," Yerin said, vaulting over the railing and landing on the first floor instead of taking the stairs. Cassias took them carefully, one at a time. "Don't know what I'd do if I wasn't practicing the sword. You think I'd rather put down roots, or what?"

"That's not what I meant to imply," Cassias said, unbuckling his belt and tossing it and his sheathed saber onto a nearby rack designed for the purpose. "Only that it often helps in a fight if you have something to fight *for*."

Preserving her own life had always been enough to push Yerin along in fights. Should be enough for anybody.

But that wasn't always the truth, was it? She wanted more than that.

The Sword Sage had always said the pursuit of perfection in the sacred arts was a lonely pursuit, and anything else was a distraction. She'd come to think that advancing alone wasn't just boring, it was painful.

Which had made it such a stab to the gut when Eithan told her she couldn't come to watch Lindon fight. Especially when he'd taken Fisher Gesha, of all people.

"She won't be allowed to watch either," Eithan said. *"I'm bringing her for her unique talents. And I can't carry two people."*

That had sounded like an excuse to Yerin.

Cassias stepped up to the wooden console at the front of the room, before a massive wall of paneled glass. He looked out, through the clouds, over a series of strange mountains that rose from the ground like a forest of spears. One of the closer ones had something that looked like a temple on the top.

"I only ask you to consider...expanding your interests," Cassias said, moving his hands over the script-circles on the wooden panel. They lit up, and *Sky's Mercy* shuddered in response. "Even your master was a famous refiner, in addition to being an accomplished swordsman. Many experts find that splitting their focus can actually increase their results."

Yerin folded her arms, considering. She *did* spend all her time practicing the sacred arts in some way. Made it hard to care about anything else, when that was her world.

Problem was, she didn't know anything about the world outside of her training. It was the only thing the Sword Sage had raised her to do.

She needed a breath or two to think, but the floor shuddered again, and Orthos came stomping in.

The turtle was so tall and wide that he couldn't pass through most of the doors in the house without tearing holes in their frames, so he stayed in the corner of this main room. He'd walk out of the larger outer doors when he needed to relieve himself or vent his madra, standing on the Thousand-Mile Cloud. But he was tender as a newborn chick when it came to heights, so Yerin usually had to guide him out so he could close his eyes.

For a massive, black reptile with a shell that smoldered with dragonfire, he didn't have much of a spine. Even now, he glanced from side to side with his black-and-red eyes wide. "We're not on the ground yet?" he demanded in a deep, rumbling voice. "We were supposed to land. Why haven't we landed?"

Cassias turned around, his hand reaching into his pocket. Beneath his outer robe, he wore a shirt and pants, which still looked strange to Yerin in a fight. Everyone she knew fought in either a sacred artist's robes or armor.

"I apologize, Orthos," Cassias said. "I should have given you your medicine already."

Orthos shifted from one leg to another like a wobbly stool, his eyes flicking from one window to another, staring at the clouds. "We're not…it's not…why are we so high? Hm? Why do we have to be all the way up here?"

Cassias held out a violet pill streaked with blue. "Take your medicine, Orthos. It won't be long now. We're on approach. When you wake up, you'll be with Lindon."

"He was weak," Orthos mumbled, stretching out his head to snap up the pill in Cassias' hand. "So weak. He's probably dead. I'll be going back to the way…I was…"

In seconds, he drifted off, withdrawing his head and his limbs into his shell. Now there was a great black mound in the center of their living room, smoke drifting up from him as though from a dying fire.

"He's cheerier than a ray of sunshine," Yerin said. She'd already heard about Lindon's bout of weakness following his duel, but Orthos admitted that he might feel the same way if Lindon had died. He'd never felt a contractor's death before. He thought Lindon's madra had recovered since, but he couldn't be sure—maybe he was just getting used to the sensation.

So she couldn't shake a little worry. Not enough to distract her, of course, but some.

"Well, at least the pills still work," Cassias said, eyeing Orthos' sleeping form. "They've kept his madra quiet as well, even when he's awake."

"He hasn't torn the house apart. That's a prize and a half, if you ask me."

Cassias turned back to the console. "That was our last pill, so we'll have to rely on Eithan and Lindon for the trip back. One breath of dragon's fire, and we'll hit the ground like a meteor."

He had angled the house down slightly, so that the cloud was now drifting toward the temple at the top of the mountain. She walked up to stand beside him.

"That it?"

"Eithan's down there," Cassias confirmed. "I believe I saw some Remnant parts set out in a room as well, so Fisher Gesha must have set up."

That, or some Remnants died in a cave. And she noticed he didn't say a word about Lindon, one way or another.

She turned to go find a seat—she'd learned it was best to be sitting during a landing. As she did, she felt a surge of power miles away to the south, the opposite direction of the mountain. Only a few miles, and it gave off the familiar feeling of blood madra.

At least it wasn't any closer. A sudden battle between experts could be like an earthquake in a ceramics shop. Maybe that fight would—

Her Blood Shadow unraveled.

That quickly, the knot tied behind her slipped free. The seal her master had left for her was gone. No warning.

Her belt loosened, uncoiling like a serpent.

No time to panic. She dropped to the floor with Orthos' heat behind her, focusing on her spirit. A bloody red light was already stretching deep into her, its roots questing for the silver light of her core. She pushed her madra through its cycles, her breath coming too fast, silver light forcing back the red.

It wanted to slither inside. Infect her.

And her master's protection was gone.

The thought made her breath come even faster, but she calmed herself before she lost control over her madra, pushing back, forcing the Blood Shadow to retreat. She was a Highgold now, and it hadn't quite caught up yet. She was still ahead of it. She could still keep herself under control.

Something shifted on her waist, and she snapped her eyes open.

The Shadow reached for Cassias.

It stretched out from her like a questing limb, the end of its blood-covered length splitting into fingers. A hand. It was actually reaching for Cassias now, its fingers grasping for the back of his head. Its fingertips were sharp as knives—shaped by her sword madra.

She croaked out some kind of warning, but it was hard to talk while every part of her was straining to hold back her uninvited guest. She even seized it with both hands, trying to pull it back, but it dragged her seated body a few inches across the floor.

The parasite's knife-edged hand closed on Cassias' golden curls.

And without turning around, he slid away.

With one punch, he drove a spike of silver madra from his fist and into the center of the crimson palm. Blood madra spattered on the ceiling and then dissolved into essence with a hiss.

Yerin was still trying to push out her warning, sweat streaming down her face, but she finally closed her mouth. An Arelius might as well have eyes in the back of his head.

The Shadow moved again, a blur of red, and Cassias stood his ground. Both of his hands struck, blasting pieces away from the Blood Shadow.

But when the exchange ended, there was a scratch on his arm. It oozed a single drop of blood.

"Get away," she managed to grunt out, hauling on her uninvited guest. "Blood!"

Cassias looked from her to the parasite and dashed back without asking questions, but the drop had already fallen to the ground.

The Blood Shadow fell on it like a hawk taking a fish, slapping its palm down on the droplet on the floor. Blood aura and madra flared, twisting with one another into a horrible and complex technique, even as the parasite relaxed. It retreated, allowing her to haul it back a few feet.

She knew why. She had seen this technique before.

It had destroyed her home.

As though that single drop of blood had been a seed, a creature sprouted in seconds. It was a doll of pure crimson, formed as though from solid blood, shaped like a man but only half the height. It had no features on its head, but it turned to Cassias like a hunting dog. It loped toward him, using its arms for balance, like an ape.

Her master had called them bloodspawn, and they were the stuff of her nightmares.

She shouted a warning to him, still hauling on her Shadow. Cassias kicked off, away from the console, a flash of silver driving a hole in the floorboards. His Silver Step technique brought him forward with such speed that he vanished, reappearing behind his opponent. He slashed his hand back, trailing silver light, passing through the bloodspawn's head.

Its head was blasted apart, but it was made of ooze. It latched onto him, grabbing him by both shoulders and across the chest.

Each bloodspawn was different, but this one had been grown by a Shadow that fed on *her* madra. She knew what would happen next, but it still caught her off-guard with its speed.

It sharpened into a forest of blades, like it had sprouted razors.

Cassias let out a sound like a grunt, soaked in his own blood in an instant. The bloodspawn dissolved, having poured its own power into the technique, but the wounds remained. His shirt was shredded, and a stain slowly spread over his chest. He staggered, even as a sheet of blood fell from his wounded scalp and covered his eyes like a waterfall.

He looked up to the window, where the mountain temple had

grown huge in his sights. He stumbled to the controls, leaving a bloody handprint on them, starting to level off their flight.

Guilt squeezed Yerin's gut. This was her fault.

But no, she had to focus. If she let the Blood Shadow take over her spirit, things would only get worse.

She tightened her grip on the parasite, both physically and spiritually. But it seemed to sense Cassias' wounds...or perhaps the blood aura.

It surged toward him, transforming into a razor-edged mace that smashed down at his back. She managed to shout a warning this time.

He turned with both his hands raised, filled with silver light, driving forward with spikes of sword madra. The technique blasted into the Blood Shadow, splattering power onto the walls, and turning its course aside. He was able to take one unsteady step to the side, avoiding its strike.

But it smashed straight into the console, blasting it to splinters.

The parasite had lost much of its strength in confronting Cassias, so Yerin was able to lever herself to her feet...but all she could see was the mountain in the window. Growing closer and closer.

The Blood Shadow drew itself back in, like a pet falling asleep, twisting itself around not only her waist, but her shoulders and hips as though it would never let go.

She shuddered, but at least she was in control over herself now. She dashed forward, seizing the wounded Cassias. He struggled against her for a moment, but he was too weak.

Yerin ran out the door, dashing onto the deep blue cloud as wind tore past them. She cast a glance back at Orthos, but he was withdrawn into his shell—she hoped it would be enough to protect him from the crash. Whether it was or not, there was nothing she could do.

She leaned over the edge of the Thousand-Mile Cloud and forced herself to wait. Her every instinct told her to jump out now, abandoning the doomed house, though it would splatter her like a...well, like anything dropped from this height.

The temple loomed closer, and she refused to blink, staring straight into the wind as they approached.

When the edge of the mountain was finally beneath her, she jumped.

With Cassias over her left shoulder, she drew her master's sword, slashing at the air in the only Forger technique she knew. She Forged a blade beneath them—it would be thin enough to see through if viewed edge-on, but of course she didn't want to fall on the edge of the blade. They fell onto the flat side.

Her master had used a variation of this technique to fly. She only hoped she could do half as well now.

She couldn't. The sword shattered like glass and they tumbled down toward the rock, barely slowed at all.

She tried again, crashing through it once more, and then she drew her sword back to try a third time.

They hit the stone.

She couldn't feel her limbs. A disturbing sense of cold passed through her, and darkness pressed into the edges of her vision. A roar sounded nearby, and some part of her guessed that had to be the house crashing.

Before she lost consciousness, she realized there was one thing she could still feel: the power rising from behind her, like a blood-red sun. It was getting closer.

Something was coming, and it had given her Blood Shadow its strength.

Pai Ren had joined the Skysworn to see the world look up to him.

Not only was the green armor of the Skysworn among the most respected uniforms you could wear in the Blackflame Empire, you also got the chance to *fly*. People watched him from below as he flew over, and they looked up at him in jealousy. Until today, he had considered it the best decision of his life so far.

Now, he thought it might be the worst—and last—decision he ever made.

Death had come to Lastleaf Fortress, where he had been stationed. He was only investigating the Empire's southern border. It was a standard inspection, and the sacred artists in Lastleaf had welcomed him like an honored guest. He had spent the last three weeks feasting on the products of the southern jungle, which he had been honored to visit.

Now, somehow, the sun had been stained red. He stood on his personal Thousand-Mile Cloud, looking out over the rest of the fort below him, horrified. Blood aura choked the air, so that he had to close his Copper sight and withdraw his spiritual sense, lest he lose his lunch.

The fortress was a vast complex, wider than it was tall, spread out beneath him in layers like the rings of a tree. Each ring was walled, and the strongest sacred artists lived in the heart of the fort.

The sacred arts of this School, the Path of the Last Leaf, turned trees into deadly weapons. Vines and trees had been planted within the fortress for the purposes of cycling aura, dotting each layer. The innermost layer was almost a forest.

Ordinarily, there was a natural flow of students and experts flowing throughout the fortress, passing between walls and going on a thousand different tasks. It had been soothing to watch.

Today, it was a horrifying scene of carnage.

Beneath him, the artists of the Lastleaf School tried to stand in desperate pockets against an army of...not Remnants, exactly, nor sacred beasts. Were they constructs? He couldn't be sure.

He'd call them monsters.

Creatures of blood, born of blood. Every wound created another one—a faceless, shambling creature that sacrificed itself in order to kill another sacred artist. They would latch on to a Lastleaf artist, split into a thousand crimson vines, and then strangle the man or woman to death.

It looked disturbingly similar to a technique from the Path of the Last Leaf, as though these blood-creatures used the sacred arts of those they killed. Or perhaps they took the sacred arts from the blood when they were born.

Ren's mind tried to unravel the puzzle even as his body stood, frozen and horrified, stuck to his Thousand-Mile Cloud. He was a Truegold, stronger than most in the Empire, but he couldn't imagine himself doing anything about the tragedy he saw unfolding beneath him.

A trio of women stood with weapons in hand, standing against a tide of crimson creatures. One slashed a green sword, and leaves were Forged from nowhere, slashing against them. Another raised a construct device, which flashed green, to no apparent effect he could see. A third swung a hammer, smashing a single monster to a splatter. A wave of creatures overwhelmed them in seconds.

He could probably have heard their screams, if they didn't blend into everyone else's.

A couple pulled their child between them, running from a line of red monsters. They wouldn't make it.

An elder directed a tree to raise its branches in a fist, smashing down on the blood-creatures and reducing them to paste. A group of disciples huddled behind him, frightened, but there seemed to be a new batch of enemies born from every human death. There was no end to them, and the elder's madra could only last so long.

Similar stories played out all over the fortress, such that he found it harder and harder to focus on any individual detail. It was just a mass of horror, like a nightmare spread out beneath him.

He could descend on that elder who was holding out. Perhaps save a disciple or two on his cloud.

But...

He glanced behind him, where the red light had condensed into a shaft of what looked like a beam of crimson sunlight. He had withdrawn his perception already, but he still felt something from back there: dread. Horror. Overwhelming power.

There was something only a mile or two south of this fortress, something ancient and powerful. It had caused this, he was sure.

And if he died here, the Skysworn would never know about it.

There was a sealed box on his thigh, scripted and reinforced so that it was almost impossible to open by accident. Among the Skysworn, it was considered shameful to open this box.

He flooded it with his madra, unlocking it. It popped open, causing a stone to fall into his gauntleted hand.

This green egg-shaped stone was, in fact, a simple construct. He crushed it, releasing the power inside.

The power gathered into a small, winged creature like a four-winged hummingbird made entirely out of green light. The construct flitted around his head for one lap and then streaked into the distance, heading for Skysworn headquarters.

The messenger would alert the Underlord, drawing reinforcements, but it couldn't carry any detailed information. He would have to tell that story himself.

He retreated into the sky, urging his Thousand-Mile Cloud forward. Away from that disturbing shaft of red light…and from whatever it was shining on.

As he flew away, he spotted someone standing on the outer wall. A young man, with utterly pale skin and black hair that fell down almost to his waist. Even among the brutal scenes below, he stood out. Ren slowed, wondering if he should pick the boy up. He didn't look older than eighteen, but something warned him off.

The young man wasn't watching the fighting around him. His eyes were calm, and on the sky. Watching Ren.

Ren gained some distance, rising into the sky. The young man was wearing a shapeless black coat that covered him from shoulders to feet, but he reached out a hand.

The hand was solid red, as though it had been dipped in blood. With one sharp gesture, the young man made a fist.

A lance of pain shot through Ren's heart.

He clapped a hand to his chest, his lungs freezing up, and the break in his concentration made his cloud shudder. An instant later, the script in his armor flashed, breaking off the blood Ruler technique that had almost killed him. The red aura was pushed away from him, his heart relaxed, and he heaved a huge breath.

This time, he flew as fast as he could. There was no thought in his head besides escape.

He made it a few more yards before something seized him around his ankle and dragged him off his cloud.

Before Pai Ren hit the ground, he screamed one last time. No one heard him.

Lindon hobbled out into the sunlight to see what the noise was about. He and Gesha had been preparing his new arm when the mountain shook with an overwhelming crash.

He still hadn't fully recovered from the fight, his body still sore, his madra still weak. Little Blue had cleansed some of his madra channels, but they were still scraped raw. His body felt as though it was made of clay, and he was pushing it through each step with sheer willpower. Gesha had tried to keep him in his bed, assuring him that he needed his rest, and that she would investigate the noise.

But Yerin was supposed to arrive today.

Fisher Gesha held the door open for him, but she was distracted. Her bun of gray hair was in his face as she stared out the door.

Before he saw anything, he was distracted by the feeling of a huge power to the south. He looked that direction first, and it was as though the sunlight had been filtered through a lens of red glass only a few miles to the south.

But when he realized what was lying right in front of him, all thoughts about that distant power were pushed from his mind.

The wreckage of *Sky's Mercy* was strewn all over the side of the mountain, with dust and smoke rising from the debris. Blue wisps of cloud were still dissolving in the air, and here and there he could see something he recognized: a chair lying upside-down, a twisted piece of what had once been a dragon-headed banister.

Then he spotted a figure in black robes, and he shot forward, his wounds forgotten. Yerin was lying there on the stone, bloody and broken, with Cassias next to her.

His spirit told him Orthos was nearby, but only a quick glance assured him the turtle was fine: his limbs and head had been retracted into his shell, and he was sitting at the center of the wreck like a smoldering coal. If Lindon was reading his spiritual sensations correctly, his contracted partner was sleeping.

But when he looked at Yerin's condition, his throat tightened up. She was lying on her side, blood pooled beneath her head, with her legs twisted around one another. Her arms were limp, her fingertips twitching, her bare sword lying twenty yards away. At least she hadn't fallen on it. Even her belt had come undone, somehow, twisting around her body instead of coiling around her waist.

He knelt beside her, raising trembling fingers an inch away from her lips to feel for breath.

An instant later, he felt her exhale, and he released his own breath. As long as she was alive, she could be saved.

Cassias' corpse was a few steps away. Lindon only looked him over once before knowing he was a lost cause. He didn't need to check for a pulse; the man was covered in wounds and soaked in blood. No one could—

Cassias stirred, raising a hand to his head. Lindon jolted, hurrying over to the older man to help him sit up.

"Don't push yourself," Lindon advised. "We're here." He had no idea what they would *do*, but it seemed important to soothe a man who had just survived a violent crash.

When it seemed Cassias could sit up on his own, Lindon began to walk back to Yerin, but the Arelius seized his arm.

"Stay away," Cassias said, voice rough.

He was shaky from the crash. Lindon had seen this before, back in his clan, on people who had survived battles. He tried to pry himself away gently, but Cassias' grip was like an eagle's talon. He staggered to his feet, pulling Lindon away from Yerin.

Toward Eithan.

Eithan had, of course, made it here before Lindon and Fisher Gesha had even made it out of their rooms. But Lindon hadn't noticed until now that the Underlord had made no effort to help his family member or his disciple.

Instead, he stood on the very edge of the cliff, staring at the red light in the distance.

Which, now that Lindon thought of it, seemed a little closer than it had been a moment ago.

Wind tugged at Eithan's hair, and for once he wore no smile. He stared into the red light like a man contemplating the approach of an advancing army.

"Her Blood Shadow has awakened," Cassias reported to Eithan.

"It's no wonder, considering what's coming," Eithan said, still looking to the south.

"We should remove it. We should have removed it before now, I can't imagine what you were thinking."

"No, you can't," Eithan said, pulling out his black iron scissors. With one swift motion, he sliced open the tip of his finger.

Then, without warning, he turned on his heel and headed for Yerin.

Yerin's belt stirred and struck like a serpent when Eithan moved closer, which startled Lindon. Fisher Gesha scuttled away on her spider's legs, looking terrified, but neither Cassias nor Eithan seemed surprised. The Underlord simply let the end of the blood-colored rope strike him on the neck, where it did no more damage than a limp string.

Eithan pulled Yerin's robes apart.

He tore the cloth easily, exposing about a foot of her belly. There were thin scars even there, though not as many as on the skin of her arms and face. It was just her stomach, but Lindon still thought about looking away.

But the sight stopped him. The bloody rope that she had always worn like a belt stretched out from her navel, as though it was made of her intestines.

Or, a more disturbing thought: as though it stretched into her core.

Eithan sketched on her skin with his blood, writing a circle of symbols around her navel. It must be a script, but Lindon recognized none of it. He took in a breath, and then a gray fire ignited the symbols. Soulfire: the power of an Underlord.

Lindon still didn't understand it, as Eithan refused to explain, but soulfire was the hallmark and the signature of a Lord. This script used it as power.

And the red rope crumbled away. It wilted and shriveled like a dying plant, dissolving into what looked like flakes of dried blood before it finally evaporated to red essence.

Just like that, it was gone. The circle of symbols on Yerin's stomach had been blackened, as though they had been burned into her flesh.

She woke up only a second later, coughing. She groaned. "Somebody find the ox that trampled me."

Lindon hurried over to her, but Eithan had returned his gaze to the south. "You'll feel worse in a moment," he said. His scissors were still in his hand. "Battle is upon us."

Lindon was going to ask what he was talking about, then he saw the wall of red had pressed against the edge of the mountain. His eyes widened.

Then red light swallowed them all.

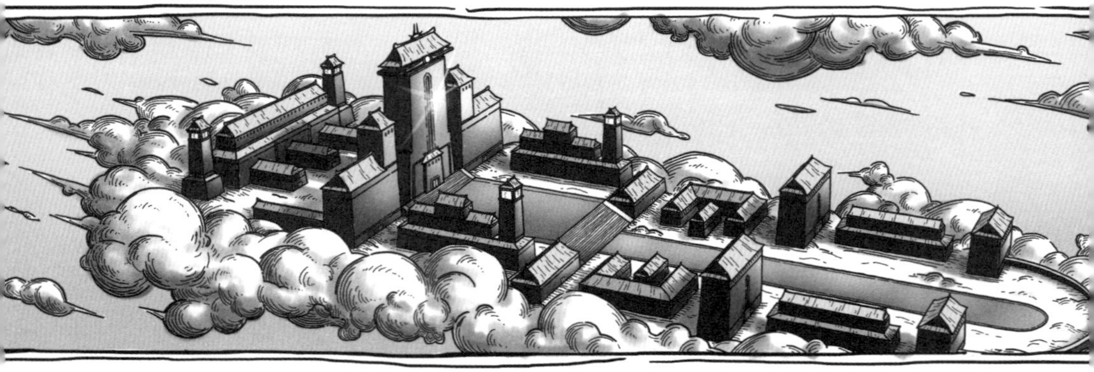

IX

It was as though the sun had turned red.

Even in Lindon's Copper sight, everything was dyed crimson. His stomach heaved, and bile rose in his throat—this felt like being submerged in a pool of blood.

He closed his spiritual sight before he lost himself, but what he saw in reality was even more disturbing.

Where Cassias and Yerin had been lying on the stone, *creatures* rose from their blood like Remnants from corpses. They were only half the size of a person, with featureless faces, and their bodies had been formed from gelatinous blood.

There were six of them in an instant, turning their heads toward Lindon and the others as though they could smell living flesh.

They lurched forward, but Eithan blurred through their ranks, his scissors sweeping through the air.

Blood madra sprayed into the air and dissolved into essence, and all six of them deflated.

Fisher Gesha pointed a trembling finger at the sight. "That! What is that? Hm? Did you bring those back with you?"

"These are bloodspawn," Eithan said, shaking the last stains off his scissors as the liquid madra evaporated. "They are the least of the Bleeding Phoenix's creations."

Gesha seemed to shrink into herself even more, though she didn't have much size to lose. "The...the Bleeding Phoenix? Did you...are you saying..."

Cassias grasped at his hip as though feeling for a sword that wasn't there. He frowned at the space, then fumbled at his other hip. Of course, there was still no weapon. The crash had shaken him.

"What happened here, Eithan?" he asked, finally giving up on his saber.

"Jai Daishou opened a door he should not have," Eithan said, moving his head as though watching something move through the air. Something that Lindon couldn't see. "Someone noticed."

"Dreadgods," Fisher Gesha repeated, shaking. "Dreadgods..."

"Bloodspawn rise from spilled blood," Eithan said. "When it's still inside you, or on your skin, your madra still has control. The Phoenix's power can't do anything with it until it leaves the influence of your spirit."

"Unless the Phoenix itself rises," Cassias pointed out. He was leaning against the back of an upturned couch that had fallen from *Sky's Mercy,* and he still didn't look balanced.

Eithan nodded absently, still watching something in the air. "A Dreadgod doesn't care for the protection of your meager spirit. This isn't its full attention, just a side effect of its awakening."

More bloodspawn formed from the drops spilling from Cassias and Yerin, but Eithan dispersed them with a couple of quick blasts of pure madra. Lindon needed to learn that technique.

"Forgiveness, but we should leave," Lindon said at last. He felt like he was stating the obvious, but no one else had said it. If the red light was the extent of the Phoenix's influence, they had to escape it.

Eithan responded without turning. "I could take myself out of here. I could take Yerin with me, and perhaps Cassias. You, with your Thousand-Mile Cloud, could take Fisher Gesha. But what about Jai Long and Jai Chen."

Lindon started. They were still here?

"And what if we have to fight our way out?" Eithan continued. "Do we abandon our charges? If we are to run, we first have to clear some space."

Yerin rose unsteadily to her feet, clutching one arm as though it pained her. "Then let's stop jabbering and do it," she said, hobbling over to her master's sword. Leaning over and picking it up was an agonizing production. "Better than sitting here."

"Don't worry. They have come to us."

A young man appeared beyond the edge of the cliff, his pale face framed by black hair that stretched down to his waist. He wore a dark, shapeless coat that covered his shoulders, and as he slowly rose up the side of the cliff, Lindon saw that the cloak covered even his feet.

He was standing on a rising tide of blood.

The newcomer stepped from his red platform onto the edge of the mountain without a word, his gaze locked on Eithan's. "Underlord," he said, his voice a whisper. He sounded as though that single word pained him.

"An emissary of Redmoon Hall, if I'm not mistaken," Eithan said. His voice was cheery, but he still wore no smile. His scissors were held ready in his right hand.

"I am Longhook," the emissary said. A gleaming red hook appeared at the end of his right sleeve, as though it were made of crimson-dyed steel. In that light, everything looked red, so its color could have been nothing more than a trick of the eye.

Though he doubted it.

The hook slowly slid to the ground, revealing link after link of red chain. In a moment, the hook hit the ground with a clink.

Eithan looked from his enemy's weapon to his own. "Longhook, is it? You can call me Tiny Scissors."

Longhook didn't seem to appreciate the joke. He stood like a statue carved from ice.

"What does your master want?" Eithan asked, casually strolling away from the other members of the Arelius family.

"North," Longhook whispered. "He wants the treasure of the north."

"By all means, go around us," Eithan offered.

Lindon wondered what Eithan was doing. Why was he trying to make a deal with the enemy? Eithan often preferred to talk his way around problems, but he had already said they would have to fight. And he had dispersed the bloodspawn with no problems. Why didn't he knock this newcomer off the mountain?

Gingerly, feeling as though he were submerging his arm in sludge, Lindon extended his perception.

Only an instant later, he understood the truth.

Longhook blazed with the power of an Underlord.

"No," the emissary responded. "A piece of the treasure...here." His breath rasped, so many words apparently having been too much for him.

Eithan froze a moment, then his smile reappeared. "Well then, I think we can come to an—"

In the middle of his own sentence, he exploded into motion. The air clapped behind him when he moved, driving his scissors at his enemy.

Lindon couldn't follow what happened next, only the explosion of sound, a rush of wind, and a flash of red light.

A column of stone exploded under Longhook's weapon, the hook having missed Eithan and slammed into the building behind him. Eithan avoided even the chain as though it were red-hot, vaulting over it, and slamming his fist into Longhook's chest. A ripple of colorless power surged out, blasting past the Redmoon Hall emissary.

This exchange of blows was still too fast for Lindon to follow, but the emissary didn't seem slowed down by Eithan's attack at all. It ended in Eithan leaping backwards, and Longhook with one arm extended. It stuck out from his coat, and his arm was sheathed in solid red.

Was that his Goldsign? Or was he covered in one of those bloodspawn?

He'd hauled his hook back to himself, and now he whipped it at

Eithan. It struck with an impact that hurt Lindon's ears, carrying the sound of steel-on-steel as Eithan blocked with his scissors.

The impact sent him flying back toward the building on the mountain, and Longhook was after him in an instant.

From start to finish, the whole exchange took perhaps two seconds.

Lindon stared after the crashes and explosions coming from inside the building. He shivered.

He couldn't have blocked a single one of those strikes. He would have died in an instant.

He'd started to think of Jai Long as close to Eithan's level, but the first step toward Underlord was nothing compared to the real thing.

"I say we leave," Lindon said, moving to help Yerin walk. She waved him away, though she winced at the motion and her arm was starting to swell. He stayed next to her, just in case.

Cassias was in even worse shape, his eyes distant. Fisher Gesha nodded to Lindon's words, scuttling off to the side entrance of the building—the sounds from Eithan's fight had already grown distant, but she was still careful.

Slowly, Cassias shook his head. "Not yet. There are more coming."

Lindon scanned the ground, but no new bloodspawn had risen. It looked as though the blood from Yerin and Cassias' injuries had been exhausted.

"Not ours," Cassias said, and pointed to the edge of the cliff.

Where Longhook had first appeared, there were now a host of featureless heads popping over the edge. They clambered up with their malformed arms, but these seemed somehow different from the ones before.

The others had been slightly angular, with sharp features and long limbs. These were still made of blood madra, and still had no faces, but their bodies were twisted and gnarled. As though there were a skeleton of wood underneath. There was even a pattern in the flow of their crimson "skin," where Lindon caught an impression of fluttering leaves.

His guess was confirmed an instant later, when one of the bloodspawn exploded into a branch of crimson vines covered in scarlet leaves. The vines rushed across the ground for them, like a nest of hungry snakes.

Next to him, Yerin shuddered. Her skin was even paler than usual—although that might have been the blood loss—and she clutched her master's sword in both hands. He had never seen her so panicked before.

"No, no, no," she said. "Not this time."

With a desperate shout, she slashed her white blade at the grasping vines. Lindon heard a sound like a bell, and something sliced at the edges of his robes.

The vines splattered to liquid madra, which quickly began to dissolve.

So did the ranks of the bloodspawn.

Lindon caught her with his left hand as she sagged, exhausted, but his sudden motion pulled loose the scripted band around the stump of his right arm. Pain flared back again, dull but immediate, and his eyes lost focus.

He fell to his knees, taking her with him.

She shook for a moment, then her eyes fastened on the space where his right hand had once been. "Your arm," she said, looking up to him with wide eyes.

He forced a smile. "Better than my life, isn't it?"

"Doesn't make it smiles and rainbows just because you lived," Yerin said. "Heavens know, I'm sorry. I'm just..." She looked back to the splashes of blood and shuddered again. "I am sorry."

In mortal danger they may have been, but her sympathy warmed him even as it caught him unprepared. He thought she would say he should just bear it and stop complaining.

"I've been down that road," she said, rolling her sleeve up to reveal a scar around her left elbow. "Lost both of them, to tell you true." Another scar ringed her right wrist. "And chunks out of both legs so they hung there, useless as rust on a blade. It's no joke. Nothing worse than an itch on a limb you've already lost."

"How did you get them back?" Lindon asked. As interested as he was in the powers of a Remnant arm, if he could get his own arm back...

"Master had a pill for everything. He could regrow a limb faster than a flower. Expensive, though, so he always made me work for it."

She stood on her own now, and despite the blood running down her face, she seemed more like herself now than she had only a moment before. Lindon's missing arm had shaken her out of whatever had taken hold of her.

He looked to the still-vanishing puddles of blood madra. "Pardon, but have you seen these before?"

She went still for a moment before giving him a single nod. That lost expression returned. "I've seen them. Too much of them, when this showed up," she said, clapping a hand to her stomach. "I guess it's time to—"

Then she seemed to realize her belt was missing. She stared down, dumbfounded, and felt around her waist. "Where is it? It can't just...crawl off..." She was starting to breathe quickly, and she squeezed her eyes shut.

A moment later, her breath returned to normal, but her shoulders slumped. "It's still there. Coiled like a worm in an apple." Her lips twisted in disgust. "But somebody bottled it up. Eithan?"

"Eithan."

Another explosion in the back of the mountain led to a rising column of smoke. "Let's go. We should be ready to leave when he wins."

Another bloodspawn poked its head up the cliff, and Fisher Gesha threw a web of purple light at it. It was jerked down the side of the mountain as though she'd tied a weight to its ankles.

Carefully, Cassias stepped up to the edge of the cliff and glanced down. Almost instantly, he staggered back.

"We have to leave. Right now."

He marched back toward the entrance into the mountain, though every second or third step he swayed as though he stood on the deck of a ship.

Yerin and Gesha followed him, but a strange curiosity took hold of Lindon. He walked to the edge and peered down.

Dozens—perhaps hundreds—of bloodspawn were stuck to the side of the mountain. Some of them looked like gnarled trees, others like clouds of gas, and still others like a mass of jagged crystals. Most of them weren't moving quickly, but they all crept up the side of the mountain.

But beneath them, covering the hills, was an ocean of writhing red figures. Lindon couldn't begin to guess how many there were. An army.

He ran back, hurrying after the others. There were so many. *So many.* And if they fought, new ones would be created every time a human was injured.

They would be overwhelmed in minutes, dragged down and torn apart by monsters.

His exhaustion and the mental burden of losing his arm seemed to retreat in the face of a rising tide of panic.

One of the doors to the sanctuary had been blasted off its hinges. Red-stained sunlight streamed in through a hole in the ceiling.

A bloodspawn was forming right in front of them, from a tiny splatter on the wall. It was transparent as red glass, and it seemed taller and thinner than the others.

Cassias drove a spike of silver madra through it, but the bloodspawn didn't seem to mind the hole in its chest. It held its arms wide, trying to catch the Arelius in an embrace.

Lindon moved up, cycling pure madra.

His madra channels still pained him whenever he cycled, and he had to improvise a different pattern to use his technique with his left hand. He usually used his right.

But a second later, he had driven an Empty Palm into the bloodspawn's midsection.

It popped like a bubble, spraying him with liquid madra. The madra burned slightly, tingling against his skin, but it started to evaporate almost immediately. No one commented; they were all on high alert as they moved through the red-lit halls, heading for the entrance to the complex below.

So many walls had been blown out by the battles between the two Underlords that Lindon wondered about the sanctuary's structural integrity. As he watched, a few boulders bigger than his head crumbled from a hole in the ceiling, smashing into the ground.

The wind, whistling through the walls, now sounded ominous.

After an agonizing minute or two of navigating through the fractured halls, they finally came upon a door at the end of a hall. Debris was lying against it, holding it closed, but at least they hadn't run into another bloodspawn. Lindon would count that as a success.

Fisher Gesha lashed lines of purple madra to the debris, hauling them back with her power. With a single palm strike, Cassias shattered a block bigger than he was, though he had to lean against a wall and take a breath afterwards. He looked as though he'd bathed in blood, and his wounds were obvious. More than any of them, he needed to get out of here.

Yerin simply grabbed chunks of stone and hauled them away with her bare hands. Lindon switched to Blackflame and joined her, though the Burning Cloak was better for sudden, abrupt motions than for sustained strength. He ended up kicking stones away, then shattering the door open.

He was relieved when he saw the steady runelight of the script-circle in the stairway behind the door. It led down, toward the chamber where his pack waited. Once he retrieved Little Blue, his belongings, and his new arm—which was still in the process of being created—they could all leave. Fisher Gesha had some belongings of her own as well, which she couldn't leave behind. She wasn't even carrying her goldsteel hook.

They started heading down when Eithan crashed through the ceiling behind them.

A red hook had been driven into his shoulder, and the Redmoon Hall emissary had hauled him down *through* the ceiling. Longhook was standing behind them, on the ground floor, and none of them had noticed him show up. Now he stood over Eithan's squirming body, holding his chain in two crimson hands.

Eithan forced his eyes open, though they were hazy with pain, and both of his hands were holding the hook in his shoulder. He craned his eyes back to see Longhook, though from his perspective the emissary must have looked upside-down.

He revealed a grin of bloodstained teeth. "It's not too late for you to surrender," he said, pulling the hook from his shoulder with a sick, wet sound. He shuddered as he did so.

Longhook had a cut along the side of his neck, and his coat had been sliced in a few places. But otherwise, he seemed the same as when he had first appeared.

Lindon gripped the edge of the doorway, rekindling the Burning Cloak.

A loud voice in his mind urged him to run down, grab his belongings, and leave. But Blackflame pushed him to action, which is why he kept it surging through him.

He had to help...without getting destroyed by a single casual backhand from an Underlord.

He gathered a dark fireball in his one remaining palm, focused on Longhook. Fisher Gesha shook her head frantically when she saw what he was doing, but he was staring at his target. Blackflame madra was known for piercing defenses. He had blasted off a

Truegold's hand and threatened Jai Long. He could at least distract an Underlord for an instant.

As long as he didn't draw *too* much of his attention.

Eithan flipped up, slamming a foot into Longhook's face, but the emissary dodged and caught Eithan in the ribs with a red fist. The blow launched Eithan five feet in the air, where he twisted and fired a Striker technique down at his opponent.

A colorless wave washed over the Redmoon Hall emissary, and just a hint of it splashed on Lindon, destabilizing his technique. His ball of Blackflame swelled to twice its size in an instant as his control shook, and it was all he could do to compress it once again before it exploded.

The fight between Underlords had continued in a long, ear-shattering roar of strikes and counterstrikes, but Eithan was clearly getting the worst of it. If Lindon couldn't do something, he was going to die.

Then Longhook froze.

And the world darkened.

The crimson light streaming in from the holes in the ceiling was cut off, swallowing them in shadow. Lindon looked up, startled, only to see a deep green mass covering the sky. It rolled like distant storm clouds, or the surface of a lake seen from beneath...

No, those *were* clouds. A massive bank of green clouds.

Longhook withdrew his chain, and it slithered back into his sleeve, the hook following. He turned to dash off, but there was another wave of transparent power. He stumbled.

When it washed over Lindon, his Blackflame technique was snuffed out like a candle. The purple lights connecting Gesha to the rocks vanished, and Cassias and Yerin both sagged to their knees as the Enforcer techniques they used to keep themselves upright failed.

"So rude, to leave in the middle of a conversation," Eithan said, though his words were slurred and his smile was still bloodstained.

Longhook's head swiveled on his neck independent of the rest of his body. His hook peeked out the edges of his sleeve again.

Then a figure fell from above. It fell through one of the holes in the roof, folding its emerald wings, and landed with an impact that shattered stone.

Naru Gwei looked up through the veil of his greasy, gray hair, burn scars twisting his face. His old, battered armor was no worse for his hard landing, and his wings folded up impossibly small as they vanished into slots in the back of his armor. He knelt with one hand pressed against the broken stone.

The other held his massive black sword.

"In the name of the Blackflame Empire, and by the authority of the emperor, you are under arrest," the old man said. His voice still sounded bored, if not sleepy.

Longhook hurled his weapon. Not toward Naru Gwei; the hook shattered the far door, breaking the way out to the arena where Lindon and Jai Long had fought. The chain continued, impossibly long, until the end of the weapon hooked one of the columns still standing.

Without a word, he hauled on his chain, pulling himself down the hall so fast he may as well have been flying.

Naru Gwei lifted his free hand from the stone, making a gesture as though grabbing something.

Longhook froze like a bird trapped in mid-flight.

"I thought I said you were under arrest," the Skysworn said, rising to his feet.

The emissary of Redmoon Hall craned his neck with great effort to look back at them. No, not at *them*.

He looked straight at Yerin.

Yerin's head rocked back as she noticed, and she drew in a breath. With a barely perceptible motion, he nodded to her.

Then he twisted his body, fighting Naru Gwei's Ruler technique, and moved his hands in a strange pattern.

Red light twisted, and pain stabbed through Lindon's limbs. He fell to the ground, because the weight of his body was too much for the agony in his calves. Even Naru Gwei grunted, flinching back.

A blood Ruler technique, Lindon was sure of it. He was using the power of blood aura to affect their bodies directly. Normally, it might be too weak to harm an opponent, but the power of blood was so strong it was twisting the light. He had more aura to work with than Naru Gwei possibly could.

The Skysworn's technique broke, and Longhook shot off again. In an instant, he had vanished beyond the cliff.

Naru Gwei looked sharply to Eithan, who was struggling to sit up while leaning against the wall, a bleeding hole in his shoulder.

"He has friends," Eithan said, his smile twisting. "He's headed straight for them. I can't be sure if they're coming to us, but I'd rather not find out."

The Skysworn Captain nodded. With a casual swipe, he destroyed a bloodspawn that was rising from the pool beneath Eithan.

"Fifteen minutes," he said. "See to your injuries and gather your things. Then we're leaving."

Eithan glanced up at the vast green clouds overhead. "You brought your whole fortress along, did you?"

"Never thought I'd need it," he said heavily. "No one should have to plan for a day like this." Eithan started struggling to his feet, but Naru Gwei scooped him up with one hand. "The rest of them can join us, or they can take their chances with the Bleeding Phoenix's mercy. But you, Arelius, you're coming with me. The Emperor needs us both."

Jai Long spun his spear, driving the white-edged point of his spear through a blood-creature, reducing it to a rush of liquid. After every one he defeated, he glanced back to his sister.

His instincts urged him to carry her, but he fought back the thought. She could move on her own now.

Although not by much.

The rush of unstable madra from Jai Daishou had swollen her core with powers he didn't understand. If not for the Arelius Underlord's assurance that she would be fine, Jai Long would have tried his own hand at first aid. Though he knew so little about healing the spirit that he might well cripple her again.

She was following behind him, and to the physical eye she looked healthier than ever. Her wide eyes were focused, and she wore lavender sacred artist's robes that had been stained with red liquid madra. She had her hands out as though trying to use a technique.

And that was where the problem came in.

Her breath was ragged and heavy, and she was extremely focused on the area between her hands, but she couldn't control her madra.

A nearby monster exploded into a cloud of red spores, and Jai Long was almost caught off-guard. He spun his spear in a circle, trailing serpents of white madra.

The spores met the snakes and sizzled like water droplets hitting a hot grill, and the serpents moved of their own volition to devour more of the blood madra.

They'd run into fourteen of these since they sensed Underlords fighting above them and decided to run. Remnants, perhaps? If so, where had so many of them come from?

There were a series of tunnels leading down from the chambers inside the mountain to ground level, and they'd hoped to escape the Arelius family while Eithan fought off...whoever it was.

Eithan Arelius may have promised them safety, but they were still enemies and rivals of the Jai clan. It was best to be on their own.

Except Jai Chen had been stumbling after her brother, attempting to control her madra, for far too long now.

"Don't force it," he reminded her. She could strain her madra channels and cause greater spiritual damage than she'd struggled with in the first place. "I can get us out of here."

But he was less and less sure of that.

The red light that flooded the world made him shiver. This wasn't the work of a mere Underlord; perhaps a foreign Overlord, or a Sage, or some ancient weapon. No matter what it was, he had to escape it.

They rounded a corner, and six more creatures raised their featureless heads to fix on the living humans.

Jai Long evened out his breath, focusing on his cycling technique as he spun his spear. His core was dimming, running dry, but he'd seen early on that he couldn't spare his effort. These monsters favored suicide attacks, exploding into a mass of whatever power had been used to create them. They were easy to destroy individually, but if he were to miss even one of them, more could swarm him in seconds.

And, as they'd learned, more could be born from even a single drop of spilled blood. He was fighting against a tide, and running out of power.

But he would use what he had.

He stepped forward, gathering up his madra for a technique.

Then the red light receded before a bright tide. He spun his spear around, looking for the creature that had gotten behind him, only to see his sister holding a dragon by its tail.

A serpentine dragon roared, surging from the space between her hands. It was like one of his snakes, only far more detailed: he could see a pair of whiskers on its face and scales on its body. It was tinged pink, like the light of dawn, and it raged into the bloody creatures with a majestic cry.

They were splattered across the floor with the sheer momentum of its charge.

Awed, Jai Long extended his spiritual perception. The substance of this creature felt like nothing he'd ever seen before. It was something like his own madra, corrupted by that Remnant long ago, which explained life in a creature that wasn't a Remnant. But at the same time, it was also...refined, in a way he couldn't describe. Like Jai Long's power had been boiled down, purified, perfected, and then strengthened. And there were elements that reminded him of a storm.

It was a confusing, overwhelming mass of impressions, and he couldn't make sense of them before the dragon burst in a massive flash of essence, dissolving almost instantly.

"I did it," Jai Chen said, her smile broad.

Then she collapsed.

Jai Long hurried over to her, checking her spirit. Her madra channels were strained and dim, and her core was almost exhausted, but there was no further damage. He let out a breath of relief and threw her over his shoulder.

There was still a long way to go before he escaped.

When he sensed someone behind him, he whirled, readying his spear in one hand.

It was Wei Shi Lindon.

He didn't have the black-and-red eyes he'd used for most of their fight, but his gaze still smoldered with anger. Although that could be Jai Long's imagination; he didn't know Lindon well, but the young man apologized too much to be the angry type. He just *looked* like he was spoiling for a fight, with his rough face, tall build, and broad shoulders.

Now, he wore his large canvas pack on his shoulders, and he was holding out another, smaller pack in one hand.

The only hand he had left.

"Forgiveness, but we don't have much time," he said, holding out the small pack. "The Skysworn have arrived. They've offered to take us from here, and it's not safe to stay. I think you may have noticed."

Jai Long ignored the offering. "We will make it on our own."

Lindon didn't withdraw the pack. "I assumed so, but there are hundreds of bloodspawn at ground level. There's another way."

Slowly, Jai Long reached out with the tip of his spear and hooked the strap of the pack. He was still wary of some sort of trick. "Where?"

Now that his hand was free, Lindon pointed down a stone hallway that ramped gently back up. "That tunnel is connected to a bridge that leads to another mountain. That one isn't surrounded by bloodspawn."

"Have you told the Skysworn about us?" Jai Long asked, still searching for a trap. Wei Shi Lindon was full of tricks, and not to be trusted. The Skysworn would be hunting down anyone connected to Jai Daishou, and this could all be a plot to lead Jai Long and Jai Chen into capture.

"They're not looking for you," Lindon said. "They have bigger problems. But no, of course I have not told them."

After a moment of silence, he added, "Please, accept my gratitude. For your...mercy." He shrugged his right shoulder.

Jai Long stared at him, but despite his generally surly appearance, he seemed sincere.

"You could have killed me, so I appreciate your restraint." He rubbed at the remainder of his right arm. "Forgive me, but I hope you'll make it far away from here."

Jai Long returned the sentiment. He shrugged the pack over the shoulder that didn't have his sister on it and began to walk away.

Jai Chen spoke from his back. "We're going to the very outskirts of imperial territory," she said. Jai Long hadn't realized she'd regained consciousness. "People there have forgotten about the Empire."

Awkwardly, Jai Long turned her so that she could see Lindon without straining her neck. The young man gave her a smile. "That sounds like it's for the best."

She shifted on Jai Long's shoulder, and he realized she was trying to give him a polite bow. "I hope the heavens will allow us to meet again."

"Maybe they will," Lindon said, lifting his hand. "In the meantime, travel safely."

A tiny blue Remnant climbed up onto his shoulder. It looked like a sapphire woman only a few inches high, and she lifted a hand in imitation of him, waving to Jai Chen.

Without another word, Jai Long took off.

He couldn't sense any trap in the pack. There was nothing in there that gave off any power. No sealed Remnants or easily triggered constructs, which he had expected. Still, he'd have to check it for mundane traps when he had a chance.

Even if Wei Shi Lindon really had helped them out of goodwill, they had quite a journey ahead of them. Their cursed valley was little more than a legend, though evidence suggested it did exist somewhere to the west. If nothing else, they could find a peaceful place for Jai Chen to grow familiar with her new spirit.

And they would escape the net of the Jai clan. That was the important part. This was a new start.

Whether the heavens allowed it or not, they would never see Lindon again.

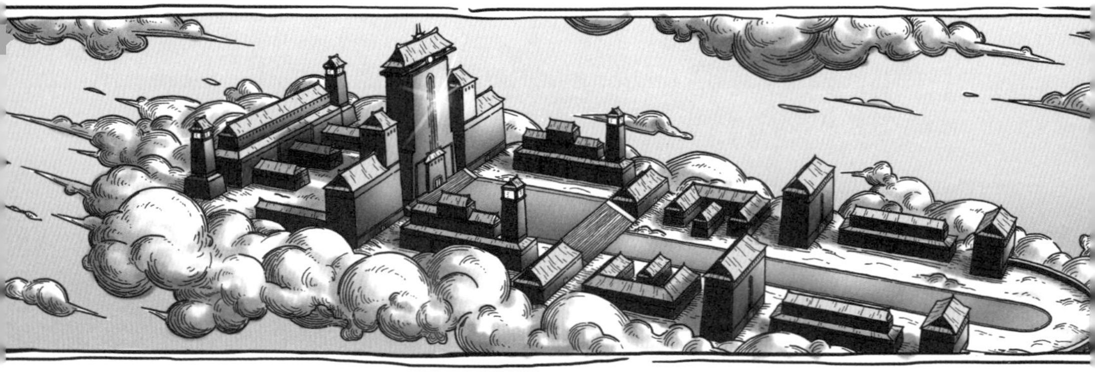

X

The Skysworn didn't refer to their enormous cloudship as a *ship*. It was more like a floating city on the clouds, and they treated it as such.

It looked like a jagged fortress of midnight-black stone, each building peaked and sharp. The largest facility was in the center of the cloud, a broad tower that loomed over all lesser structures. It matched the image Lindon had of a dark lord's stronghold, and the rest of the city was his evil fortress in the sky.

It was not at all the image he would usually associate with the Skysworn, a group of sacred artists dedicated to preserving justice and the rule of law.

Renfei and Bai Rou had come down to gather Lindon and the others to bring them onto the clouds above. Lindon wasn't sure if they were chosen as familiar faces, or if they were simply the only two with free time, but he was strangely glad to see them. He didn't know them well, but at least he knew their names.

The massive Bai Rou, his face shaded beneath his woven straw hat, marched in front of them down the paved streets. He pushed his way through the crowds, clearing the way for the people behind him.

Renfei followed behind, the cloud over her head bobbing with every step. She seemed far less serious and more relaxed now that they were aboard the heart of Skysworn power, and she quickly explained why.

"We call this city Stormrock," she said, as they walked past row after row of tall obsidian buildings. "Costs a fortune in wind scales to keep it aloft every second. If the empire didn't have so many Underlords on wind and cloud Paths, we would never be able to fly it at all. This is the home to almost two million people, when it needs to be, and only about five thousand of those are Skysworn or trainees. The rest are our families, as well as the merchants and farmers and such that we need to be self-sustaining. The Redflower family has quite a presence here, and in times of emergency it actually serves as their family headquarters as well."

Lindon vaguely remembered the Redflower family: just as the Arelius served to clean and sanitize the Empire, the Redflowers provided food and irrigation, even to those corners of the Blackflame Empire where farming would usually be impossible.

Sure enough, the streets were bustling. People cried out greetings when they saw the green armor of the Skysworn, or else they tried to entice Renfei or Bai Rou into buying some trinket or another. If not for the fact that their party needed medical attention, Renfei said, they would normally have stopped and interacted with at least a few of the city's people.

Yerin lay on Lindon's rust-colored Thousand-Mile Cloud and Cassias lay on a green one provided by the Skysworn. Yerin insisted that she could walk on her own, but she didn't get up. Cassias didn't struggle at all, and Lindon thought he might be asleep.

The people swarmed around them, all going about their ordinary lives, and only the passage of a couple of Skysworn could break their routine.

Well, that, or Orthos' irritation.

The sacred beast had woken up sore and irritated. Not only was he bruised and battered from the crash, but now he was on *another* cloud instead of solid ground. Only the size of this cloudship had appeased him; when he was inside the city walls, he couldn't tell that he was in the sky at all. Still, he snorted smoke at anyone who passed, and every once in a while pulled up a chunk of the street and munched on it. No one stopped him.

Lindon had thought they would make a strange sight; they had two Skysworn with them, a giant lumbering dragon-turtle, and an old woman drifting on spider's legs. Even he and Yerin would stand out in a crowd, and Cassias was always visible thanks to his golden hair among the sea of black. Not to mention that two of their number were covered in blood and using floating clouds as stretchers.

But despite the admiring looks at the Skysworn and the fearful ones at Orthos, they didn't stick out as much as he would have imagined.

Paths of all kinds were represented here on the streets of

Stormrock. A woman passed over their party without looking down from a book she was reading, a half-dozen tentacles extending from her back and swinging her from building to building. A pack of fiery dogs passed through the middle of the street, following their leader, who had a golden crown on his head. They were conversing in quite ordinary human speech about which of them should guard their territory that night. A set of triplets wrapped in identical white ribbons watched the party pass, their eyes in eerie sync.

Words floated in midair, as though the characters had drifted up of their own volition: "Mother Lin's Parlor," "Goldhammer Soulsmiths," "The Restaurant in the Sky." It took Lindon longer than he cared to admit to realize that they were floating business signs, and that realization explained the *other* signs that were etched in physical material above each building's mantle.

"Second-ranked Soulsmith in the city available for commissions."

"Ranked number one of all mixed bowls in the city (vegetable-only category)!"

"Number four purveyor of Thousand-Mile Clouds for civilians, but number one in value!"

The experience of the city reminded him of his first arrival in Serpent's Grave: he'd been overwhelmed by the sights, sounds, and smells of the city then too.

But this time, it didn't take him long to notice a key difference: a level of consistent unease. They were high enough that the red light was beneath them, so there were no bloodspawn here, but they must have picked up on something.

Each salesman who called out to the Skysworn also asked them what was going on. Almost half the shops they passed were in the process of packing up and closing. And most of the looks they encountered were nervous and unsteady rather than hostile or curious.

It remained so until they made it to the center of the city, where the Skysworn's true headquarters were. That overwhelming spire that Lindon had noted earlier towered over the rest of the city, and its entrance was guarded by a quartet of men and women in green armor. Two of them also had emerald wings, and they were spread as though to stretch them.

Orthos snorted smoke at one of the guards, but the young man didn't seem to notice. Instead, he asked Bai Rou if there was any news from outside. He seemed as nervous as any of the civilians outside, but Bai Rou reassured him in a steady voice.

Renfei had been keeping up a steady history of the city as they walked in, but Lindon paid closer attention now that they were within the heart of Skysworn power.

She whispered to one of the guards, who flew off over the wall. Skysworn hurried everywhere, the courtyard bustling like a wasp's nest, but Renfei stood calmly in their center.

"We wait here for the healers to arrive," she said. "Ordinarily we could take them right in, but we're preparing for a new class of Skysworn applicants, and we don't have anyone in urgent danger of death." She glanced at Cassias as she said this.

"In the meantime, let me tell you about the Starsweep Tower. All these facilities are exclusive for Skysworn and trainees." Jerking her thumb over her shoulder, she indicated a door of swirling blue light behind her. Lindon only knew it was a door because of the bronze framework and the goldsteel handle at the center. Otherwise, he would have thought it was a portal or a barrier of madra.

"Soulsmith's foundry," she said. "State-of-the-art. All of our Thousand-Mile Clouds and our weapons are made and maintained in there. We have the most complete dream tablet library of Soulsmith legacies in the entire empire, including one left by an ancient Herald for his descendants."

Fisher Gesha's breath caught. Lindon wasn't sure what half of that meant, but he was still aching to take a look inside.

"Our armory is over there," she said, indicating a door banded in steel. "We offer public tours, because our weapons cannot be stolen. They're keyed to either the individual Skysworn using them, or to the Skysworn armor in general. They can all be located or deactivated remotely. Confiscated weapons and our suits of armor are stored elsewhere."

Lindon wondered how the weapons could be deactivated remotely. He could imagine how you might track a unique weapon down, but how would you deactivate them? Unless they drew from a central power source, instead of being powered by the substance of the weapon itself, and you could simply shut off the power link.

Speculation was useless. There was too much he didn't know. Perhaps there was a Path with a technique that could reach across the city and disable any weapon. But the question intrigued him, and he longed to open the door.

She nodded to a tall set of copper doors. "That's our technique library. It's more extensive than our Soulsmith library, but it's only ranked third, Soulsmith tablets being so rare. There are Paths that exist only here in the city, thanks to original techniques we managed to salvage in our library."

Lindon realized he'd taken a step toward the door. When had that happened?

"We've also assigned as much space to cycling rooms as we have to bedrooms," she continued. "Skysworn can't spend all their time focusing on advancement, like many sacred artists do. They have combat training, study, and assignments. We have to accelerate the advancement process as much as we can, so our cycling regimens are brief but intense."

Lindon wondered if there was a cycling room that would work for the Path of Black Flame. He imagined there would be—it was a Path unique to this empire, after all. But maybe they had gotten rid of it after the Blackflame family fell. Would it be sealed up? He could probably find it...

"It's thanks to these facilities, and the prestige of the Skysworn, that our recruitment has gone so well," Renfei said. She seemed as proud as if she'd built the city herself.

"You're recruiting?" Yerin asked.

"Only a week ago, our dream-readers agreed that we would soon need to add more to our ranks, so we opened ourselves to applications. In that week's time, we have received over six hundred qualified Lowgold and Highgold applicants, both from inside the city and outside."

"What does an applicant need to be qualified?" Lindon asked, eyeing the Soulsmith's door.

"Twenty years of age or younger for Lowgolds, thirty years or younger for Highgolds, and they have to be ranked highly enough. Top one thousand for Highgolds, and top three thousand for Lowgolds. Even so, they have to pass our application process."

"What if they aren't ranked by the Empire?"

She gave him an odd look. "Everyone is ranked."

"I'm not."

Renfei pulled a purple card from a slot over her wrist, touching her fingers to it. Wisps of purple rose from it, and Lindon thought he could see shapes in it. Dream madra.

"After your duel with Jai Long, you are ranked…" She shook her head, sliding the card back in. "Twenty-fourth among Lowgolds. They must value you highly. Though that only takes individual combat power into account, of course. Your skill, aesthetics, and influence are all lower."

"Twenty-fourth," Lindon repeated. He couldn't suppress a little excitement. "I don't mean to overstep myself, but that sounds high."

"Too high," Bai Rou grunted.

"It's high," Renfei confirmed sourly.

"Forgive me if this is a rude question, but what are most Skysworn ranked?" He really wanted to ask them what their ranks had been when they were Lowgolds, and from the look on Renfei's face, she knew it.

"Lower than that," she responded.

He wanted to dig for more details, but his Thousand-Mile Cloud zoomed around, and Yerin's scarred face peeked into their conversation. "While we're all singing and sharing together, why don't you tell us about Redmoon Hall?"

Bai Rou straightened and folded his arms, yellow eyes blazing within the shadow of his hat. Renfei's businesslike mask returned, and she glanced around as though looking for listeners. Within the headquarters of the Skysworn.

"That's for your Underlord to tell you," she said firmly.

Lindon wanted to learn more about his ranking, but he couldn't pass up an opportunity to dig up sensitive information. "Underlord Arelius was the one who shared the information with us. He said it was important for us to know, but unfortunately he was wounded against one of their members before he could give us all the details."

Renfei hesitated, the cloud above her head rolling as she glanced at her partner. Lindon sensed weakness and pushed.

"We only wish to serve. We can't contribute to the Arelius family if we don't understand the situation."

Lindon didn't know much about Renfei, but he assumed that a woman who proudly served as a Skysworn would accept a plea based on duty.

Reluctantly, she leaned in. "It's the cult of a Dreadgod," she said, so softly that he wouldn't have been able to pick up her words without his Iron body. "Usually, they operate beyond the Empire's southeastern border. They are people who sought out a fragment of the Bleeding Phoenix. They call it a Blood Shadow."

She shook her head, in disgust or sympathy. "They're betting they could control it, but nine out of ten can't. Those are just puppets, little better than bloodspawn themselves. The ones who can control it...they're the ones to watch out for. They're still in the thrall of the Phoenix, but they have their own goals as well."

"What is it they want?" Yerin asked, eyes sharp.

"To feed their master," Bai Rou responded, but before he could say more, a third Skysworn reappeared. Renfei spoke to her for a moment, then turned back to them.

"We've cleared out a pair of rooms for your wounded, and

our healers will see them within the hour. The rest of you can follow me."

A new Skysworn walked in front of Cassias and Yerin, controlling Cassias' cloud directly and leading them through a plain-looking door that Lindon had overlooked before.

Fisher Gesha followed Renfei, as did Orthos, though he took a bite from the frayed end of a nearby tapestry as he did so. Lindon hitched up his pack and prepared to join them...

Then he thought once more about Yerin's reaction to seeing the bloodspawn.

"I'm going to join the wounded for a while, if that's permitted," Lindon said, following Yerin's cloud. "I'll find my room later."

Renfei looked as though she would object, but Bai Rou just waved his hand and kept walking. Eventually, she said, "Settle in before sunset," and followed her partner.

"They can't all be Underlords," Yerin muttered from her cloud. "You don't find an Underlord under every rock and tree stump." The Skysworn in the lead was probably close enough that he could hear them over the clanking of his armor, but he was polite enough not to say anything.

"They're from outside the Empire. Maybe where they come from, everyone's an Underlord."

She tried to sit up, winced, and ended up rolling onto her side and propping her head up on one arm. "My master's feet started to itch after two nights in the same place, so I've spent more time outside this empire than in it. I've never seen a place where Underlords are common as Lowgolds. Besides…" One hand drifted down to her stomach before she stopped it.

"I wouldn't call us strangers," she said at last. "They wore a different name, but they still had—" She glanced up at the Skysworn. "Some things in common. My master used to fight against these people. It was how he found me."

Lindon looked from their Skysworn to Yerin. "Is this a conversation we should have in your room?"

"Won't be easy, no matter where we have it," she muttered, but she didn't object. Cassias was taken to his own room, where a healer was already waiting. Apparently Renfei had communicated that he was the more urgently injured.

Yerin's room was more like a closet, or a prison. It had a single red-painted mat against the wall, blankets folded on the surface. A lidded chamber pot sat nearby, and that was all.

When Yerin drifted inside and the Skysworn guide left, it was actually difficult for Lindon to step inside for a moment. He had spent too much of the last year and a half locked inside small spaces. He was irrationally afraid that he would walk inside and be sealed within, though the only entrance was a sliding door of flimsy wood. He could break through it without an Enforcer technique.

Yerin eyed him, then the door. "You want me to send you a formal invitation, you'll have to write it yourself." Ever since revealing that she couldn't read, she had made several jokes about it. The subject was starting to make him uncomfortable.

Finally, he took a deep breath and stepped inside, sliding the door into place behind him. He fixed his gaze on the small window high up in the wall, though it just revealed another nook of the complex. Focusing on the outside let him forget how small the room was.

Yerin clambered from her cloud to her bedding, wincing and hissing at every movement. He would have helped, but he was still trying to keep the queasy sensation in his stomach under control.

When she had finally settled herself, she looked up and began again. "You remember my...uninvited guest, true?"

"It was your belt, wasn't it?" Lindon asked. He had come to that conclusion through implication and inference, but she'd never told him.

She grunted, and he took that as affirmation. "Some people call it a Blood Shadow."

A few things slid into place for Lindon at that moment: her reaction to the bloodspawn, the Redmoon Hall emissary looking straight at her, Eithan sealing her belt.

One of the silver blades sprouting from her back began tapping lightly on the wall, and Lindon wondered if that was a nervous gesture while she waited for him to finish thinking, or if the Goldsign was out of her control.

"But you'd never heard of Redmoon Hall," he said.

"Not by that name. Sacred artists would sometimes hunt down these parasites and take them like pills. Hoped they would get stronger." She sneered as though she were looking down on those sacred artists right then. "Only one in every ten made it, but every sacred artist thinks they're the special exception. For them, it'll work. Problem is, it doesn't just put *you* in danger."

"You didn't do that," Lindon said confidently. That seemed more like something *he* would do than something Yerin would. In fact, he'd already started wondering what specific benefits a Blood Shadow offered. Longhook had been strong, certainly, but he was an Underlord. Or did the Shadow perhaps allow you to create bloodspawn? No, that seemed to be an effect of the red light. Could they generate that red light?

A flicker of a smile crossed her face. "You're starting to learn. A little. No, I didn't look for it. It looked for me." The smile faded as quickly as it came. "The Dreadgod gives birth to...a litter, I guess you'd say...of Blood Shadows at one time. They run around like Remnants, looking to find a host before they starve. When they find somebody, they usually drain them dry and take their power back to the Bleeding Phoenix. Every once in a rare moon, you run into somebody who takes them over instead."

"When did it get to you?" Lindon asked, kneeling to face her.

"Can't be sure how old I was. Seven, maybe? Eight? They called me a genius." She smiled bitterly. "Everybody in town said how shiny my future was going to be. The star of my town. Made me stick out, as it ends up. Even to a Dreadgod."

She was silent for so long that he wanted to prompt her with a question, but he curbed his curiosity and sat quietly, waiting.

"Didn't know what it was, but I fought it," she said at last. "It was trying to...burrow into me. To my spirit, more than my body. My dad tried to pull it out, and it cut him. His blood fell on the ground."

Lindon had fought the bloodspawn only a few hours earlier. He could picture what happened next, and the bottom fell out of his stomach.

"Spawned those...things," she said, though he'd guessed it already. "Cut through town like fire through a dry wood. I'm just standing there, holding on while everybody died. If I let it get inside of me, I figured something worse would happen, so I just held it off. Don't know how long I sat there, holding it, before Master found me."

She had started to shake.

Her wounds had been wrapped, but not thoroughly bandaged, and some of them had begun to bleed again, but she didn't notice, staring into the distance.

There was nothing Lindon could say to help her. The past had already left its wounds.

But he could do something she'd done for him once before.

Without a word, he squeezed in next to her, sitting side-by-side though her Goldsign jabbed him in the side of the head. Sweat covered his palm, and he eyed her for any sign that she was uncomfortable or in pain. She didn't even seem to notice him, staring ahead with a blank gaze.

He reached across her shoulders and gave her a light squeeze. When she didn't object, he just sat there, holding her with his one arm. Reminding her that someone was there.

Back in Sacred Valley, when things had been at their worst, this was all he had wanted. Someone to sit with him and remind him that they were with him, that everything would be okay. Sometimes his sister or his parents filled that role. Sometimes they didn't. Sometimes, they were the problem.

But today, Lindon could give that to Yerin.

After a minute or two, she leaned into him. "We're going after them," she said at last, her voice confident. "They can't all be Underlords. I'd say we could stop any of them under Truegold, or we could find a way to deal with them. Together. We have to stop them."

Lindon leaned away, turning to see her expression. "Yes, we should do whatever we can. We just need to be...careful."

She turned to him and the blades on her shoulders shifted. He had to withdraw his arm or risk getting cut.

"You're in this with me, true?"

"Of course," he said without hesitation. "But we should have a plan."

She nodded, her eyes focused intensely on some point beyond him. "Yeah...we have to track down a Truegold, don't we? Cassias could tell us where it is. He points it out on the map, and we slip in like a shadow's whisper. Maybe we could get Orthos in, too, that would ease the fight somewhat."

Lindon cleared his throat. "That could certainly work, *but* I'd like to propose an alternative. We could push Eithan to make us Truegolds. He must know a way to do it, don't you think? If the Ancestor's Spear could take Jai Long from Highgold to Truegold so quickly, there has to be some solution for us."

His new arm might be exactly that solution, but there was no telling until the construct was completed.

She backed away, turning to face him head-on. "You want me to sit around on my hands until I advance again? If Eithan can make me a Truegold tomorrow, sure, I'm not going to spit on that. Short of that, I'm not waiting. I'm going with whoever's raising their swords against Redmoon Hall."

"But who *is* that?" he countered. "Who's going to take us? Who can use us? What can we even *do?* We have to know what we can do before we—"

"The Skysworn," she interrupted, folding her arms. "They'll jump to take us."

Lindon wasn't sure they would jump to take *him*, but he had to admit he was tempted by the facilities he'd seen in Starsweep Tower.

Then again...what did the Skysworn have that Eithan wasn't already giving him for free?

"Let's not rush into anything," he said in a reasonable tone. "We can wait until Eithan gets back, at least."

"Eithan's out there fighting Underlords and emissaries and heavens-know-what right *now*," she said fiercely. "When he gets back, we're out of time."

A bearded man in hooded green robes slid open the door, peeking his head inside. "Excuse me, I'm here to see the patient?"

Yerin gave Lindon a razor-sharp stare, but she took a breath. "Turn over what I said, see if it looks any better to you. I'm going to see Cassias tonight. If I don't hear what I like, I'm gone. The door's open for you to join me."

After Lindon left, he continued turning her words over in his mind. She was rushing to a decision too quickly. There was no reason to take this fight personally; Redmoon Hall wasn't after *them*. At least they could weigh out their options, they didn't have to dive straight in.

No matter how he thought of it, there was nothing to gain from going after Redmoon Hall. It would be a foolish move.

Maybe Cassias could talk Yerin around.

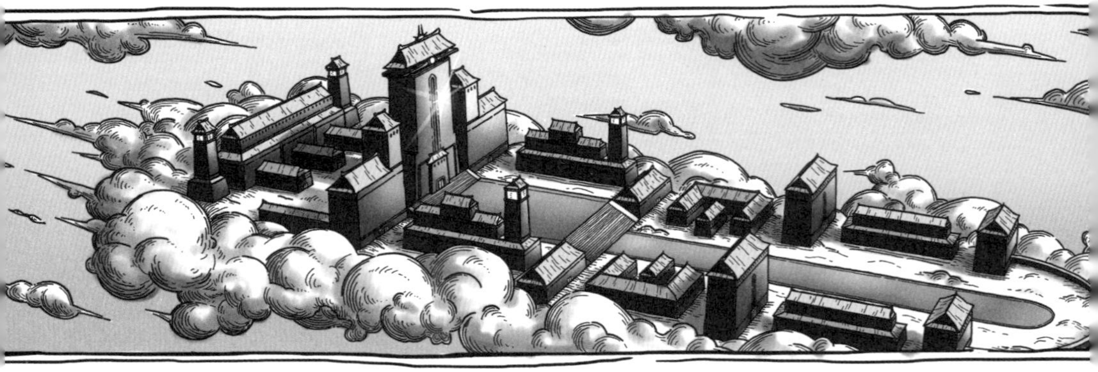

XI

Cassias sat on his mat, covered in bandages, with a frog's tongue stuck onto his wrist. The fat, blood-red bullfrog sat on a little dais, an ornately carved platform the size of Lindon's hand, and pumped blood through its tongue with every exhale.

It was one of the most fascinating sacred beasts Lindon had ever seen, and he couldn't help wondering what sort of blood Path had produced it. The healer had said that it would slowly replace the blood Cassias had lost, as well as purging any remaining influence from the bloodspawn, but that he had to rest. And, if possible, he should avoid strenuous activity or stressful conversation.

They were putting that last advice to the test.

"I'll be fighting Redmoon Hall if it's just me and my sword," Yerin said, arms crossed. To Lindon's eye, she still looked odd without the red belt, as that had been the brightest splash of color about her. "Don't have the legs to go very far if I'm not Truegold, but I'd go if I were Copper. You get me to Truegold, you'd be lending me a hand up."

Lindon recognized his opportunity. "The sooner we reach Truegold, the sooner we'll be ready to contribute to the Empire. And the more useful we would be to you."

Cassias glanced at the frog and took a deep breath. "I don't have the full list of training materials you've used in the time since you've been with us, but it's extensive. Running the Blackflame Trials alone cost the equivalent of two top-grade scales a day, not to mention my own time. That's more than the training budget for all our other students combined. And then there are those Four Corners Rotation Pills we provided. We could have hired five new workers for the same price. Yerin, you've been using our sword aura cycling room so extensively that we had to replace some of the aura sources and upgrade the scripts."

"That's a fair point, but most of those decisions were made by Eithan," Lindon pointed out. "He obviously thought we were worth the expense."

"He did, which is why Eithan paid for most of that personally," Cassias responded. "If he spent his time doing nothing else, he could generate three or four top-grade scales a day, which is absolutely stunning. Most Underlords could not do the same. So additionally, we have the cost of his time when he went to the Desolate Wilds to retrieve you. Every day he spent on you has cost this family a sizeable amount of income."

Yerin turned as though to leave. "I've heard my fill. I need to track down Eithan, not you. Is he on the battlefield yet?"

"Eithan has been recalled to a secret location by order of the Emperor," Cassias said, carefully watching the frog. The frog croaked and gave him a stern look, so Cassias settled back against the wall. "If you want help before he returns, you'll have to go through the family system."

"System?" Lindon asked, intrigued.

"Workers are paid for their living expenses, of course, but anyone who contributes to the family beyond the scope of their job receives additional resources. We invest in those who provide a benefit to us."

"And how are those benefits measured?"

"There's an extensive chart in any of our facilities," Cassias said, and Lindon perked up. A clear-cut list of tasks and rewards sounded perfect. "Essentially, we want you to advance as quickly as possible if you're serving the family."

"Sounds like a load of fetching and carrying for nothing, if we're already getting the same from Eithan for free," Yerin said.

Cassias looked to Lindon. "Yerin has already earned several rewards from the Arelius family, for tasks she performed while you were…isolated. She earned a set of pills that condensed several months' worth of sword aura, five thousand sword scales, quite a bit of time in our highest-level sword cycling room, and time with our most experienced sword Path instructor. Which so happens to be me."

Lindon looked to Yerin, astonished. He imagined that she spent all her time cycling and training alone. That was most of what he'd seen her do, when she had the choice. "What did she do for the family?"

Yerin gave an impatient sigh. "Killed a Remnant, killed another

Remnant, pushed away some guy who was needling the cleaning crews a little, stopped a big lizard from running through the sewers...Probably more, I don't know, it slips through my mind."

"Those sound like things I could do," Lindon said eagerly.

"That's the point," Cassias said. He sounded exasperated. "Most employees of the Arelius family join us because they are not suited for combat. If you can protect them from rivals or remove obstacles—such as Remnants—that pop up in the course of their ordinary duties, you are rewarded. There are other ways to demonstrate excellence than fighting, but I imagine this is the area in which you will excel."

"I don't have time for more of the same," Yerin said. "I know what bloodspawn can do to a town. Someone's getting run over while we're locked in here chatting."

The red frog croaked at Cassias, who took another deep breath. "This is the problem with how Eithan treats you. Neither of you have an appreciation for the expense that has gone into your training."

"You think so? I grew up paying for it all myself," Yerin said proudly. "My master made sure I know what sacred arts cost."

"And yet a minute of your master's time was worth more than a day of Eithan's."

She scowled at him.

Cassias closed his eyes, clearly waiting for them to leave. "I'm happy to provide you with the same support we would to any of our disciples. As long as you earn it."

"This is it," Lindon said in the hallway outside Cassias' room. "He has everything we need. If we see the family rules, I'm sure we can find a way to make them work for us."

"The family rules can go rot," Yerin said, gripping her sword and marching down the hall. "The Skysworn will let me fight."

Lindon stopped in place, forcing her to spin and eye him. "...that's it?" he asked. "We're leaving the Arelius family? After all this?"

Yerin's scars stood out in the pale white rune-lights of the hall. "Not joining another family, are we? The Skysworn don't ask you to throw your family away. We're just serving the Empire, like good and proper boys and girls. Now let's go."

Lindon didn't move. "I...really don't think we should."

Color rose into her cheeks. "I'm not just *thinking* about it. I'm doing it. Thought you were with me."

Lindon felt like a Remnant had reached into his chest and made a fist, but he swallowed. "I am," he said, "of course I am. But I don't understand why we're rushing into this. If you'll just give me a few more days..."

"Don't have 'em to give," Yerin said, and she kept walking.

Lindon stayed where he was.

Yerin found Renfei and Bai Rou talking intently over a low table, which was heavy with food. Empty plates were piled around Bai Rou, and he was sucking the meat from a chicken bone as she approached.

Both of them were in full armor, though they had stayed close to the Arelius family guests. No one had taken them off babysitting duty yet, and as the days passed, they were starting to get restless.

Yerin had no news of the outside world. That was part of the weight she felt pushing down on her—what was Redmoon Hall doing now? How many towns had the bloodspawn ruined?

Grabbing a chair from a nearby table, Yerin spun it around and sat down, joining them. Renfei eyed her as though trying to figure out whether to be amused or irritated, but Bai Rou just kept eating.

"You mentioned you're recruiting. What do you need the recruits for?"

Renfei frowned. "You've seen them. Redmoon Hall is washing over the southern Empire like a tide. We've lost contact with three cities on the southern border, and have confirmed bloodspawn sightings a hundred miles north. People all over are beginning to panic, and that's when you need order. If we had five times as many Skysworn as we do, it wouldn't be enough."

"And here we are," Bai Rou said between bites, "waiting."

"You're fighting the bloodspawn? And Redmoon Hall?"

"Of course we are. What do you think we do with our time?"

Bai Rou swallowed. "When we're not trapped here."

Yerin nodded sharply. "All right. I'm in."

Renfei and Bai Rou exchanged glances, then Yerin felt a whisper of power tickle her soul. She was being scanned.

"We don't usually take people on slaughter Paths," Renfei said, and Yerin gave an inward sigh of relief. The Skysworn had sensed the presence of the Blood Shadow inside, but had assumed it was just a part of Yerin's power.

Sacred artists on Paths of blood and the sword weren't the most popular people around. They were known for murdering anybody they came across just to cycle. It had earned them the nickname "slaughter Paths," though Yerin had heard others.

"...but you're a Highgold," Renfei continued. "We're not in the business of turning down eager Highgolds while we're in a state of emergency. But we'll be checking your rank, and you still have to go through the same qualification process everyone does."

Yerin had no problem with that. She'd never been afraid of trials.

Officially, Eithan was on a private cloudship on his way to the capital.

The cloudship had actually departed from Stormrock that morning, and the city's records showed him aboard. From beneath a hood, and with a veil over his core to make him seem like an ordinary Gold, he had waved good-bye to the ship himself.

The Emperor had commanded his presence.

Naru Huan, Patriarch of the Naru clan and sole leader of the Blackflame Empire, was officially on a tour of their southern defenses. He was addressing this crisis personally.

In reality, that was almost correct. He was just doing it a bit more...directly than the public believed.

He waited at the top of the Starsweep Tower at the center of Stormrock. When Eithan entered, the Emperor had his back turned and wings spread, looking out vast windows over the city. From here, they could see the edge of the green cloud that supported all of Stormrock. And below them, a dome of hazy red light.

Eithan was the last to arrive.

The other Underlords were already there.

There was a table in the center of the room, laden with fruits and drinks, but no one sat. They all stood separately, each man and woman an island, though many in the room were related. A control console of ornate gold stood a few feet from the Emperor, though no one was manning it. Its script-circles were dark, and the city was still.

Eithan made his way to the food as the Emperor spoke. "We have chosen you to serve us in the most important tasks. We will address the others later, but you are the ones who will truly defend the Empire."

Naru Huan turned, spreading his vast, shimmering emerald wings for effect. He cut a heroic figure, with a jaw like a brick and eyes like knives. His royal robes didn't hide his muscular figure, and the outfit was impressive in its own right. His robes had a green dragon and a blue one twining around each other, the cool colors complementing his wings, and his hair was pinned up with a jade pin.

Eithan nodded at the presentation even as he took a bite of a steamed bun. Naru Huan wasn't a *master* of capturing an audience, but he had presence, personality, and a flair for style. He'd learn.

There were seven others around the table, including Eithan: the top seven Underlords in the Blackflame Empire. Only a few months ago, Eithan had been rated merely eleventh, but his confrontations with Jai Daishou had raised him a few spots up the ladder.

Had he not been invited, he would have been forced to eavesdrop on this meeting. And that would have been rude. Besides, it was much harder to advance his own plans if he wasn't in the room.

"This has been nothing less than a betrayal by one of our number," the Emperor said, spearing each of them with his gaze. "He has risked the very existence of our nation for selfish greed." When it was Eithan's turn, he raised his half-eaten bun in salute, and he caught a brief twitch of Naru Huan's eyelid.

When he had let the moment sink in with appropriate gravity, the Emperor made a sharp gesture with his right hand. Wind aura surged, and a box drifted up on a cushion of air. It was sealed with layers of script-circles, and even the Emperor had to use three different keys to open it.

With great ceremony, he turned the box toward them and lifted the lid.

Several of the others gasped or muttered at the sight of the Archstone, sitting on a cushion. The dull light within swirled as though with motion, and Eithan could sense its hunger tugging at their spirits even from so far away.

After only a second or two, the Emperor shut the lid. Its scripts shone, sealing away its power once more. "The Archstone, as described in the Draconic Records. It was sealed deep in the western labyrinth, where Jai Daishou retrieved it."

The Emperor inclined his head toward his uncle, and Naru Gwei stepped forward. The second-ranked Underlord in the Empire had positioned himself near the door, as though hoping he could leave as soon as possible. His hair was even more matted and dirty, if possible, and it seemed to be wet this time. He still wore his battered Skysworn armor, though he hadn't brought his sword along this time. Perhaps he felt safe in the heart of his headquarters. He had withdrawn his wings as well, so there was nothing to mark him as one of the elders of the Naru clan.

"We believe the Underlord of the Jai clan entered the western labyrinth to retrieve a weapon that would allow him to settle a personal grudge," Naru Gwei recited, as though reading from a dull schoolbook. "We cannot confirm how long the seal was breached, but it was long enough to alert the Bleeding Phoenix."

Another general murmur swept through the room, though they all must have known as much already. A crack came from the edge of the table as the Emperor's sister lost control of her strength.

"Based on the movements of Redmoon Hall and the influence of the Phoenix, we believe that it has nested only a few miles south of our border this time. Our dream-readers suggest we have weeks, perhaps months, before it is fully conscious and able to move."

"Will the Skysworn be enough to stop Redmoon Hall?" Eithan asked through a mouthful of food. He didn't have to be subtle here. Very few of the others considered him important enough to care what he was doing, and the ones who did wouldn't stop him.

Naru Gwei gave him a look, though it lacked impact coming from his dead face. Eithan wasn't exactly sure what that expression was supposed to be.

"We will serve the Empire with honor," Naru Gwei said, raising his fingers to touch the burn scars on his left cheek. "And we are recruiting as we speak. But we could use as many applicants as we can, if only to keep the peace while we focus on the real battle."

Eithan nodded thoughtfully, sipping a crystal goblet of blazewater. It was a popular drink in the East, and he enjoyed the novelty. Every sip made him feel like his mouth was on fire, but with no actual pain. It was infused with spirit-fruits and dream aura, he heard. Some Paths considered it invaluable for cycling.

Naru Huan fixed his imperial gaze on the third-ranked Underlord. "Underlord Kotai, what is your assessment of our situation?"

Kotai Shou walked up to the table, pressing his fists together in a salute—one of his fists was five times bigger than the other—and then standing straight with hands at his side to report. Shou was a grizzled old sea captain with his head shaved except for a dangling gray braid in front of each ear. He had storm-gray skin, and he had lost his left arm in battle as a child, replacing it with the limb of a massive stone-madra Remnant.

"We've got three problems," he barked. "The bloodspawn are the first. They're part of the Phoenix's power, so they will only show up in the red zone around the nest. But they will spread further as the Dreadgod wakes, until every drop of blood inside a hundred miles will hatch into a monster. I'd call that a regional emergency on its own.

"Second, Redmoon Hall. They've got two levels. The *vassals* are the ones who let their Blood Shadows take control. They can be managed. They can raise bloodspawn if they want, but they're mindless and weak enough to be taken over in the first place. We can handle them. And they'll stay close to either the Phoenix itself or the emissaries."

His gray-skinned face remained calm, but his prosthetic arm gripped so tightly that the madra creaked. "That's the real threat of Redmoon Hall: the emissaries. They were powerful sacred artists even before they controlled their parasites. With a Blood Shadow, they can each fight beyond their stage. Battle reports we've received from the Akura clan, based on their encounters with Redmoon Hall outside of the Empire, confirm multiple emissaries at the Underlord level."

A few of the others had already started muttering again, but Eithan knew he hadn't finished.

"...as well as at least one Overlord." The muttering intensified. "And, supposedly, the Sage of Red Faith."

This time, the room was quiet for a long moment.

"Then we have the third and final problem," Underlord Kotai continued. "The Dreadgod itself."

In the ensuing silence, Kotai Shou bowed to the Emperor once more and backed up.

"We have plans to handle each of those issues," Naru Huan assured everyone. "First, let us hear from the only one to have fought a Redmoon Hall emissary. Underlord Arelius, if you would?"

Eithan walked forward, giving an exaggerated wince and touching his shoulder as though it pained him. In truth, it was just a little sore. The Underlady of the Jade Eye School had treated him herself, so he was healthier than before his battle. In fact, she was in the room, and he was sure she was rolling her eyes at him. Unfortunately, it was hard to make out anything of the old woman's expression under her thick black veil.

"I crossed swords, so to speak, with an emissary of Redmoon Hall only yesterday," Eithan confirmed. "I can confirm that he was indeed an Underlord. A skilled and powerful one, at that." He hadn't even relied on the power of his Blood Shadow, and he had still knocked Eithan around the mountain.

It had been embarrassing, not to mention painful. He had almost forced Eithan to resort to a contingency plan.

"If he was the only one of his kind, we could manage. Honored

Chon Ma could surely have destroyed him," Eithan said, dipping his head to the number-one Underlord in the Blackflame Empire.

He was the head of the Cloud Hammer School, and the dark cloud hanging over his head seemed to indicate the Underlord's perpetual mood. The bearded man scowled, folding his arms and revealing the hammers he wore at each hip.

Supposedly, he doted on his only daughter, who had the potential to become an Underlady herself one day. Eithan had trouble imagining him softening enough to dote on anyone.

"...but he was not alone," Eithan continued. "He had allies in the mountains, and though I could not measure their strength accurately, the fact that I could sense them at all from so far away suggested that they had at least as much raw power as I."

That wasn't necessarily true, but it could be, and it suited Eithan's purposes.

"With so many Underlords in the enemy's forces, it seems right to me that we should count ourselves as the front line of defense for the Empire. I know it will be difficult to set aside our own agendas for the duration of this crisis, so in the interests of unity, I propose that we should assist the Skysworn directly."

Eithan projected absolute sincerity, but he hadn't pierced the cynical looks on most of the others. It was just as well; someone would have proposed it anyway, but by being the one to bring it up, they would make sure he was forced into participating. So he could nobly accept the role of a temporary Skysworn officer.

Where, he gathered, at least one of his beloved disciples was about to enroll.

Naru Saeya pounded the table with her fist, sending a crack

through the polished wood. The Emperor's little sister was tall and strikingly beautiful, with smooth skin and a delicate face that had "inspired" any number of ambitious painters in the Empire. She, the Emperor, and Eithan were the only ones in the room who appeared younger than fifty.

She wore a fan of peacock feathers over one ear—they were either powerful constructs or nothing more than decorations, because Eithan had never sensed any power from them. Her wings, spread in agitation, were much smaller and thinner than her brother's or uncle's, and her agility in the air was almost unsurpassed. She had been the youngest Underlord in the Empire before Eithan, and her senses rivaled those of the Arelius family.

Which was almost a shame, because her *sensitivity* was comparably lacking. She had a reputation of bulling her way through problems headfirst.

Now, she was rolling her sleeves up as though getting ready to punch through a wall, pacing in agitation. She looked restless for a fight. "We know what to do. We have the Underlords and the Overlord, we just need to find a Sage. Then we can take the fight to *them*. We might be able to destroy Redmoon Hall in one stroke!"

"Then we only have to deal with the Dreadgod," Chon Ma said, still scowling beneath his cloud.

"We'll evacuate! People do it all over the world, all the time. Without its servants, it has nothing to weaken us before it wakes up."

Mentally, Eithan had to applaud her plan. It was vague on the critical details, but the general outline was good. If they simply weathered this storm without destroying Redmoon Hall, they would be inviting another apocalyptic crisis in the future. It was never good to leave enemies behind you.

Of course, they didn't know the enemy's full strength. And they didn't have the power to deal with the forces they knew about.

"Finding a Sage might be tricky," Eithan said. "I have it on good authority that the Sage of the Endless Sword was killed not so long ago, which leaves..."

"Frozen Blade and Silver Heart," Underlady Li Min Redflower put in, her voice creaking behind her dark veil. She was the one who had healed his shoulder, and from his understanding, she rarely spoke in these meetings. She was the only one with a chair.

Kotai Shou turned his gray face to Eithan, flexing his stone fingers as he spoke. "What about the Arelius homeland? The Sage of a Thousand Eyes has an honorable reputation. She would come to our aid."

Eithan winced. He hadn't been to the homeland for seven years, but memory of his last failure was still harsh. "I'm afraid the doorway doesn't open for another three years. Besides...last I saw them, they didn't have any help to spare for anyone else."

If the Sage of a Thousand Eyes was still alive after all this time, then she was much wiser than he had given her credit for. Or she'd found a powerful ally. Somewhere.

The Emperor reached out a hand to the golden console beside him, and one of the circles shone. Starsweep Tower hummed to life around him, but the enormous cloudship went nowhere.

Eithan extended his senses, confirming that they were indeed hovering over Lastleaf Fortress. This must be their target.

Once the meeting was over, the battery of launcher constructs on the bottom of the floating city would fire at once, in a barrage that would reduce anything beneath them to dust. The Underlords would be expected to contribute their power to that effort.

"We have all the facts we need," Naru Huan said, staring out the window. "At the least, we must beg the help of a Sage...and a Monarch."

Good luck to you, Eithan thought. Monarchs were practically myths. It would be hard enough to find a Herald, and very few Monarchs could be reached at all. By mortals, anyway.

Those few that stayed in one place and ruled steady kingdoms all had something...wrong with them. Not that Eithan would ever say so aloud; some of them could hear their names spoken from all the way across the world. Still, supplicants had an equal chance of being ignored for centuries, granted an audience, or unmade. It was like begging the help of a volcano.

No one else could drive off a Dreadgod, it was true, but the Blackflame Empire could employ the strategy that had served humanity for millennia in front of overwhelming natural disasters: fleeing like mice.

"Underlord Arelius," the Emperor said, spearing him with that sword-sharp gaze. "You will be our representative to the Akura family. Using our name, you will beg an audience with their Monarch, as one of her loyal servants. They have shielded us from the dragons for generations, and they might grant us grace this time as well."

Eithan's mind froze. The room came into focus as it did when he was in battle, his emotions chilling. The smile slipped from his face.

"You're sending me to die," he said. His voice had an edge.

As befit the sole Overlord in the country, the Emperor did not back down an inch. "We do not waste resources in times of war.

But if your death will grant us the chance at an audience with a Monarch, yes, then your blood is cheap to us."

Eithan stared down Naru Huan for a long moment as he considered.

The logic was sound. It took a moment for his feelings to catch up, but he accepted the decision. It was the right move.

Eithan's smile came back as though it had never left, and he bowed before his ruler. "Your command is my heart's desire. However, you have never sought the Akura family's support before. Why now?"

"In our reign, the Empire has never faced such a crisis." The rampage of the Blackflame family had occurred during his mother's rule, so technically Naru Huan had never faced a true crisis. Well, this could be considered a test for him.

The Emperor paused a moment, then added, "We may also reveal that the Akura family has recently asked a service of us. As we have agreed to their terms, currently we are on better footing with their clan than we ever have been before."

Fascinating. Eithan had been unaware that there was any more than incidental contact between the great Akura clan and the relatively unimportant Blackflame Empire. The Akura protected the Empire from dragons simply because they were both humans, but otherwise they were utterly apathetic. Only their lack of motivation kept them from enslaving the entire populace or razing them for cultivation resources.

What favor could the Emperor possibly do for a Monarch's family? Eithan was dying to find out.

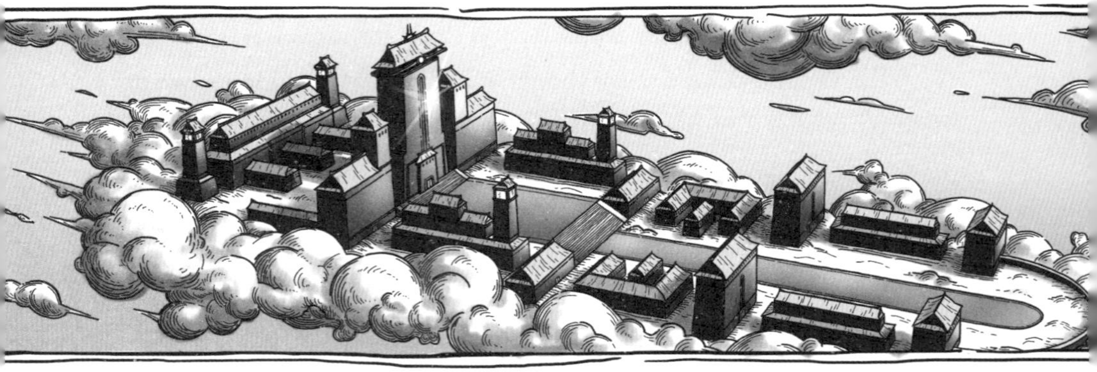

XII

The Soulsmith foundry in the Skysworn's tower was advanced enough to support the creation of Truegold and Underlord constructs. Lindon had picked up a rumor in the city that suggested the Emperor's Overlord-stage weaponry had been created here.

He wasn't allowed to use those facilities. Instead, he and Fisher Gesha had been pushed to one of the apprentice rooms.

It was barely big enough for the two of them and their tools. Fisher Gesha stood next to her drudge—the huge purple spider—rather than riding it around, as she was used to. Little Blue clutched Lindon's hair, piping up every once in a while in a high-pitched burble.

The foundry had a basic set of tools on the wall, though they were goldsteel-plated instead of made from pure goldsteel, and they were chained to their rack to prevent theft. In the center of the room was a boundary formation in the shape of a large bubble. It would keep the project suspended so that Lindon and Fisher Gesha could work on it together without letting their construct rest on a table.

Lindon wondered what a higher-level foundry would have allowed him. Could he have made his new arm stronger? Fisher Gesha had assured him that he would have to replace this one when he became an Underlord (though she found that possibility unlikely). It was made of Gold-stage components, so it wouldn't handle the stress of a transition to Underlord.

Then again, when he was an Underlord, maybe he would find the materials for an even *better* arm.

Fisher Gesha floated the Shifting Skies arm into the center of the boundary field. It floated there peacefully, gleaming like glass in the light, its spiked fingertips drumming against the air.

Then she sat cross-legged on the ground. "Cycle," she commanded. "It calms the mind and the soul, hm? You should be at your sharpest when you Forge a new weapon."

Lindon followed her lead and began cycling his pure madra, but he couldn't contain his excitement. His imagination kept providing all the things he would be able to do with his new arm.

And the alternative was to focus on the fact that he was missing a limb. He preferred daydreaming.

Their preparation seemed to stretch on and on, but finally Fisher Gesha levered herself out of her cycling position—moving stiffly—and started to limber up her shoulders. "Well, it's not naptime. Let's get moving."

She sounded nervous, eyeing her chest which sat in the corner. Lindon knew why: even through the restrictive scripts on the box, he could sense the power of the white binding. It felt like intense hunger.

The more they prepared it for use, strengthening it with pure madra as though watering a flower while attuning it to Lindon's soul, the stronger it felt. Now it shone with power, which even the chest couldn't contain.

Using a set of halfsilver tongs, which would disperse any stray madra, she withdrew the small book-sized box that contained the binding itself. Then she shut the large chest, placing the small box on top. Reaching into her robes, she pulled out the notes that they had taken from the Transcendent Ruins along with the binding.

She and Lindon had both practically memorized those notes in preparation for today. They tended to be very technical, though they referred back to a "Subject One" as the source of the hunger madra. Lindon very much wanted to know about Subject One, as it seemed the entire purpose of their research in the labyrinth was to duplicate Subject One's unique madra.

"Soulsmithing is blending three elements," she said. She had given him this lecture before, but he still focused on every word. A mistake here might mean weeks of going without an arm. "You have the binding, the material of the construct itself, and the Soulsmith's madra, hm? But unlike blending physical materials, you are working with the stuff of souls. Madra lives. It changes. Even the same Path, taken from two different people, can have subtly different properties."

She traded her halfsilver tongs out for her goldsteel set. These could seize immaterial madra without damaging the subject. She opened the small box, which let a feeling of ravenous hunger wash over the both of them.

Then she withdrew a finger-sized shard from within. It was one of the pieces left over from the Ancestor's Spear.

"A Soulsmith must learn to predict those changes, hm? It's no good making a weapon that will turn on its owner. But even with the best drudge in the world and years of experience, we are working with living components. No two constructs are exactly the same."

Gingerly, she placed the shard of white within the bubble at the center of the room. The transparent arm and the shard of bright white orbited one another, though the smaller piece seemed to be squirming through the air toward the larger.

Gesha crossed her arms. "Now," she commanded.

Lindon reached out with his perception, sensing both the arm and the piece of hunger madra. They gave him very different impressions, but he didn't focus on that, instead pouring pure madra into combining them.

They drifted together faster than he'd expected, and he focused on Forging them like he would a scale. He held the shape in his mind, pushing it together with his will.

The shard entered the clear-as-glass surface of the arm, staining six inches of the forearm white. Pale strands ran through the limb like veins, and the sharp fingers shuddered.

Fisher Gesha gestured, and her spider scurried up beneath the floating boundary field. It lifted two legs, poking at the substance of the construct, spinning it around as though spinning a web.

After a moment, it hissed in three sharp patterns and withdrew its legs.

"Unstable," Gesha reported. "Keep holding it." She produced another shard of the Ancestor's Spear, and Lindon repeated the process.

The stress of holding onto the construct felt like cycling the Heaven and Earth Purification Wheel for too long: his soul was under pressure, every breath was heavy, and he was having trouble holding onto the appropriate breathing pattern. Sweat had begun to bead on his face.

But there was a distinct difference. The *presence* of the arm had begun to change, as the Shifting Skies madra in the original limb was suffused with the power of the hungry white madra. Instead of tapping, the fingers now flexed, grasping, and he sensed...

Well, he wasn't sure what he was picking up on. Maybe Fisher Gesha could tell him, if he could spare the attention to ask. It felt as though the arm *wanted* something, and it twisted in the floating bubble like a hunting snake.

It must have been an effect of the hunger madra, as she added more samples inside and Lindon used his pure madra to Forge them together into one. With every piece, it seemed to become more aware, like they were building a Remnant instead of a Remnant arm.

This time, when Fisher Gesha's drudge tested the limb, it gave a high whistle. Immediately, she withdrew a shiny, twisted form of pure white light with a corkscrew pattern. The binding.

A crystallized technique, the binding was the heart of any construct. Without it, a construct would only have the properties of its material and whatever scripts they added on top. That would make it no better than any scripted object.

Ideally, this binding would allow him to feed on someone else's madra, though Fisher Gesha insisted that it would only allow him to pull another's power into his arm and then vent it elsewhere.

Either way. Both ideas intrigued him.

As the binding approached, the arm squirmed toward it, fighting against the hold of his spirit. He tried to ask her to wait, but the word came out as a croak.

Then the binding slid into the arm, and he had to absorb it.

The actual process of completing the arm was simple. He worked it into the Forging, and the arm flared with a brilliant white. Now it was all spotless and pale, and the claws had smoothed out into fingertips—Lindon didn't want to use an arm with needle-sharp fingers. It looked almost skeletal in shape, though it was thick enough to fit on his arm.

Fisher Gesha let out a breath. "Good. Now, normally we would add scripts at this point, but it will be attached to your body. Your own spirit will do the maintenance, protecting it from decay. It seems stable, but for a while you'll have to…prepare for…"

Her words drifted off as she watched the arm.

Lindon was staring at it too.

It had gone wild, twisting and writhing as it pushed its hand at the edge of the boundary field. He could almost hear a snarling in his head, as it sought to devour…something.

An instant later, the boundary field vanished.

The hand lunged for Lindon's head. No…not for his head. The link he shared with the arm gave him an instinctive understanding, and rather than ducking, he threw himself to the side.

It wasn't after him. It was after the Sylvan Riverseed.

Little Blue scurried down the side of his head, hiding in his robe, peeking her sapphire head out of his collar and trembling. Lindon reached out with his power again, but the arm wouldn't respond to him anymore. All he could sense from it was a boundless hunger.

"What now?" he asked, his voice creaking from disuse.

"It's out of control," Gesha said sourly, pulling the goldsteel hook from her back. Sharp on the inside and as big as her torso, it was more of a sickle than a hook, and it gleamed white in the light of the room. "This is why you don't use unique parts, hm? Something goes wrong, and you can't learn from it and try again. You have to give up all your wasted time."

She stepped forward, preparing to swing her weapon, but the arm was still scurrying across the floor on its fingertips. Toward Lindon.

Lindon kept his attention on the limb. There had to be something he could do to salvage this—it would be a waste of not only irreplaceable materials, but also far too much time. And a unique opportunity.

He held out a hand to Fisher Gesha, begging for restraint, even as he studied the arm. What he called *hunger* wasn't just that. It felt similar to hunger, but it was more textured, with deeper layers. He felt ambition, greed, gluttony, an endless desire to reach for more and more.

The hand lunged at him, but he caught it by the wrist. It burned his palm, as though he'd grabbed onto solid ice, but he kept his attention on it.

Without context, the arm was out of control. It needed a mind to control it. A will to keep it in check.

And it fit him. There was a little of this hunger in him already.

He focused on that, stoking his desire for power, the feelings of envy and awe he'd felt when Suriel had demonstrated absolute authority, the aching helplessness of living as Unsouled and his desire to get stronger. As strong as he could.

The arm stiffened, like a dog catching a new scent.

Lindon threw more at it. His feelings as he looked over the Heaven's Glory School's treasures: he wanted it all, but even that wouldn't be enough. He remembered the sensation of Blackflame, the desire of a dragon to conquer and to destroy.

Then he shoved the end of the arm onto his stump.

The construct didn't resist him, but pain blacked out his memory for a moment. When he came back to himself, he was on the floor, his back propped up against a cool wall. Fisher Gesha was muttering, her hook on the ground next to her, holding her wrinkled hands over his elbow.

Where flesh met pure white madra.

"Dangerous," she muttered. "Too dangerous. Could have devoured you, you know that? Hm? And you made *me* Forge it on, so that will hurt your compatibility. An impulsive Soulsmith is a dead Soulsmith, I can say that much for certain."

He forced a smile. "Forgiveness, and thank you. I can only tell you that I thought it would work. I felt...like it would," he finished, though it sounded limp when he put it that way.

She grunted and thwacked him on the forehead with her knuckles. "You have to stay open to your instincts when you're Forging a construct. That's important. But don't go sticking things on your body just because you feel like it, hm?"

Full of expectation, Lindon flexed his new white arm.

It twisted backwards, fingers twitching, reaching for Fisher Gesha's face.

She stepped back, sighing. "It will take you some time to adjust so that you can control it naturally. Scripts could speed the process up, but they would eventually restrict you, so it's better to adapt over time."

Lindon nodded, focusing on his spirit. The arm's madra wasn't flowing into his body, but his power was flowing into *it*, and it was quite a burden. It took more madra to maintain his arm than to Enforce the rest of his body together.

"Don't try to use the binding yet," she warned him, sticking a finger in his face. "Lindon? I could not be more serious. Your madra channels are having enough trouble with the load of a Remnant's arm. If you try to use the binding, your spirit might tear itself apart. You have to get used to your new arm, and preferably strengthen your channels, yes? You should really wait as long as possible before you try to use the technique. At least four to six weeks."

Lindon nodded attentively, but his mind was focused on controlling his new arm. Finally, he got it to run its white fingers over the floor.

Sensation was...odd, through the new limb...as though the arm were talking directly to his brain and spirit instead of his body. Like he *knew* the floor was rough and cold, rather than feeling it as he would through a hand of flesh and blood.

But at least he could tell if something was hot or cold, smooth or rough. He would take it.

Forcing the arm to move as he wanted it to was stressing his spirit, and Little Blue seemed to react to that. She reached up from his collar, slapping her tiny hand on his chin. A cold spark traveled through him, soothing his channels and giving relief to his spirit. When the spark reached his arm, it shuddered and stilled for a moment.

"That's better, thank you," he said, smiling down at little blue. She dipped her head in respect and then gave him a broad grin. Where had she learned that?

No matter how much trouble it caused him, he had an arm. He could be careful for a few weeks if it meant having two hands again.

He leaned his head back against the wall, exhausted, and met Fisher Gesha's face. She seemed concerned.

"Gratitude, Fisher Gesha. I'm excited to see what I can do with this."

Gesha watched him quietly for a few seconds before folding her arms and addressing him with the look of a strict grandmother. "What is wrong with you, boy?"

That wasn't the first thing he had expected her to say. "Honored Fisher, I humbly apologize for anything that I—"

"You've been running at a full sprint for more than a year. Well, I guess I can understand it at first, considering your fight with the Jai boy. Afterwards, I thought you'd settle into a routine, hm? No, it's adventure after adventure with you. You're going to burn yourself down to ash if you keep this up."

Lindon held his hands out in a pacifying gesture, trying to reassure her. Well, he held one hand out. The other squeezed into a fist and shook itself aggressively.

"I have a lot farther to go," Lindon said reasonably. "If my goal was only Jai Long, then certainly, I could have given up and gone home by now."

"You think you hike up a mountain by sprinting all the way, do you?" she snapped. "You need a place to rest as much as anyone, if you don't want to crack like bad steel."

"I can't afford a break yet. I started too late; only last year, I was still Copper. If I don't try as hard as I can, I can't catch up."

She threw her hands in the air. "Catch up? Who exactly are you trying to catch up to, hm?"

Only two names flashed through his mind, but he was embarrassed to say them out loud.

"They call you the twenty-fourth ranked Lowgold on the combat charts," she said. "You know what that means?"

"That there are twenty-three Lowgolds stronger than I am," he said immediately.

"That you're ranked higher than three quarters of the Empire! If you settled down and lived in the Arelius family, you'd be Highgold by twenty-five. Considering it's you, probably Truegold ten years later. You could be an Underlord in your fifties. And that's living peacefully! You could settle down, rest, find a nice young lady, raise a family. You don't have to live every day like you're looking to die!"

She was shouting by the end, and Lindon winced as every word landed.

Because they hit him too close to home.

Since leaving Sacred Valley, he had risked his life almost daily. He'd given everything to move forward. He didn't regret it—if anything, his only regret was that he'd advanced too slowly.

But it was scraping him raw.

He felt like a man who had started to run down a hill, going faster and faster until he couldn't stop. Now he had to keep accelerating or stumble and fall.

The problem was, he really couldn't stop. As enticing as that vision was, he could never return to his homeland as an Underlord. Not if it took him more than thirty more years.

His home would be gone by then.

Lindon started to speak, and was surprised to find his voice rough. His vision had blurred—were those tears? Fisher Gesha looked down on him sympathetically.

There came a single knock at the door, and then Yerin pushed her way in. "They said you'd be fussing around with constructs in here," she said, glancing around the room. "Didn't want to bump your sword-hand, so I knocked." She saw the white arm and brightened.

"Skeleton arm! Scarier than a tiger's teeth, I love it. With your black eyes, that'll have them messing themselves before you ever throw a punch."

That hadn't been Lindon's actual goal, but he was glad she was pleased. And it did remind him of another issue: he had to test the arm with Blackflame. All of the tests performed on samples by Fisher Gesha's drudge had suggested the two types of madra wouldn't interfere with each other, certainly not after his soul acclimated to the limb, but there was no way to be sure without testing.

"I'll take any advantage I can get, in a fight," Lindon said, surreptitiously swiping at his eyes and rising to his feet.

Yerin straightened her back, the silver Goldsigns over her shoulders rising. "That wasn't why I came. I have news for you, and the sand's running down." She met his eyes with a firm gaze. "Skysworn are going sword-to-sword with Redmoon Hall. I'm joining them."

Lindon's new arm twitched as he lost control of his breathing technique. He had known she'd spoken with the Skysworn, but not how it had turned out. She hadn't told him, and he'd been afraid to ask.

But now...Yerin was going. And he wasn't.

"Already?" he asked, and he sounded like he'd swallowed sand.

"Told you I wasn't burning time," she said, meeting his eyes. "They've got some test or something coming up. Could be my last chance, and I'm not planning to miss it."

He wanted to say he was going to join her, wanted to leave Fisher Gesha and walk out alongside Yerin. They'd traveled together for so long, it felt wrong to be parting ways now.

But she was still rushing, he wasn't wrong about that. The smart thing to do was wait.

If only it didn't feel like slicing into his own chest.

"There will be another test, though? Perhaps I can join then."

"Could be," she said, with half a smile. "Couldn't tell you when it is, though."

Then, at least for now, he needed to say good-bye. He bowed at the waist, as deeply as he could. "This one thanks you for your long guidance. He could never have made it without you."

She scratched the back of her neck with one hand. "Yeah, well... wouldn't have made it out of the Valley without you, would I? And having you around kept me busy."

Lindon straightened and looked into her eyes. "Thank you, Yerin. I can't...ah, thank you." It wasn't adequate, but he was afraid that if he said any more, he would embarrass himself.

She nodded, shifting her gaze. They stood in silence for a few moments before Yerin finally waved and turned on her heel. "Don't need to make this any fancier than it has to be," she said as she walked out. "I'll see you soon, won't I? Not gone forever."

"I'll see you then!" he called after her, even as the door shut.

Fisher Gesha eyed him. "I'm sorry, boy."

Lindon didn't hear her.

The excitement of his new arm had been completely dampened. He packed up his things in a haze, and the next thing he knew, he had returned to his room. It was simple—less appointed even than the cell where the Skysworn had kept him before, but mercifully bigger. It was connected to a kind of stable, where Orthos slept.

He stood in the center of his room, lost.

When Gesha had asked him who he was trying to catch up to, only two faces had popped into his mind: Yerin and Eithan.

Both of them were too embarrassing to say aloud. Yerin was the apprentice of a Sage, and a prodigy. Eithan was an Underlord and the Patriarch of a great family.

But they had both treated him as though he could catch up to them. They had made him believe it.

Now he was on his own.

Without knowing what he was doing, he grabbed his pack with his left hand and slipped it on. He froze halfway through, realizing he didn't need it, but it comforted him. Made him feel prepared.

Then, aimlessly, he drifted over to Orthos' room. It was broad, empty, and its walls were plated in dark, scripted metal. It had been designed to hold contracted sacred beasts, or so Lindon had been told.

Orthos hadn't been asleep, which Lindon had expected from the feel of his spirit. Instead, the turtle was munching on a pile of rocks and broken chunks of street that Lindon had scavenged from around the city. The red circles of his eyes pivoted to Lindon as he entered, but the turtle didn't say anything. He just kept chewing away.

Lindon hugged his pack to himself—with one arm, because the other had rebelled again—and sat down.

Orthos felt confused and weak again. The years he'd spent with a damaged spirit had left their mark on his mind. Now, he was struggling to think.

Little Blue popped up from inside Lindon's robes, eyeing Orthos. With a quick glance at Lindon, she hurried across the floor, resting her blue hand on one of the turtle's forelegs.

His spirit and body shuddered as the Sylvan Riverseed's power cleansed his madra channels, but he kept munching away on the rock.

"Lin...don..." he said, through a mouthful of gravel.

Little Blue gave him a mournful whistle and then drifted back to Lindon.

"Good morning, Orthos," Lindon said.

"...arm," the turtle forced out.

"It's a new one," Lindon said, holding it up and twisting it with difficulty. "But it should be an improvement."

Orthos' consciousness was growing sharper by the second, but he was still having trouble with speech. After a moment, he gave a single nod. "Good. Like it."

Well, he'd gotten approval from Yerin and Orthos.

"I think you and Yerin will be happier the more frightening I look," Lindon said, idly opening his pack.

"Dragons...are frightening," Orthos said, the red in his eyes shining.

"That doesn't mean *I* want to be," Lindon said, flipping through his belongings. He was taking inventory.

Here, in this room, was everything he had left.

Little Blue, Orthos, and the contents of his pack. Eithan would still help him, but Eithan was gone. Who knew when the Underlord would return? He had been fickle even before the Emperor had needed him to resolve an imperial crisis.

He dug down past a portable rune-light, a spare set of clothes, and a ball of string. Counting everything in his pack calmed him, gave him a sense of control. He had prepared for everything he could, and these were the fruits of his preparation.

After only a moment, his fingertips brushed old, yellowed paper. He pulled it out: *The Heart of Twin Stars,* the cover said.

Inside, he had written on the blank sheets the manual had included, and had added more pages within as necessary.

The Path of Twin Stars, he had written, in his own handwriting.

Here, he had recorded every step of his advancement. The uses of pure madra. Notes on the performance, range, and feel of the Empty Palm technique. He had recorded his experience splitting his core, and how he had used scales he Forged himself to expand his capacity. He recorded when he'd moved on to the Heaven and Earth Purification Wheel technique—though he was vague on those details, following Eithan's advice to keep that cycling method a secret.

After that, his notes were sparse. He'd recorded the pills Eithan had given him to train, and how he had refined Lowgold and Highgold cores for Lindon's digestion. That was the method Lindon had used to reach Lowgold in his pure core.

But that was all. There were still more blank pages left.

Lindon sat for entirely too long, holding the manual in his hand. The feel of the old paper, the smell of it, brought back old feelings.

How he'd felt when Yerin taught him that an Unsouled was a fabrication of Sacred Valley. How he could carve out his own Path.

"Orthos," Lindon said quietly. "Yerin went to join the Skysworn."

The turtle grumbled for a moment before forcing out, "Why?"

"They're fighting against Redmoon Hall."

Rage boiled up in Orthos' spirit. Lindon could feel it, pushing against the sacred beast's restraints. He had heard about the bloodspawn, what they'd done while he slept, and that they'd come from a Dreadgod. In his mind, Redmoon Hall had made a fool of him while he slept.

Orthos kept himself under control, but he rose up to his full height, turning his head to face Lindon. "And you? You will allow them to do as they wish, unopposed?"

At least he was back to full sentences.

"The smarter choice is to stay with the Arelius family," Lindon said. "Get stronger first. If I went to fight now, I wouldn't offer anything. I'd be going to lose, or to die."

Orthos backed him against the wall, looming over him. Lindon felt a pang of fear, though he could sense that the turtle was totally in control. He had fought against the wild Orthos too many times to be entirely comfortable.

"A dragon does not allow fear to make his decisions for him," Orthos rumbled. "A dragon decides for himself."

Lindon glanced down at the manual in his hand.

His own Path.

What did *he* want to do?

Little Blue looked up at him from somewhere around his shin, her ocean-blue body shimmering in Orthos' smoldering light. She reached up to pat him, giving him some comfort.

He reached down with his flesh arm, scooping her up, and she scampered up to sit on his shoulder. Then he stood.

"Let's go," Lindon said.

Orthos stomped out the door. "You don't need to tell me we're going. Of course we are." He snapped up a chunk of the floor, munching on it as he spoke.

"A dragon always fights."

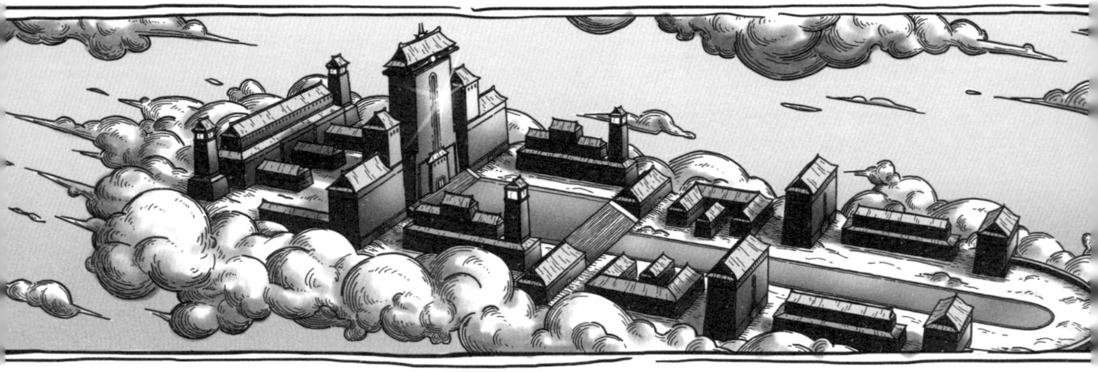

XIII

Renfei and Bai Rou led Yerin away from Starsweep Tower, toward the class of applicants. Bai Rou loomed over her in a way that made her want to knock him down a peg, if only he weren't a fully armed and armored Truegold. Renfei had a more reasonable height, only an inch or two over Yerin herself. Yerin couldn't help but like her more.

"As we return to the capital, Stormrock will pass over Serpent's Grave. The rest of the Arelius family will be sent home then," Renfei said.

Yerin nodded. She had been a little worried that they would stay here, so that she might crash into them during her Skysworn training. She itched at the thought of them seeing her train to leave them.

And at the same time, she ached when she thought about them

leaving her. Her feelings were too twisted to think about for very long; clearly, she needed more training.

"There are only fifty other qualified Highgold applicants," Renfei went on. "You'll be competing with them for ten spots."

"I thought you'd be begging for as many bodies as you could squeeze into green armor," Yerin said.

"We can't let our standards slip," Renfei told her proudly, the cloud over her head lightening. "Now, more than ever, we need the Skysworn to be excellent." She waited a moment before adding, "However, we won't dismiss the other forty, like we might under other circumstances. We will give them a chance to re-apply, or to serve in other ways. And the basic training program for those who join will be accelerated."

Yerin translated to herself. They were cutting corners all over the place, but not in places where they had to admit it. So they *were* desperate, they just didn't want to look that way.

She had another question, but before she could ask it, the crowd parted behind them as random passersby were shoved out of the way. A tall, broad figure loomed behind her, and the brief flash from her spiritual perception showed her a great power moving toward her at speed.

Her sword was in her hand immediately, the blades over her shoulders poised. Her master's memories drifted to the surface, sketching the outline of combat in her mind. Not that she needed his experience—she had scars from enough fights herself. She wasn't so raw and unformed that she'd lock up at the first taste of combat.

Then she saw who it was and completely locked up.

Lindon stumbled up to her, out of breath, dipping his head in apologies to all the people around him he'd shoved out of the way. Orthos rose over him like a smoking mountain, his eyes glaring at her. He looked even angrier than Lindon usually did, though it fit his black, leathery turtle's face.

Lindon's pack was hanging awkwardly from one shoulder, Little Blue seated on his head, his arm twisting and bucking like it had slipped his leash. Wasn't a tough guess to see he hadn't mastered it yet.

He met her gaze, and his eyes were black with red circles. But that darkness faded as he switched away from Blackflame, looking to the Skysworn.

"I'd like to join as well," he said. "To serve the Empire."

Bai Rou marched forward, yellow eyes shining in the shadow of his hat, and seized Lindon by the arm. "You *idiot*," he said in a low voice, dragging him into a nearby alley. The citizens stared after them, and Orthos followed, growling like he was prepared to attack.

Renfei's cloud was a solid black as she joined them in the alley, one hand on her hammer as though she expected to use it.

"A Blackflame?" Bai Rou snarled, shoving Lindon up against the wall. "In Stormrock?"

Orthos stepped up, growling, his eyes blazing red and Blackflame madra flaring from the plates of his shell.

Yerin had her own sword out. She'd aim for the back of Bai Rou's neck first, above the armor, while he was focused on Lindon. If she and Orthos killed him quick, then they could turn to Renfei together.

The woman stabbed her finger toward the mouth of the alley. "You didn't even hide yourself! What do you imagine *they're* thinking right now?"

Wary of a trap, Yerin shot a quick glance at the opening, but she didn't take her eyes off Bai Rou for more than an instant.

The people had run, peeking in from around the corner. They looked terrified. A shop owner shut his door with a bang.

Lindon held up his hands...or his hand, as his white arm rebelled halfway through and started reaching for Orthos. With visible effort, he knocked it down. "I...humbly apologize for causing a scene, but surely you see why I can only join the Skysworn. How can I fight for the Empire when merely revealing my contracted partner causes a panic? *Unless* I work for the Skysworn."

Yerin saw a shred of reason in it. If people knew the Skysworn had a Blackflame under control, it would make them look stronger. Lindon would look weaker, too, but he didn't care what every random person on the street thought. At least, he shouldn't.

Renfei was still furious, Bai Rou still had Lindon pushed against the wall, and Orthos' growl was growing louder. Yerin held her sword at the ready, careful not to send any madra flowing through the weapon. If Renfei sensed it, the battle would begin too early.

"How did you get out of the tower?" Renfei demanded. "The guards would have stopped you."

Lindon looked genuinely confused. "We just...walked out. They seemed busy."

Other than Renfei and Bai Rou, every other Skysworn Yerin had seen in the city was scampering around like a scared rabbit. She still couldn't swallow that he'd walked straight out with Orthos following him. She wondered what had really happened.

Bai Rou turned to exchange a glance with Renfei. He released Lindon, abruptly taking a step back.

Yerin sheathed her sword as though she'd never drawn it. Her Goldsigns withdrew.

Somewhere around her core, her uninvited guest sent out a pulse of disappointment. Like a craving gone unmet. It pushed against the seal on her skin, but that dam held.

How long will that last? she wondered. If Eithan didn't come back in time, she'd have to find a solution herself.

He'd hinted and teased about a way to get this parasite out of her, but he'd also made it clear as glass that he'd rather she *use* it. He wanted her to be one of these emissaries, or whatever she'd be called if she didn't work for Redmoon Hall.

She had no interest in that. She'd rather walk away from the sword forever than lose to this…disgusting thing inside of her. She couldn't end such a long fight by giving up. Not even by taking it over herself.

A handful of her master's memories dealt with her guest—it seemed like every other memory she pulled from his Remnant had to do with her. Eithan said that it was easier to pull up memories that touched you in some way, but she was disappointed. She'd hoped to learn things about her master she didn't know.

Still, she knew what he'd felt about her Blood Shadow: disgust. He thought the parasite was a burden on her, and he'd only been waiting until she advanced enough to be rid of it.

While she was lost in thought, the other four had gone back to an uneasy standoff.

"We have to bring him to the Underlord either way," Renfei said at last. "If he wants to invite a Blackflame to try out…well, that's up to him."

Lindon nodded along. "I believe I'm qualified to apply for one of the Lowgold positions. I know the application process is today; we could try that before meeting with the Underlord, if time is an issue."

"He's at the testing grounds," Bai Rou said, ignoring Lindon.

"We'll have to circle around, by the walls," Renfei responded, looking into the shadows of the alley. "We would be even more visible in the air. Just have to take it fast."

Bai Rou turned to look at Lindon, face in shadow. "Keep up," he commanded, then took off with a splash of golden liquid madra.

"You first," Renfei said. "Try to escape or deviate from the course, and I will take care of you myself."

Lindon gave Orthos a nervous look. He'd be wondering what Yerin was: whether Orthos could keep himself under control as they ran. After one reassuring pat on the turtle's head, he scooped Little Blue off his head and into his palm.

The Sylvan Riverseed caught Yerin's eye as she was lowered, and Yerin waved.

The spirit turned away as though suddenly frightened, huddling on Lindon's palm. Yerin sighed.

An instant later, Lindon's eyes were dark again, and the Burning Cloak ignited around him like a red-and-black shroud in the air. He kicked off, Orthos trotting after, and Yerin filled her body with madra.

The Path of the Endless Sword didn't have a full-body Enforcer technique, but her Iron body was strong. She fed madra to her limbs in a general Enforcement, which was nowhere near as good as a true technique, but she had no trouble keeping up with Lindon.

They ran side-by-side for a while as she tried to sort out what to say, but the words got tangled up inside her. She couldn't seem to push the knot out past her tongue.

As a group, they were darting through damp alleys, vaulting short walls, dodging piles of trash and hopeless-looking people crouched on the sides of the road. She'd seen the decay of cities before, and it almost comforted her to see that the sickness extended even here, to the city of the Skysworn.

She had remained silent too long, the tangle of words keeping her frustrated. Finally, she just blurted it out.

"You followed me," she barked as she hopped up on top of an eight-foot wall and waited for him to come after her. "Why? Ten seconds ago, you didn't want to fight."

He shrugged as he landed next to her, though his white arm folded up with the motion and wouldn't unlock. "You've followed me for the better part of two years," he said at last, taking off and trusting her to keep up. "You didn't have to stick with me after Sacred Valley, and you didn't have to help me through the Blackflame Trials. It seemed like my turn."

He gave her an embarrassed smile. "When I stopped looking at all the problems, and I just asked myself what I wanted to do…I realized I wanted to come with you. So here I am."

Yerin kept her eyes focused on Bai Rou's broad back, because she could feel heat rising up through her neck and into her cheeks. Her words were stuck in her throat again, but for a different reason this time.

"Well," she said at last. "Glad you finally saw it straight." Then, to change the subject, she asked him, "How did you really get past the guards?"

"It's a good thing the applications aren't back in the tower," Lindon said, voice low. "Orthos burned a hole in the wall."

Lindon was losing track of the number of times he'd been imprisoned.

Bai Rou walked around him, producing a pair of manacles joined by a short length of chain. They looked like iron, but pale specks like stars deep in the metal told him that they included halfsilver. They would disperse madra on contact, preventing him from burning his way out of the restraints.

Not that he was drawing on his Blackflame madra at the moment. He had switched to his pure core as soon as Renfei and Bai Rou had dragged him into this squat, nondescript building. The Path of Black Flame made him aggressive, made him want to move, to act.

If he was filled with Blackflame madra, he was sure he would have tried to run. That would only have resulted in a short chase followed by Bai Rou dragging him down the hall anyway. He could sense that was what Orthos wanted to do; the turtle was safe, but growing restless. Wherever he was, he wouldn't stay there long. Little Blue had crawled back in her case, and though they'd taken his pack, they'd left her inside.

The manacle was uncomfortably cold on his wrist of flesh, but it positively *burned* his Remnant arm. He managed to slip the edge of his sleeve inside, to protect his artificial limb. If he hadn't, Bai Rou would have been dragging his limp body inside.

Past an ordinary door was yet another bare, nondescript room. He was growing used to those. At least this one didn't have a bed, so they wouldn't keep him here for too long.

There was another door on the opposite wall, and a smooth wooden chair in the center of the floor. A circle of script on the ceiling glowed softly white.

Otherwise, it was empty.

Bai Rou walked him to the chair and clipped the chain between his restraints to a hook in the floor. Lindon sat down, because it was that or stay uncomfortably hunched. There wasn't enough slack in the chain for him to stand up straight.

"You don't need to speak respectfully," Renfei said. "He appreciates direct answers more than good manners. But you should be respectful."

"Tell the truth," Bai Rou added from his post by the door.

Lindon's breath sped up as he pictured the Skysworn Underlord. The man had shown him no mercy during the duel...but he had, in the end, allowed Lindon to go free.

It made him feel better about being cuffed and chained to the floor of what was most likely an interrogation room.

The far door swung open and Naru Gwei entered, the man shuffling inside in his beaten armor as though dragging a weight behind him with every step.

Renfei and Bai Rou bowed slightly and pressed their fists together. Lindon mimicked them as best he could in his position.

"I am Wei Shi Lindon, sir," Lindon said. He had to force himself not to refer to himself as 'this one.' "I was not able to properly introduce myself last time."

The man slipped a long leaf into his mouth, chewing it for a while before saying, "You're part of the Arelius family."

"I have that honor, sir. If I could only—"

"But you weren't born to it."

"No, sir. Underlord Arelius was kind enough to take myself and my companion under his wing."

The old Skysworn didn't ask about his companion. "Where *were* you born?"

"Sacred Valley," Lindon said. "It's far to the west, past the Desolate Wilds."

For a long moment, he chewed his leaf. "Are there more Blackflames hiding in Sacred Valley?"

Lindon forced a polite laugh. "No sir, no. There aren't even any Golds."

"So this was something that Eithan Arelius taught you."

The old man was drilling for something, and Lindon wasn't quite sure what; surely he'd known all about Lindon's situation before even the duel with Jai Long. The uncertainty made him wary. "I entered a contract with a sacred beast known as Orthos. You have him captive here, somewhere, and I'm sure he could give you a further explanation."

Orthos would know more about this situation than he did, though Lindon doubted the turtle would cooperate with any questioning.

Only the wet sounds of the leaf between the man's teeth broke the silence of the room. Eventually, he reached out and shut the door behind him.

The snap of the door closing echoed in the tiny room.

The Skysworn Captain folded his arms and leaned against the wall.

Bai Rou took a respectful step away, but the old man didn't seem to care. He examined Lindon through a curtain of matted gray hair.

"Did you ever break that arm as a kid?" he asked. "Back when you had it, I mean."

Whatever Lindon's interrogator wanted, he was coming at it from a different direction. Lindon only wished he understood where this was headed. Why hadn't he waited for Eithan before trying to join the Skysworn? Maybe the Arelius Underlord could have persuaded them to hold another round of applications.

"Both of them, yes," Lindon said. He'd broken one falling out of a tree, and the other had been broken *by* a tree.

"And how did they treat that break, back in Sacred Valley?"

"We weren't the richest family in the clan, sir. We had simple elixirs and a scripted sling."

"No life artists?"

"Only for more severe injuries, honored sir." Lindon's father had his leg treated by a life artist, but the woman hadn't been on hand soon enough to restore the limb completely. Without her, he wouldn't have kept the leg at all.

The man nodded slowly, flipping the leaf over between his lips. "And burns? You ever burn yourself?"

Lindon's eyes flicked to the scar on the side of the man's face. "Minor burns only, sir." His voice had grown quiet, and he wasn't sure why.

"Well, since they didn't heal burns back in Sacred Valley, I'll tell you how we do it here." Lindon stayed focused on the raised patch of ridged, reddish scar tissue that ran from his temple down to his chin. It only missed his eye by a quarter-inch.

"Blood madra removes unhealthy tissue and grows some more. Life madra smooths it all out, heals it together with the rest of your body so that you'd never know you'd been burned at all. And that's just a general picture. If you get a specialized healing Path, or some decent elixirs, the whole thing can be done in a breath."

He ran his little finger across his scarred cheek. "Black fire hurts a little worse."

Lindon sat, more and more conscious of the chain locking him in this room. He looked to the more familiar Skysworn for comfort, but Bai Rou had his arms crossed, his yellow eyes staring at the far wall. Renfei kept her eyes on her Captain.

"They tell me you're requesting entry into the Skysworn," Naru Gwei said, without leaning away. "Did Eithan tell you to do that?"

"No! No, I...I probably should have waited for his permission, but I didn't. He doesn't know."

"But he was the one who turned you into a Blackflame," Gwei said. His expression still looked tired, as though he hadn't slept in three days and wanted nothing more than to go home and sleep. His tone, by contrast, betrayed no impatience.

"He helped me along this Path, yes," Lindon said, hoping this wouldn't reflect too badly on Eithan. The Arelius Underlord had never told him to keep his involvement a secret.

The Skysworn Captain gave no sign whether he thought this was good or bad. He kept leaning against the wall, chewing his leaf. "Did he do that to your core?"

From his previous conversations with Renfei and Bai Rou, Lindon gathered that they assumed his pure core was a sort of disguise to cover the Path of Black Flame. "I split my core on my own, sir. Before I met Eithan."

"And what did he want you to do with this new Path? What purpose did he have for you?"

Finally, Lindon saw what the Underlord was getting at. Naru Gwei assumed this was all part of Eithan's plan, and wanted to know what that plan was.

"For the duel, sir. I asked him for a Path that might allow me to fight someone stronger than I was."

"The way I've heard it," Gwei said, "Eithan allowed the duel. Even proposed it."

"His favorite training method is…I guess I would call it extreme duress."

The Skysworn Captain swallowed the leaf and withdrew a long straw from within his armor. He placed it between his teeth and continued chewing. "So he proposed this duel, held you to it, and then held out the Path of Black Flame as your only salvation. That doesn't sound like a plan to you?"

"He's pushing me forward," Lindon insisted. "He's helping me grow."

Naru Gwei unfolded his arms and leaned closer. "Into *what?*"

Lindon had no answer to that.

"What did he say you would do after the duel?"

"Nothing I know of. He's helping me advance." Lindon felt less confident than he had before.

The Underlord stared at him for a long moment, then jerked his head toward the door. His two subordinates traded looks, though they couldn't do anything but leave. Bai Rou ducked his woven hat beneath the doorframe, and the cloud over Renfei's head passed through with plenty of room to spare.

They didn't look back at Lindon.

"The duel is over," Naru Gwei said. "Now, in the middle of an imperial crisis that he helped cause, he's trying to slip a Blackflame into my Skysworn. While he tries to take over himself. I know what he's doing, linking Underlords to the Skysworn. He's trying to win them over from me."

The Underlord had loomed over Lindon, the air in the room swirling and picking up into a windstorm. His scarred face was hostile: he was working himself up into a fury. Whatever was happening out there had put too much pressure on the Skysworn Captain, whether it was the threat of Redmoon Hall or whatever Eithan had done.

Either way, Naru Gwei had decided Lindon was part of it.

Lindon's right arm started straining against its restraints, and he almost wanted to help it.

The Underlord leaned toward Lindon, his dirty gray hair swinging closer. Lindon shut his mouth. Naru Gwei's weather-beaten face somehow looked both weary and intense, as though he were bracing himself for an unpleasant task that he had performed hundreds of times before.

"Lower your head," the Underlord commanded, and Lindon could hear his death in that command.

"It's not Eithan!" Lindon said desperately, tapping his Blackflame core. His eyes heated, and he knew from experience that they would have transformed into a copy of Orthos' eyes: pure black with red irises. The Path of Black Flame flooded into his left hand, and his right remained mercifully untouched and intact.

He poured that power into his cuffs even as he Enforced his muscles. If he melted them, they would burn through his wrists, so he had to hope he could tear his hand free before the damage was too great.

Instead, the madra broke to steam on contact with the cuffs. A spike of cold shot up Lindon's arms, as though he'd driven an icicle through his wrists.

Halfsilver in the cuffs. He'd remembered, but hoped against hope that there was some flaw.

"A friend wanted to join! Yerin, I mentioned her earlier, she's the companion that Eithan adopted. She wanted to fight Redmoon Hall, so she insisted on joining the Skysworn! I didn't want to, but I couldn't let her down!" He was babbling as though every word out of his mouth would slow down the Underlord's blow.

Considering that he was still alive, maybe there was something to that theory.

"She just wanted to help! And...ah, so do I! Of course!" As Naru Gwei's hand drifted upward toward the hilt of his sword, Lindon's breath came faster and faster. His breath started to blur, and the ice in his wrists grew sharper as he poured more effort into breaking the shackles. Even his white arm was writhing with desperation. Just a little more, he was sure. He had to believe that. Just a little more...

"Eithan adopted her too," the Captain said quietly, and Lindon forced himself to take deeper breaths. He could feel Orthos growing agitated in his own cell, feeding on Lindon's fear—if it went too far, or if Lindon was killed, the turtle would go on a rampage.

"Why?" Naru Gwei continued. "What was special about her?"

"She was apprenticed to a Sage," Lindon blurted out. Yet again, he wondered if he should be sharing this, but Yerin had never kept it a secret. She would proudly tell anyone.

"Which Sage?"

"The Sword Sage!"

Naru Gwei's green-armored fingers wrapped around his sword hilt. "*Which* Sword Sage?"

There was more than one?

"I don't know!" Lindon insisted. "I don't know! She's on the Path of the Endless Sword, and she learned it from him, but I don't know if he had another name, or…"

After a moment, the Captain's hand moved down. He stared at the wall, and Lindon felt a light brush on his spirit as the Underlord's perception moved through him…and kept going.

He was looking for Yerin.

◇

Naru Gwei wasn't an Arelius, so he had to rely on his spiritual perception to find someone. He'd long been jealous of their bloodline legacy; it was wasted on them, he felt. The world's best scouting tool, and they wasted it on civic maintenance.

But there were some things that an old-fashioned spiritual scan did best.

He found a nearby Highgold sword artist almost immediately. Her madra moved in smooth, steady rhythms—she was cycling. That would be Yerin. There were other sword artists nearby, but none of them so close.

He'd read reports that had mentioned Yerin, but he hadn't paid them much attention. He had been focused on Lindon, the Blackflame. He'd even seen her once himself, briefly, though she hadn't stood out to him.

But now he'd found yet another seed that Eithan had tried to plant in the Skysworn.

At first, he felt nothing out of the ordinary. She had a powerful soul, with madra that was potent for a Highgold. She may be on the verge of Truegold, or she might have used some elixir. None of that was cause for alarm.

But upon closer inspection, he felt something: a seal. Fueled by soulfire.

The seal was like a cage embedded in her soul, and it must have been made recently. Soulfire couldn't last forever.

What was inside?

He ran his perception around the box, probing for gaps, but he found none. Instead, he sat there with his attention on the box itself, waiting for an impression to drift through.

After a few breaths of time, he felt a wisp of something from inside the seal: blood. Like a monster that had spilled an ocean of blood and was hungry to spill more.

He jerked away, his head actually snapping backward as he broke the connection.

Could Eithan have done this intentionally? No, he must have picked this girl up months before Jai Daishou had opened the western labyrinth. And he couldn't have known the Jai Underlord would attract the attention of Redmoon Hall.

Or could he? How far ahead had Eithan's plan gone?

If not for Naru Gwei's vigilance, Eithan would have slipped a Blood Shadow into the Skysworn.

The Underlord wasn't surprised no one had caught it before. Even without Eithan's seal, most people had never encountered a Blood Shadow before. Renfei must have scanned her before allowing her into the Skysworn, but she could easily have mistaken that impression as a blood Remnant or perhaps part of her Path.

But Naru Gwei could tell. If she wasn't part of Redmoon Hall herself, she was well on her way.

Now, the Blackflame and the Blood Shadow's host were in his power. He could rid the Empire of both of them.

He stood still, thinking, as Lindon squirmed against his manacles beside him. He *could* kill them both in an instant.

And then what would happen?

He would provoke the Arelius family at least, on the verge of a national crisis. Everyone expected the Arelius to replace the Jai clan in the ranks of the great clans, now that Jai Daishou was dead. This would be the worst possible time to make new enemies.

Even if he were willing to face that problem, there was a greater one: the Sage of the Endless Sword.

Eithan said he was dead, and if he had adopted the Sage's disciple, he would be in a position to know. But could Naru Gwei accept anything Eithan said?

No, he couldn't. If the Sage showed up alive, and his disciple had been killed by a fellow Highgold, he would have no one to blame. But if she had been killed by an Underlord...

Naru Gwei wouldn't last any longer against an Archlord than a Copper would. And the Sages were the greatest of the Archlords.

No, he couldn't kill her himself. And he would prefer not to antagonize the Arelius family by executing Lindon either. Now he had two enemies with backgrounds he couldn't afford to offend.

Wait, not two...*three.*

A new face popped up in his memory, and he remembered the request from the Akura clan.

Take good care of our errant daughter, their messenger had said. *Treat her as you would a favored disciple, and place her where the battle is hottest. If she is to fall, there will be no reprisals. Your cooperation will be rewarded.*

The Akura clan had entrusted their Empire with this request only months ago, and Naru Gwei himself had been assigned to oversee its execution. The Emperor was counting on him.

There was no reason he couldn't fold two more enemies into the plan.

Lindon and Yerin would still have to apply. They could go through the evaluation process like usual, and Eithan Arelius couldn't complain. If they failed, they would join the reserve, and Naru Gwei could still find a place for them.

And if they succeeded, so much the better. They would share a fate with all the Empire's enemies.

Before Lindon could react, Naru Gwei pulled free his sword and struck through the young man's manacles. Halfsilver had its uses, but it was brittle, and it practically crumbled under the force of his blow.

"You're free to go," the Captain said.

Lindon's expression looked dissatisfied, as though he'd missed the opportunity for a fight, but he sounded only relieved. "Gratitude, Underlord, gratitude."

"Better hurry," Naru Gwei said, returning his sword to his back. "The application begins precisely at noon."

Without a backward glance, Lindon scurried out of the room. He would be headed for his contracted partner and to Yerin.

And, soon, to his death.

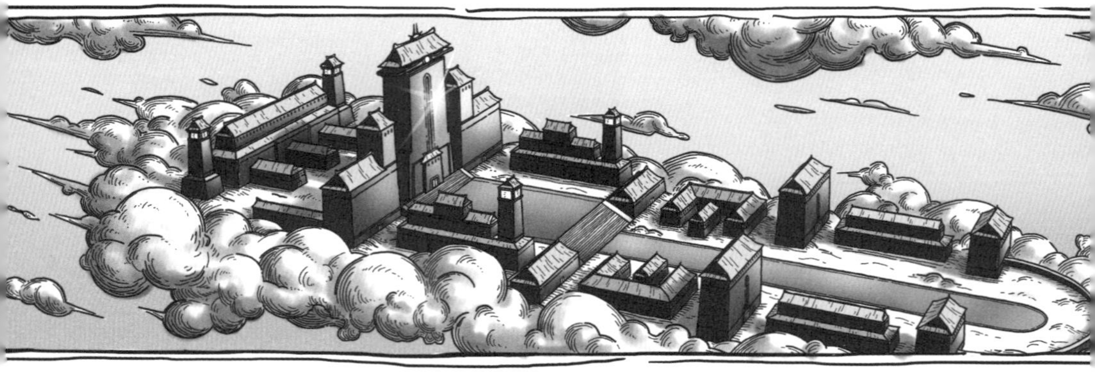

XIV

The two Skysworn guided them to a fairground just inside the city walls. Hundreds of people had gathered out in the open, bustling and mixing, and the sheer variety of different sacred artists made it a riot of color and motion. Birds, winged Remnants, and hovering constructs filled the sky. Lindon saw Goldsigns of every description, from shining tattoos to floating clouds of eyes, and weapons Forged from solid fire or living dreams.

It was an overwhelming sight, but Renfei and Bai Rou eventually dropped them off by a pair of tents. Each had a pair of characters floating overhead, projected on cloud madra. They spelled out the words "Lowgold" and "Highgold."

Yerin made her way to the Highgold tent, and Lindon started to make his way toward the Lowgold area.

He stopped almost immediately, when the green-armored guards saw him and their faces went hard. One of them drew a sword, and the other's hands started crackling with lightning.

Bai Rou stood with his arms folded, as though whatever happened to Lindon was no business of his, but Renfei stepped up and spoke to them. What she said must have worked, because they backed away, but they still didn't look pleased.

"This is foolish," Orthos grumbled, tearing up a chunk of grassy soil and swallowing it whole. "We surround ourselves with enemies."

Lindon glanced over at the Highgold tent, where Yerin's silver Goldsigns bobbed over the crowd. "The Skysworn treat their students well. One day inside their Soulsmith library will pay for itself."

He was trying to convince himself, and Orthos' skeptical grunt said he knew it. Lindon was still shaking from his encounter with the Skysworn Captain, and his decision to apply for the Skysworn now felt like the most impulsive and stupid decision he could possibly have made.

The woman sitting inside the tent was motherly and soft, and she had a miniature sparrow of crackling yellow sparks sitting on her shoulder. "Name," she demanded.

"Wei Shi Lindon."

She scanned down a scroll, and her eyes widened when she found his name. Or perhaps when she saw his Path—Lindon couldn't tell what information was written on the scroll, but her eyes flicked to Orthos, at which point they widened even further.

The woman looked from side to side for help, but the other people working in the tent were all dealing with other applicants.

Finally, she pulled out a small wooden chit with the number "537" stamped onto it.

"This is...your, ah, participant number? Please do not lose it...um, if you don't mind. You are one of the final applicants we're accepting today. If you are one of the first fifty participants to reach the end, you will be considered to have passed."

It had the sound of something she'd said many times today, but she was too flustered to deliver it smoothly.

"The end of what?" Lindon asked, but the woman was staring at Orthos again. That reminded him of a different question. "He's not a Lowgold. Will we have to apply separately?"

She shook herself as though waking up. "Ah, no, of course not. As your contracted partner, he is considered part of your strength. He will be competing with you."

Suddenly, Lindon wondered if this application might be incredibly easy.

On her directions, he and Orthos made their way to a massive group of other Lowgolds. Hundreds of young sacred artists huddled in small groups, matched with people they recognized. Some of them looked nervous, others projected confidence, and still others were seated on the ground cycling to steady themselves.

As he and Orthos pushed through the crowd, the turtle earned more than a few angry glances. Followed by second looks, and spiritual scans. Which invariably led to even angrier looks.

Orthos may not have noticed, but Lindon grew more and more nervous each time it happened. He was hoping they were upset because he was bringing a Truegold-level sacred beast into a Lowgold competition, but he suspected otherwise. They could recognize Blackflame in the sacred turtle at a glance, and they weren't happy about it.

"Orthos," Lindon said, "can you veil yourself?"

The turtle snorted out a puff of smoke. "Do you know how to open and close your eyes? I was veiling myself before your grandfather ever laid eyes on your grandmother. When the Skysworn were nothing more than a sect of servants, I was—"

Lindon cut him off before he gained too much momentum. "I think it would help us both if you did."

There was a wide circle around them now, and most of the Lowgolds surrounding them were giving them hard looks. Some of them held their weapons in hand, bringing them to life as they filled the blades with madra.

Orthos' dark eyes flicked up to him. "You want me to hide before a mob of angry hatchlings? They will make good targets for you to practice Void Dragon's Dance. The survivors will cast their eyes to the ground, and they will know that we are to be respected!"

Lindon cleared his throat, trying to think how to phrase this for the turtle's benefit. "I'm trying to infiltrate their ranks, Orthos. To benefit from their unique resources. It would hurt my cause if I killed their young on the way in."

Orthos rumbled deep in his chest, clearly displeased, but finally the strength of his spirit weakened. Now, he blended into the feel of the crowd, instead of standing out like a bonfire among candles.

Not that it helped the looks they were getting.

Lindon had started to identify some patterns among the young men and women surrounding him. Many of them had the emerald wings of the Naru clan's Path: the Path of Grasping Sky, if he remembered correctly. Their wings were not as fully formed as Naru Gwei's, looking more like they were made out of vivid Remnant parts rather than real feathers.

Almost as common was gray skin, though he didn't know what family or Path that represented. He even spotted two or three with the shiny metallic hair of the Path of the Stellar Spear, and those sacred artists all had their spears in hand and stared at him avidly.

Finally, one of the boys with gray skin stepped out. He carried a round shield on one arm, and held a long knife in the other—the knife rippled, as though seen from underwater. A pink-and-white fish swirled through the air around his head. Lindon assumed that was his contracted partner, as the boy's pink gemstone eyes matched those of the fish.

He held his chin high, looking down on Lindon despite being head-and-shoulders shorter. "Blackflame," he said loudly. "You should leave. For your own safety."

A general murmur of agreement and soft laughter rose from the crowd.

Lindon leaned over to Orthos. "Is he going to attack me?"

He had run into situations like this back in Sacred Valley. A number of boys would take out their frustrations on Lindon simply because they could, but the scenario was different here. He didn't understand what was likely to happen—would the young man give up after posturing for a while, or was he actually looking for a fight?

Red-and-black flames rose slightly from Orthos' shell as he considered the gray-skinned boy in front of him. "He is looking to stand out by provoking one of the Empire's villains in front of everyone," the turtle said, not bothering to keep his voice down. Everyone heard. "He is not confident enough in his results to let them speak for him, so he has to distinguish himself in another way. He is the weakest sort of scavenger, crawling along the bottom and looking for scraps. Crush him."

The words echoed in the ensuing silence, and power slowly gathered and mounted inside the gray-skinned youth.

Lindon regretted asking Orthos anything.

He plastered on a smile, raising his hands in a show of peace. "I apologize for him, honored brother. Please, can I know your—" His own right hand cut him off. Not satisfied by staying in the air, it instead lunged for a gray throat, grasping with white fingers.

Lindon managed to pull it back before anything happened, but the gray young man had raised his shield. He lowered it, pink eyes blazing. "You face Kotai Taien of the great Kotai clan, Blackflame! Defend yourself!"

The meeting with Naru Gwei had only been an hour ago. Lindon still hadn't recovered from *that*, and all he wanted was a peaceful tryout. He bowed carefully, spending most of his madra on keeping his arm under control. "I humbly apologize," he said, and someone kicked him in the back.

He stumbled forward a few steps, turning to see who it was, but there was no telling. It was a circle of hostile faces.

For the second time that afternoon, he started to sense real danger. There were more than five hundred Lowgolds around him, and none of them had any love for the Blackflames. If it hadn't been for his confrontation with the Skysworn Captain, he may have tried to run.

But this time, he'd reached the end of his patience.

Against an Underlord, he had no choice but to beg and whimper. There was no standing up against overwhelming strength.

These...were not Underlords.

Lindon shifted the pattern of his breathing, tapping into his Blackflame core. He could see those nearest him flinch as his eyes filled with black and red.

He turned to see Kotai Taien, resolving to try one more time. "I have no reason to fight you, Kotai. We are not enemies."

But he'd miscalculated. He'd hoped to push the boy away, but he should have known that he was giving Taien exactly what he wanted: a villain.

Pink eyes brightened, and he held up his shield, reversing the long knife in his right hand. "This Empire is no longer yours!" he declared, and charged.

Orthos' laugh was like that of a hungry dragon.

Lindon ignited the Burning Cloak before Taien had taken a step, launching himself forward. He drove a punch at the gap around Taien's shield, fully expecting him to shift and block the strike. The momentum should knock him back, giving Lindon time to…

Taien's ribs crumpled like a cage of dry sticks.

His body slammed backward into the crowd, tossing aside a group of other gray-skinned Lowgolds. His weapons tumbled from limp hands, his fish swam in agitated circles above him, and blood sprayed from his lips in hacking coughs.

Lindon stood, staring, from within the black-and-red haze of his Burning Cloak.

Orthos' laughter grew until it deafened the entire crowd, and he stomped the ground, howling in mirth. His eyes were almost closed, and if he were human, Lindon was sure he'd be crying with laughter.

Everyone in the crowd took a step back.

Still chuckling, the turtle walked up and sniffed at the fallen boy's shield. "Spoils of war," he said, snapping it up and chewing. The sound of twisting metal cut through the air even louder than his laughs had.

Taien hacked up blood again, letting out a loud moan, and tried to roll on his side. Abruptly, Lindon realized that he hadn't canceled his Burning Cloak yet, and finally let the technique fade.

He had only intended to show everyone that he couldn't be pushed around. He hadn't wanted to kill anybody.

Everyone in the group of Lowgolds seemed allergic to him all of a sudden. Even the other gray-skinned sacred artists backed away from Taien, as though to help him was to associate themselves with him.

The crowd rippled as someone pushed through, and Lindon turned, readying his madra in case it was another challenger. He sincerely hoped it wasn't; he had never had to adjust his strength to *avoid* hurting someone before. If they attacked, he couldn't hold back.

From the wall of people, a girl stumbled out. She was slender and a little taller than Yerin, with her hair pulled back into a long black ponytail. She wore white-and-black sacred artist's robes, with a breastplate of smooth purple armor over her chest. The armor matched her eyes, which were a startling, vivid purple. The eyes looked human, not as though she'd borrowed them from a sacred beast through a contract, but he couldn't be sure.

She carried a staff in one hand. It was as tall as she was, thick as her wrist, and made of smooth-looking black tendons. The tendons coiled up to the top of the staff, which was capped by a dragon's head.

The girl stumbled as she came out of the crowd, steadied herself, and then dropped to her knees next to Kotai Taien. "Oh, wow! You really hammered him, didn't you? Just..." She gave the air a little mock jab. "He's on the Path of the Unstained Shield, too. Must have been skipping his training, huh?"

She looked around at the other gray-skinned youths standing around. They shifted in place, clearly unsure how to respond.

Taien coughed again, blood splattering his lips.

"Are you his...friend?" Lindon asked hesitantly.

"I try to be friendly, when I can!" she chirped, brushing a lock of hair away from her eye and smiling brightly. "But no, I can't say that I've ever met him before." She put two fingers to his ribs and winced. "Sorry, you must be in pain. Give me a second."

She removed a pouch tied at her waist, rummaging inside. Her hand seemed to dip further into the pouch than it should have, and Lindon noticed that she wore tight black gloves up to her wrist. They seemed to be made out of the same substance as her staff, as though she had dipped her hands in glossy black liquid. Her Goldsign, perhaps?

After a moment of rummaging around, she brightened, withdrawing a smooth white bottle with a cloth tied over its opening. She untied it in one swift motion, popping out a round green-and-gray pill.

Lindon could smell it from where he stood, like a rainstorm in a pine forest.

"Open up," she called down. When he didn't respond, she propped his head up and shoved the pill into his mouth. He gagged for a moment, his face turning red, but she held his mouth closed and he eventually swallowed.

The effect was immediate. Light of green, red, and purple burst from his chest in long strings, and the aura inside of his body was ignited into a storm. He sat up as though someone had pulled him on a string, gasping loudly, pink eyes wide. The fish flying in the air around his head grew excited, bobbing up and down and all around his face.

The girl slapped him on the back, smiling proudly. "There we go, good as new! Try not to eat for an hour or two, or you might start vomiting up living creatures. I've done it, it's not pretty."

Only a few seconds later, Taien was conscious again, breathing steadily. He glanced once at Lindon and then looked away, turning instead to the young woman who had saved him. "I thank you. The Blackflame attacked me before I was—"

At the sight of her eyes, he froze. She waited patiently, seeming to expect what was coming.

"...Akura?" he asked, voice hoarse.

"Akura Mercy," she said. "I'm honored to meet you."

If everyone had taken a step back when they'd seen Lindon crush the other guy's ribs, they *fled* at the mention of Mercy's family name. Even the other gray-skinned members of the Kotai clan abandoned their fallen cousin, scrambling to get away.

There were two types of people who stayed: the ones who looked as confused as Lindon felt, and the ones who were bowing too deeply to run. Not everyone had heard of the Akura name, it seemed. But all of the students from major clans had: none of the Jai, Naru, or Kotai remained.

Except for Kotai Taien. His gray face went ashen, and he planted his forehead on the ground. "Forgive me my disrespect," he said. "I am not worthy of your help."

Mercy pushed herself to her feet and swayed for a second as though unused to her own legs. She leaned on her staff for balance, and the dragon's head at the top shone with purple light. Its eyes were glowing purple pinpricks, and Lindon thought he heard it snarl.

"No atoning necessary," Mercy said with a smile. "Just don't bow to me anymore, how about that?"

Taien jumped up as though the ground had become red-hot, and vanished into the crowd just as quickly.

Mercy looked after him for a while, then sighed, and walked into the distance idly twirling her staff.

"...what just happened?" Lindon asked Orthos.

No response. Lindon looked to the turtle on his left.

Orthos had withdrawn his head and all his limbs into his shell. His core seemed small and quiet, though that could have been because of the veil over his spirit. After a moment, his voice echoed from within the shell. "Is she gone?"

"She didn't seem so bad to me," Lindon said, watching Mercy's ponytail vanish into the crowd. Every few steps, she tripped over her own feet and had to catch herself on her staff.

Orthos peeked out of his shell, confirming that she really was gone, before he finally emerged. "If she's really a descendant of the Akura clan, we're lucky she was in a good mood. Her family owns three-quarters of the continent."

"Not the Empire?"

"The Blackflame Empire is one of their territories," Orthos said, still staring at where Mercy had vanished. "And not their most valuable. She might receive the Empire as a coming-of-age present."

"Then why doesn't the Emperor come from the Akura clan?"

Orthos snorted smoke. "The Emperor runs the Empire. They *own* it. They don't put one of their own on the throne because they don't have to. Naru Huan knows enough to do whatever they want him to."

Lindon rested a hand on the turtle's head. Though Orthos would never acknowledge it, Lindon knew he found it comforting. "She must be impressive, to get a dragon to back down."

"Even dragons," Orthos said, "know when to bow."

***

Eithan stared up at the fortress of death and wondered how he had gotten in so far over his head.

The heart of Akura clan territory was clearly designed to intimidate anyone who laid eyes on it. The wall—which rose high over his head and stretched for miles beyond sight—was made of absolutely black Forged madra and topped with man-sized sword blades. He was fairly certain that the material of the walls had at least some aspect of death madra to it, from the icy cold dread that pressed against his senses and the cold howls that he heard from deep within.

And that was just the outer wall. The Emperor had a gatekey

that had transported Eithan over ten thousand miles straight to the entrance, but even such a key couldn't get him in the door. The Akura family Matriarch must have created the gatekey herself, or one of her close disciples, because no one in the Blackflame Empire had such control of space.

The guards were even more intimidating than the wall they guarded. The two Remnants were the dark green of murky swamp-water, and they looked like dried lizard-corpses. Only they were fifteen feet tall, and each of them carried a halberd that blazed with black-and-violet flame. A different breed of dragon's fire than Blackflame, but just as deadly.

They each rested on piles of bleached human bones that were undoubtedly there for effect.

...not that they were a deception. They had just chosen to leave the bones of those the guards killed as a declaration to future visitors.

Remnants they may have been, but they looked down on Eithan with cold intelligence. They had been left by Lords on the same Path and slowly cultivated by the Akura clan until they could match Heralds for power. The signs were there, if you knew what to look for.

It was enough to make Eithan painfully aware of his status as an Underlord. Or rather, his lack of status. If the guards were to blast him to vapor, word would never reach the Blackflame Empire. Even if it did, the Emperor would be the one to apologize.

Even in mortal danger, Eithan had never been one to give in to intimidation. He smiled brightly, pulling the gatekey from his pocket and holding it forth. It was made of purple-tinted black crystal, and it pulsed like a heart in his hand.

"I represent Naru Huan, Emperor of the Blackflame Empire," he declared. "I seek an audience with the highest-ranking member of the Akura clan available to me."

He certainly couldn't request a meeting with their clan leader directly. Disrespecting a Monarch by implying that he was worthy of her time would kill him on the spot, and might even spread to the rest of the Arelius family.

The Remnants inspected him with unreadable reptilian gazes. Even his bloodline powers were of no use to him here, as the spirits gave no physical clues for what they were feeling.

However intelligent and advanced they were, they were still Remnants. They would act according to their nature unless given reason to do otherwise, and these had clearly been given guard duty. One sent out a spiritual pulse—the heft of which felt like it would push Eithan to the ground—in an obvious signal.

Eithan waited. Somewhere behind the wall, the fortress itself spewed fire into the air.

He hoped they wouldn't ask him to go inside. It would severely derail his plans if he was captured in an Akura holding cell for a hundred years.

Finally, a center section of the wall dissolved into a black puddle. An old man with a long, wispy beard and purple eyes strode out of the gap, hands crossed in front of him. Those hands looked as though they'd been dipped in tar up to the elbow: the Goldsign from the Path of the Chainkeeper. He would be a blood descendant, then, as though the purple eyes weren't enough of a clue.

He walked out with stately dignity, but he did not carry himself with arrogance. His black-and-white robes were simple, and he met

Eithan's eyes with a placid gaze. Eithan liked him already; a different member of the Akura clan might have made him bow and scrape for an hour before deigning to hear a word.

Eithan did not scan him directly, as that would have been an appalling breach of manners, but he did gingerly reach out his spiritual perception to get a sense of the man's advancement. As he suspected, he couldn't tell. The man might as well not have been a sacred artist at all.

That meant he was *at least* an Underlord skilled in veils. Most likely, he was far above that stage.

Eithan bowed deeply, pressing his fists together. "As an unworthy servant of the Blackflame Empire, I greet the representative of the honored Akura clan."

The old man dipped his head in acknowledgement. "I am Akura Justice. The clan welcomes you, Eithan Arelius."

Eithan was not at all surprised that the Akura clan knew his name, but he was somewhat surprised that Justice had chosen to use it. "I am honored that you have taken such notice of me," he said, without straightening from his bow.

"Our Matriarch, eternal and all-knowing, employs the greatest dream artists in the world," Justice said calmly. "They have seen you. It seems there has been a great shift in fate recently. The currents of destiny change rapidly these days, and the dream-readers have seen you in their flowing currents."

Eithan began to sweat. Though their talents all varied, the legendary Monarchs could see far. Depending on what they decided about his destiny, he could be killed here. Or worse.

"*She* has left words for you," Justice said, and his voice was awed.

He must have been a descendant of his clan's Matriarch, so he was talking about his own mother, grandmother, or great-grandmother, but his tone suggested he was referring to a divinity made flesh. "In other circumstances, we would have a feast for anyone so honored, but time runs short."

Eithan fell to his knees, pressing his head to the ground three times in the direction of the fortress. He resisted the urge to grimace while facing downward—Justice might not have been able to see it, but a Monarch would. If she were watching.

Better to play it safe.

"I am not worthy," Eithan said. And then, far more sincerely, "I will engrave the Monarch's words onto my heart."

That, at least, was true. Whatever she had gleaned from the future, it would be invaluable to him.

"The following words are not mine, but the Monarch's." Justice drew himself up, words rising in a proclamation. "Once, and once alone, will I defend your empire from the fiend that rises against it. Soon, I will have greater concerns...so you must raise protectors of your own. They will defend us all from the great calamity that follows. I await your success, Underlord."

"She left those words for me?" Eithan asked, raising his head.

"For you, by name. She has seen your plans, and knows that you have a chance of success."

Eithan tried not to shiver. A Monarch's help could make everything infinitely easier...but no one at that stage was selfless. She might take over, and there would be nothing Eithan could do to stop her.

However, any information about his fate was invaluable. "I cannot express my gratitude in words. If the time does come where I may defend the Akura clan's territory, I will do so." He was careful not to admit debt. His soul might hold him to such words, especially when he was dealing with a Monarch.

Justice nodded, gesturing for Eithan to rise. He did so, trying to ignore the mudstains on his outer robe.

"I do not wish to overstep my station," Eithan said, turning up the charm in his smile. "But are there any instructions I should pass to my Emperor?"

Justice ran a black-gloved hand down his beard. "We have made our will known to your Empire regarding our fallen daughter, and they have interpreted our instructions in an acceptable manner. It is important only that the daughter is pushed to the brink. Whether she learns to fly or falls to her death, the imperial clan will be rewarded."

Eithan was doubly glad that he had researched the Akura clan's "fallen daughter" before coming here. Otherwise, he would have been completely in the dark, and there was little he hated more than ignorance.

He bowed once more, extending his gatekey in both hands. "I regret the inconvenience, but if I could beg you for one further favor..."

Justice smiled in a grandfatherly way and extended one finger to touch the crystal key. "Good-bye, Underlord. Until we meet again."

Eithan vanished.

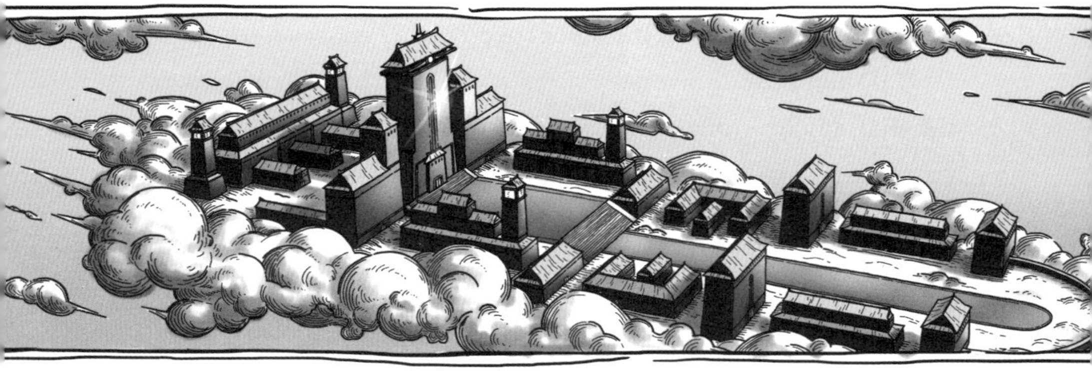

XV

The "application process" was a race.

It was more of an obstacle course, Lindon had heard, similar to the dummy courses Eithan had used to train him. The course was so wide that it took up three-quarters of the fairground, broad enough that all five hundred and fifty-two Lowgold participants could line up shoulder-to-shoulder to begin.

The course itself was shrouded in an orange cloud meant to obscure the obstacles. He supposed they wanted applicants thinking on their feet, and he'd caught a few snatches of conversation as people speculated on what could be inside.

Although very few of the Lowgolds were actually *on* their feet at all. They rode sacred horses, or stood on flying swords, or spread their wings, or were carried in elaborate cages by constructs. He spotted Mercy, who had straddled her staff as though she were riding a horse, leaning forward and bracing herself on the weapon with both hands. It hovered a few feet over the ground, though she wobbled so much he wondered if she would fall off. The dragon's head at the end of the staff snarled, violet lights shining where eyes should be, as though it were eager to proceed.

He glanced over at the Highgold course, which was much smaller and swallowed by a white cloud. There were only fifty participants there, and fewer of them were mounted, as though they trusted more in their own speed. He couldn't see Yerin, though he did notice sunlight glinting on steel and wondered if he'd spotted her Goldsign.

"Everyone else is riding," Lindon muttered softly. "I won't be able to catch up to them on foot."

Orthos' eyes blazed. "Of course. Climb on my shell, and we will destroy any obstacles in our way."

Lindon didn't want to question his good fortune, but he was shocked at how quickly the turtle had agreed. "Gratitude, Orthos."

"You sound surprised."

"I only thought you might consider carrying me to be, ah... demeaning? Not that *I* think it is, of course, only that you might see it that way."

Orthos looked at him as though looking at a particularly simpleminded child. "When a horse carries a man, which of them is the stronger party? It is only suitable that a dragon should carry lesser creatures."

Lindon couldn't argue with that.

His shell was hot, spiky, and uncomfortable. Lindon had to cycle and push back against the Blackflame madra rising from Orthos in order to stop from burning a hole in the seat of his pants. Every step the turtle took as he shuffled around at the starting line jostled Lindon so badly that his badge bounced on his chest. It was so uncomfortable as to be almost painful, but before he could get down and take his chances with the Burning Cloak, a Skysworn rose above the crowd.

Lindon had never seen her before, but she had a single horn rising from the top of her head and she floated on an emerald Thousand-Mile Cloud. Her armor gleamed, pristine, as she raised one hand.

"You are the greatest of all those who desire to serve in the Skysworn," she announced, voice thundering. "The first among you will have the honor of keeping the peace in the name of the Emperor. Fight hard, and let nothing stand in your way."

Lindon looked to his fellow competitors, who had either formed into groups or were casting suspicious glances at the others. They had picked up on the same thing he had: nothing prevented them from fighting each other inside the cloud. It was a pure competition, and the judges cared only about who emerged from the other end.

What did it say about the Skysworn, that they taught their next generation of protectors to compete with one another first and foremost?

The judge high in the sky raised her palm, and a crackling field of yellow and blue formed in her hand. "Prepare yourselves!" she declared. Lindon leaned forward, gripping the edge of Orthos' shell.

The field exploded with a crack, and they were off.

The orange cloud swallowed him in a second as Orthos dashed forward with blurring speed. It felt warm on his face instead of cool, as he would have expected.

On the other side, the first thing he saw was a ball of shining chrome headed straight for his head.

He ignited his Burning Cloak, striking the ball away with an explosive punch. The ball hurtled into the orange distance, and Lindon got a better look at this obstacle.

It was a broad field of flying, whirling metal balls. There must have been thousands of them, all circling in seemingly random patterns. It didn't look like they were targeting competitors, but the air was so thick with them that the mass of Lowgolds crashed into them like a wall.

They were fighting through, but with only a few exceptions, they were forced to slow themselves and proceed slowly and carefully. He could see Mercy among those who were hurtling through, her ponytail streaming behind her. She was still wobbling as though her staff would fall to the ground at any second, but she always adjusted her balance, narrowly avoiding a chrome ball each time. It looked like chance, but she hadn't slowed at all.

And neither had Orthos.

Perhaps because he was used to the protection his shell offered, he didn't seem to see any threat in hurtling spheres of metal. He galloped through the cloud in a straight line.

Lindon screamed for him to slow down, clinging to the shell. His knuckles ached where he had punched the first chrome ball, so he switched hands, grabbing on with his flesh hand and using his skeletal Remnant arm to defend himself.

His new hand was only a day old, and it still wouldn't do as he commanded.

...fortunately, it seemed only too eager to help. It hauled him closer, catching the metal balls in its palm without Lindon's direction. It seemed to draw something out of the spheres, because they dropped to the ground, lifeless, after it caught them. It must have been a property of the madra, because the binding in the arm didn't activate.

That was the good news.

There was a dark side, though. The arm focused on one ball at a time, preferring to feed than to protect him. One steel ball smashed into his ribs, another crushed his elbow between it and Orthos' shell, and still a third slammed into the heel of his foot.

As the pain took his breath away and his Bloodforged Iron body siphoned madra to deal with the injuries, he reflected that the pain in his ribs might be divine justice for Kotai Taien.

They were through the field of balls almost too quickly, and he gasped in relief, holding onto the shell with both hands. He was clinging desperately to Orthos, plastered belly-down on the smoldering shell. He was most focused on staying stable and conscious, but keeping his clothes from burning off was a strong secondary concern.

The second obstacle was a brick wall.

Orthos still didn't slow down. Lindon barely had enough time to form dragon's breath and burn his way through; he almost lost control of the technique, without a second hand to contribute. He finally managed it, sending out a liquid-looking bar of Blackflame madra that sliced through the bricks as though they were made of butter...

Carving a line straight down. He might have been able to edge his way through, if he didn't mind red-hot bricks pressing against him, but there was no way he would squeeze through riding on Orthos.

He drew madra together desperately, though he knew there was no time for the technique before they hit.

Then Orthos opened his mouth and blasted a hole in the center of the wall.

They went through with no more damage than a smoldering patch on the back of Lindon's outer robe. He could feel it burning, but he couldn't spare any attention to put it out.

So far, he understood the reasoning behind the obstacles. The flying balls tested your awareness and reaction time. The brick wall tested your raw power—it was already re-forming behind Lindon, so the only way to pass through was to tear a hole in it.

The third obstacle was a cloud of wasps.

He almost cried. *What does this have to do with enforcing the law?*

Devoutly, he swore to himself that he wouldn't go through any more trials without learning more about them ahead of time. He could have cheated his way through here without a problem.

Riding Orthos was something like cheating...though far, far less comfortable.

The wasps began stinging him, and he both thanked and cursed Eithan for his Bloodforged Iron body. There was nothing it handled better than poison, but without its help, he would have passed out.

There were four more obstacles after that.

○

Yerin could have passed the Highgold application in her sleep. The Blackflame Trials had pushed her harder than this, and her training with Cassias and Eithan even harder. She had passed through in first place, earning astonished looks and not a few people trying to snatch her up for their organizations.

She ignored them all, strolling over to the end of the Lowgold course. If she had passed the Highgold so easily, Lindon should have blown through the application like a spring breeze. He loved having time to plan for things like this, but it wasn't as though he really needed it. Not in her estimation, anyway. Planning for a fight was important, but he used a plan more like a crutch. That was how the weak did things.

The Lowgold course was longer than hers had been, so Yerin arrived in time to see the first person emerge from the orange cloud. To her surprise, it wasn't Lindon.

A girl on a flying...broomstick?...blasted out, tumbling onto the grass at the end. She flipped heels-over-head, rolling to a halt and looking around in a daze. Her hair had been tangled from the fall, her ponytail had dead grass in it, and her purple eyes were hazy.

She sat up, looking around, and saw no one. Then she put her hands up in victory—they were gloved in black—and collapsed onto her back, breathing hard.

Yerin gave her a quiet scan, sneaking a glimpse at her soul. Her madra was rock-stable for a Lowgold, deep and quiet as a winter pond. Yerin couldn't figure why she hadn't advanced to Highgold yet. With power that solid, she should have been able to do it in a snap.

The girl seemed to notice something, glancing around until she saw Yerin. Yerin didn't look away—if she had been caught, she'd been caught. No use playing around about it.

Rather than looking offended, the girl gave a cheery wave and let her head fall back down against the ground.

An instant later, a new batch of students came through the clouds. The first flew on green wings, though one of them was broken and his eye was swollen shut. The next was covered in a cloak from head-to-toe, and flew on a jet of streaming blue sparks.

The third was Orthos.

She was surprised they'd let Lindon take him. Sure, contracted beasts were normally considered like a weapon or construct, but they didn't normally have a two-stage difference from their contractors. Sacred beasts didn't advance like sacred artists did, but Orthos still had power on the level of a Truegold.

Which surprised her even more, because he had only come in fourth.

He trotted out, not seeming to hurry, carrying something in his mouth. It took her a breath or two to see it was Lindon, limp and covered in blood. There were slices in his outer robe, pieces of it were on fire, and his face was covered in lumps like bug bites.

But he groaned and moved in Orthos' mouth, so she reasoned he was fine.

She walked up to the turtle as the remaining members of the successful fifty made it through. "What rolled him over?" she asked.

Orthos spat him onto the ground, where Lindon groaned upon landing.

"He needs a shell," Orthos said.

Three days after the qualification, there was a ceremony to welcome the new generation of Skysworn trainees. In consideration of the red light that was swallowing more and more of the horizon each day, the usual feast and celebration were cut short.

Each inductee was handed a green pin marked with a cloud, which would identify them until they graduated their training and received the Skysworn armor. They were then given a brief, personal greeting by the Skysworn Underlord. He had made himself presentable for the occasion, so his hair was washed and clipped back, baring the scar high on his left cheek. He was even out of his armor, wearing instead a crisp layered outfit that had the look of a uniform.

For Lindon and Yerin, he practically threw their pin at them and gave them no greeting, but Lindon didn't mind. He was eager to minimize any future contact with the Underlord; that seemed to be the best way to live a long and healthy life.

Finally, when all sixty trainees had been given their pins, they sat down for instruction. Twenty full Skysworn, Truegolds all, lined the walls of the room, looking in at the student tables.

They stood in pairs, which Lindon took to be partners when he saw Renfei and Bai Rou among them.

The Highgold table and the Lowgold tables were separate, with five Lowgolds for every Highgold. More than one of the students at Lindon's table sent jealous glances at the higher table. Some of the more advanced trainees gave smug looks back.

Yerin looked as though she were falling asleep. Her bladed arms sprawled, threatening the people seated on either side of her.

Naru Gwei stepped between the tables, looking as though he

would rather be anywhere else. Lindon's white arm struggled to escape from the table, but he wrestled it back down. Orthos, seated next to Lindon, fought to stay quiet and still. Lindon could feel the effort in the turtle's soul and in the thickening pillar of smoke that rose from his shell.

"You'll be separated into teams," the Captain said at last, nodding to the full Skysworn around the walls. "Every pair of Skysworn gets five Lowgolds and one Highgold. Normally we'd get you started by finding lost pets or delivering messages, something suited for your level of advancement. We don't have the luxury of that this time."

It was so quiet that Orthos' breath sounded like a bellows. None of the trainees seemed willing to make a sound.

Their system was easy to understand: sixty trainees, and ten pairs of Skysworn mentors. Six to a team.

But what about Renfei and Bai Rou? They stood apart from the line, and with them, that would be twelve teams of five each. But he had clearly said they would be six-man teams. Were they expecting extra students?

"We always choose the better fighters among the young. We have to, because the bigger your weapon, the less you have to draw it. We've got the biggest hammer in the Empire, and everyone knows it."

A halfhearted cheer rose from the Highgold table, but Naru Gwei ignored it, so it died quickly.

"If we were at peace, I'd have higher standards for your training. I'd want you to be familiar with imperial policy, and the names of all the political players." He waved that aside. "It's a luxury. We're in a crisis, so we're cutting everything down to the bone. We only need one thing from you: to fight. When and where we tell you. The Empire's scurrying like a kicked anthill, and there are always snakes and rats who want to take advantage of that while we're looking away. We'll need to defend the Empire from those traitors...and from the real enemy to the south."

He pulled a long straw out of his chest pocket and started chewing on it. "We're baptizing you in fire. There's plenty of fight to go around. We'll be taking you from battle to battle, and in between, you're expected to spend every second pushing for your next advancement. The Empire has no time for you to waste.

"At the end, if we all make it, I'll be looking over all the reports from your mentors. Those of you who follow orders and distinguish yourselves...well, I look forward to calling you Skysworn."

He nodded sharply to one of the green-armored Truegolds in the back and then walked away, hands tucked into his outer robe.

The speech actually encouraged Lindon. Going from fight to fight, with nothing but a stop to train in between, was essentially what Eithan had for him every day. If the Skysworn would be pushing him to advance faster, that was all he could wish for.

Though it wasn't as though he was eager to rush into battle with Redmoon Hall. At least Yerin would be happy.

The first pair of Skysworn read out a series of names, calling up five Lowgolds and a Highgold. The team of eight filed out, leaving all the young sacred artists in the room excitedly waiting their turn.

That included Lindon. He wondered if they would pair him with Yerin, given their history of working together, or if they separated those who came from the same sect or family.

As the selection process continued, he noticed two things. First, most of the sacred artists in the room were from the three major clans. Kotai and Naru were the most common names, followed in a distant third by Jai.

Second, the math didn't add up.

There were twenty full Skysworn in the room: ten pairs. They were selecting from a pool of ten Highgolds and fifty Lowgolds, so there should be five Lowgolds, one Highgold, and two Truegolds to each team.

But one team took only four Lowgolds. A few picks later, another team skipped a Lowgold. Toward the end, an irritated-looking pair turned down a Highgold.

With three teams left to pick, there were fifteen trainees remaining. Including Lindon and Yerin.

From the way Yerin was glaring, she'd picked up on it too.

Renfei and Bai Rou were the pair at the end, so it was possible they'd been left in order to join the team of Skysworn they knew. But neither of them had made eye contact with Lindon through the whole process, so they weren't doing anything to help Lindon's unease.

When it came their turn to pick, Lindon knew something was wrong. There were only three trainees left: Yerin alone at the Highgold table, and he at the Lowgold table together with Akura Mercy.

Mercy sighed with a resigned look on her face, as though she'd expected this, and pushed her way up with her staff before Renfei had even said a word. It wasn't as though anyone had to hear their picks anyway.

Renfei and Bai Rou were selecting students after all: the dregs. They had been left with a team half the size of the others.

"Something's crooked here," Yerin said. She didn't bother to keep her voice quiet.

"You think so?" Naru Gwei asked. He shrugged. "Quit."

With that, he turned and walked out of the room.

The cloud over Renfei's head seemed especially dark today, as she looked over the three of them. She seemed paler than usual, with shadows under her eyes.

"You're not stupid," she said to them, when the Underlord had left. The other teams had filed out when they were chosen, leaving the room empty but for the five of them. "They've singled you out."

"What for?" Yerin asked, glaring.

Renfei looked from Lindon to Mercy and back to Yerin. "I don't think I need to answer that."

Mercy swung her staff up onto her shoulder and walked up to Yerin, though she tripped over nothing and almost fell on her face. When she righted herself, she smiled. "Akura Mercy," she said. "But my clan doesn't *entirely* approve of my being here." She tapped her chin with a black-clad finger. "I'd guess they either let it be known that they wouldn't avenge anything that happened to me, or offered a reward for placing me in mortal danger."

Renfei remained stony-faced, giving nothing away, but Bai Rou glanced to the door before nodding once.

"There are more than a few people who would take any opportunity to settle things with an Akura who can't fight back," Mercy said with a sigh. She pointed to Lindon. "Then we have a Blackflame, who the Skysworn don't like very much, and..." She hesitated when she reached Yerin. "Wait! I don't know your names!"

"Wei Shi Lindon of the Arelius family," Bai Rou said, before Lindon could speak up. "And Yerin. Emissary of Redmoon Hall."

He gave her a yellow glare, and Lindon's spirit screamed with the sudden tension in the air. Orthos was on his feet and cycling Blackflame, and Yerin was ready to draw her sword. Her face had paled during her introduction, and her Goldsigns blazed with silver light.

Lindon stepped forward, holding one arm out. The other couldn't be bothered. "Wait! Wait a second, I think there's a misunderstanding here that we can resolve!"

"I'll cut your Truegold tongue out," Yerin said, which didn't help his efforts.

Mercy was looking curiously at Lindon. "Wei clan?" she asked. "Not the Blackflame family? You must have an interesting story."

She didn't seem to see the fight brewing behind her, though the dragon's head on her staff hissed.

"This isn't an execution squad," Renfei said. Her voice was calm, but she kept one hand on her hammer. "Not unless you make that necessary. We are here to keep you under control, and to squeeze as much use out of you as we can."

Why tell us? Lindon wondered. *Why not put two more trainees in our squad, and pretend everything was normal, then abandon us on a mission?*

He realized the answer almost immediately: because they didn't need to lie. Part of it could be due to a sense of honor on the part of the Skysworn, but for the most part, the three students were no threat. If they left, they would be deserting their duty and would be hunted down. If they fought, they would lose. They were battling two Truegold Skysworn inside the heart of Skysworn power; reinforcements would arrive almost immediately. And even if they succeeded, they would be executed.

And then there was Mercy. Her family had disavowed her, or exiled her, or whatever they wanted to call it, but clearly the Skysworn couldn't kill her flat-out. Yerin and Lindon, too, were backed by the Arelius family. Anything the Skysworn did to them had to at least appear legitimate.

Lindon held his hand out steadily. "Correct me if I'm wrong," he said, "but we *will* be given a chance to do our jobs, won't we?"

Bai Rou's yellow eyes blazed, still fixed on Yerin. "We won't put you anywhere you can hurt the Empire," he said. He must have taken Yerin's Blood Shadow personally. Maybe it hurt worse because he hadn't spotted it himself; the Underlord must have told him, or he would have reacted this way the very first time he met Yerin.

Renfei answered him directly. "Yes. We are only to supervise you. So long as you follow our instructions and contribute to our cause, we have been instructed to treat you as any other trainees."

"Until we give you a shot at our backs," Yerin countered, still holding her sword in both hands.

"Until you betray us," Renfei corrected. "We will not give you the safety net we give to the other students. One instance of insubordination, one refusal to fight, and there will be no disciplinary action. We are authorized to execute you on the spot."

They had to be holding something back. Lindon was sure of it. With only the strength of two Truegolds, they couldn't be sure of removing Lindon's group quietly. Orthos alone could match one of them, which left the other three to deal with a single opponent. It wouldn't be easy, but it wasn't a sure victory for the Skysworn.

Which meant they had a reason for their confidence. Either that armor did more for them than Lindon expected, or they had some weapons in reserve.

So fighting wasn't an option, but they had time. And the Skysworn needed something from them.

That meant there was a way to win.

He was exhausted, and wished he could sleep as long as he wanted without worrying about another life-threatening battle popping up.

But there was a small part of him that was focused and excited. They hadn't killed him from behind, so this was a puzzle with a solution.

He moved over to Yerin, ready to calm her down.

Then the light turned red, and the world was cast into chaos.

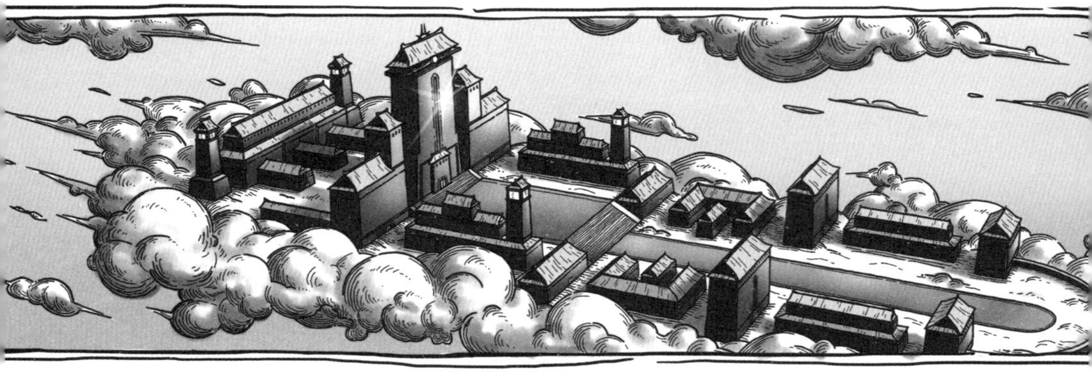

XVI

Cassias walked through the barn, waving to the workers. His team of cleaners was preparing it, shoveling manure and dirty hay, sweeping cobwebs, and building temporary pens for the livestock. The Arelius employees would be staying here, for the time being, unless and until they could reclaim their former territory.

Their homes had been ravaged by bloodspawn.

Cassias passed families where only one parent wore the dark blue outer robe of the Arelius, but the others worked just as hard. He was squeezing forty-two people into this barn, and he might have to find room for even more before this was done. Considering that virtually all of their branches in the south had been closed by the advance of Redmoon Hall and the rise of the Bleeding Phoenix, he was dealing with as many as fifty thousand people either evacuated or displaced. And those were only the ones attached to the Arelius family. The Empire as a whole was in a crisis even if the Phoenix never rose.

He moved out of the back of the barn and looked to the south, where blood-colored light hovered like a permanent sunset.

It had grown. When he had left Stormrock, only a few days ago, the light wasn't visible from this far away. In the worst-case scenario, he might have to pack everyone up *again*, and find room for them even farther north. He didn't have a way to transport so many people so far, unless Stormrock agreed to help, and he suspected they would be packed to capacity as well.

Well, that wasn't the *worst* scenario. The Dreadgod might decide to go on a rampage and kill them all, without a Monarch to turn it aside into the eastern wasteland or the uninhabited sea to the west.

If it marched straight north, killing everything in its path and spreading bloodspawn, no evacuation would matter.

He reached the back of the barn and stood beneath a particular tree.

"We don't have to meet in secret, Eithan," he said without looking up. "These are your employees."

Eithan sat with legs dangling over the edge of a branch, staring south. "You don't think this is more exciting? Besides, I don't want to deal with greetings and farewells and all the ceremony."

"You never do," Cassias said, stretching his shoulder. Despite the attentions of the Skysworn, his wounds were still sore, especially when he moved around for too long. "Have you come to help with the evacuation?"

Eithan laughed as though Cassias had made a joke. "I actually received some new information that deserves prompt action. Suffice it to say that this will not be the only disaster of this scale in the coming years. We may be heading for interesting times ahead, little brother!"

"I'm not your brother," Cassias said, his mind racing. First of all, he had to know if Eithan had gotten this information from a reliable source, or if he was relying on his own guesses. Knowing that a disaster was coming could make all the difference.

He said as much, and Eithan nodded along.

"A wise question," Eithan responded. "I cannot reveal my source, but it is...worthy of trust."

"Then we need to suspend normal operations immediately. We should pull back to our strongholds, prepare for sieges... can you convince the Empire that we're in danger, or should we accept censure?"

"*Instead* of that, we're going to send teams south and west."

Cassias looked up to stare at his Underlord, horrified and disbelieving all at once. The South was a slaughterhouse, and the West was the home of the crumbling Jai clan. "You want me to send families to die."

"Not if you do it right," Eithan responded lightly. "I'm not asking our clansmen to throw their lives away, but these are the places where we are needed. We're equipped to help rescue and repair efforts, as well as to gain information. On Redmoon Hall, the Bleeding Phoenix, and the western labyrinth. That information will soon be very valuable, as will the allies our assistance will earn us."

"It's not worth the risk." Cassias gestured behind him, to the barn that was halfway through its transformation into a shelter. "We'll have enough trouble keeping these people alive if we're *not* walking straight into the Phoenix's nest. You can't ask them to—"

Eithan dropped to the ground, landing as though he weighed nothing. "I am not *asking* them to do anything. Put the best face on it, and certainly don't feed anyone to the Dreadgod, but I am commanding them to take a riskier path for greater reward to the family." He clapped Cassias on the shoulder. "Make it so, Cassias."

Cassias' heart boiled. Personally, he was still grateful to Eithan. But as the one-time heir to the Arelius family, he itched at the Underlord's attitude. He would always do things according to his own whims, and would never listen to anyone else.

Now, it fell to Cassias to tell these people that they had to leave their families and head back into danger.

After Eithan left Cassias to his simmering thoughts, Naru Jing returned. She was carrying their three-year-old son in one arm and a basket of firewood in the other, eyeing the sky.

One of her eyes and one of her wings had been replaced with glowing orange Remnant prosthetics, which meant one of her wings could no longer be fully retracted. It stuck out over her left shoulder, folded up.

Both her soft brown eye and her bright false one scanned the sky. "Was Eithan here?" she asked curiously.

Cassias dropped to the ground, leaning his back against the tree, and told her everything that had happened.

When he'd finished, she'd set the firewood down and was examining him with a steady gaze. "I owe Underlord Eithan the same debt you do," she said at last, "but we can't let gratitude overshadow our duty to the family."

Cassias nodded along. He'd let Eithan overwhelm him, causing him to forget his other options. Although...did he really have any?

"You have to take this to your father," Jing said, spelling out what he already knew.

Sighing, he nodded. The elders of the Arelius family could rein in the Patriarch, if they wanted to.

But would they oppose him after he'd brought down the Jai clan, leaving an opening among the great clans that the Arelius could fill? They might, considering that Lindon had lost his duel to Jai Long, which had cost the family some reputation for no reason.

Cassias knew his father, though. The former Patriarch of the Arelius family had never approved of all the time and resources Eithan spent on his own whims.

Though he felt like he was betraying Eithan, he had to ask his father's approval. For the family's sake, it was the right thing to do.

A screech cut off his thoughts. Glass shattered next to him, but he didn't hear it. Instead, he stumbled over to his son, clapping his hands over the boy's ears. Jing had already woven a barrier of wind around them to cut out the deadly sound.

A crimson light shone from behind him, and he didn't need the horrified look on his wife's face to understand what had happened. He already knew.

The floor tilted and Lindon scrambled to grab onto one of the bolted-down tables as Stormrock accelerated as quickly as possible.

The whole city shook, the table in Lindon's arms shaking as though in an earthquake.

All from the force of a scream that was *more* than a scream, as though the sound had been given life. It was layered, like a thousand birds shrieking at once, so loudly that he felt a sharp pain in both ears.

A moment later, warm liquid trickled down both sides of his face. His Iron body drew madra to his ears, but there was a moment of blissful silence where he couldn't hear...he could only hear the cry in the rest of his body.

He didn't even dare to listen to his spirit, which trembled under a force much greater than the sound.

The Bleeding Phoenix had awakened.

The stench of blood filled the red-tinged air. His heart beat more heavily than usual, as though it were hammering on his ribs, and his veins seemed to boil. He opened his Copper sight—not south, lest he blind himself, but at the room around him—and everything was tinged red. Even the pale green of the wind was tinged with wet red.

Mercy was sitting on the ground, both of her palms stuck to the floor as though nailed there. She squinted south, staring into the bright red light. Her ears had been stoppered up with the same black goo that seemed to coat her hands and staff; her madra, Lindon guessed. Renfei stood on dark platforms of solid cloud that she had generated with her madra, face horrified, and Bai Rou was clinging to his emerald Thousand-Mile Cloud like a drowning man clinging to driftwood. Blood ran from their ears as well. Orthos had let himself fall, slamming the side of his shell into the far wall. His sanity had fled before the Dreadgod, his madra raging up, and it was taking all his self-control to keep from breathing fire in the general direction of the Bleeding Phoenix.

However badly off the rest of them were, whatever changes the Phoenix's aura was making in their bodies, Yerin was worse.

She lay on the floor, collapsed on her back. The only things keeping her from sliding down the slope were her silver blade-arms, which had been driven into the stone. She shook even worse than the ground around her, her back arching and her eyes rolling up into her head.

Blood spilled from her stomach.

Despite his total lack of any medical ability, Lindon looked for a way to slide over to her before she bled out. At least he could keep pressure on the wound, even if his pack—which he'd kept in the back of the room during the ceremony—had slid to the opposite wall. Little Blue's case must have cracked in the impact, but he couldn't worry about that now. There were bandages in there.

It was only at that point that he realized it wasn't blood. It was a Blood Shadow.

Sparks of gray soulfire hissed from the broken seal over her core. The Shadow reached tendrils out, sliding over her body, questing about, looking for something.

Bai Rou let out a roar when he saw her. Lindon's ears had just healed enough to hear. The Skysworn struggled onto his cloud, kneeling on it and flying over to Yerin.

With one hand, he scooped her up. The Blood Shadow latched onto his arm, but a sheath of liquid yellow madra protected him.

With the other hand, he sprayed a geyser of his madra at the window.

The glass dissolved as though eaten away by acid, and he soared free, dragging Yerin along with him.

For a long, frozen second, Lindon panicked.

Where was he taking her? What was he doing? The Dreadgod's scream had quieted, but Stormrock was still rushing away. Why was Bai Rou flying around?

One thing was clear: he'd taken Yerin. And Lindon had to follow.

He released the table, letting himself slide down the slanted room. He bent his knees as he hit the far wall, his legs Enforced by pure madra, landing between Orthos and his pack.

His right arm betrayed him then, grasping at the air to the south, so he had to open his pack with one hand.

"Orthos," he said, as he dug through his belongings. "I don't know if you can hear me right now, but I have to go after Yerin. If I'm not back soon...please don't kill anyone."

Nothing in his spirit told him if the turtle heard him or not, but he couldn't spare any further thought. He'd found the scripted box that contained one of his most valuable possessions.

His own Thousand-Mile Cloud.

He slung the pack on his back even as he spilled out the cloud, hopping onto it immediately. Unlike the Skysworn's, his was a rusty red, made a vibrant ruby by the light.

With no more hesitation, he poured his madra into the construct, hurtling out the hole in the window after Bai Rou.

Wind tore past him as he flew out of the building, and it took most of his effort to keep up with the flying city. After one frantic look around didn't reveal a huge, armored man on a green cloud, he reluctantly opened his spirit.

He was drowning in blood.

Life, vibrant and powerful, had been spilled here. The power that anchored his soul to his body was in his blood, and it was overwhelming him, choking him.

Strangely, the overpowering sense of the Dreadgod actually made it easier to sense what he was looking for. There was only one spot of power that was hanging in the air instead of cowering in a building, and Lindon headed straight for it.

It was to the south.

The red light was almost blinding, but within it he could see a shape. A monstrous shape.

It was so large as to defy description, swallowing half the sky and stretching into the clouds. Each of its feathers was an oozing, flowing blob, as though it had been made from clumps of crimson gel pushed together. Its beak was curved like a scythe and razor-sharp, and its eyes were shapeless masses of white-hot power.

The Bleeding Phoenix spread its wings like a wound stretching from one horizon to another. Then it opened its beak and cried again.

Lindon sent madra to his ears to protect them, but it didn't save him. That stabbing pain returned, blood dribbling down his ears.

This time, a pair of bloodspawn formed beneath him in midair.

They hadn't sprouted earlier, inside the building, though he wasn't sure if that was due to some scripted protection on the Skysworn fortress or if the influence of the Dreadgod simply hadn't been strong enough yet.

These bloodspawn—made of liquid, but clear as red glass—clawed at him as they fell, splattering against the street below and re-forming.

Even when he went deaf again, Lindon kept his eyes locked on the distant green speck. It had reached the southern end of the city, the part that was trailing deep emerald clouds and tilted downward.

He closed on them as the other cloud began to slow down.

Then Bai Rou released Yerin.

Her Blood Shadow clawed for him as she fell, but he defended himself with yellow madra. Without waiting to see her fall, he turned and started flying his cloud after the city.

Lindon tore after her.

She was falling through natural clouds now, and he pushed his Thousand-Mile Cloud harder than he ever had before. She was too far below him. He wouldn't make it.

For months, he'd been stretching his core using the Heaven and Earth Purification Wheel. He had more madra in his core than he could possibly use at one time.

He strained his madra channels, shoving as much out as he could, flooding the construct's core with power. He didn't need the cloud to last beyond today. Just now. Just one last time.

She was close now, her tattered robes blowing in the wind, her Blood Shadow flailing. He reached out his right hand, trying to grab a fistful of her robes.

His arm betrayed him.

The Blood Shadow reached for the white madra of his arm, seeking it, and his arm flinched away.

Desperate, he tried to push the Thousand-Mile Cloud even harder, but the cloud was already dissipating beneath him. The script at the core had overloaded and warped, and now he was flooding the cloud madra with his own. It would fall apart any second.

Which was only fitting, because they would hit the ground any second.

A searing pain hit him in the shoulder, and he shouted, though even he couldn't hear it. He had only a moment to see what it was: a black arrowhead, sticking out from the front of him.

Then, from the tip of the arrow, burst a net.

It looked like a spider's web made of tar, blasting out from the arrow and swallowing Yerin. It covered her from neck to hips.

The Blood Shadow wrapped around the net immediately, seeping into it, but it remained intact. Yerin's weight pulled at the arrow impaling his shoulder, and he was tugged downward, but he grabbed onto the black web with his left hand and hauled her aboard the cloud.

As he swooped below the trees, he managed to level off their flight. Only then did he see what they were falling into: a broken village, with barely a single building left intact. The ground was dotted with fresh corpses.

And shambling bloodspawn.

The Thousand-Mile Cloud burst apart when they were only five feet from landing, but he'd managed to slow them enough. Yerin slammed into the grass back-first, and Lindon fell onto his hands.

He caught a glimpse of the glowing mass of Forged madra at the heart of the cloud construct before it dissipated into essence.

His body flooded with relief, though it was likely premature: they were still caught out in the open, surrounded by bloodspawn, still within the Dreadgod's influence. The sheer size of the creature made it hard to estimate, but they might have been over a hundred miles away. It only *felt* like it was looming right over them.

Also, he still had an arrow in his shoulder. He couldn't stand up straight or move away from Yerin, because the weight of her body kept the black string between them taut.

His ears healed again in time for him to hear someone land behind him. He turned with horror, part of him expecting to see Bai Rou, but it was Mercy.

She was standing on her staff, which drifted down to the ground. She stumbled as she landed, but smiled as if she'd done a trick. "Sorry for shooting you," she said. "It was the only shot I could get." Black madra unraveled from her ears as she spoke.

Lindon stared at her. "I don't know how I can repay you. I wasn't going to make it, I..." He shook himself. "I can't believe you followed me at all."

"I'm not the only one," she said, turning and pointing to the north.

A smoldering red-and-black meteor plunged to earth. It was a few miles away, but Lindon knew exactly what it was. Or rather, *who* it was.

He had no idea if Orthos' shell could withstand such an impact, but the turtle would know better than anyone.

Lindon tapped the arrow on his shoulder as some of the blood-spawn oozed closer. "Could you remove this, please? We need to go."

Mercy reached out and touched the arrow, whereupon it melted, along with the web over Yerin. Her Blood Shadow surged up, an excited mass of tendrils seeking food. They leaned toward Lindon's right arm, which flinched back.

Lindon had expected more pain when the arrow vanished, but all discomfort vanished with the arrow. His skin was untouched.

He found that fascinating, but he held back his curiosity about her madra until later.

"He's your contracted beast, isn't he?" Mercy asked. She spun her staff idly in both hands, eyeing the approaching bloodspawn. They were acting sluggish, perhaps blinded by the Phoenix's influence, but all of them focused on the living humans. "It might be better if we let him come to us."

"I'm not certain he can," Lindon said, feeling the rolling rage in Orthos' core. He was heading quickly for Lindon, but there was no telling how long he could hang on. "When I'm not around, he doesn't always stay…himself."

Mercy's eyes grew sad. "If he loses himself, I will help you find him and bring him back. But I'm afraid none of us will make it if we're out in the open when the fight begins."

Lindon tapped his Blackflame core, feeling the warmth in his eyes and in his spirit, the low-level sizzling pain as his body strained to contain the destructive power. It seemed even wilder today, more difficult to control, as though it fed on the blood aura. His Burning Cloak ignited as he faced down the first of the bloodspawn.

"I've fought these before," he said. "We can't let them bog us down, but we can force our way through."

Mercy shot a black web from her fingertips, binding three bloodspawn together, then she drove her staff through one of their heads. The headless creature still grasped at her, and she danced backwards, tying up another.

"I don't mean this fight," she said. She nodded south, and her voice grew heavy. "I mean that one."

Lindon wanted to follow her gaze, but he couldn't bear to look upon the Dreadgod again. It was too bright, and reminded him too much of carnage and slaughter. Although letting it hover over him like a weight about to fall may have been worse.

"What is it going to fight? Us?" Lindon couldn't imagine that being much of a contest.

"Not us," Mercy said. "We should get inside."

Carrying Yerin ended up being the hard part, with Mercy dragging her along in a case of webbing, wrapping up the Blood Shadow whenever it struggled free. Lindon was forced to face most of the Bloodspawn himself, and with every one he killed, he regretted his lack of a weapon.

The bloodspawn burned on contact with his fist, and he could only use Striker techniques every few seconds. He took several cuts and some burns just because of how close he had to get, and came very close to death as one of the creatures had burst into thorns when he got close. Mercy managed to haul him out at the last second.

Fortunately, his Remnant arm was only too happy to devour these bloodspawn.

It seized any of the spirits that came too close, gripping them by the throat as though they were made of flesh. The bloodspawn froze when the white claw took them. They trembled, flashed with power, and eventually dissolved into dark, dried flakes. The arm always glowed brighter when it did so, and the sense of hunger radiating from it grew stronger.

It was taking *something* from the spirits, but he couldn't figure out what. The arm wasn't turning red, and there was no hint of blood madra in his channels. It was either taking something other than madra, or it was processing the power so efficiently that Lindon couldn't sense any waste.

He would question it later. For now, he was simply glad of it. Without its help, he would have been overwhelmed in an instant. He had to get too close to his opponents, and these enemies could burst into suicide attacks. Mercy couldn't always cover him, and his dragon's breath took too long to muster.

Yerin would tell him his training was lacking. He needed a way to deal with a mass of opponents, when he couldn't approach to arm's length. A reliable Striker technique and a weapon would go a long way.

In his opinion, it was preparation he lacked. He needed to stop plunging headfirst into situations where he had no reliable information.

Although, in this case, it wasn't as though he had another choice.

They fought their way to a building that may have been an inn. Its windows were broken out, but Mercy found a door to the cellar. They pushed inside, and she webbed up the edges of the door. Lindon pulled out a knife from his pouch and scratched a quick Remnant-repelling script into the door's wooden surface. He didn't think bloodspawn were exactly Remnants, but they were composed of madra, and that should be similar enough. He hoped.

When they finally came to a stop in the cellar, surrounded by sealed jars and sacks, his breath came so fast that he had almost released his cycling technique. Sweat drenched him, and he heaved in air. Mercy was in the same state, leaning on her staff as though it were the only thing keeping her upright.

At last, Lindon had a moment to check on Yerin.

He didn't need to be a healer to tell she wasn't doing well.

Beneath the layers of black web covering her, she still bucked, limbs thrashing. He slipped a mass of folded-up bandages between her teeth to stop her from biting her tongue, but he wasn't sure that he would be in time.

The Blood Shadow wrapped her like a second robe. He didn't know anything about it, but that couldn't be good.

He pulled Little Blue out of his pack—her container had indeed cracked, but only slightly, and not enough to spill any of the water within. She saw the Blood Shadow and flinched, letting out a piping scream. Then she ran from Yerin, tucking herself back inside his backpack.

He hadn't expected her to help anyway. Her power washed madra channels clean, she didn't expel parasites, otherwise Eithan could have used Little Blue to free Yerin from the Blood Shadow months ago.

Bloodspawn slammed against the door, and the circle flared. It wouldn't hold against them for long. Every time the circle expended power, it would push against the material of the door, until eventually the wood broke and snapped, the circle deforming. Scripts engraved in metal or stone lasted longer, but they weren't appropriate for all aspects of madra. Also, they often took more power to operate.

He switched to his pure core, reluctant to touch the parasite, but he had to try.

Gathering power, he slammed an Empty Palm into Yerin's core. He felt the pure madra penetrate, disrupting the flow of power through Yerin's body. She bucked again, but the Blood Shadow didn't seem to mind.

It wasn't anchored in Yerin's core, but around it. He could feel that now, though the haze of the Bleeding Phoenix still hung in the aura around him.

He couldn't shake it loose. His Sylvan Riverseed couldn't cleanse it.

There was one more thing he could try.

The closer he got, the more the Shadow reached for his arm. His skeletal white hand, which had fed on the bloodspawn, was too frightened of this parasite to get close.

Lindon wished he had a drudge. It could help detect and measure the interactions of madra, so he wouldn't have to rely on feelings and guesswork. Instead, he had to rely on blind experimentation.

There was some relationship between the Blood Shadow and the material of his arm. It almost made sense: the Bleeding Phoenix was awakened by the power hidden in the same labyrinth where he'd found the Ancestor's Spear and the binding of hunger madra.

It seemed as though this piece of the Phoenix's power wanted to feed on his arm, rather than the other way around. But the binding in his arm was supposed to devour madra.

It was possible that he could tear it free.

There were risks. First, he didn't know what the Shadow wanted with his arm. It was possible that he was feeding it exactly what it needed to grow strong enough to consume Yerin completely.

Second, he had used the arm for less than a week. It still wasn't bound to him completely. He couldn't even control its motion all the time, and he was supposed to wait for three to five more weeks before he activated the binding.

Third, there was the danger to him. He didn't want to pull a mass of self-aware blood madra into his core...but at least he had one to spare. It was better than leaving it free to control Yerin.

But that was if it went into his core at all. It wasn't in Yerin's. If it attached itself to his spirit, or embedded itself inside his arm, he wouldn't be any better off than Yerin was. Less so, considering her years of experience.

Another bloodspawn slammed on the door, and the circle flared again. Mercy stood below the door, staff in both hands, ready to protect them.

It was time for Lindon to do his part.

He placed his palm on the bloody surface of the parasite, then triggered the binding.

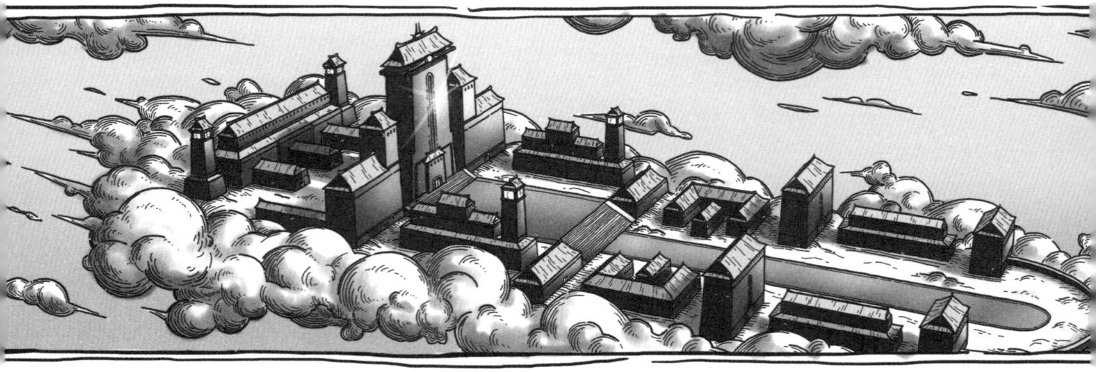

XVII

Deep in a trance, Yerin fought for her soul. And for the lives of the people around her.

She didn't even know where she was. Her body had been moving, she knew, but she couldn't tell where she was or what was happening. She might be all clear to stop struggling. To let go.

That thought whispered to her, and it was too sweet. Too sweet to trust. Out of sheer stubbornness, she clung to her uninvited guest. Ever since she was a little girl, she'd been fighting to keep it from taking over her body. From draining her dry and wearing her like a suit.

Now, she fought to keep it from leaving.

The Blood Shadow wanted nothing more than to tear itself away from her. It strained for freedom, pulling away from her spirit, but she poured the whole force of her spirit and mind on keeping it trapped within.

Why? That was a puzzle and a half. Maybe the Dreadgod was spraying so much power everywhere that the Blood Shadow was getting thirsty. Maybe she was about to beat it, and it was trying to run. Maybe it was finally leaving her alone.

But she didn't need to know why.

The Blood Shadow wanted it, so she was going to stop it.

She almost lost her grip on it when something drove a hole in her madra, but lucky for her, the Shadow itself took the brunt of that hit. It was stunned just as much as she was, so she kept hold. In fact, for a moment, she had the upper hand.

Then something started pulling.

Arms of blood madra wrapped around Lindon's pale right arm. They stuck as though they were covered in suckers, and the madra burned where it made contact. Being a Remnant arm, it felt more like burning his spirit than his body, but that was an ache all its own.

His madra channels, already strained by what he'd done with the Thousand-Mile Cloud, felt like tendons on the brink of tearing. The arm was already a burden on his spirit, and activating the binding was worse.

But it was working. The technique embedded in his arm had fastened itself to the heart of the Blood Shadow, and he was pulling it away from Yerin. It peeled back, inch by inch, as he stretched his spirit to its limit.

The binding had released a vortex of white light, which was meant to devour the Shadow, but the parasite fought to feed on the arm instead. They were stuck together as though nailed, but Lindon couldn't pull the Shadow the last few inches. There was still a short tether connecting the Blood Shadow to her core.

A crash came from the door as a bloodspawn exploded through and into the room. The rest of its brood followed, only to meet Mercy's vast black web.

Lindon was out of time.

With one last, wrenching effort, he pulled the Blood Shadow free.

Yerin's body shuddered and shrunk back to the ground, limp. Her chest was heaving, which led him to let out a sigh of relief. His one other concern had been that pulling the parasite free would somehow kill her.

Now, he stopped powering the binding, but the Shadow was still attached to his arm. It was a huge mass, easily half the size of Yerin's body, and most of it was a bulbous shape stuck to Lindon's palm. The rest was wrapped around his arm like the roots of a tree, and he could feel it trying to burrow inside.

It hadn't succeeded yet, but he only had a moment. Focusing the pure madra of his core, he squeezed a little more out of his exhausted spirit. His core was still half-full, but his madra channels were as ragged as old clothes.

In a focused wave, as though striking with an Empty Palm, he thrust as much pure madra as he could out of his right arm.

The Blood Shadow blasted away, losing its grip on him, and Lindon thought he could hear it hiss.

An instant later, he realized it wasn't his imagination at all.

The spiritual parasite *was* hissing, and snarling, and burbling like a boiling cauldron. All at the same time. It was also contorting into a roughly humanoid shape. *It's becoming a bloodspawn,* he thought, but he almost immediately realized that was wrong.

Or at least incomplete.

This was darker, thicker, and more real than a bloodspawn. It stood on two feet, not two oozing shapes meant to resemble legs. It had two arms and two hands, not the vague outlines of arms. It still had no face, but it looked as though it had hair. Hair cut straight across the back of her neck.

He was starting to have a bad feeling about this.

Its body inflated to twice its original size, so that now it was more Yerin's size. In fact...

Exactly Yerin's size.

His stomach dropped when a pair of blood-red, razor-sharp blades sprouted from behind its shoulders.

Lindon's spirit was tender as an open wound, and though he tapped into his Blackflame core, he felt as though five more minutes of combat might actually kill him. "Mercy," he called, without taking his eyes from Yerin's Blood Shadow. "Can you spare a little help?"

"I'm...doing...the best I can...over here," she said, her words punctuated by crashes. Blood madra sprayed close to him, but it missed him.

As the Shadow examined its hands, Yerin's eyes snapped open.

"...what did you do?" she whispered.

That struck Lindon like a kick, but he'd already ignited his Burning Cloak. Yerin's sword was lying nearby—they had taken it from her for fear that she would hurt herself with it, and he pulled it out of its sheath.

He had no idea how to use a sword, but he'd learned his lesson from the bloodspawn. Any weapon was better than none. He wasn't about to fight this blood-clone of Yerin with his bare hands.

Lindon lunged, the motion powered by the explosive movements of Blackflame. He slashed through the Shadow...or tried to, as one of its blade-arms caught his white sword with the sound of steel on steel.

"We're dead and buried," Yerin said, struggling to her feet. "It's free."

"We can kill it," Lindon said, with more confidence than he actually felt. Mercy pinned a bloodspawn to the wall, where it exploded, but neither the Blood Shadow nor the other two gave it any notice.

"This is its favorite dance. It drains what it needs, then brings that whole mess back to its mother." Yerin stood frozen, staring at it. "It's how the Dreadgod feeds."

The Blood Shadow finally looked around, though it didn't seem to have eyes. It walked over to the splatters left by one of the bloodspawn and stood in the puddle before the madra dissolved. An instant later, the puddle vanished, and a light slipped up the Shadow's legs.

"It usually kills its host, doesn't it?" Lindon said, keeping his sword trained on it. He was determined to keep his focus on any ray of hope he could find, because the alternative was to sit down and wait for death.

"Kills you or wears you like a mask," she responded dully.

The Blood Shadow's head tilted toward his arm. Mercy cried out, and something sounded like the beating of a drum. There came a great splatter like a dropped bucket of paint.

He glanced back to see her panting and exhausted, seated on the floor, her dragon-headed staff resting on her shoulder. The entire front half of the room was covered in sticky black madra, but there were no more bloodspawn.

"There's one more outcome," Lindon said, still trying to scrape together a hope. "How do the emissaries—"

The parasite moved, and his Burning Cloak ignited once again. It felt like tearing his soul in half.

She knew about the emissaries of Redmoon Hall, or people like them. They had gone by different names in different countries, but she'd never met one who had survived the Sword Sage.

Eithan had made it clear as glass that he saw the Blood Shadow as an opportunity for her. A step forward.

But all of those sacred artists had hunted down their parasites with purpose. They had prepared scripts, treasures, and traps. And the least of them she'd ever met was Truegold.

She couldn't do it. This was the demon that had haunted her from the inside for most of her life; she hated it with a burning passion.

And it was the one thing that frightened her.

Under the Burning Cloak, Lindon moved in bursts of speed. The

Blood Shadow's motions stopped and stuttered, like it was getting used to its new shape, but it was faster than Lindon. Easily faster. And Lindon used a sword like he'd never seen one before.

She had to fight with him. Together, they might be able to drive the Blood Shadow away.

But her spirit was as exhausted as his was. She'd strained every ounce of her soul trying to keep the Shadow from taking over. In the Dreadgod's light, the parasite was stronger than it had ever been. Fighting would kill them both.

This wasn't her first hopeless fight. She could go down swinging. Maybe the heavens would send them a miracle.

But she could sense bloodspawn overhead, more and more every second. Whatever the new girl had done—Mercy, Yerin thought her name was—it had kept them out for a breath or two. Wouldn't hold for long.

Orthos should be on his way, but she couldn't feel him yet. The Phoenix was choking out her perception, so maybe he was closer than she thought. That was her only hope.

That, or...

If she could control the Shadow, that was one enemy down. One less thing to worry about. And it might make her strong enough that she could keep fighting.

That, or I could be giving them another enemy to worry about, she thought.

The Blood Shadow rushed forward, grabbing Lindon's collar and slamming him into the far wall. The blades on its back knocked the sword from his hand, and grabbed him by the shoulder.

It lifted him by the right shoulder as though he weighed no more than a child. His pale arm thrashed like a trapped snake, but the Blood Shadow stared it down.

Mercy stood up. A bloodspawn exploded at the top of the stairs, its power eating through the black web that protected them, but she didn't look to the sound. The purple in her eyes spread out until it stained the whole eye. Looked like she had gems stuck in her face.

She was about to do something, Yerin reasoned. Too bad she was late.

Yerin's anger and fear had finally come to blows, and she realized which one had always been stronger.

The rage.

She kicked off and dove for the mass of blood that had stolen her shape. It turned, slashing out at her with the blade over her left shoulder.

Yerin had one of those herself.

The two Goldsigns met with a clash, sending up red-and-silver sparks of essence. She grabbed the Blood Shadow, tearing it away from Lindon.

It had taken enough from her. Whatever it wanted, she was going to take.

Right now, it wanted freedom.

The spirit let itself become fluid again, and her hands sunk in to the wrists. The blood madra started to break down her skin, which she felt as burning. Blood madra was good at that; it controlled the body, usually tearing it apart.

That was okay. She could work better from inside.

With her will as much as her spirit, she *pulled*.

The Blood Shadow resisted, but it was actually easier to haul it back inside than it had been to keep it inside in the first place. It felt like the Dreadgod's aura was helping her, like it was pushing the parasite to take a new body.

It flailed, its blades slashing at her, but she stopped it with her own. With his flesh arm, Lindon seized one of its Goldsigns, wrestling it back.

Yerin gritted her teeth, still pulling. Half of the Shadow had vanished, merging inside her, sinking into her like a statue into a lake. But the top half still fought, reaching for Lindon's arm or stabbing at Yerin's face as though berserk.

Lindon pulled his arm back, and—looking like he was tearing his own skin off—he slammed an Empty Palm into its face.

Stunned, the Shadow slipped into her spirit easy as a sword into a sheath.

Lindon fell back, relaxing, though a troupe of bloodspawn were marching down the stairs. Yerin's spirit was in tatters, but she had succeeded.

Almost.

"Get out," she said, her voice little above a whisper. Mercy looked at her, frowning in confusion, but Lindon seemed to have heard. He just didn't *move*.

A rope of red madra burst from her core, stretching for Lindon's arm.

She barely caught it with both hands, the force dragging her across the floor. "*Why?*" she hissed. "Why aren't you running?"

Lindon ignored the Blood Shadow and moved to pick up her sword, walking like a crippled old man. "I'm waiting for you."

He glanced up to the creatures on the stairs, then added, "...hurry, though."

She stared after him.

"If the emissaries of Redmoon Hall already did it, you can," he said reasonably.

With that, he ran to support Mercy on the stairs.

When you put it like that, it didn't sound so bad.

Instead of trying to push it back into place with her unsteady and failing madra, Yerin reached out to the Blood Shadow like it *was* her madra. Her spirit. Part of her.

It resisted her, of course. But this didn't have to do with advancement level. It was pure grit.

As far as that went, she wouldn't lose to anybody.

***

Lindon knew Mercy didn't really need his help. Not as long as her madra lasted, anyway, though based on her heavy breathing and the fading sense of her spirit, that wouldn't be much longer. She held the stairway with webs, keeping the bloodspawn back.

She didn't actually destroy any of them, but she locked them up. When they destroyed themselves unleashing their power, they'd break through, but she put up more barriers.

It was good that he didn't have to do much. Yerin's sword felt like it weighed a thousand pounds.

Mercy wiped sweat from her forehead, shooting a brief glance back at Yerin. She had been standing in one place, spirit and body still, for...too long.

"Is there anything we can do for her?" Mercy asked, sounding worried.

"We won't need to," he said. Oddly, he *was* confident. Eithan had implied he thought Yerin could control the Blood Shadow, and others had managed it. Yerin could do it.

And if she didn't...well, then the parasite in her body would kill him, so he wouldn't know any differently.

A bloodspawn compressed itself to slither through a gap in the web—none of them had done that before, and he wondered why. He drove his sword through it, and it froze, then shattered.

That was...strange. The Blood Shadow hadn't done that. Maybe it was a property of the madra that had gone into making the sword's blade; it had always given him the impression of icy cold.

Whatever the reason, he was glad he had a weapon that could oppose the bloodspawn without using his own madra. Because Mercy was running out.

The spirits seemed endless, and as far as he knew, maybe they were. More and more slipped through, and he had to use the sword.

It wasn't long before he could barely hold up the sword, and Mercy was breathing so hard she could hardly speak. "I...have...one more trick," she said, panting. "Hoping...to save it...sorry."

Lindon couldn't imagine what she was apologizing for, but before she could do anything, the bloodspawn froze.

They didn't turn to ice, like they did at the touch of the Sword Sage's blade. Instead, they simply...stopped. Like constructs that had run out of power.

Relieved, he turned.

Yerin stood with hand held out, trembling.

And a red shadow stood behind her.

The Blood Shadow wasn't as distinct this time—it looked more like an actual shadow cast by the Dreadgod's bloody light. But it was very clearly standing an inch behind her, mimicking her every move.

"It's about time I gutted that fish," Yerin said, and though she swayed on her feet, her smile was radiant. "Stone simple. Who's in control now, huh?"

Lindon sagged down, sitting on the lid of a nearby jar. His right arm was limp, like it was made out of nothing more than wood and string, and he thought he might have actually torn open a wound in his spirit.

"Knew you'd do it," he said, using what seemed like a great effort to push a smile onto his lips. "Knew you would..."

Finally, a warm presence approached, crashing through the web on the doorway with a roar. Mercy stood abruptly, but he flopped his hand in the air to wave her down.

Orthos stomped through the bloodspawn, splattering them on the stairs, snarling. Two of them burst into dark flames, but the others were just destroyed.

"On time like a rising sun, you are," Yerin said, releasing her Blood Shadow.

Orthos growled, but shook his head to show he couldn't speak. He chomped into a nearby jar, crunching mouthfuls of the uncooked rice within.

Finger on her chin, Mercy looked at Yerin. "Does that let you command the bloodspawn?"

"Just cut them off from the mother," Yerin said, then winced. "...the Dreadgod." She brightened. "And I can do this."

The Blood Shadow formed fully this time, as though it were going to attack, and Lindon couldn't help but flinch. It stood next to Yerin...but this time, a red line stretched between their feet. The Shadow jumped up and down, waving its arms.

"It's a new weapon," Yerin said, re-absorbing the spirit. "I'll need practice."

"That's amazing," Mercy said in awe. "Can you—" She cut off, her head whirling to one side. "Oh no..."

Lindon didn't need another "oh no" in his life.

Mercy threw herself onto the ground. "She's here!" she shouted. "Get down!"

A new presence stabbed into his spirit like a light seared into his eyes. He let himself fall to the ground.

And the house above them was torn away.

It was as though a shovel the size of a mountain had scooped out the ground in a second. Between one instant and the next, the view above Lindon transformed from a dirt ceiling to a red-stained sky.

He had seen nothing but a wave of dark purple. Felt nothing but overwhelming, *crushing* power.

Mercy was pulling on his left arm, urging him to get up, to run. He stumbled after her, though Orthos was actually leading the way. He had bolted up the stairs like a spooked rabbit.

"Can't stay here," Mercy shouted over the rushing wind. "We need to find another—"

Whatever she was going to say was obliterated by an unimaginable crash. The sun went dark.

A wall of purple-edged darkness covered everything to the west. An enormous tower of crystalline amethyst rose from one end of the wall. And there was something above even that, something that blacked out the sky...

Mercy pulled on him again, and Yerin lurched out in front, so he followed.

An instant later, the wall vanished.

Wind actually pulled him off his feet, sending him tumbling down the street, so he lost himself for a moment. When he looked up again, the tower was gone.

No...it had moved.

The Dreadgod had taken to the sky, farther away now, but still incomprehensibly vast. Its sickle-like beak opened, and though its screech still pained his ears, it was nothing like before.

Now, it was focused on its opponent.

A giant stood beneath it, holding a spear. A giant covered from head to toe in armor of dark purple crystal. From the smooth facets of its face, a pair of violet pinpricks shone with light.

It was many miles away—how many, Lindon couldn't begin to guess—and he could still see it clearly. How large *was* it? There was a mountain by its knees, and when it adjusted its stance, half of the mountain crumbled away.

His brain finally snapped the pieces into place, and his jaw slackened. What he had taken as a wall covering everything to the west was just one of its boots. The tower had been its leg.

There came a flash of color and power as the two monsters exchanged blows, but he couldn't even catch a glimpse. A wall of heat and pressure pushed against Lindon's face. The skin of his scalp pressed back against him, and his eyes spiked with pain.

He fell back, but raised two fingers to his eye. Blood ran like tears.

As his Iron body pulled the last of his madra to heal his eyes, he saw bloodspawn rise from the ground...until Yerin reached out a hand and dispersed them to nothing.

First his ears, then his eyes. Though his Bloodforged Iron body had healed him so far, that still couldn't be good for him.

A black web snagged him and dragged him along the dirt road. Mercy and Yerin hauled him in, stuffing him down into a cellar door.

He fought them, though none of them had much strength at the moment. "Please," he begged them, "please, I have to see."

This was *real* power. These were the sacred arts that could stand over the entire world.

In this case, literally.

Mercy pushed him deeper, casting fearful glances behind her. "If we don't get down, we will die. Trust me."

He still struggled. "I beg you! I have to see this."

She halted for a second, though the wind grabbed her ponytail and tossed it around. "She'll be fighting for days."

Lindon stared at Mercy. Yerin, who had most of her body down the stairs already, looked up and peeked out.

"How do you figure that?" she asked. The armor covered the figure completely, and there was nothing to say if it was a man or a woman.

"I think she knows who it is," Lindon said, watching Mercy's expression.

"I should," she responded. "That's my mother."

A blazing crimson light crashed into a shining amethyst blur, and Mercy shoved Lindon the rest of the way inside. The last he saw was a wall of dust and debris headed their way before the door shut it all out.

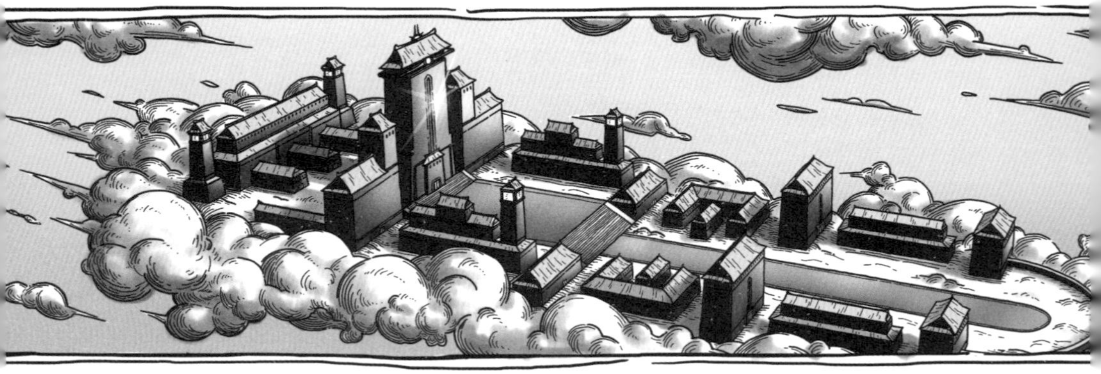

XVIII

They huddled in the shelter of the broken village's cellar for three days.

Most of the homes here had stockpiled some food, so they were able to feed themselves easily. Water was harder, at least at first, until they ventured outside and realized that one of the blows from the distant battle had torn open a spring. They filled as many jars as they could carry, hauling them back to their cellar while avoiding as many bloodspawn as possible.

After the first day, the sounds of battle had faded to those of a thunderstorm. By the end of the second day, they'd disappeared entirely, and the red haze had vanished from the sun.

Only then did the bloodspawn completely vanish. Most of them had been torn to pieces in the wake of the titanic conflict, but stragglers still formed until the red aura withdrew.

It was for the best, because Lindon couldn't fight. He couldn't even cycle.

Little Blue had worked on him, with every spark improving his shattered spirit, but each of her touches caused him agonizing pain. Each time, it was like setting a broken arm.

She hated that he was in pain, but she still tried her best. But he wasn't her only patient—Yerin and Orthos needed help as badly as he did.

Her power was stretched thin, and the store of pure scales in his pack wasn't endless. Eventually, she paled and had to curl up in her case again, the crack hovering over her like a frozen lightning bolt.

If his madra channels had been in better shape, he could have shared his power with her. As it was, he needed to feed her if he wanted her to help, but she needed to help him before he could heal her.

So they were stuck, waiting.

He was awakened on the third day by someone tearing the door open. He tried to extend his perception, but it was like trying to touch something with a broken finger. He shied back.

Not that it matters, he thought. *I know who it is.*

There was only one person who could find them. And, for that matter, only one person who would have gone looking for them.

Eithan stuck his head down, hair gleaming in the shaft of sunlight he was letting in. He jerked back, lips twisting in disgust.

"An apocalyptic battle is no excuse not to bathe," he said.

Lindon rose, apologizing, but Mercy laughed, her voice light with relief. Yerin rolled her eyes, and Orthos extended his neck from his shell, snorted, and withdrew it again.

Despite the smell, he hopped down the stairs, examining them with hands on his hips. He addressed Yerin first. "I see you managed to follow my advice after all!"

"No choice," she said. "Bad luck pushed me into a corner."

"You'd be surprised how often people listen to me when they're left with no choice. I'll have to fulfill one of those many rewards I've promised you."

"Cheers and celebration," she muttered.

Then he turned to Lindon. "Why is it that I so often find you locked in a dark place, filthy and exhausted and covered in blood?"

"At least Yerin didn't have to kick me this time."

"Does that happen often?" Mercy asked.

Her comment pulled Eithan's attention to her, and his smile broadened. "I don't believe I've had the pleasure," he said.

Lindon couldn't quite see how, but he got the impression Eithan was lying. Somehow.

Mercy stood and propped her staff on one shoulder, bowing and pressing her fists together. "Akura Mercy. I cannot thank you enough for coming to rescue us."

Eithan didn't mention her family name, though Lindon was sure he knew what it meant. All the clan members among the Skysworn trainees had known, though the lower-class students hadn't. He doubted those Lowgolds would have information that Eithan did not.

"Not at all, young lady, not at all. I was simply retrieving some of mine." He beamed over at Lindon and Yerin. "I have some news that you will enjoy, and some that you will not. Which would you prefer first?"

"I could use some cheer," Yerin said.

"Bad news first, then! I do not know how the Skysworn will react to your absence. It could be that you are wanted for capture."

Capture. Again.

Lindon had rarely longed so badly for advancement in the sacred arts. The stronger he was, the harder it would be to keep him imprisoned.

He couldn't imagine anyone keeping Mercy's mother in a box.

"Allow me to follow with the good news: I have successfully completed a difficult task for Naru Gwei, and he owes me a favor... although it was not actually difficult for *me*, but that was not a relevant detail to share with the Empire. They will punish you lightly, just for the sake of appearance, but then they will allow you to continue serving the Skysworn."

Yerin scoffed. "Maybe when the sun cracks and falls. They dropped me from the sky." Lindon had shared that story with her during their time in the cellar.

"Alas, they won't let go of you. You are still, officially, Skysworn. Even I cannot pry you loose, now that you have committed to them." He spread his hands. "If it eases your mind, at least know that they won't be trying to kill you so aggressively anymore. Not now that I'm openly in favor."

Mercy heaved a deep breath before saying, "They think we're the enemy. We just have to show them we're all on the same side."

Yerin and Lindon stared at her.

Eithan pointed. "That's the spirit. Another piece of good tidings: the Bleeding Phoenix has retreated for now."

A chill ran down Lindon's spine. "She didn't kill it?"

"Kill it? If anyone could kill a Dreadgod, they would not have survived for so long. No, there's a reason behind the Bleeding Phoenix's name." He paused a moment. "I think you've figured out the *Bleeding* part, but the *Phoenix* half is just as important. It disperses its Blood Shadows all over the world, then it builds itself a new body from the power they gather. Unlike most of the other Dreadgods, Monarchs can destroy its body temporarily, but it always forms again.

"Although, in this case, that isn't what happened."

Eithan was milking the moment, Lindon could tell. Unfortunately, he couldn't pretend not to be interested. The Underlord had them on a hook, and he knew it. Even Orthos had poked his head out of his shell.

"The honored Monarch fought for two days and nights, until her armor was cracked and leaking essence. She would surely have had to retreat in only another hour or two, and the Phoenix had sustained no injury. Their battle had spilled into the eastern wasteland, but it would be nothing for the Dreadgod to turn back and return to our lands."

He shrugged. "Then the Phoenix fell apart. I saw it myself. It just...split apart."

Mercy let out a huge sigh of relief, perhaps thinking about her mother, but Yerin looked skeptical. "Gave up and went home, did it?"

"A battle on that scale takes huge quantities of madra," Eithan said. "Even a creature like the Bleeding Phoenix cannot fight forever.

I have only a theory, you understand, but I believe it a likely one: it is biding its time."

Lindon sucked in a breath. "So it's still around."

"It always is. But usually it is sleeping, and this time...this time I believe it's still awake. I think it realized it was fighting for no reason, that the objective which had pulled it out of its long slumber was no longer obtainable. So it decided to wait."

"For what?" Mercy asked, eyes wide, clutching her staff.

"For its brothers," Eithan said, and his voice was suddenly grim. As though he'd heard himself, he lightened almost immediately. "I'm sorry. That falls in the category of unpleasant news, doesn't it? This was supposed to be the time for good tidings. Speaking of which, Lindon, I have something of a mixed bag for you."

He faced Lindon, the fingertips of both hands pressed together. "You mentioned that you saw several doors into the great labyrinth in your homeland. Sacred Valley, as you said. Could you describe to me the vision your heavenly messenger shared with you? In more detail than you have shared before, I mean."

Lindon was prepared for this. "I'd be happy to exchange our stories. Perhaps part of your vision will remind me of details I've forgotten."

His encounter with Suriel was the one bargaining chip he had to trade. He wasn't giving it up for free.

Eithan inclined his head, acknowledging the point, before withdrawing the void marble from his sleeve.

"I hereby swear on the heavens, my soul, and the grave of my second cousin that I will share my account with you in return." He flipped the marble up and caught it. "In fact, I was prepared to do so in any case. I received some...reliable advice...that suggested I no longer have as much time as I'd assumed."

Lindon searched that statement for any hint of deception, but it seemed airtight. If Eithan was going to wriggle out of it, he would, but he hadn't left himself any obvious loopholes.

His oath shouldn't hold much real weight unless Lindon closed the circle by returning a promise of his own, but sacred artists as powerful as Underlords were still wary of false promises.

Besides, Yerin and Mercy were both staring at him with interest. Yerin had heard most of this already, but Mercy looked like a child awaiting a bedtime story.

"She showed me my future," Lindon began. He glossed over the personal details, especially the parts with his family. Until he came to his death.

"Something marched into Sacred Valley," he said. "My home. It was just a shadow, blotting out the sun, but it waded through the mountains like they were made of sand."

Like the giant in armor he'd seen only a few days before. Mercy's mother.

"That's how I was supposed to die," Lindon said. "Suriel gave me a chance to avoid that. And she showed me some people who could have saved me." He had long since committed the names to memory. "Luminous Queen Sha Miara. Northstrider. The Eight-Man Empire."

Mercy sucked in a breath. Even Yerin gave a low whistle, though Lindon was sure he'd shared this detail with her before. Hadn't he?

Eithan ran a thumb along his chin. His smile was gone, but he didn't look cold or angry. Just thoughtful.

"Those are some of the most powerful people in the world," the

Underlord said. "Though you figured that out already. They are practically myths. In fact, I have it on good authority that Northstrider died almost seven years ago, and the reputation of the Eight-Man Empire is supposedly exaggerated. Though if this Suriel rates them so highly, then presumably popular opinion is in error."

He sat thoughtfully for another moment before raising a finger. "Placing that together with those doors in your valley, I have a theory. I believe it is the return of one or more Dreadgods that leads to the destruction of your home. They hunger for whatever is in this maze. On their way to it, they—or perhaps one of the Monarchs doing battle with them—was destined to crush your valley underfoot."

Lindon thought back to the impossibly vast wall of blood and power that was the Bleeding Phoenix.

He had to stop *that*.

"Thirty years," he said. "That was how long she said I had, and that was the summer before last. Is that enough time?"

"Ah...by conventional wisdom, most lifetimes are not enough." Eithan gave a polite cough. "And I believe I mentioned that I no longer had as much time as I expected. Somewhere along the line, fate has been twisted."

Dread filled Lindon's stomach. "What does that mean?"

"No one predicted the rise of the Bleeding Phoenix until a matter of weeks before it happened. An event of that magnitude should have showed up in their premonitions for *years*. Sometimes generations. All over the world, that is how sacred artists deal with Dreadgod attacks: we predict them, and then we run.

"Something changed this time," Eithan said. "We'll have to consult experts in the subject, but I think it's best to assume you have less time than you thought."

Lindon's heart sunk further.

"...perhaps much less."

They sat in silence for a while. Mercy looked like she was still piecing stories together in her head, Yerin was brooding, Eithan cleaned his nails, and Orthos munched on fragments of pottery.

Lindon was wondering how much he could trust Eithan's guesses. Suriel had descended from the *heavens* to show him the future. Surely, she was the most reliable source.

But she had emphasized how fate could always be changed…

"Now it's my turn," Eithan said, evidently having grown bored with waiting. "But first, I have to ask. Lindon, has your resolve been shaken?"

Had it? Lindon thought about it for a moment.

If he didn't really have thirty years, then he should go back to Sacred Valley as soon as possible. Borrowing help from Eithan and Yerin, he could warn everyone to leave. They should do what most people did before a Dreadgod attack and run. He was powerful enough now that even the elders and clan leaders should listen to him.

But…

Assuming he did clear everyone out, would he give up and go home? Would he pack it in, once his goal was achieved?

No. He'd seen too much. There were sacred artists whose steps covered miles, who traded blows with Dreadgods and blotted out the sky.

If he settled for less than that, he was giving up. Suriel had transcended this world entirely; he couldn't forgive himself if he didn't at least try.

He shook his head, and Eithan accepted it, turning to Yerin. "How about you, Yerin?"

Yerin seemed surprised that he addressed her at all. "Is Redmoon Hall still around?"

"Like their master, they remain awake and aware," Eithan said. "They are here, now, in the Empire. Longhook, the gentleman we met before, has been sighted more than once. I fear we will see them again even before the Phoenix returns."

"Then I'll be there too."

Eithan cocked his head curiously. "For that reason alone? What if you were to defeat Redmoon Hall completely? What if they *did* retreat? Would your spirit fade away, and your resolve crumble to nothing?"

Yerin sat and thought, rather than delivering a snap answer, as Lindon had somewhat expected. Slowly, a light grew in her eyes, until a smile slid onto her scarred lips. "I've got a lot of road left to travel, but...even my master couldn't keep up with a Dreadgod. Sure would be fun to go sword-to-sword with one."

"It is my intention," Eithan said, "to do exactly that."

Mercy frowned up at him. "But you're so weak," she said.

Yerin snorted a laugh, and Orthos gave a deep chuckle.

Eithan winked at her. "I have a secret weapon. A great expert has peered into my future and determined that I have at least a *chance* of success. I traveled all the way to your home, where Akura Malice gave me her blessing. She told me she was counting on me."

Mercy scooted back a few feet and looked up at the ceiling.

A few breaths passed.

"I swear on my—"

"You're telling the *truth!*" Mercy said in a mixture of disbelief and awe.

"How do you know?" Lindon asked. If there was a way to catch Eithan in a lie or an evasion, he wanted to know.

"Because he's still alive," she said simply.

Lindon shivered. Monarchs could do that?

Eithan seemed a little shaken himself, from the glance he shot upward, but he continued on. "No matter where you are, the strong write the rules. But even if you're the most powerful in the world, there are limits to what you can do alone." He clenched his fist. "They say the sacred arts are lonely. The higher you climb, the more alone you become. That is the first rule I'd like to rewrite."

Mercy tapped her staff against her shoulder, eyes narrowed. "Let's say you do make it to my mother's level," she said, and Eithan didn't so much as twitch at the word 'mother.' So he *had* been pretending not to recognize Mercy. "There are a lot of things you could do with all that power."

"I think of myself as a fairly shrewd judge of character," Eithan said. "I have chosen very carefully who I want to take with me on this journey. They are people who, I believe, have the potential to make the world a better place." He gave a wry smile. "You'll notice I've only found two. And they have years to grow. Their choices will determine whether I was right or wrong."

Mercy looked sheepish, but she didn't give in. "Everyone thinks they're making the world a better place," she said quietly.

"Then we have come full circle," Eithan said, flipping out his marble again. The void pulsed in the center, a hole of endless darkness. "Now I will fulfill my promise."

He tossed the glass ball to Lindon, who clapped his hands around it.

The world vanished as a vision consumed him.

⬡

A man stood against a background of endless, textured blue. He wore black armor of rounded, eggshell-smooth plates that looked almost like a liquid. His skin was pale, his face long and angular...but his features were perfect, without a blemish or wrinkle anywhere. His eyes were pure blue, and his hair a long, streaming white.

He seemed familiar for a moment before Lindon, with a shock, recognized him. He looked like Eithan.

Not *exactly* alike. His chin was a little sharper than Eithan's, his hairline a little further back, his nose a little thinner. But if someone had told him this was Eithan's brother, or perhaps a younger version of Eithan's father, Lindon would have believed them.

It was somewhat disconcerting going straight from sitting in a cellar to floating in a sapphire void, but Lindon's experience with Suriel had somewhat prepared him. It was comforting, in a way: this was independent confirmation, if he'd needed any, that Suriel's visit was more than just a hallucination.

"I am called Ozriel," the man said, turning to fix Lindon with his stare. "If you have found this, that means you are one of the descendants I've left behind. Lucky you." His voice was far more animated than Lindon would have expected—in his black armor, with his pale hair, he looked like he should speak in grave whispers.

"I left behind this message in case one of you, any of you, inherits some spark of my desire. I determined that there must be more beyond the world I could see. And I was not content to stay trapped, like a fish in a pond."

He waved his hand, and the blue fabric tore. He stepped out into the sky over a city Lindon had never seen before: a landscape of towering spires in all the colors of the rainbow, as though each had been hewn from gemstone. Amethyst and sapphire and emerald shone in the sun, with glittering crystal bridges crossing from one to the other.

Sacred artists traveled through the sky, standing on Thousand-Mile Clouds, riding sacred birds, or pulled by Remnants.

Ozriel looked out over the city, and his voice turned sad. "Everything you know, everything you have ever known, is but one world. One island in a vast ocean."

He made no gesture, but he began to rise, and Lindon felt once again that sickening lurch that came when his eyes told him he was moving, but his body told him he was standing still. They rose into the sky, until the city was but a dot beneath them...and they kept rising.

Into the stars.

Lindon's eyes couldn't widen enough to take it all in. The land curved away from him...endlessly. He couldn't even see the city below him anymore. He could barely make out what he thought was the country.

The world spread out in front of him, blue and green and yellow.

There were so many clouds! And so much ocean…how much of the world was covered in water?

He almost didn't notice the curve. The world was…bent?

They continued to drift into the stars until Lindon could see the whole thing. It was a *ball.* He'd read his natural history before, and more than one natural philosopher claimed that the world was a ball, but it had never caught his thoughts before.

How did the people on the bottom stay on?

"It's an overwhelming sight," Ozriel said softly. "This is the central planet of the world we call Cradle. Iteration 110. It is larger than average for an inhabited planet, with vital aura making it both harder and easier for humanity to spread. At the moment of this recording, over six hundred billion souls call this place home."

He spread his hands. "And this planet is but the central fragment of the world called Cradle. Your moon, your sun, each of the stars… they exist only here.

"There are thousands of realities just like yours," Ozriel said, tearing open another rift in reality. An instant later, they had popped into another Iteration. This planet was also blue and green, but the shapes of the land were all different. It didn't *seem* much smaller than Cradle had, but Lindon's mind was still twisting to try and comprehend the scale involved.

"Each of them with their own population," Ozriel said, popping into another. This world was a series of jagged chunks floating in darkness, as though the planet had been torn to pieces and left to drift. But Lindon could see city lights on each of them. Even some in the ground beneath the surface, as though humans had made those islands into their own personal molehills.

The world went blue again. "I belong to an organization called the Abidan," he said, and now new figures appeared in the blue. Rank upon rank of white-armored figures, drifting in color. Arranged in regiments, some of them had symbols on their armor, and still others carried strange tools.

Eagerly, Lindon watched for Suriel. He didn't see her, but it was hard to pick any individual out from the crowd.

The Abidan were formed into seven distinct ranks. Above each of them now hovered a single individual.

This time, Lindon finally saw Suriel.

She stood over the sixth division, purple eyes staring forward, her hair drifting emerald as though underwater.

Tears welled up as he saw her, though he couldn't quite explain why. He swept them away as though Ozriel might see him and laugh.

The sole black-armored Abidan stared out over the ranks of thousands of Abidan, and Lindon thought he seemed...lost. Though who could read the expression of immortals?

"We draw our power from the Way," he said. "This is what you see all around you now. It is the power of order that runs through all Iterations. With that power, we defend you all. Without us, all would fall to chaos."

Suddenly, without Ozriel making a gesture or tearing open another gateway, the scene changed.

The Abidan were gone. The blue light of the Way had vanished, and now Lindon stood on a vast, dusty plain.

All around him, people were dying.

They had once been an army, with armor and swords and shields, but now they were on the ground, writhing and choking.

Their bodies grayed and dried by the second, as though they were aging decades before his eyes.

Every time one of them died, he could pick them out, though he couldn't tell how. It pierced him through the heart, as though each was a friend.

Tears streamed down his face now, and he averted his eyes, but there was no escaping from the pain.

"Like all power, ours has rules," Ozriel said sadly. "This is a necessary truth. One of those rules restricts our interference. For centuries, I have watched worlds die…and the pain you now feel, I feel with each death. Over and over again, in worlds without end."

Now they were in another world, as people were run down by monsters. Another, where the air had become too toxic to breathe. Another, where men and women starved or died of thirst. A world where great rocks fell from the sky and devastated cities. A world where great beasts rampaged. A world on fire.

Over and over again, time blurring in Lindon's head. Each death speared him as though he had personally caused it.

Finally, when Lindon was on his knees, they returned to the calm of the Way. Ozriel met his eyes. "This is one part of my plan," he said softly. "Only one seed planted of many, in the hopes that some might one day bear fruit. I need you to join me."

He raised black-armored fingers to his head, and Lindon could see endless weariness written there. "Not as Abidan. I want to raise you outside their rules. I want you to go where we can't: into dying worlds, to save those we have abandoned."

Now a mantle of darkness billowed from the back of Ozriel's armor. Suddenly, he loomed like the end of all things. "You are one of my children," he said. "You have inherited my sight. To you, the world is open.

"You *can* step out of the Cradle. You can grow up.

"And join me."

Eithan had touched Yerin with the marble as well. It would be awkward for Mercy, sitting around watching the other two sit motionless and stare into space, but she would adapt.

If he accepted her early, he would seem too eager. Best to reel her in.

He knew what Lindon and Yerin were seeing—the message's contents never changed—and he could imagine how overwhelmed they felt. He had felt the same way, once.

Speaking of messages...

Reaching into his pocket, he pulled out an envelope that had been sealed with wax. It was a foreign way of sending messages, from the Arelius homeland. And indeed, this wax was marked with the Arelius family's crescent symbol, alongside two ancient characters indicating power.

The mark of the head family. Cassias' father had appropriated it without cause. How would he feel if he knew Eithan had a marble containing a vision from their family's First Patriarch?

Although, if the *real* head family had been wiped out, Gaien Arelius had as much claim to the seal as anyone. Eithan would have to wait another three years to find out.

Eithan, Cassias had written.

The family elders are not pleased with the way you have handled recent matters. Lindon's lost duel, they meant, although they had seen the benefits of that. And the orders he'd given Cassias before the Bleeding Phoenix rose, though Cassias had never had a chance to carry those out.

In reality, they just didn't like his way of doing things. They wanted him to consult them before every single decision. He understood. This stemmed from his own, old failing: he kept too much control. It made him difficult to work with.

But the sun would burn cold before he let himself be ordered about by men like this.

It personally gives me great pain to deliver you this message with my own hand, but the family elders would like you to temporarily step down as Patriarch. You will still hold all the rights and privileges of a family elder, and of course our only Underlord.

I am here with my father, who provides his stamp at the bottom. He concurs, and we have received imperial approval. If you are unsatisfied, I urge you to appeal to the elders. I believe you are the one to lead this family into the future, when you settle down and put the family's needs above your own.

In pain and regret,

Naru Cassias Arelius

The paper was stamped with characters for both Cassias' name and his father's. Eithan flipped over the envelope, looking at the wax seal that he'd left intact.

The symbol of his family.

They had rejected him.

A gust of wind picked up, and he let it take the letter away.

INFORMATION REQUESTED: CURRENT STATUS OF THE DREADGODS.

BEGINNING REPORT...

The Bleeding Phoenix, its consciousness scattered over thousands of pieces, settles in to wait. Many of its fragments go dormant, but many others go looking for hosts. To hunt, and to build up their mother's power. It is biding its time, for the moment when it senses its lost brother again.

The Silent King stirs in its dreams as it senses the Phoenix in battle. For hundreds of miles, spirits and Remnants feel its influence. Though they do not know the source, they are disturbed.

The Weeping Dragon sleeps in the upper atmosphere, on a miles-long bed of clouds. It has not been long since it last woke, and it is still weary. Though the power of the Phoenix prickled its spirit, it will take more enticing bait to rouse the Dragon from its slumber.

In a chasm on the ocean's floor, the Wandering Titan rolls its stone joints. They have stiffened from long disuse. It wakes slowly, but steadily.

Soon, it will rise.

Suggested topic: Makiel's full influence on the fate of Cradle. Continue?

Denied, report complete.

THE END
of Cradle: Volume Four
Skysworn

LINDON'S STORY CONTINUES IN

GHOSTWATER

CRADLE : VOLUME FIVE

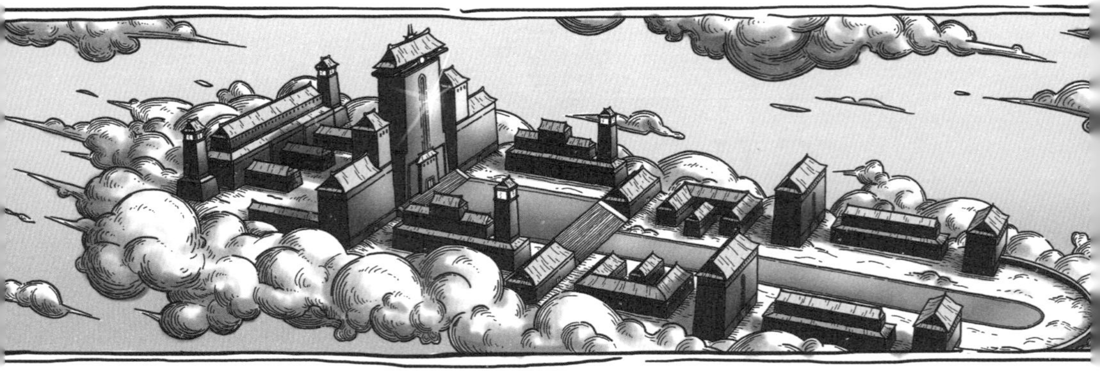

BLOOPERS

The Emperor looked over his gathered Underlords gravely. "I could assign one of you the dangerous task of meeting the Akura Monarch, but this is a decision we must make collectively. Let us leave it to a vote."

"I vote we make Eithan do it," Naru Gwei said immediately.

"Eithan," Naru Saeya agreed.

"Hold on just a moment," Eithan protested, but he was overridden by a cascade of other Underlords.

"Eithan."

"Underlord Arelius."

"Can I vote for Eithan twice?"

Eithan threw up his hands. "Wait! For such a momentous occasion, certainly we should use a more objective approach. Why don't we draw straws?"

"I just so happen to have some right here," Naru Gwei said, holding up a fistful of wooden sticks. "I've written a name on each one myself."

Eithan scowled at the sticks. "Those all say 'Eithan.'"

"No peeking."

"Prosthetic limbs," Fisher Gesha said, "are among the easiest constructs for a Soulsmith to create. If we had to replace one of your organs, I would be singing a very different tune right now, hm?"

"But you could do it if you had to?" Lindon asked. "Replace my organs, I mean."

"What?"

"If we're already upgrading me, why stop at an arm? Let's give me rocket legs! Laser eyes! Missiles in my liver!"

Gesha frowned at him for a moment, then shrugged. "Well, who am I to say no to a patient, hmmm?"

Three days later, Fisher Gesha hung her head before Eithan in shame. "I did get carried away."

Lindon crawled in on the legs of a spider-construct, eyes glowing bright red. He spoke with the voice of a machine. "FROM THE MOMENT I UNDERSTOOD THE WEAKNESS OF MY FLESH, IT DISGUSTED ME," Lindon said.

Fisher Gesha winced. "I may have gone a bit too far."

"We've got the biggest hammer in the Empire, and everybody knows it," Naru Gwei said.

A cheer rose from the Highgold table.

"And there it is now!" the Underlord cried, pointing out the window of Stormrock.

Far in the distance, propped up against two mountains, was a gigantic hammer.

◇

"Tell me how you avoided our security," Renfei said coldly, refusing to let Eithan evade. She couldn't intimidate this man, but she exerted as much pressure as she could to squeeze some kind of answer out of him.

Eithan shrugged. "Sure, I'll tell you. You see, as long as I'm not onscreen, I can do whatever I want."

"Onscreen?" Renfei repeated, incredulous.

"Yes, I mean, as long as the readers aren't watching. Here, I'll show you. Try setting up a flashback."

"What?"

"Focus very hard on a memory that's important to you."

Renfei hadn't always wanted to join the Skysworn. As a girl, she'd sifted sand in the desert, dreaming of treasure. She remembered the sun beating down on her neck, shielded only by the shade of her hat. The other children panning at her side.

And Eithan, squinting into the sun and holding up a hand for shade. "This is unpleasant. Flash back to somewhere with a cool breeze."

Back in the present, Renfei's eyes snapped open. "How did you do that?"

"I don't have to explain anything," Eithan said. "It happened offscreen."

Jai Long sliced through Lindon's arm. "I'm sorry, Lindon. I win."

Lindon returned a bar of dragon's breath with his remaining hand. "You win? We've barely gotten started!"

"You really want to keep fighting while you're down one arm?"

"Unless you're ready to surrender!"

Jai Long cut off his other arm. "You made me do this. Now the battle's over."

"You wish!" Lindon leaped in, sending a kick at Jai Long's head.

With one spin of his spear, Jai Long sliced cleanly through both of Lindon's legs. "Let's be done with this."

"Quitting already, coward?" Lindon shouted from his back. "This is only a flesh wound!"

"How are you going to keep fighting now?"

Lindon fired a dragon's breath from his mouth.

Mercy was looking curiously at Lindon. "Wei clan?" she asked. "Not the Blackflame family? You must have an interesting story."

"Well, the first two volumes can be a little slow," Lindon said. "People say it picks up in book three."

◯

Naru Gwei slid the leaf back into his lips and continued talking, but now it no longer sounded like he was quoting. "Even though this is a Lowgold against a Truegold, it's still a fight between two great families. It will reflect official rankings, as well as the reputation of both powers. State your grudges so we may see if they can be settled."

He didn't sound like he had much hope for that to happen.

"I don't have a grudge," Lindon said. "I obviously don't want to do this."

Jai Long dipped his red-wrapped head. "I'm obligated to fight for the Jai clan. I no longer blame you for Sandviper Kral's death.

"Hold on," Gwei said. "You challenged him to a duel over Sandviper Kral?"

"Originally, yes. But—"

"Let me get this straight. Your friend tried to murder him, so now you're trying to murder him because he defended himself?"

"It was for honor!"

Gwei narrowed his eyes and chewed for a moment on the long stalk of grass between his teeth. "That's the dumbest thing I've ever heard. Case dismissed."

Lindon raised both his healthy arms and cheered.

The world spread out in front of him, blue and green and yellow. There were so many clouds! And so much ocean...how much of the world was covered in water?

He didn't notice any kind of curve. From up here, it was so obvious. The world was...flat.

"How?" he wondered aloud. "I thought the world was a ball, and we stick to its surface because of gravity."

Ozriel's voice scoffed. "A ball? That's ridiculous. How would the people at the bottom stay on?"

Eithan lay on the ground, groaning and bleeding after the beating Longhook had given him. He could hardly move.

Worse, the sleeve of his fine robe had been caught by some embers left in the battle. It began to smoke and, a moment later, caught fire.

Eithan coughed as he called for help. "I seem—ahem, I seem to be on fire! Someone!"

To his great relief, rain began to pour in through a crack in the ceiling. He squirmed to one side, angling himself so that the water would put out the fire.

But something stretched over him, blocking the rain. Eithan focused his eyes to see Naru Gwei standing above him.

Holding an umbrella.

WILL WIGHT is the *New York Times* and #1 Kindle best-selling author of the *Cradle* series, a new space-fantasy series entitled *The Last Horizon*, and a handful of other books that he regularly forgets to mention. His true power is only unleashed during a full moon, when he transforms into a monstrous mongoose.

Will lives in Florida, lurking beneath the swamps to ambush prey. He graduated from the University of Central Florida, where he received a Master of Fine Arts in Creative Writing and a cursed coin of Spanish gold.

Visit his website at *WillWight.com* for eldritch incantations, book news, and a blessing of prosperity for your crops. If you believe you have experienced a sighting of Will Wight, please report it to the agents listening from your attic.

HIDDEN GNOME PUBLISHING

Want to always know what's going on?

With Will, we mean.

The best way to stay current is to sign up for
The Will Wight Mailing List™!
Get book announcements and…

Well, that's pretty much it.* No spam!

SIGN UP HERE!

*Ok, *sometimes* we'll send an announcement about something that's only book-*related*. Not a lot, promise.

We thought there'd be more space for jokes back here, too. Maybe in the next book.